## ALSO BY J.A. JANCE

ALI REYNOLDS MYSTERIES

*Edge of Evil*

*Web of Evil*

JOANNA BRADY MYSTERIES

*Desert Heat*

*Tombstone Courage*

*Shoot/Don't Shoot*

*Dead to Rights*

*Skeleton Canyon*

*Rattlesnake Crossing*

*Outlaw Mountain*

*Devil's Claw*

*Paradise Lost*

*Partner in Crime*

*Exit Wounds*

*Dead Wrong*

J.P. BEAUMONT MYSTERIES

*Until Proven Guilty*

*Injustice For All*

*Trial by Fury*

*Taking the Fifth*

*Improbable Cause*

*A More Perfect Union*

*Dismissed with Prejudice*

*Minor in Possession*

*Payment in Kind*

*Without Due Process*

*Failure to Appear*

*Lying in Wait*

*Name Withheld*

*Breach of Duty*

*Birds of Prey*

*Partner in Crime*

*Long Time Gone*

*Justice Denied*

WALKER FAMILY THRILLERS

*Hour of the Hunter*

*Kiss of the Bees*

*Day of the Dead*

HAND

J.A. JANCE

A TOUCHSTONE BOOK

PUBLISHED BY SIMON & SCHUSTER

NEW YORK LONDON TORONTO SYDNEY

TOUCHSTONE
A Division of Simon & Schuster, Inc.
1230 Avenue of the Americas
New York, NY 10020



*Designed by Mary Austin Speaker*

Manufactured in the United States of America

ISBN-13: 978-1-4165-3753-3
ISBN-10: 1-4165-3753-8

*For TLG.*

# HAND OF EVIL

## { PREFACE }

When the car door slammed shut on his hand, the universe came to a stop and nothing else mattered. Nothing. He dropped to his knees, howling in agony while a nearby coyote, startled by the sound, responded with a howl of its own. Rigid with pain, at first he couldn't even reach for the door handle. By the time he did, it was too late. The door lock inside the vehicle had already clicked home.

"Please," he begged. "For God's sake, open the door."

But the answer to that was no—an unequivocal no. The engine turned over and the car began to move.

"You can't do this," he screamed. "You can't!"

By then the pavement was moving beneath him, slowly at first, then faster and faster. He held out his other hand, trying to brace himself or somehow pull himself back to his feet. For a moment that almost worked and he was close to upright, but then the speed of the car outdistanced his scrambling feet and he fell again, facedown this time, with the full weight of his body pulling on the exploding pain in his fingers.

As the speed of the vehicle increased, so did his agonized

screams. The parking lot's layer of loose gravel scraped and tore at him, shredding his blue-and-white jogging suit; shredding his skin. By the time the hurtling car bounced over the first speed bump, he was no longer screaming. Plowing face-first into the second one momentarily knocked him unconscious.

He came to when the car door opened. Once his trapped hand was released from the door frame, he fell to the ground. He couldn't actually see the car or even the ground for that matter. He seemed to have been struck blind. Nor could he differentiate the pain in his crippled hand from the agony in the rest of his tortured body, but his ears still worked. He heard the car door slam shut again and felt the spray of gravel from the tires as it drove away into the night, leaving him in absolute darkness.

He lay there for a long time, knowing he was barely alive and feeling his life's blood seeping out through layers of damaged skin. He tried crawling, but he couldn't make that work.

"Help," he called weakly. "Somebody, please help me."

In the wilds of Phoenix's South Mountain Preserve, only a single prowling coyote heard the dying man's final whispered plea for help. The coyote was on the trail of his dinner—an elusive bunny—and he paid no attention.

No one else did, either.

• • •

Sybil Harriman strode through the early morning chill and reveled in the sunlight and the clear crisp air. Across the valley, she could see the layer of smog settling in over the rest of the city, but here it was cold and clear—cold enough to see her breath and make her nose run and her eyes water, but not cold enough to scare her away from walking the full course of the park's Alta Trail and back to the parking lot along the Bajada.

She had been warned that Alta was "too difficult" for someone her age, and that she certainly shouldn't walk it alone. So she did so, at least twice a week. Because she could. And as she walked along, huffing and puffing a little, truth be known, she was also drinking in the view and the cactus and the birds—birds so different from the ones she'd grown up with back in Chicago—and she was also thinking about how wrong she'd been and wishing things had been different.

Herman had wanted to move here the moment he retired from working for Merck. She was the one who had fought it, saying they should stay where they were in order to be closer to the kids and grandkids, although a lot of good that had done. Finally, when Herm's arthritis had gotten so bad that he could barely walk, she had relented. Now she was sorry they hadn't come sooner, while Herman would have been able to reap some of the benefits of desert living.

His arthritis had improved so much once they were in Arizona it was unbelievable, but then the rest of it had happened. The dry climate could do nothing at all to stave off the ravages and gradual decline that was Alzheimer's. As for the kids? Once Herm died, it had been plain enough that what they wanted more than anything was to get their greedy little hands on their father's money. Well, thanks to the trust Herm had wisely insisted on setting up, they weren't getting any of that, not until Sybil was damned good and ready. And that was another reason she walked every single day. She was determined to live as long and as well as she could.

*Let 'em wait,* she told herself fiercely as she marched along. *They can wait until hell freezes over.*

When she returned to Chicago for Herm's funeral, her friends there hardly recognized her. They thought she had dropped the excess weight she had carried all those years in a fit of sudden grief. In actual fact, the process had been much less abrupt than that—and much more permanent. She had started by walking four miles each day on the flat but circular streets in their Awatukee neighborhood. Later she had forced herself up and down the steeper grades and gradually more and more difficult trails throughout South Mountain Preserve.

Sybil was one of the early birds this crisp January morning. She had seen not a soul on her morning walk—at least no other humans—in the course of her almost three solitary hours. There had been plenty of bunnies, however, and scads of other early birds—doves, quail, skittish roadrunners, breakfasting cactus wrens, finches, colorful hummingbirds, hawks, and even an ebony-feathered, red-eyed phainopepla. Now, as she approached the spot where the trail crossed San Juan Road, it was close to midmorning and the sun was high.

San Juan Road had been closed indefinitely for some strange reason, so there shouldn't have been any traffic. Still, Sybil was too much of a city girl to cross a road or a street without looking both ways. And that's when she saw it—what appeared to be a pile of rags or trash lying in the middle of the roadway some thirty or forty yards northeast of the now abandoned San Juan parking lot.

Offended that someone would toss out a load of garbage and leave it there in the road, Sybil headed in that direction. She was determined to clean up the mess and haul it off to the nearest garbage containers. Ten yards or so away from the debris field, however, she saw the blood.

With a trembling hand, she pulled out her cell phone and dialed 911. "Emergency operator. What are you reporting?"

Sybil was closer to the mess now—much too close—and

wished she wasn't. There was blood everywhere. It was hard to tell that the flayed and bloody pulp inside the pile of shredded clothing was even human, but she knew it was.

"A body," she managed at last. "I've just found a human body lying here in the middle of the road."

She didn't hear the panic in her voice, but the operator evidently did. "Calm down," the operator advised her. "What is your name and your location?"

Sybil took a deep breath and forced herself to get a grip. "Sybil Harriman," she replied. "I'm in the park—South Mountain Preserve. The body is just to the east of the abandoned parking lot on San Juan Road."

"Units are on the way," the operator told her briskly. "Are you sure the person is dead? Did you check for a pulse?"

Sybil looked at the mound of bloody flesh, searching for wrists. One hand, virtually skinless, was little more than a bloody stump. The other hand contained a relatively recognizable thumb, but the four fingers seemed to have been mashed flat. Sybil knew at once there would be no pulse in either one of those two mangled wrists nor would there be any possibility of bringing the bloodied victim back to life.

"He's dead," she whispered to the operator. "Sorry. I've got to hang up now."

Sybil snapped the phone shut. Then, gagging, she staggered over to the edge of the road and promptly lost the single banana she had eaten for breakfast.

As she straightened up and waited, listening for approaching sirens, Sybil Harriman knew it was the last banana she would eat for a very long time.

# { CHAPTER 1 }

With her laptop asleep and perched virtually untouched on her crossed legs, Ali Reynolds stared into the flames of the burning gas log fireplace. She was supposed to be working on her blog, cutlooseblog.com, but on this chilly January morning she wasn't. Or maybe she was. She was trying to think of what to say in today's post, but her mind remained stubbornly blank—right along with her computer screen.

Ali had started cutloose in the aftermath of the sudden and almost simultaneous ends of both her television newscasting career and her marriage. Back then, fueled by anger, cutloose had been a tool for dealing with the unexpected bumps in her own life. To her surprise, what had happened to her was far more commonplace than she had known, and what she had written in cutloose had touched chords in the lives of countless other women.

Since the murder of Paul Grayson, Ali's not quite, but nearly ex-husband, cutloose had morphed into something else entirely. For weeks now it had focused on grief and grieving—on the pitfalls and setbacks that lie in wait for those attempting to recover from the loss of a loved one or even a not-so-loved one. Ali had learned enough from her readers that she could almost have declared herself an expert on the subject if it hadn't been for the inconvenient reality that she had zero perspective on the topic. She was still too deep in grief herself. As her mother, Edie Larson, would have said, drawing on her endless supply of platitudes: She couldn't see the forest for the trees.

Because Ali was back in her hometown of Sedona, Arizona, grieving. She grieved for a phantom of a marriage that had evidently never been what she had thought it was and for a job she had loved but which had come with zero job security and no reciprocal loyalty.

Having people write to her and tell her that "someday you'll be over it" or "it doesn't matter how long it takes" wasn't helping Ali Reynolds. She couldn't yet tell what she was supposed to be over. Was she supposed to be over Paul's death or over his many betrayals? How long would it take her to move beyond the shock of learning of the child—a little girl—her husband had fathered out of wedlock while he was still married to Ali? Ali hadn't even known of Angelina Roja's existence until after Paul's death, and looking out for the financial welfare of the child and her mother had made tying up Paul's estate that much more complicated.

There were times Ali felt downright resentful when she heard from widows—real widows whose husbands had been faithful, honorable men—who were struggling with their own overwhelming sense of loss. It was all she could do sometimes to keep from writing back to them and saying, "Hey, you, don't you know how lucky you were? At least your dead husband's not driving you nuts from beyond the grave."

Sam, Ali's one-eyed, one-eared sixteen-pound tabby cat,

shifted uneasily on the back of the couch behind her and let one paw fall on Ali's shoulder. Sam's presence in Ali's life was supposed to have been temporary. Sam had belonged to Matt and Julie Bernard, children of Ali's murdered friend, Reenie Bernard. When the children had gone to live with their grandparents, Sam had been unable to join them and Ali had taken Sam in. Ali had never liked or particularly disliked cats. She had never thought about them much one way or the other—and Sam was anything but outgoing or sociable. But now, almost a year since Sam's unexpected arrival, Ali had started thinking of the animal in terms of "my cat" rather than "their cat."

Ali turned and scratched the seemingly permanent frown lines on Sam's ugly forehead. "How about if you do the blog this morning?" she asked.

Sam simply yawned, closed her one good eye, and went back to sleep. When the doorbell rang, Sam leaped to life. Spooked by newcomers of any kind, the cat scrambled off the couch and disappeared from view. Ali knew from past experience that it would probably be several hours before she'd be able to coax the wary feline back out of hiding.

Putting the laptop on the coffee table, Ali hurried to the door. She was expecting Kip Hogan, her parents' handyman, to drop off her refinished bird's-eye maple credenza. That and the comfy leather sofa were the two pieces of furniture she had brought to her mountaintop mobile home with her from her former home digs in L.A. The top of the credenza had been damaged when someone had carelessly deposited a wet vase on it. Now, after careful sanding and varnishing, Ali's father assured her that the wood had been restored to its former glory.

Except, when Ali looked out the peephole, Kip Hogan was nowhere in sight. The man on Ali's front porch, a wizened but dapper-looking elderly gentleman in a suit and tie, was holding a small envelope. He looked somewhat familiar, but she couldn't quite place him. In the old days, growing up in small-town Arizona, Ali wouldn't have hesitated at opening the door to a stranger, but times had changed in Sedona. More important, Ali had changed. She cautiously cracked the door open but only as far as the length of the security chain.

"May I help you?" she asked.

"Ms. Reynolds?" the man asked. He wore a brimmed leather cap, which he tipped respectfully in Ali's direction.

"Yes."

"A message for you, madam," he said politely. Removing a soft leather driving glove, he proffered the envelope through the narrow opening. "From Miss Arabella Ashcroft."

Ali recognized the name at once. "Thank you." She took the envelope and started to close the door, but the man stopped her.

"If you'll forgive me, madam, I was directed to wait for an answer."

Using her finger, Ali tore open the creamy white envelope. It was made from expensive paper stock, as was the gold-bordered note card she found inside. Written across it, in spidery, old-fashioned script was the following: Dear Alison, Please join me for tea this afternoon if at all possible. 2:30. 113 Manzanita Hills Road. Miss Arabella Ashcroft.

A summons from Miss Arabella, one of Sedona's more formidable dowagers, was not to be taken lightly or ignored.

"Of course," Ali said at once. "Tell her I'll be there."

"Would you like me to come fetch you?" the messenger asked, gesturing over his shoulder at the venerable bright yellow Rolls-Royce Silver Cloud idling in Ali's driveway.

"Oh, no," Ali told him. "I can get there on my own. I know the way."

And she did, too, despite the fact that it had been twenty-five years earlier when she had last had afternoon tea with Arabella Ashcroft and her equally daunting mother, Anna Lee, at the imposing Ashcroft home on Manzanita Hills Road.

Ali's visitor bowed slightly from the waist and backed away from the door. "Very well," he said. "I'll tell Miss Arabella she can expect you." He tipped his cap once again, turned on his heel, and marched away. Once he drove out of sight, Ali closed the door. Then, with both the note card and envelope in hand, she returned to the couch lost in a haze of memories.

On a Friday afternoon two weeks before Ali had been scheduled to graduate from Cottonwood's Mingus Mountain High School, she had bounded into her parents' diner, Sedona's Sugarloaf Café, for her after-school shift. All through high school she had helped out by waiting tables after school and during Christmas and summer vacations. As she tied on her apron she spotted an envelope with her name on it propped up next to the cash register. There was no stamp or return address, so obviously it had been hand delivered.

"What's this?" she had asked Aunt Evie, her mother's twin sister and her parents' full partner in the restaurant venture.

"It's still sealed, isn't it?" Aunt Evie had asked. "How about if you open it and find out?"

Ali had opened the envelope on the spot. Inside she had found a note card very similar to the one she had received just now: "Please join my daughter and me for tea, this coming Sunday, May 21, 2:30 P.M. at our home, 113 Manzanita Hills Road, Sedona, Arizona." The note had been signed *Anna Lee Ashcroft,* Arabella's mother.

"Tea!" Ali had exclaimed in disbelief. "I've been invited to tea?"

Taking the note from Ali's hand, Aunt Evie examined it and then handed it back. "That's the way it looks," she said.

"I've never been invited to tea in my life," Ali said. "And who all is going? Are you invited?"

Aunt Evie shook her head.

"Is anyone else I know invited, then?" Ali asked. "And why would someone my age want to go to tea with a bunch of old ladies in the first place?"

"You'll want to go if you know what's good for you," Aunt Evie had said severely. "But this doesn't give us much time."

"Time for what?" Ali had asked.

"To get down to Phoenix and find you something appropriate to wear," Aunt Evie had answered.

Ali's high school years had been tough ones for the owners and operators of the Sugarloaf Café. Things had been so lean during Ali's junior year that she had turned down an invitation to the prom rather than admit she didn't have a formal to wear and couldn't afford to buy one.

By the end of her senior year, things were only marginally better, but she was astonished when Aunt Evie took the whole next day—a Saturday—off work. She drove Ali to Metrocenter, a shopping mall two hours away in Phoenix, where they spent the whole day at what Ali considered to be the very ritzy Goldwater's Department Store putting together a tea-appropriate outfit. Aunt Evie had charged the whole extravagant expense—a stylish linen suit, silk blouse, and shoes—to her personal account. The loan of Aunt Evie's fake pearls would complete the outfit.

At the time, Ali had been too naive to question her aunt's uncharacteristic behavior. Instead she had simply accepted Aunt Evie's kindness at face value.

The next week at school, Ali had held her breath hoping to hear that some of her classmates had also received invitations to the unprecedented Ashcroft tea, but no one had. No one mentioned it, not even Ali's best friend, Reenie Bernard, so Ali didn't mention it, either.

Finally, on the appointed day, Ali had left her parents and Aunt Evie hard at work at the Sugarloaf doing Sunday afternoon cleanup and had driven herself to Anna Lee Ashcroft's Manzanita Hills place overlooking downtown Sedona. Compared to her parents humble abode out behind the restaurant, the Ashcroft home was downright palatial.

Ali had driven up the steep, blacktopped driveway and parked her mother's Dodge in front of a glass-walled architectural miracle with a spectacular view that encompassed the whole valley. Once out of the car, Ali, unaccustomed to wearing high heels, had tottered unsteadily up the wide flagstone walkway. By the time she stepped onto the spacious front porch shaded by a curtain of bloom-laden wisteria, her knees were still knocking but she was grateful not to have tripped and fallen.

Taking a deep, steadying breath, Ali rang the bell. The door was opened by a maid wearing a black-and-white uniform who led her into and through the house. The exquisite furniture, gleaming wood tables, and lush oriental rugs were marvelous to behold. She tried not to stare as she was escorted out to a screened porch overlooking an immense swimming pool. Her hostess, a frail and seemingly ancient woman confined to a wheelchair and with her legs wrapped in a shawl, waited there while another somewhat younger woman hovered watchfully in the background.

Ali was shown to a chair next to a table set with an elaborate collection of delicate cups, saucers, plates, and silver as well as an amazing collection of tiny, crustless sandwiches and sweets.

"So," the old woman said, peering across the table at Ali through a pair of bejeweled spectacles. "I'm Mrs. Ashcroft and this is my daughter, Arabella. You must be Alison Larson. Let's have a look at you."

Feeling like a hapless worm being examined by some sharp-eyed, hungry robin, Ali had no choice but to endure the woman's silent scrutiny. At last she nodded as if satisfied with Ali's appearance. "I suppose you'll do," she said.

*Do for what?* Ali wondered.

"Your teachers all speak very highly of you," Anna Lee said.

Ali should have been delighted to hear that, but she couldn't help wondering why Anna Lee Ashcroft had been gossiping about her with Ali's teachers at Mingus Mountain High. As it was, all Ali could do was nod stupidly. "Thank you," she murmured.

"I understand you want to study journalism," Anna Lee continued.

Ali had discussed her long-held secret ambition once or twice with Mrs. Casey, her journalism teacher, but since going to college seemed like an impossible dream at the moment, Ali was trying to think about the future in somewhat more realistic terms—like maybe going to work for the phone company.

"I may have mentioned it," Ali managed.

"You've changed your mind then?" Anna Lee demanded sharply. "You're no longer interested in journalism?"

"It's not that," Ali said forlornly, "it's just . . ."

"Just what?"

"I still want to study journalism," Ali said at last, "but I'll probably have to work a couple of years to earn money before I can think about going to college." It was a painful admission.

"My parents really can't help out very much right now. I'll have to earn my own way."

"You're telling me you're poor then?" Anna Lee wanted to know.

Ali looked around the room. Even out on this screened patio, the elegant furnishings were far beyond anything Ali had ever seen in her own home or even in her friend Reenie Bernard's far more upscale surroundings. Ali had never thought of herself or of her family as poor, but now with something for comparison she realized they probably were.

"I suppose so," Ali said.

Without another word, Anna Lee Ashcroft grasped the handle of a small china bell and gave it a sharp ring. Almost immediately a man appeared bearing a tray—a silver tray with a silver tea service on it. Remembering the scene now, Ali couldn't help but wonder if that man and the sprite who had delivered that morning's envelope weren't one and the same—albeit a few decades older.

The man had carefully placed the tea service on the table in front of Anna Lee. She had leaned forward and picked up a cup. "Sugar?" she asked, filling the cup to the brim and handing it over with a surprisingly steady hand.

Ali nodded.

"One lump or two?"

"Two, please."

"Milk?"

"No, thank you."

Arabella moved silently to the foreground and began deftly placing finger sandwiches and what Ali would later recognize as petit fours onto delicately patterned china plates. Mrs. Ashcroft said nothing more until the butler—at least that's what Ali assumed he was—had retreated back the way he had come, disappearing behind a pair of swinging doors into what Ali assumed must lead to a hallway or maybe the kitchen.

Ali juggled cup, saucer, napkin, and plate and hoped she wasn't doing something terribly gauche while Anna Lee Ashcroft poured two additional cups—one for her daughter and one for herself.

"I don't have a college education, either," Anna Lee said at last. "In my day young women of my social standing weren't encouraged to go off to college. When Arabella came along, her father sent her off to finishing school in Switzerland, but that was it. Furthering her education beyond that would have been unseemly."

No comment from Ali seemed called for, so she kept quiet and concentrated on not dribbling any tea down the front of her new silk blouse.

"But just because my daughter and I don't have the benefit of a higher education," Anna Lee continued, "doesn't mean we think it's unimportant, right, Arabella?"

Arabella nodded but said nothing. Sipping her tea, she seemed content to let her mother do the bulk of the talking, but there was something in the daughter's wary silence that made Ali uneasy.

"You must be wondering why you've been asked to come here today," Anna Lee continued.

"Yes," Ali said. "I am."

"This is the first time I've done this," Anna Lee said, "so it may seem a bit awkward. I've been told that most of the time announcements of this nature are made at class night celebrations or at some other official occasion, but I wanted to do it this way. In private."

Ali was still mystified.

"I've decided to use some of my inheritance from my mother to establish a scholarship in her honor, the Amelia Dougherty Askins Scholarship, to benefit poor but smart girls from this area. You've been selected to be our first recipient—as long as you go on to school, that is."

Ali was stunned. "A scholarship?" she managed, still not sure she had heard correctly. "You're giving me a scholarship?"

Anna Lee Ashcroft nodded. "Not quite a 'full ride' as they say," she added dryly. "What you'll get from us is enough for tuition, books, room, and some board. If your parents really can't help, you may need to work part time, but you shouldn't have to put off starting. In fact, you should be able to go off to school this fall right along with all your classmates."

And that's exactly what Ali had done. The scholarship had made all the difference for her—it had made going on to college possible. And everything else in Ali's life had flowed from there.

So Alison Larson Reynolds owed the Ashcrofts—owed them big. If Arabella Ashcroft wanted to summon her to tea once again some twenty-five years later, Ali would be there—with bells on.

## { CHAPTER 2 }

It was late morning when Phoenix PD homicide detectives Larry Marsh and Hank Mendoza arrived at the crime scene in South Mountain Preserve. "What have we got?" Hank asked Abigail Jacobs, the patrol officer who along with her partner, Ed Whalen, had been the first officers to respond to Sybil Harriman's desperate call to 911.

"We've got a dragger," Officer Jacobs told them. "From what I'm seeing it looks like somebody slammed this poor guy's left hand in a car door and then dragged him for the better part of a mile—through the parking lot and over several speed bumps. The bloody trail starts way back there by the park entrance."

"Any ID?"

"Not so far. From what's left of his clothing, it looks like maybe he was out jogging. We've got no ID and no cell phone, either."

"Too bad," Hank told her. "These days cell phones work better than anything. Any idea when it happened?"

"The witness found him here about ten A.M."

"You're sure it's a him?"

"Yes, and whoever he is, he's wearing the remains of a fairly expensive watch," Abbie Jacobs replied. "A Patek Philippe, and that's still working."

"A what?" Larry Marsh said.

Hank Mendoza laughed. "The poor guy's beaten to hell but the damned watch is still running. But then again, you wouldn't know a Patek Philippe from a hole in the ground. You're still wearing your Wal-Mart special Timex."

"It works," Larry replied. "And nobody's tried to steal it."

"Turns out nobody tried to steal this one, either," Abbie said, looking down at the mangled hand. "And I for one don't blame them."

"Blood's all dry," Hank observed. "My guess is this happened sometime overnight. Isn't the park supposed to be closed at night?"

"Supposed to be," Officer Jacobs agreed with a shake of her head that left her thick, braided ponytail swinging back and forth. "But declaring it closed and keeping it closed are two different things," she said. "Kids manage to get in here overnight all the time. Last Halloween we had to rescue a bunch of kids. They were here having a midnight kegger and ran afoul of a herd of javelina. The javelina were not amused."

"So you patrol out here a lot then?" Hank asked.

Abbie Jacob nodded.

A van with the medical examiner's logo on the door slowly made its way up the road and stopped nearby. Associate ME Todd Rangel, still munching the last of a Sonic burger, heaved his bulky frame out of the van.

"Sorry to be late to the party, boys and girls," he said to the group gathered around the battered and bloodied corpse. "But a man's gotta eat. What have I missed?"

"Not too many meals," Hank muttered under his breath. Larry elbowed him in the ribs, warning him to silence. Of all the people in the county ME's office, Todd Rangel won no popularity contests with the homicide cops who were obliged to work with him. The man was overbearing and self-important with a tendency for bossing people around. He was also uncommonly lazy. Todd Rangel's idea of teamwork was to order someone else to do the heavy lifting.

"Officer Jacobs here says she thinks it's a dragger," Larry told the ME, moving aside to allow Rangel access to the corpse. "She says she followed a trail of blood for the better part of a mile from back toward the entrance."

Shading his eyes with one hand, Rangel looked in the direction Larry was pointing. "I'll check that out by car a little later," he said.

Hank Mendoza shook his head and rolled his eyes. "Big surprise," he mouthed to Abbie Jacobs, who barely managed to suppress a grin.

"Robbery?" Rangel asked.

"Could be, but probably not," Larry said. "His wallet's missing, but as you can see, the watch isn't."

Rangel nodded. "Or maybe it was too bloody and the perp didn't want to risk taking it off."

"Maybe."

"You guys got what you need from right around here or can I go to work?" Rangel asked.

"Go ahead," Hank said. "Knock yourself out."

While they had been talking, several uniformed officers, including Abbie's partner Ed Whalen and a crew of crime scene techs, had been moving along the roadway and using traffic cones to mark off the bloody strip in the pavement. Leaving

Todd Rangel alone with the body, the detectives walked over to Whalen and the others. One of the techs was wielding a camera and snapping photos of bloodstained tire tracks. Another was carefully making plaster casts.

Suddenly, a few feet away, another crime scene tech raised a shout. "Hey, come look at this," he said.

Led by Officer Whalen, the detectives hurried over to the edge of the pavement. There, on the shoulder of the road and partly concealed in a clump of dried grass, lay a shiny handgun.

"No rust," the tech told them. "That means it hasn't been here long."

Whalen leaned down and threaded a pencil through the trigger guard and lifted the weapon out of the grass. "Smith & Wesson Chief's Special," he said.

"Has it been fired?" Detective Marsh asked.

Whalen raised the revolver to his nose and sniffed. "Not anytime recently," he said.

"Bag it anyway," Hank Mendoza ordered. "Just because no one's fired it doesn't mean it isn't related."

"Where's the witness?" Larry asked.

"She wasn't feeling too well," Abbie replied. "I offered to call an ambulance and have her taken to a hospital to be checked out, but she said she just wanted to go home and lie down. I have her address in Awatukee. Want to stop by and see her?"

"Absolutely," Detective Marsh told her. "Hank and I will pay her a visit and find out what she knows."

"It won't be much," Abbie said. "She was just out walking and, like, found the body."

Larry cringed. Cops who overused the word *like* tended to make him feel older than his years.

"Come on, Hank, let's go and see if she'll, like, tell us something."

Hank rolled his eyes again. Fortunately, Officer Abbie Jacobs didn't even, like, notice.

• • •

**CUTLOOSEBLOG.COM**
*Tuesday, January 10, 2006*

Sometimes, when you're trying to get out of a hole, the first thing you have to do is stop digging. And maybe, in the course of the last few weeks, we've all fallen into the same rut and have been digging it deeper day by day. I know for sure *I've* fallen into a rut.

Yes, grief is important. It's also tough. And depressing. And draining. And it's very hard work. For weeks now I've felt as though both my feet were nailed to the floor. My mother has hinted that perhaps a visit to a doctor and a prescription of antidepressants might be in order, but I'm not there yet. Give me another few months. If I'm still in the same fog, maybe it will be time to reconsider.

But this is my blog, and for right now, I'm changing the subject.

When I was in high school, finances in our family were very tight—and I do mean *very*! I had wanted to go to college, and I had a GPA that made my going to college a reasonable assumption, but my family didn't have the financial wherewithal to make that happen. Both my parents had lived through enough hard times that they were adamantly opposed to my taking on any kind of debt. Since student loans were out of the question, then, and since I wasn't anywhere near National Merit Scholarship material, I had pretty well decided that I'd have to take time off from school long enough to earn some tuition money.

But then a miracle happened. Someone I didn't even know offered me a scholarship—an unexpected scholarship, one I hadn't heard of much less applied for. And that scholarship made all the difference. When my friends went on to college that fall, so did I.

This morning I received an invitation to tea from the daughter of the woman who gave me that helping hand so long ago. And I'm going. This afternoon. As soon as I finish posting this, I'm going to shower and put on my makeup. I'll dress up in my Sunday-go-to-meeting clothes and go there to say a much deserved thank you to someone whose unsolicited kindness opened up a world of opportunity for me.

I'm hoping that while I'm out there counting my blessings, maybe I'll find that some of the clouds that have been obscuring my view of the sky come complete with silver linings.

*posted 11:14 A.M., by Babe*

Ali was out of the shower, dressed, and mostly made up when the doorbell rang again. This time Kip Hogan, his customary Diamondback baseball cap pulled low over his eyes, stood waiting outside her front door. Beside him, resting on a four-wheeled dolly and swathed in a layer of quilted gray moving blankets, stood Ali's fully restored bird's-eye maple credenza.

"Hi, there," Ali said, opening the door. "Come on in."

"Afternoon, ma'am," he returned, lifting the brim of his cap. "Sorry I couldn't get here earlier. Something came up. Where do you want this?"

"Right here," Ali told him, pointing. "In the entry. Are you sure you can move it by yourself? Chris will be home from school in a little while. I'm sure he'd be glad to help."

Christopher, Ali's son and current roommate, was a recent UCLA graduate and a first-year teacher at Sedona High School.

"No need, ma'am," Kip told her. "I can handle it just fine on my own."

Ali moved back out of the way and made room for Kip to bring the credenza inside. Now he was a familiar and far less scary character than he had been months earlier when Ali's father had first brought the man home.

In the aftermath of one of the year's final snowstorms, Ali's father, Bob Larson, had taken his grandson snowboarding. While grandstanding for Chris, Bob had attempted a flawed turn that had resulted in a terrible spill. Bob's injuries had been serious enough that he had been thrown into the hospital briefly and then confined to a wheelchair on a temporary basis. Needing help with the most basic of tasks and loathe to listen to Ali's mother's not undeserved blitz of "I told you so's," Bob had found Kip Hogan.

Ali had no idea how long Kip Hogan had been living rough in a snowbound homeless encampment up on the Mogollon Rim before Bob Larson dragged him into the Sugarloaf Café for all to see. Ali and her mother were accustomed to the fact that Bob

Larson brought home various human "projects" on occasion. At first glance, Kip had definitely looked the part. He had been gaunt and grimy, unshaven and taciturn. Ali's initial expectation had been that he'd eat a square meal or two and then be on his way. That was what had happened to any number of Bob Larson's new friends, but Kip had defied the odds. Ali's father had been off the injured list for months now, but Kip had stayed on, staying clean and sober. He had made himself indispensable, helping Ali's parents with chores around both the house and the restaurant.

Months of eating decent food had put flesh on the man's scrawny frame. Still, Ali was surprised to see Kip was strong enough to singlehandedly wrestle the credenza off the dolly and move it into place. When he finished, he stood back and admired his handiwork. Then, frowning, he removed a hankie from his pocket and used it to wipe a speck of invisible dust off the refinished top. After stuffing the hankie back in his pocket, he ran a single finger along the smooth grain of the wood.

"Thank you so much," Ali said admiringly. "It's absolutely beautiful."

Kip looked at her and grinned. In all the time Ali had known the man, this was the first occasion she ever remembered seeing his face with an expression even vaguely approximating a smile. And that's when she realized what was so different about him on this particular day. Kip's nose still looked like it had been broken half a dozen different times in as many directions, but the gaps where teeth had been missing had now been filled by a partial plate. He looked years younger—and almost civilized.

"Never tried my hand at this kind of work before," he said, self-consciously erasing the unaccustomed grin. "I couldn't have done it if your dad hadn't showed me how."

"You're right," Ali agreed. "Dad's a good teacher, but I know you're the one who did all the work, and I'm so grateful."

Nodding, Kip picked up the dolly. "You're welcome," he said. "I'd best get going."

Ali watched while he loaded the dolly back into Bob Larson's beloved 1970s vintage Bronco. As Kip drove away, Ali remembered her father mentioning that someone he knew up in Flagstaff was thinking about starting a low-cost dental clinic. While Kip had been busy repairing the water damage to Ali's credenza, Bob Larson had been busy repairing Kip.

Ali's scholarship from Anna Lee Ashcroft had seemed to her like a bolt out of the blue. Now she wondered if maybe it hadn't been an example of karma in action. Bob Larson had spent a lifetime evening the score for that unexpected scholarship with his own countless random acts of kindness to people less fortunate than he.

With her blond hair freshly blow-dried and with a coat of properly applied makeup on her face, Ali left her house half an hour later to drive to Arabella's place on Manzanita Hills Road. The sky overhead seemed bluer and the rock-lined canyons redder than she remembered seeing them in months. Maybe the curtain of gray that surrounded her was starting to lift just a little.

Ali drove uptown and then on up into what had been one of Sedona's pioneering subdivisions, dating from the early 1950s. In the intervening years since her last visit, lots of houses had sprouted on the winding streets and cul-de-sacs on the lower part of the hillside. Those various homes, nice though they were, somehow betrayed their dated heydays like so many beads on a retrospective architectural necklace. But the Ashcroft place, situated at the top of the ridge and overlooking them all, was by far the oldest and still the undisputed top of the heap.

Ali saw the first small differences almost at once. The paved surface of the narrow, steep drive had once been a ribbon of pristinely smooth blacktop. Now the pavement was scarred with numerous webs of patched cracks and pockmarked with all sizes of potholes.

She pulled into the circular driveway at the top of the hill and gazed out at Arabella Ashcroft's unparalleled view. As a high school senior, Ali had been dazzled by the low-slung house with its massive windows set in deep, shady overhangs. She hadn't been experienced enough back then to recognize the stylish home's origins. Now she did. Clearly the Ashcroft place was a variation on a Frank Lloyd Wright theme—a Frank Lloyd Wright copycat if not the real thing.

In Ali's memory the place had loomed large so as to seem almost palatial. Compared to where her parents lived in a humble two-bedroom apartment behind the restaurant, the Ashcroft place was still large and lush. What had really changed was Ali's own perspective. She had spent almost a decade living in the oversize grandeur of Paul Grayson's Beverly Hills mansion, in a place where appearances always outgunned substance. It was that experience that accounted for the startling reduction of Anna Lee Ashcroft's once seemingly massive house.

There was still an undisputed air of quality about the place, but there were also signs of slippage. Some of the paint in the window surrounds was chipped and flaking. A few of the red roof tiles had evidently come to grief. The replacements didn't quite match the color of the original, giving the roof a somewhat spotty, freckled look.

The aged wisteria Ali remembered still covered the wide front porch, helping to shade it from the afternoon sun. Now, though, it wasn't blooming. Instead, its gnarled limbs were bare and gray in the high desert's January chill.

Ali stepped onto the porch, where the front doors could clearly benefit from some of Kip Hogan's newly acquired refinishing skills. The varnish was faded and peeling. This time, when she rang the bell, no uniformed maid appeared. Instead, the door was opened by the white-jacketed, white-haired man who, in a somewhat different outfit, had also delivered Ali's invitation earlier that morning. Seeing him this way confirmed Ali's earlier suspicion that this was the selfsame butler who had served tea on Anna Lee Ashcroft's screened porch all those years earlier. Back then, as a high school senior, Ali had thought of him as downright ancient. Years later, he didn't seem to have changed all that much.

"Good afternoon, madam," he announced with a stiff but polite half bow. "So good of you to come. Miss Arabella is waiting in the living room. Right this way, please."

The foyer was familiar but surprisingly chilly. The entryway rug was the same one Ali remembered. Back then she hadn't been all that impressed by it. Now she realized she should have been. It was a fine old Aubusson, thin and threadbare in spots, its intricate designs faded and worn down by decades of use. Ali recalled that a massive crystal vase had stood on the inlaid wood entryway table facing the door, and a similar-size vase stood there now. On Ali's previous visit, the vase had brimmed with a huge bouquet of fresh-cut flowers. Now it stood empty and forlorn. A thin film of dust fogged the surface.

The butler turned to his left, pushed open a pair of heavy double doors, and led Ali into a living room that, although still spacious, seemed much smaller than Ali remembered. The furniture and rugs, though, were virtually unchanged—at least the fabrics and placement were the same—but again Ali noted subtle differences. Thirty years ago the silk-upholstered couches and chairs and polished wood end tables had been evidence of a stylish elegance. Now, like the well-used rug in the foyer, these things, too, had a dated and somewhat shabby air. For a moment Ali felt as though she had wandered into a time capsule—a museum diorama devoted to some long faded glory—rather than into a house occupied by living, breathing inhabitants.

All those small details, taken together, left Ali thinking that perhaps Arabella Ashcroft had fallen on hard times. Yes, there was a shiny Rolls-Royce stowed in the garage and it might well tool around town driven by a trusted family retainer who filled in as butler and chauffeur and probably chief cook and bottle washer as well, but the look of the place made Ali wonder if there weren't times when Arabella Ashcroft had difficulty finding the wherewithal to fill the gas tank. Maybe, in the course of all those intervening years, there had been a complete reversal of fortunes between the well-to-do, sophisticated Ashcrofts and the awkward, small-town girl who had benefited from their largesse.

The living room was considerably warmer than the foyer had been, and the air in the room was alive with the sharp scent of mesquite wood smoke and the crackle of a roaring fire. Roving wintertime burn bans may have caused most of Sedona's wood-burning fireplaces to morph into ones fired by gas, but not this one.

At the far end of the room, two overstuffed leather chairs sat in front of the immense river rock fireplace. What appeared to be a tree-size log blazed on the hearth. A gray-haired woman, dwarfed by the huge chairs, sat upright in one of them. In front of her, on a rolling cart of some kind, was the one thing in the room that didn't quite fit—a sleek white computer monitor. Coming closer, Ali recognized the computer as an iMAC. The computer was almost identical to the one in Chris's room and included a wireless keyboard and mouse.

"Ms. Reynolds," the butler announced with all due ceremony.

The woman immediately moved the computer aside. Smiling and looking for all the world like her mother, Arabella Ashcroft stood to meet her arriving guest, pulling a shawl around her shoulders with one hand and offering the other one in greeting. Her dark gray hair was pulled back in a simple French roll. She peered at Ali through thick, eye-distorting horn-rimmed glasses. She wore a pair of slacks and a blue cashmere sweater with a matching cardigan. Her outfit was topped by a single strand of pearls. Ali guessed that the pearls, unlike Aunt Evie's, were real, and she didn't doubt for a minute that the sweater set had cost a bundle at one time, too. As they shook hands, however, Ali noticed that the wrist of one sleeve of the cardigan had been carefully mended. Not even Ali's thrifty mother did that kind of mending anymore.

"My goodness," Arabella exclaimed, staring at Ali for a long moment. "How extraordinary! I had forgotten how much you resemble your Aunt Evelyn!"

Ali Reynolds was Scandinavian on both branches of her family and had inherited a full complement of tall, blue-eyed blondeness that had served her well in her television news career. And she was accustomed to being told how much she resembled her mother just as Arabella Ashcroft favored hers. Ali wasn't nearly as used to being told she looked like her Aunt Evelyn.

"Since my mother and Aunt Evie were twins, I don't suppose that's too surprising," Ali observed with a smile.

"No," Arabella agreed. "I suppose not. Please, sit down."

Ali sat and so did Arabella. During that previous visit, Arabella had lingered in the background while her mother did the talking. Now it appeared as though Arabella had come into her own and moved out of Anna Lee's shadow.

"Evie and I were good friends at one time," Arabella continued wistfully. "We drifted apart the way friends sometimes do. Still, I was terribly saddened to hear of her passing."

The fact that Aunt Evie and Arabella Ashcroft had once been friends was news to Ali, but surprise was quickly overtaken by a renewed sense of loss. Growing up Ali had felt blessed to have two mothers rather than one. Edie Larson and her never-married sister, Evelyn Hansen, had not only looked alike, they had worked together on a daily basis as partners in the Sugarloaf. In many ways—including their devotion to Ali—they had been very much alike, but they had also been subtly different.

Edie Larson was always the solid, practical one of the pair—quiet and down to earth. Edie never took shortcuts. She cooked everything from scratch, and her recreational reading consisted almost entirely of cookbooks. She liked to see art films—tea-and-cookies films, as Bob called them—and documentaries occasionally, but that was about it.

Aunt Evie had been a vivacious and outgoing Auntie Mame kind of character. She was someone with eclectic tastes, a fondness for practical jokes, and a real sense of fun. She had loved movies and books—all kinds of movies and all kinds of books. She had read voraciously, everything from potboilers to highbrow literary fiction. She had devoured musicals and knew the lyrics to countless Broadway hit songs. Even though Ali had been living in California at the time Aunt Evie had succumbed to a massive stroke, Ali had felt her lively aunt's loss more than she would have thought possible. To this day Ali's MP3 player was filled with the songs and music from Aunt Evie's huge collection of tapes, records, and CDs. Chris had spent most of a previous Christmas vacation loading them into his mother's player.

Hearing Aunt Evie's name mentioned in passing brought back afresh the pain of losing her. "I miss her, too," Ali said.

"I'm sure you do."

Arabella turned to the waiting butler. "You may bring the tea now, Mr. Brooks."

"Very well, madam," he said, nodding his assent. With that, he turned and disappeared the way he had come, silently closing the heavy double doors behind him.

"So," Arabella said.

Ali remembered that other long-ago interview. Anna Lee had begun hers in exactly the same way, but back then, Ali, dressed in her unaccustomed finery, had been ill at ease and unsure of what she should say. This time she was far more confident.

"I've been terribly remiss," Ali said at once. "I should have stopped by years ago to thank both you and your mother for what you did for me when you awarded me that wonderful scholarship. I want you to know that your single act of kindness made a huge difference in my life."

Arabella waved aside Ali's gratitude. "It's not necessary," she said. "Not at all. You may have been our first scholarship recipient, Ms. Reynolds, but you certainly weren't the last. My mother derived a lot of enjoyment from the process, and so have I."

"Ali. Please call me Ali."

"And you must call me Arabella. I have to say that searching out possible scholarship winners is a bit like having a new treasure hunt every single year," the woman continued brightly. "We've resisted having a formal application process. Mr. Brooks works with me on this, you see. The two of us are a team. We track down deserving students and ferret them out on our own by talking to teachers and students and by asking questions in the community. That way we don't end up having to ignore a deserving student just because of some hard-and-fast official guideline. In fact, although traditionally most of our recipients have been female, one of our recent winners happens to be a boy who's majoring in nursing."

The butler reappeared, bearing a familiar silver tray polished to a gleaming finish. In addition to the tea service and a collection of sandwiches and sweets there was also a silver cocktail shaker and a pair of long-stemmed glasses.

"Care for a pre-tea martini?" Arabella asked.

"No, thanks," Ali said. "It's a little early for me."

"Not for me," Arabella said, smiling her thanks as Brooks poured her drink from the shaker and handed it over. "One of my little indulgences," she added.

There was something almost sly in the way Arabella said the words. Then, once the glass was in her hand, she stared into its depths for a long time without saying anything more. The silence went on long enough that it left Ali feeling slightly uncomfortable and made her wonder what, besides the freshly poured martini, Arabella Ashcroft was seeing there.

# { CHAPTER 3 }

Once tea had been properly served, Brooks politely retreated once more. Only then did Arabella pick up the threads of their conversation.

"As I was saying, we've had many scholarship winners over the years. Two doctors, several teachers, a psychologist. One of our girls just got tapped to do some work for the human genome project—you know, that X-prize thing. I've tried to keep up with that DNA stuff, but I just can't wrap my mind around some of it. Your exploits are a lot more interesting to me and a lot more understandable. I have your blog bookmarked on my iMAC," Arabella added. "I read cutloose every day. It's been a real eye-opener for me, an eye-opener and an inspiration."

*Exploits!* Arabella's unexpected use of the word caused a hot flush of embarrassment to bloom at the base of Ali's neck. It spread from her collar to the roots of her hair. She had never given much thought as to how what was going on in her life—her very public firing and her equally public divorce proceedings—might play back home. Yes, she had realized that her family members—her parents and her son—would be affected by all of that, but she hadn't considered that it might also reflect badly on people like the Ashcrofts, who had demonstrated such faith in her when they had awarded that very valuable college scholarship.

"Surely people don't think you and your mother are somehow responsible for the things that have happened in my life."

Arabella laughed. "Oh, no. Nothing like that. Not at all. But it is why I wanted to speak to you today," she added. She paused long enough to refill her cocktail glass, emptying the shaker in the process.

Mystified and still more than slightly embarrassed, Ali waited, wondering where the rambling conversation was going.

"I was particularly taken by the way you dodged the bullet last fall," Arabella continued. "How, when your husband was murdered over in California, the cops were so eager to blame it all on you."

It turned out there had been more than just metaphorical bullets flying back then. There had been plenty of real bullets, too, and Ali had counted herself very fortunate to have avoided being hit by one or more of them. So, although Ali didn't much like the turn the interview was taking, she answered politely nonetheless.

"For one thing, I had a whole stable of high-priced lawyers," she said. "That's always a necessary ingredient."

"Yes," Arabella said thoughtfully. "I suppose that's true. Don't get me wrong. I know there are times lawyers are a necessary evil, but I'm not keen on having what you call a 'stable' of them lingering in the background and soaking up money. As you no doubt know, they're usually far too expensive."

She sipped her drink and then continued. "I got the impression from reading cutloose that you didn't stand around holding your breath and leaving everything to your attorneys, either. It seems to me you were quite . . . I think these days the term is called 'proactive' . . . about the whole situation. I believe the relationship between you and your husband had been troubled for some time prior to his death. I happen to know from personal experience that when someone is busy making our lives difficult, it's not so surprising that we might occasionally wish them dead."

Ali nodded but said nothing.

"So when someone like that does die—someone like your good-for-nothing husband, for example—I trust you don't go around carrying a load of guilt over it. That would be completely unnecessary—and, under the circumstances, entirely counterproductive."

Arabella looked at Ali sharply, as though waiting for an answer or a denial or something. In fact Ali was too struck by Arabella's comment to respond at all. It seemed to her that Arabella had read cutloose, looked beyond the words, and glimpsed the darkest part of Ali's soul, a blemish no amount of soap could wash away.

Ali had indeed wished Paul Grayson dead on more than one occasion, thinking that having him dead would somehow make things easier for her. Now that he was dead, Ali was stuck with all the accompanying consequences. Not only was Paul dead, as were his fiancée and their unborn baby, but there was also another mother and another young baby fathered by Paul to consider. And even though none of that was actually Ali's fault, still . . .

"Yes," Ali admitted finally. "I guess I do feel somewhat guilty."

"You shouldn't," Arabella told her cheerfully, "but I suppose that's all to your credit. In fact, I'm actually glad to hear it. I've suspected all along that's the kind of person you were and are—

which is to say—relatively nice. After Bill died, I never felt a moment's worth of guilt—not a single one."

The log in the fireplace burned through and tumbled between the andirons with a resounding crash, sending a shower of sparks spiraling upward.

Ali wasn't sure where the conversation had gone. She seemed to have missed something. "Who's Bill?" Ali asked. "Did you have a husband who died, too?"

"Good heavens no," Arabella said with a laugh. "Not a husband. Thankfully I've never had one of those. In my case it was a brother who died—a stepbrother, actually, an older stepbrother. And I didn't kill him," she added hastily. "Not that I didn't want to, but in the end he took matters into his own hands and saved everyone else the trouble. He got himself all drunked up and drove off the side of a mountain. I understand in your case that someone else got rid of Fang for you without your having to lift a finger, either. I loved that you called him Fang, by the way. I thought that was inspired, and I always loved Phyllis Diller. You must have, too."

At a loss and not quite able to make the connections, Ali reverted to her old journalism training and asked questions. "When did your stepbrother die?" she asked. "Recently?"

"Oh, no," Arabella replied. "It's years ago now—right around fifty. I was actually out of the country when it happened, and I didn't hear about it until much later, so I've managed to blot out the exact date. After all, at my age I'm entitled to a few senior moments. Still, I'm sure I'll be able to track down all those gory details should I need them. Mother kept a file I'll be able to use for research, but that's one of the things I wanted to ask you about—changing names and details. When you're writing about an ugly situation—a real-life situation—is it preferable to write it as it happened, or are you better off changing names and such to keep the legal beagles from coming after you?"

"I'm sorry," Ali said. "I'm not sure what you mean."

"I'm thinking about writing a book, you see," Arabella said. "And I'm wondering if I should fictionalize some of it or all of it—you know, change names to protect the innocent and all that?"

*That depends on whether or not what you're writing is the truth,* Ali thought.

She said, "Look, we're getting into some pretty murky territory here. What you're talking about could have legal ramifications—adverse legal ramifications. You should probably consult an attorney, one who specializes in libel."

"I've already told you, hiring attorneys isn't an option at this time," Arabella replied. "But I will say that the idea that I might decide to write a book is the very last thing Billy thought would happen when he came barging in here asking for a handout."

Now Ali was really confused. "Billy?" she interjected. "I thought you just told me he was dead."

"Bill Junior is dead," Arabella replied. "Billy is his son, my nephew, and a chip off the old block if ever there was one. Every bit as contemptible as his father and his grandfather. DNA is spooky that way, don't you think? I wonder if the human genome project is looking into that? Billy's my nephew, but until he showed up Sunday afternoon, I hadn't ever laid eyes on him. Looks just like his father. That gave me a bit of a shock."

"How old is he?" Ali asked.

"Billy? Late fifties."

"And you'd never met him before?"

"Never."

"So why did he look you up after all this time?"

"Money," Arabella answered. "He's gone through what my father left him. He came here under the mistaken impression that I still had loads of Mother's money, and that I'd be happy to give him some of that, too. It turns out, of course, that Mother's money is pretty much gone, and I wouldn't give him any of it even if it wasn't. When I told him he wasn't getting a dime's worth of what I had left, things went from bad to worse."

"How so?" Ali asked.

"He threatened me."

"With bodily harm?"

"It sounded like bodily harm to me. He said that someone in my condition, whatever that is, shouldn't be left living on my own with only an aging butler to look after me. I told him Mr. Brooks is quite capable—he's only seventy-six by the way—and we're managing quite nicely. Have been for years. At which point Billy ran his finger across the table and said the place could use some dusting—the arrogant twit. Who cares about dusting anyway?"

Ali immediately regretted her own critical thoughts about how things were slipping a bit in the housekeeping department. She said nothing.

Arabella continued. "He went on to tell me that if I was going to insist on staying in this big, drafty old house, I should let him do a reverse mortgage on the place so I could hire some adequate help and do some fix-up kinds of repairs. That was when I told him I wasn't interested and he could put his reverse mortgage scheme where the sun don't shine."

Ali managed to suppress a smile. "What happened then?"

Arabella sighed. "That's when the nicey-nice long-lost nephew act ended. The gloves came off, and he went downright ballistic. I'm afraid having a dreadful temper is DNA-related, too. His father was the same way. Billy came right out and told me that if I refused to listen to reason and do what he said, he'd go to court to have me declared incompetent. He said that once that happened he'd see to it that I was locked away in one of those dreadful assisted living places."

She shivered slightly and rubbed the tops of her arms as though a chill draft had blown across her shoulders. "I wouldn't last a week in one of those," she added.

"Wait a minute," Ali objected. "You're anything but incompetent."

Arabella smiled a little sadly. "Thank you for saying that," she said.

"I didn't just say it; I mean it!" Ali declared. "It sounds to me as though Billy was trying to blackmail you, and blackmail happens to be illegal. Did you call the cops?"

"No," Arabella answered.

"Why not?"

"Because, if I did, I'm sure he'd convince them that, as my last living blood relative, he was just watching out for my best interests, that he was looking after his dotty old auntie."

"People who know you would never believe that," Ali said.

"They might," Arabella allowed. "Billy came off as a really slick operator. Probably a good salesman as well. If he takes me to court, he seems entirely capable of convincing some unsuspecting family court judge that I'm a complete nutcase—which I am on occasion, I'm told. And it would be that much easier if he brought up my past, which, of course, he's threatening to do."

"Your past?" Ali repeated. "What about your past?"

Arabella sighed. "I was institutionalized for a number of years when I was much younger," she said. "It was a very dark period of my life. Once it was over, Mother and I never spoke of it. Mother liked to tell people I'd gone to finishing school." Arabella gave a short, brittle chuckle. "I suppose that was close to true. That place almost finished me, all right, and I've spent years trying to put it behind me. Billy's showing up here and threatening to put all that unpleasantness out in public . . ." She shook her head and drifted into silence.

Ali was outraged. "Your nephew has no right to bring all that up."

"But he did," Arabella said, sipping her drink. "He has. And now I have to figure out what to do about it."

"You could just ignore it," Ali said. "Of course, I'd beef up security around here. Billy sounds like a bully. If you don't engage, maybe he'll just go back under his rock."

"And maybe he won't," Arabella returned. "I ordered him out of the house. I rang the bell and asked Mr. Brooks to show him out. The last thing he said to me before I sent him packing was that he'd be back."

"When was that?" Ali asked.

"Sunday afternoon, late."

"And have you heard from him since?"

"No, thank heaven. I thought I would have by now, but I've been thinking about him this whole time and thinking about what happened. There are times when not remembering takes a lot more effort than people think, and I've been doing that for years. But here, in less than an hour, that spiteful little worm brought it all back up. He's such a little know-it-all, but that's the thing. He only *thinks* he knows it all. He doesn't, and I do."

She took another sip of her drink, emptying the glass in the process. "I've barely slept the last two nights," Arabella said. "And when I have managed to sleep, the nightmares are back. And so, sometime in the middle of the night, I made a decision, and that's why I wanted to see you today."

"What decision?" Ali asked.

"I'm not going to sit around waiting for the other shoe to drop. Instead of letting Billy tell the story, I'm going to tell it myself. Who knows, if I manage to sell it to a publisher, I might even make some money on it. There's not much of that left, and a little infusion of cash wouldn't hurt the bottom line. What do you think?"

Ali took a deep breath. It seemed to her sometimes that almost every person she met was writing a book. "What kind of book are we talking about?" she asked.

Arabella shrugged. "One of those family sagas," she said. "One with all the usual ingredients—madness, mayhem, infidelity, incest."

"All of it based on your own family's history," Ali said.

"Of course." Arabella beamed. "With a family like mine, I wouldn't have to make up a thing."

Ali wasn't at all sure what was going on between Arabella and her long-lost nephew. There was a good chance that Billy's unexpected visit was part of some long-simmering family dispute that came complete with potential extortion and other disgruntled would-be heirs as well. It seemed reasonable to think that there were family secrets involved that might be better off left secret.

"Do you think that's such a good idea?" Ali asked.

"What?"

"Doing this kind of family exposé?"

Arabella stiffened. "Why shouldn't I?" she demanded. "Who would it hurt? My parents are both dead. My stepbrother is dead. I'm not. If I want to tell the story, it's my business and my story, not Billy's."

"Why?" Ali asked.

"Why do you write cutloose?" Arabella asked in return.

Ali had to think about that for a moment. "Initially it was to stay in touch with my fans and to be able to write about things as I see them," she answered at last. "But once I started writing about what was going on in my life, I discovered there were a lot of people who had been through the same kinds of things I had. And sharing ideas with them helped me somehow, and I think it helped some of them, too."

"Exactly," Arabella said. "Now, what do you know about incest?"

The question took Ali aback. "Not much," she said.

"I know rather a lot about it," Arabella said quietly. "Far too much as a matter of fact. From the inside out."

For a moment Ali was too stunned to speak. Taking advantage of the silence, Arabella reached past her iMAC, picked up the small wooden-handled bell, and gave it a sharp jangle.

"Mr. Brooks," she said, when the butler appeared noiselessly in the double doorway. "I do believe this calls for another round of martinis. Would you care to join me now, Ali?"

"Yes," Ali agreed. "I believe you're right. Martinis are definitely in order." Then, once the butler left the room, Ali repeated the single word as a question. "Incest?"

Arabella nodded. Reaching across her computer keyboard, she picked up a slim leather-bound volume that had been lying on the far side of the computer table. She handed the book to Ali.

"It's my diary from back then," she said. "I've kept it through the years. It's a talisman, you see, a tiny concrete piece of evidence that proves it all happened. It isn't something I just made up."

Ali looked down at the book. The word DIARY was embossed on the cover in gold letters. "But why are you giving it to me?" Ali asked.

"Because I want you to read it," Arabella said. "And after you read it, I want you to tell me what you think."

"You were the victim of incest?" Ali asked.

Arabella nodded. "For years," she said.

"And the perpetrator?"

"Bill, of course," Arabella answered. "My stepbrother. He was almost ten years older than I was."

"Were you his only victim?"

"Probably not," Arabella said dispassionately. "I'm the only one I know of for sure, but there may have been others."

"You never told your parents?"

Arabella shook her head. "It was years before I told my mother. I never mentioned it to my father, which was probably a good thing."

"Why?"

"Because he had a sister, too," Arabella said. "A younger sister. I never knew her because she died long before I was born. She committed suicide when she was only fourteen years old. She hanged herself in a closet. I learned about her for the first time a few years ago when a second cousin sent me a copy of a genealogy study he was doing."

"Are you saying that, based on that snippet of information, you suspect that your father victimized his younger sister the same way your stepbrother victimized you?"

"I know he did," Arabella said fiercely.

"Do you have any proof?"

"Not enough to hold up in a court of law."

*And not enough proof to put it in a memoir, either,* Ali thought. "Better make it fiction, then," she said.

"But if you live in a family of monsters like that," Arabella continued without acknowledging the comment, "you know things. You know them in your soul. If you don't figure them out on your own, you don't survive."

Just running her fingers across the diary's cover made Ali wary. "Maybe I shouldn't read this," she suggested.

"Please," Arabella said. "I really need you to, so we can discuss it."

Mr. Brooks returned bearing two cocktail shakers on a tray. He poured Ali's first martini and Arabella's third and handed them over. After two martinis, Ali would have been crawling on the floor. Arabella, sipping her third, appeared to be relatively unfazed.

"What's the point of all this?" Ali asked after Mr. Brooks left them alone once again. "You said yourself that your brother's been dead for years. Why not leave the past in the past? Chances are your nephew won't be stupid enough to bring any of this up. If he does, you can counter it when the time comes. There's no need to . . ."

"Bill was my stepbrother, not my brother," Arabella reminded Ali. "And yes, he's been dead for a very long time, but I'm not dead. And as long as I'm alive, what Bill did to me isn't dead, either. What about all those other little girls who are trapped in similar situations? What about them? I used to read all those Bobbsey Twins books. Do those even still exist anymore?"

Ali shook her head. "I don't know."

"Well, the Bobbsey Twins lived in a perfect family in a perfect world. When I read those books, I kept hoping I'd find someone in the stories who was more like me, someone whose family wasn't perfect, but I never did. None of the books I read even hinted that what was happening to me had ever happened to anyone else. As far as I knew, I was the only one.

"And I believe that's one of the reasons I've been so drawn to cutloose," Arabella added. "I've read it from the very beginning. When you got fired from your job and your husband dumped you, I'll bet you thought you were the only one who had suffered those kinds of calamities, but you weren't. I've also seen you take the bad things that happened to you and transform them into good for someone else."

"But . . ."

Arabella waved aside Ali's objection.

"I know there are lots of young women out there who are in the same situation right now that I was in at their age. If I can write this book—if I can get it all down and somehow get it published, maybe they'll realize they aren't alone. I want them to be able to believe that they can overcome whatever bad stuff is happening to them; that they can go on with their lives and be successful. I also want adults to pay more attention to what's going on right under their noses."

"Writing a book is hard work," Ali counseled. "The idea of eventually getting it published . . ."

"That's why I want you to read the diary," Arabella said. "I value your opinion. After you read it, we can talk and you can tell me what you think. Maybe you'll still say I'm better off letting sleeping dogs lie. But the fact that Billy thinks he can use this as a club over my head really offends me. I was the victim, Ali. If I keep quiet about this—if I let Billy push me around—then I'm a victim again. Or still."

Ali opened the diary and fanned through the pages. A few of them had been written on. Most of them were blank.

"As you can see, reading it won't take long," Arabella added. "I was given the diary on the occasion of my ninth birthday, and I wasn't very good about keeping it up. You're far more faithful at writing cutloose than I ever was at keeping the diary."

Ali didn't want to accept this assignment. She didn't want to have anything to do with Arabella Ashcroft's benighted book project. On the other hand, considering what Arabella and her mother had done for Ali all those years earlier, she didn't feel as though she had a choice.

"All right," she agreed at last, reluctantly slipping the diary into her purse. "But I'm not making any promises that I'll be able to help."

"Wonderful," Arabella said with a brilliant smile. "I can't ask for more than that."

Just then the double doors swung open and the butler entered the room once more. "Would you like me to clear now, madam?" he asked. He had evidently decided on his own that three martinis amounted to Arabella's limit. He was cutting her off.

"Yes, Mr. Brooks," Arabella said. "Thank you. That would be very nice. And after that, feel free to take the rest of the evening off. I don't think I'll be needing anything more. I'll just toddle off to bed."

Ali noticed that Arabella's tongue seemed slightly thick—that she was stumbling over the words.

*After that many martinis, I wouldn't be needing anything more, either,* Ali thought. *I'd be comatose.*

Mr. Brooks led Ali back through the front hallway and out into the front driveway where he opened the door to Ali's Porsche Cayenne SUV. "Do come again," he said graciously.

Ali smiled and nodded. "I will," she said.

Still she drove away feeling uneasy. *What have I gotten myself into now?* she wondered. *And how much of Arabella's story was the truth and how much was drunken rambling?*

Ali's intention was to head straight home, but a phone call

from an escrow officer at the title company detoured her. Left to unload her deceased husband's real estate holdings, Ali's first plan had been to empty the house on L.A.'s Robert Lane and then list it. In talking to a real estate agent, however, the suggestion had been made that she consider selling it on a turn-key basis with all the furnishings and artwork intact. Ali had thought finding a buyer on those terms was unlikely, but in that respect she was wrong. Within days she had a full-price offer.

The buyers were people who had just won an amazing Powerball jackpot and who wanted to move up into newer and classier digs without having to do any of the work on their own. They were ready to buy everything, pots and pans and linens included. In the back of Ali's mind, the distrustful, snarky part, she wondered if her agent had been straight with her. It seemed likely that the agent must have known that those particularly needy purchasers were out there. It made Ali wonder if maybe the advice from the Realtor had been less impartial than it should have been. Maybe she could have gotten more.

But the truth was, Ali Reynolds was glad to be done with the Los Angeles house and was more than ready to let it go. She had balked at unloading a few items—the Limoges china she had chosen when she and Paul married; the leather couch from the family room; and Paul's extensive wine collection along with the water-damaged credenza. Other than those, however, Ali had accepted the purchasers' offer and had let everything else go without a second thought.

"I know our closing appointment is scheduled for tomorrow," said Linda Highsmith of Highsmith Red Rock Title. "But the papers are here now, ready to be signed. Unfortunately, I have a conflict tomorrow. I know it's late, but if you could possibly come by this afternoon . . ."

"Sure," Ali said. "I'll be right there."

It was close to five. Most of the uptown area was a maze of road construction. Once through that, the traffic on Sedona's main drag to the far side of town was maddeningly slow as well, so Ali wasn't "right there" nearly as fast as she thought she'd be, but Linda was delighted when she finally did show up.

"I really appreciate this," Linda said, ushering Ali into a conference room. "It's only a parent/teacher conference, and I didn't find out about it until just this afternoon. I suppose I could have handed the closing off to someone else, but . . ."

"It doesn't matter," Ali said. "I'm glad to get it out of the way today."

The whole process took the better part of an hour. "Once the purchasers sign and the sale is recorded, the funds will be deposited in the account you've designated," Linda explained as they finished up. "This is only our good-faith estimate of the moneys due to you. The actual amount may vary slightly from this."

Alison Reynolds looked down at the line Linda indicated. The amount written there was more than substantial. It amounted to more money than Ali ever would have imagined accumulating in her lifetime.

And Linda Highsmith, who had also grown up in Sedona, seemed to be thinking much the same thing. "Small-town girl makes good," she said with an envious smile. "It must feel pretty incredible."

Ali nodded and smiled back as best she could, but the truth was, it didn't feel all that terrific. This unexpected real estate windfall was coming to her not because she personally had earned or deserved it, but because she had married well—from a financial point of view, at least, and because Paul had died before their divorce became final. In Ali's book, neither of those two items really qualified as "making good."

"I guess that remains to be seen," she said.

## { CHAPTER 4 }

The truth was, Ali left the title company office knowing she had money coming her way, but feeling more burdened by that fact rather than less. Ali briefly considered going by to see her parents, but decided against it. She usually enjoyed being around Bob and Edie Larson, but the last time she had seen them, her mother had been all over her about being "down in the mouth." Edie had asked several pointed questions about what Ali was doing to "get herself back on track."

Not wanting to risk being lectured by the parental units, Ali drove back home where she was delighted to see Chris's Prius already parked in the driveway. Chris's energy and cheerfulness were usually welcome antidotes for her current bout with unaccustomed torpor.

"Hey, Mom," he said, looking up from the evening news as she walked in. With his blond hair suitably moussed and spiked, the six-foot-one Christopher could have easily passed for one of the new breed of weather reporters showing up on the tube. Chris had gotten in the habit of watching television news back in the old days when his mother was often on screen. Ali was pretty much over her own TV news addiction. Chris wasn't. He sat on the couch with Sam stretched out next to his leg.

"My night to cook," Chris told her. "Pizza's on the counter in the kitchen."

Ali had grown up in a household at the back of a restaurant. Her parents were both professional cooks. As a consequence learning to cook had never been a priority—she had never needed to. When she had been married the first time, to Chris's father, she had cooked enough to get by, but that was all. When she had married Paul, she had moved into a place where yet another professional cook, Elvira Jimenez, had held sway over the kitchen. Besides, Ali's news anchor duties had precluded her being anywhere near home during meal prep time.

The upshot of all that meant that not only was Ali not a capable cook, neither was her son. Between them, they subsisted on takeout and leftovers sent over from the Sugarloaf.

Ali went over to the counter and scooped up a napkin and a piece of still steaming pepperoni pizza. She stared down at the message book beside the telephone.

"Dave called?" she asked.

Dave was Detective Dave Holman, a fellow alum of Mingus Mountain High, where he had graduated a year before Ali. He had served in the U.S. Marine Corps and, along with his work as a homicide detective for the Yavapai County Sheriff's Department, he was still a member of the Marine Reserves. During the years Ali had been away from Sedona, Dave had established a firm friendship with her parents. Now he was her friend as well. Months earlier, during that awful time in California after Paul's murder, Dave had been at Ali's side every step of the way.

"Yup," Chris said. "Wanted to know if you'd be home later. Said he'd like to stop by. I told him as far as I knew you'd be here. I also told him if he's not too good to turn up his nose at pizza he'd be welcome to have dinner. Tuesday is the two-for-one special, so we have plenty."

Pizza was their usual Tuesday night fare, and Chris usually spent the remainder of the evening playing city league basketball down at the high school gym. Much as Ali enjoyed her son's company, she was also accustomed to having the house to herself on the evenings he played ball, taking advantage of the solitude to work on her blog entries and go through her readers' comments. Tonight, if time allowed, she had planned to delve into Arabella's diary. There was a part of her that resented the fact that Chris had seen fit to invite company over without consulting her first, especially when he had no intention of being at home.

"Oh," Chris added. "And Gramps called. He wanted to know if you knew where Kip went."

"Kip?" Ali returned. "I have no idea. He was here earlier this afternoon, but I haven't seen him since."

"That's what I told Gramps—that since the credenza was there in the entryway, Kip must have come by. He said not to worry; something probably came up. I could hear Grandma grousing in the background—that Kip had probably fallen off the wagon and gone out and wrecked Grandpa's precious Bronco. There'd be hell to pay if that happened."

Bob Larson's vintage Bronco was precious all right. Ali reached for the phone. "Did Grandpa want me to call?"

Chris unfolded his long legs from the couch, dislodged Sam, and came over to the counter where he collected another piece of pizza.

"Depends on how brave you are," he said. "It sounded to me like he and Grandma were going at it pretty hot and heavy. If I were you, I'd wait awhile and give them a chance to cool off."

Ali found a soda in the fridge and brought it to the counter. She was several bites into her pizza before she spoke again. "I signed the papers on the Robert Lane house," she said.

"The sale went through then?"

"As long as the buyers sign, too."

"Good," Chris said. "I'm glad that's all behind you."

Except it wasn't all behind Ali. Selling the house would go a long way toward allowing Ali to finally straighten out Paul Grayson's financial obligation to his daughter—an out-of-wedlock child whose mother had refused, on religious grounds, Paul's offer to pay for an abortion. That whole issue was still an unsettling obstacle to Ali as she attempted to move forward and consign her deceased husband to where he belonged—as a fading image in her rearview mirror.

Something in Ali's facial expression must have betrayed what she was thinking. "Are you okay?" Chris asked.

"Of course, I'm okay," Ali answered abruptly. "Why wouldn't I be?"

"Don't bite my head off," Chris replied. "And I asked because you don't look okay. You look upset. You've been upset for weeks now."

*You're almost as bad as my parents,* Ali thought.

"I'm okay," she repeated, but just because she said it didn't necessarily make it so. She got up from the table, tossed the rest of her pizza into the disposal, and made a show of loading the few dirty dishes into the dishwasher. Once that was done, she went into the bedroom to get out of the tea-drinking attire she'd worn to Arabella Ashcroft's house and into something a little more comfortable—a pair of well-worn sweats. When she emerged, Chris had disappeared.

Without knowing when Dave would show up, Ali was reluctant to start reading Arabella's diary. Instead, she reached for her laptop, but before she had time to log on, the doorbell rang. Peering outside, she found Dave Holman standing on her front porch. With his hands stuffed in his pockets, he had turned away from the door and seemed to be staring off at the last of the sunlight on the distant red rock formations.

Determined not to let him gripe at her about her current emotional state, Ali opened the door with a flourish and was going to make some smart-mouthed comment. When she glimpsed the grim set of Dave's lean, square-jawed face, she stifled.

"Come in," she said. "What's wrong?"

Stepping inside, Dave grimaced. "It's that apparent?"

"Evidently," Ali responded. "What's up?"

"It's Crystal," he said. "She ran away."

Crystal was Dave's twelve-year-old daughter. Dave's three kids—sixteen-year-old Rich and two daughters, including eight-year-old Cassie, lived with their mother, Roxanne, and her second husband, a time-share salesman with a none-too-sparkly reputation.

"From Lake Havasu?" Ali asked.

Dave gave Ali a look and then dropped heavily onto the sofa. "From Vegas," he said. "They moved to Vegas the first of October, remember? Cassie and Rich seem to have adjusted all right, but not Crystal. Roxie called me about it just a little while ago."

Listening to the news, Ali took a hit in the guilt department. She had been so caught up in her own miseries that she hadn't been paying any attention to her friend's difficulties. The last Ali remembered Dave's kids had still been living in Lake Havasu with their mother and her new husband. She had no recollection about them having moved to Vegas.

*How come I didn't know about any of this? What kind of a friend am I?* Ali wondered.

"How long has Crystal been gone?" Ali asked.

Dave's face was bleak. "Since early this morning," he said. "Rich dropped her off at school, but she never showed up for any of her classes."

"A twelve-year-old truant on her own in Vegas?" Ali asked. *Not good,* she thought. *Not good at all!*

"They've issued an Amber Alert," Dave continued. "But only just now—an hour or so ago. Somehow the school didn't notify Roxie that Crystal wasn't at school, and nobody worried when she didn't show up at home as soon as school was out. When it comes to parental supervision, Roxie runs a pretty loose ship. Until it was almost bedtime, everyone assumed Crystal was off at a friend's house. And she's thirteen, by the way," Dave added. "Not twelve. Just turned. Her birthday was last week. I'm terrified thinking about what might happen to her, and with a twelve-hour head start, she could be anywhere by now."

Las Vegas was less than three hundred miles away—a drive of a little under five hours. The way Dave looked right then, he could probably make the trip in far less time than that. Ali stood up, brought the pizza box over from the counter, and offered him some. Absently he took a slice of the cooled pie and bit into it.

"If all this is happening in Vegas, what are you still doing here?" Ali asked. "I would have thought you'd be on your way by now."

"Roxie asked me not to come," Dave replied. "Told me not to, actually. She said she had enough on her plate right now without having to worry about me showing up and making things worse."

"But you're a cop," Ali objected. "How could you possibly make things worse?"

"You'd be surprised," Dave said grimly. "You don't know Gary, her jerk of a husband."

Ali didn't know Gary Whitman personally, but what little she knew *about* the man wasn't good. He had been new to town—a hotshot time-share salesman—when he had taken up with Roxanne Holman, wining and dining her while Dave was off doing his second tour of duty with the reserves in Iraq. The affair had started then. The actual divorce hadn't happened until months later, after Dave got back home from his deployment.

Just being divorced had been hard enough on Dave, but the previous fall, when Roxanne and Gary had moved from Sedona to Lake Havasu and taken the kids with them, Dave had been devastated. Ali vaguely remembered Dave mentioning that there had been trouble of one kind or another with Gary's employment situation in Lake Havasu, but that was all she could recall. She had no idea that another move had occurred, and right that minute, none of that seemed particularly important.

"Forget about Gary Whitman," Ali said now. "He doesn't matter. What does matter is figuring out where Crystal could have disappeared to and why. And how do we go about bringing her back home?"

"I suppose Roxie's right in a way about wanting me to stay here," Dave admitted. "I can make more inquiries—official inquiries, that is—by going through channels on this end than I could as boots on the ground in Nevada, where I'd be outside my jurisdiction."

Ali knew from personal experience that being outside his jurisdiction hadn't kept Dave Holman from riding to Ali's rescue when she had needed his help in California a few months earlier. Surely, with his own daughter at risk, there could be no question now about what he should do.

"You have to go," Ali declared urgently. "I don't know what you're waiting for."

Dave blew out his breath as though trying to relieve some pressure. "Rich said pretty much the same thing his mom did when I talked to him a little while ago—that I shouldn't come. He says Gary and Roxie fight about me all the time as it is. He said if I come up, it'll only make things worse."

"All the more reason for you to go," Ali insisted. "True, you may not be able to do anything to help find Crystal, but at least you can be there as moral support for Cassie and Rich, and they're the ones who need it. What did Rich tell you, by the way? Did he have any idea why Crystal might have taken off?"

"Not really. According to him she's been quite the handful since they got to Vegas. She's already been suspended from her new school—twice."

"Suspended twice from middle school?" Ali asked. "What did she do?"

"I have no idea," Dave said. "Roxie hadn't mentioned it to me, and Rich didn't say, either. But here's what I don't understand. It used to be that, of all the kids, Crystal was the one who actually liked going to school. At least, I thought she did. Up until this year, she was always a straight-A student. I can't imagine what's gotten into her."

"Divorces are difficult for kids," Ali offered. "And middle school especially can be tough, especially if you're the new kid on the block. In that case it can be downright brutal. I'm sure you've heard about 'mean girls.' But tell me about the Amber Alert. I know a little about them, but I don't know how they work."

"It's like an all-points bulletin for missing kids," Dave replied, "except more so. The announcements don't just go out to law enforcement agencies. They're posted on radio and television and on road signs on the interstates. They also go to bus depots and airports so busline and airline personnel are also on the lookout. The problem is, for it to do any good, it should have gone out within hours of Crystal's disappearance."

"So why are you still here?" Ali asked.

Dave heaved himself off the sofa and walked over to the window, where he seemed to stare outside. With the now all-enveloping darkness, his brooding features were reflected back into the room by the windowpane.

"I didn't tell you the real reason Roxie doesn't want me to come," he said softly. "She's scared."

"Of her husband?" Ali asked. "Because of what Gary might do if you show up?"

"No," Dave said softly. "Of me. She's scared about what I might do."

"What do you mean?"

"Because I told her I was going to get in my car, come to Vegas, and kill that son of a bitch of a husband of hers. It was bad enough that the slimeball destroyed my family the first time. Then he took them to Havasu. Now he's dragged them all off to Vegas. You can't just move kids around like that, hauling them from place to place like so much excess baggage. It's too hard on them. Crystal used to be a really good kid. If she's screwed up now, I'm blaming it on him. As far as I'm concerned, it's all Gary Whitman's fault."

"You may have said you were going to kill him, but I don't think you meant it," Ali said.

"Didn't I?" Dave returned gloomily. "I'm not so sure. Maybe I did mean it. But the point is, I did say it. Roxanne heard me and so did Gary. So that's the deal. First thing tomorrow morning Roxie plans on going to court to swear out a restraining order against me. If I come anywhere near her and Gary, I'll go to jail."

"Screw Roxie and Gary!" Ali said forcefully. "And screw going through 'official channels on this end.' You need to be there, Dave. Let the cops look for Crystal. That's their job. The people who need you the most right now are Rich and Cassie. You're their father. In order to help them, you don't need to go anywhere near the house. You just said Rich took his sister to school. That means he has his driver's license now, right?"

Dave nodded.

"So go to Vegas," Ali told him. "Check into a hotel somewhere close but not too close to where they live. Call Rich and Cassie and let them come to you and be with you."

"But I'm used to doing things," Dave objected. "I'm used to taking action. If I'm just sitting around in a hotel room somewhere, I'll feel utterly useless, even more than I feel right now."

"Being there for your kids is doing something," Ali insisted. "So is setting a good example about how to behave in the face of a crisis."

Dave seemed to consider what she had said before he responded. "I just thought that if Roxanne wouldn't let me come to the house, there wasn't much point in my going."

Ali shook her head. "You mouthed off when you probably shouldn't have, but so what? From what I can see, Roxanne isn't very high in decision-making skills, either. So go. Be there for your kids—for all your kids."

Dave looked down at his watch. "If I left now, I could be there by midnight."

"Yes," Ali agreed. "You could. And if you're really worried about taking a potshot at Gary Whitman, you could always leave your gun at home. Take some more pizza and leave the gun."

Dave accepted another piece of cold pizza and gave her a halfhearted grin. "Maybe I'm not that worried," he said. Pizza in hand, he started toward the door; then he stopped and turned back. "I guess I already knew what I should do," he added. "I just needed someone to point me in the right direction. Thanks."

"You're welcome," Ali said. "That's what friends are for. But drive carefully. You won't be of much use to your kids if you end up in a wreck somewhere between here and there. And call me. The moment you hear something about Crystal, call me. Day or night, it doesn't matter."

Dave sobered, his grin disappearing as suddenly as it had come. "I will," he declared. "I'll call day or night and let you know what's happening."

For a while after Dave left, Ali sat on the couch absently stroking Sam's soft fur and wondering if she had given her friend the right advice. She had no doubt that Dave Holman was capable of using deadly force when necessary, but she also wasn't at all convinced that his threat toward his ex-wife's new husband was real. It seemed more likely that what he had said was nothing more than bluster, an empty emotional outburst provoked by his daughter's unexplained disappearance.

Faced with a choice between blogging about this current crisis or perusing Arabella's diary written sixty or so years earlier, Ali voted for immediacy by reaching for her laptop. Once it booted up, she began working on her post for the next day's installment.

**CUTLOOSEBLOG.COM**
*Wednesday, January 11, 2006*

**We've all seen the headlines and watched stories like this unfold on the airways. A young girl, a teenager, inexplicably disappears on her way home from school or from a friend's house. Eventually, con-**

cerned parents go to the police and report her missing. If they're really lucky, an Amber Alert is issued, and their child is found.

Sometimes the missing child turns out to be nothing but a common runaway. Once she is reunited with her anxious parents, the family is left to cope with whatever it was that caused her to leave home in the first place. Sometimes the difficulties seem relatively minor—problems with a friend at school, a bad report card, or maybe a case of puppy love gone awry. Sometimes the reasons are much more troublesome and the finger of blame points directly back to unsavory conditions existing in the home itself. In families plagued by drug or alcohol abuse or where domestic violence and/or sexual molestation are the order of the day, leaving home can seem like—and sometimes is—the child's only viable avenue for survival. And when runaway children are returned to homes like that, it's often only a matter of time before they bolt once more.

We're also all too familiar with other endings to this story—horrific instances where missing children disappear and never return home. They simply melt into the ether. Days or weeks or months later their remains are found and identified—close to home or far away. At that point what was once a missing persons case is suddenly transformed into a homicide.

Today a friend's thirteen-year-old child has gone missing. She never made it to school this morning even though she was dropped off right outside the campus. She wasn't reported missing until late this evening, a good twelve hours after she was seen walking in the direction of her first morning class. An Amber Alert has been issued, but her father fears too much time may have passed before that happened.

Yes, the clichés are all there. The girl is from a broken family—a divorced family—with the distraught father living in one state and with the mother, children, and new stepfather living in another. Some people are probably thinking this is nothing more than a custody dispute gone bad. But it isn't that, not at all.

It's bad enough for families to have to face this kind of crisis when a marriage is solid and intact. It's even tougher to contemplate doing so when the marriage bond has been severed and the crisis must be faced alone.

And that's where my friend is tonight—facing the loss of his daughter on his own. His former wife has a new husband, and the two of them are together in this difficult time. My friend is alone—alone and angry; alone and grieving. He came to talk to me earlier this evening. I did what I could to bolster him, but there's only so much anyone else can do.

I have no idea how these events will sort themselves out in the course of the next few days. If it is a family dispute of some kind and if his daughter has simply run away, she may turn back up on her own when she gets cold enough or hungry enough or even tired enough. But it may turn out that something else is going on here—something more ominous than that. If foul play is involved, it's likely the story will go public. For right now, and out of deference to my friend's privacy and that of the other family members, I'm not identifying any of the players. There may come a time when that will change, when posting the missing girl's information on this Web site may be used as a possible means for bringing her home.

In the meantime, though, I'm going to hope and pray that doesn't happen.

While the post took its sweet time about uploading, Ali turned to her new mail list. There, along with a mountain of spam, was an e-mail from one of her regulars, Velma Trimble in Laguna Beach, California. Under the name of "Velma T in Laguna" she usually sent correspondence to the comment section of cutlooseblog.com. It was odd for her to write to Ali directly.

*Dear Babe,*
*You're the only person I can think of to write to tonight. You see, today I went to the doctor to get the results back from the biopsy for the lump on my left breast. It took almost two weeks to get the results back. I don't know why it takes so long, but today was the day.*

*I had pretty well prepared myself for the fact that it was going to be bad news, and it was. Since I have a computer, I had gone to the various Web sites and looked up what I could expect in terms of treatment options—surgery, radiation, chemo. What I wasn't prepared for was to be told not to bother.*

*"At your age," this little whippersnapper doctor*

*told me, "there's really not much point." He's probably all of forty-five and he should count himself lucky I didn't whack him over his head with my walker. The problem is, I can't get in to see an oncologist without a referral from my primary physician. And if he does give me a referral, what's he going to say? "Here's Velma, but don't bother doing anything to fix her because she's a useless eighty-something and curing her cancer isn't going to be cost effective."*

*What I want to know is this: Did this happen because Medicare reimbursements are so low that the doctor can't be bothered? Maybe he'd rather treat full-fare patients. Or does he just hate old people in general? (Surprise, he's going to be one someday himself. I wonder how he'll like it?) Or does he just hate me? Personally.*

*Should I go to the trouble of trying to see another doctor—not easy when you have to go by cab or bus because you can't drive anymore (another bad thing about getting old) or should I just take him at his word, decide he's right, I'm a hopeless case, and that the sooner I turn toes up the better off we'll all be?*

*You're probably wondering why I'm asking you these questions. I can't very well ask my son, because he would definitely be in the toes-up corner. Unfortunately my doctor and my son are friends. They belong to the same club and play golf together. That's how I ended up with him for a doctor—my son recommended him. I even signed a form saying it was okay for him to let my son have access to my medical information. That was before all this happened, of course.*

*Please write back and let me know what you think. I really value your opinion.*

*Sincerely,*

VELMA T IN LAGUNA

Ali was absolutely outraged. When she had been in California dealing with the avalanche of crises that had accompanied Paul Grayson's death, she had been overwhelmed by everything that had been coming at her. On the night when she had been at her very lowest ebb, a single bright spot had appeared. Velma T had managed to track Ali down at her hotel. Sporting a walker decorated with patriotic items—including red, white, and blue tennis balls—the woman had caught a cab and come all the way across L.A. to offer her support and to let Ali Reynolds know there was someone in her corner.

This was a sprightly, outgoing woman. And this obnoxious doctor was writing her off because she was eighty-eight?

Ali's first husband, Dean, had died of glioblastoma when he was in his twenties and while Ali was pregnant with Christopher. During her high-profile years as an L.A. area newscaster, Ali had done lots of work with the cancer community—helping with fund-raising and doing guest appearances. One of the side benefits of that had left Ali with a good deal of knowledge and with a whole list of cancer treatment contacts she could call on for help and information.

The idea of Velma, a most likely impoverished old woman trying to fight her way through the cancer treatment morass on her own, left Ali feeling physically ill. And suspecting that Velma was spending this worrisome, sleepless night in front of her computer screen, Ali wrote back at once.

*Dear Velma*
*I'm so sorry. Receiving a cancer diagnosis is always devastating no matter how old you are or how young or how young at heart.*

*Although I've dealt with my share of medical professionals, I have no idea why your primary care physician thinks treatment options are off the table at this time. It may be that you were in such a state of distress that you simply didn't understand exactly what he was saying. On the other hand, there may be other physical and medical conditions involved that make it risky for you to undergo treatment of any kind. There's always a chance that, as you suggested, your doctor is simply an uncaring jerk. Another possibility that tends more to aluminum-foil-hat conspiracy theories would have to do with your doctor having a conflict of interest in treating you due to his chummy relationship with your son.*

*Although I no longer live in southern California, I still have many contacts in the local cancer care medical community. I'll be in touch with some of them first thing in the morning and see what, if anything, I can do.*

*In the meantime, go ahead and worry. You are right to be upset and scared, but try to take things one step at a time and let me and others do what we can to help.*

*My thoughts and prayers are with you.*

ALI

# { CHAPTER 5 }

Hoping Velma would find the note reassuring and comforting, Ali spent the next hour or so looking through her database and thinking about who she should call on Velma's behalf. In the process, something struck her. It seemed to her that Velma Trimble and Arabella Ashcroft were being plagued by similar scourges—young, overly officious males who appeared to be attempting to micromanage the lives of older female relatives.

In Velma's case her son appeared to be conspiring with her doctor to direct her medical care without bothering to take Velma's own wishes into consideration. And Arabella's nephew, Billy—a blood relation Arabella claimed to have never met prior to his unannounced visit the previous Sunday—was now threatening to expose Arabella's unfortunate history as a mental patient in hopes of having her locked away.

Ali couldn't help wondering about motive. Was it possible both these overreaching people were after the same thing—their elderly relative's moolah? She didn't know Velma's son's name, but she did know Arabella's nephew's—William Ashcroft. For Ali, turning to the

Internet for more information was as natural as breathing. Her very first attempt at Googling the name came up winners. The article, dated three weeks earlier, came from the *San Diego Ledger.*

## 1.5 MILLION JUDGMENT IN REVERSE MORTGAGE SCHEME

Reverse mortgage guru and long-time real estate developer William Cowan Ashcroft, III, was found liable for $1.5 million in damages on behalf of the relatives of three elderly clients whose families claim were defrauded out of valuable real estate holdings in exchange for promises of payments that were never forthcoming.

A jury of five women and one man assessed Ashcroft $500,000 in real damages and an additional $1,000,000 in punitive damages with the proceeds to be divided evenly among the three plaintiff families. He was also held liable for the plaintiffs' legal expenses, which are thought to be considerable.

Helen Sampson, one of the plaintiffs in the case, was jubilant with the outcome. "William Ashcroft is a worm who specialized in cheating the frail and infirm. He had zero compunction about stealing my Aunt Claire's home right out from under her and putting her out on the street. I'm grateful that the jury has given us this moral victory, but it's still only a fraction of what Claire's property was worth and what she and Ashcroft's other victims should have had coming to them."

Thomas Rago, Mr. Ashcroft's attorney, expressed dismay at the finding and declared that he would be appealing the jury's decision.

*Billy, you low-down son of a bitch,* Ali thought. No doubt the reverse mortgage offer to Arabella had been little more than a ruse. He may have taken possession of the property, but if his previous track record was any indication, his promised payments wouldn't have been forthcoming. The longer Ali thought about it, the more she understood that, faced with rising legal costs and the need to pay off the judgment, Billy Ashcroft had come to Sedona planning on talking his well-to-do old aunty into giving him the cash he needed. When Arabella had proved to be anything but a soft touch, he had resorted to extortion instead.

After printing that article, Ali returned to her search page. There were twenty-nine other entries for William Cowan Ashcroft III, and she fully intended to read every one.

• • •

As the steamy windows turned the interior of the Explorer into a cozy cocoon, Curt Uttley reclined the driver's seat, lay back, and enjoyed it. How he enjoyed it. He had known she'd be good just from watching the downloaded film clip from the BJV section of his now favorite Web site, www.afterschoolspecial.com, and this was special all right. It was very special indeed.

He didn't focus on how old the girl was because if he did that, he might end up thinking about his own kids—his two sons, one a year older and one a year younger than this very hot, hot, hot little girl on her knees before him on the floorboard of his car. What Curt thought about instead, as he moved her face ever so slightly to achieve a better angle, was how impossibly good she was at what she was doing. And he wondered how much longer he could possibly hold off before letting go. Fortunately for him, she hadn't demanded that he use a condom. That made it all the better.

He had seen the clip and then had made it his business to find her. With the help of what she'd posted on her Web page, that had been almost too easy. And it had taken only a matter of weeks after first making contact for Curt to reel her in. That was what was so wonderful about little girls—they believed what they wanted to believe.

Now, though, within seconds of climaxing, Curt was startled out of his pink haze by the unwelcome flash of headlights in his rearview mirror. He had pulled off I-17 near Mund's Park into a secluded area that he often used for these kinds of late-night trysts where it was essential not to be disturbed. He liked this spot in particular because it was far enough from town that he'd never seen anyone else anywhere around. But there was someone here now.

Terrified that a cop was coming, Curt pushed the girl away and then peered desperately through the steam-covered glass while he pulled up his pants. He could make out a single pair of headlights, but that was it. No flashing reds, thank God.

"What is it?" she asked. "What's wrong? Don't you want me to finish?"

"Shut up," he ordered. "Someone's coming. Get your clothes on."

He could see several figures making oddly jerking motions in front of the stationary headlights. They seemed to be milling around some central object, but he couldn't tell what that object was or what they were doing. While the girl wiggled back into her clothing, Curt rolled down the window and peered outside. What he saw made his blood run cold. There were at least three men standing over a fourth one who was lying prone on the ground. As Curt watched they passed something that looked like a baseball bat from hand to hand, then they took turns smashing the club into their helpless victim, laughing and jeering at him as they did so.

The ugly sound of wood thudding into flesh left Curt petrified. A cop showing up was one thing, but what would these murderous thugs do if they spotted the Explorer parked only a matter of yards away?

"What's going on?" the girl asked again. "What's wrong?" Except, she didn't just ask—she screeched really.

He hit her hard with the back of his hand, just to shut her up, but it was too late. The sound of her voice had carried, and one of the bat-wielding attackers had heard her. Still holding the weapon raised in his hand, he had turned and was peering off into the darkness—staring toward the very spot where Curt had parked.

Petrified, Curt sprang into action. "We've got to get the hell out of here!"

He turned on the engine, switched the lights to what he hoped was a blinding bright, and hit the gas.

"What are they doing to that man?" the girl wanted to know as they raced past. "It looks like they're hurting him. We need to call someone. We need to call the cops."

She was already reaching for her cell phone. "Put that thing away," he ordered. "We'll call for help, but don't call on that."

• • •

As Ali scrolled through William Cowan Ashcroft III's checkered past, time slipped away from her. She was half asleep with the computer still perched on her lap in front of her when the ringing telephone startled her awake.

A glance at the clock told her it was after eleven. In her current frame of mind a late-night phone call couldn't mean anything but bad news, especially with Chris still not home. She answered with her heart in her throat.

"Hi, Ali," Bob Larson boomed cheerfully. "How's my favorite daughter?"

Of course Ali was Bob Larson's *only* daughter.

"Hope I didn't wake you," he continued. "Is Chris there?"

Relieved that her father was on the phone and that something terrible hadn't happened to her son, Ali tried to erase the hint of panic she was sure had been obvious in her voice. "No," she said quickly. "He's still down at school playing basketball. They don't usually finish up until after ten, and he often stops off for a beer or something afterward. Why?"

Bob sighed. "That probably explains why he isn't answering his cell. I guess it'll have to wait until morning then."

"What'll have to wait?" Ali asked.

"Going to pick up the Bronco," Bob replied.

"The Bronco? Why?" Ali asked. "Where is it?"

"At Sunset Point," Bob answered.

Sunset Point was the first rest area south of Sedona on I-17. "What's it doing there?" Ali asked.

"That's what I'd like to know," her father said with a growl. "I can't imagine what got into Kip that he went off and left it there. It's a miracle somebody didn't steal it. My friend Jack Riggs called a little while ago just after he spotted it. Jack was taking his wife down to Phoenix to catch a plane. He stopped to take a leak, and that's when he noticed my Bronco sitting in the parking lot. He says it has a flat tire, but the key was still in the ignition. He said he put the keys under the floor mat for safekeeping until I can get there to pick it up. I want to go right away. Changing the tire is no problem, but I can't drive two cars by myself. I need someone else to take me there, and your mother's already gone to bed. I was hoping Chris would give me a hand so I can drag the Bronco home before someone decides to strip the damned thing."

When Bob finally paused for breath, Ali realized it was one of her father's longest speeches ever. Clearly he was very upset. After all, his one-owner 1972 Bronco was his baby.

Bob had purchased the Bronco new and at an end-of-year bargain price in early 1973. Buying it with minimum down and on credit, the Bronco was the first and only brand-new vehicle Bob Larson had ever bought from a dealer. By dint of mechanical know-how and a whole lot of stubbornness, he had managed to keep the Bronco running for decades and for more than three hundred thousand tough miles.

Ali knew that other than burning down the Sugarloaf, no betrayal on Kip Hogan's part could have hit Bob Larson as hard as the hired hand's casual disregard of Bob's beloved vehicle. Thinking about it now, Ali decided even that might not have hurt as much. At least the restaurant was insured. The Bronco was long past qualifying for comprehensive coverage. A five-hundred-dollar deductible would have amounted to full replacement value.

So clearly the Bronco needed to be brought home. Chris was out having fun, and Edie Larson's early-morning baking duties at the Sugarloaf exempted her from any late-night excursions. That left the job up to Ali.

"No problem, Dad," she said. "I can take you."

"You can?" he replied eagerly. "You're sure you don't mind?"

"I'll be there as soon as I can."

"Thanks. I really appreciate it. Don't come to the house. I'll wait out by the restaurant so we don't wake your mother."

Ali jotted off a note and left it on the counter for Chris in case he beat her home. Then she pulled on a fleece-lined jacket and hurried out to her Cayenne. When she pulled up in front of the Sugarloaf a few minutes later, she found her father pacing back and forth in the parking lot.

"You still haven't told me what your Bronco's doing at Sunset Point," she said as he settled into the seat and fastened his belt.

"How should I know?" Bob asked irritably. "The last I saw it was this morning when Kip headed out to go see you. He put that credenza in the back and took off. Then he was supposed to pick up a load of groceries and clothes and blankets and deliver them to the folks up on the Rim. He did come to your place, didn't he?"

"Yes, but not this morning," Ali said. "He didn't show up with the credenza until after lunch. He said something came up."

"Something must have come up all right," Bob sniffed. "When Kip didn't turn up this afternoon, your mother was convinced he fell off the wagon."

"Do you think Kip stole the Bronco?" Ali asked. "Did you call the cops?" she asked.

"No, I didn't call the cops," Bob grunted in return. "Why would I? What would I tell them if I did call? That I'm afraid the guy I loaned my truck to turned around and stole it from me? The cops in town already think I'm some kind of bleeding-heart, do-gooder fruitcake. And when I say cops, I don't mean Dave Holman, by the way," Bob added defensively. "Not him. No, I'm talking about the guys on the city police force. I'm guessing the local gendarmes would treat this whole thing as some kind of joke, starting from the premise that I probably deserve it. I've heard that several of them are of the opinion that by taking in street people like Kip Hogan I'm just asking for trouble. It's one thing to hear that kind of stuff from my wife. I sure as hell don't need to hear it from our local civil servants."

Finished with his second rant in a row, Bob crossed his sturdy arms across his chest and subsided into an angry, wounded silence.

"Do you think something bad could have happened to Kip?" Ali suggested.

"If it hasn't," Bob replied, "it sure as hell is going to happen once I catch up with him."

"Did you try calling his cell phone?" Ali asked.

"The man doesn't *have* a cell phone," Bob pointed out irritably. "He's a street person, remember—an ex-street person. I offered to buy him a disposable, but he couldn't be bothered. I think he actually likes being unavailable."

Ali knew this wasn't the first time one of Bob Larson's human rehab projects had gone sour on him. She also knew her mother wouldn't be out of line for pointing it out or for being upset about it, either. Driving back toward the freeway, it seemed like a good idea to change the subject.

"Your friend said that there's nothing wrong with the Bronco," she said.

"It has a flat tire."

"But it hasn't been wrecked or anything?"

"Not as far as I know," her father answered. "Maybe it's out of gas. The gas gauge stopped working years ago. Who knows? Just drive," he answered with a sigh. "There's no way to tell how bad it'll be until we get there."

• • •

Crystal Holman crouched on the toilet in the locked bathroom stall for the better part of an hour, shivering and hoping the guys with the bats wouldn't come looking for her there. She had no idea where Curt had gone. The last she had seen of him, he was using a pay phone in the parking lot.

A woman came into the restroom and tried the stall door. A few minutes later, she returned and tried again. Finally a man came in and pounded on the door. "You've gotta get out of there. Other people need to use it."

Crystal peeked out through the crack. The man was wearing a uniform of some kind—a blue shirt with the name *Jimmy* sewed on the pocket.

Finally, Crystal opened the door and walked out past Jimmy. Past the woman. Out in the mini-mart, she looked around for Curt, but he wasn't there and neither was anyone else she recognized. Pulling her lightweight jacket close, Crystal darted outside and surveyed the deserted gas pump area. In the sallow glow of the overhead lights, there was no sign of Curt or his SUV. Thankfully, there was no sign of the guys with the bats, either.

Out of the corner of her eye, Crystal caught sight of Jimmy emerging from the restroom area. Before he could spot her, she rounded the corner of the building and melted into the darkness. All Crystal Holman wanted right then was to find a place to hide.

• • •

When they pulled into the parking lot, Ali was relieved to see the Bronco sitting awash in sickly yellow light at the far end of the row reserved for passenger cars. At first glance it seemed unharmed. As Jack Riggs had reported, the right rear tire was flat. Closer examination revealed that Bob's tool chest, gas can, and spare tire had been lifted. As for the flat tire? It was much more than flat—it was in tatters. Bob squatted down to check on it.

"Looks like he drove on it flat for a long time," he muttered. "So the rim's ruined, too. That means it'll have to be towed," he said resignedly. "Thank God we belong to Triple A. A wrecked rim, no spare, a stolen gas can, and a stolen set of tools—that's bad enough. If we had to pay extra for towing, your mother would really have my hide."

*She may still,* Ali thought.

Bob hauled out his cell phone and his wallet. As he made the call, Ali walked around the Bronco looking for and not finding any sign of additional damage. "What are all those boxes in the back?" she asked once Bob was off the phone.

He placed his hands against the back window and peered inside. "So he didn't even make the delivery," Bob muttered.

"What delivery?"

"On Tuesdays he goes to Basha's and collects some of their throw-aways—outdated food they can no longer sell—and takes it up the mountain."

"Where people are still living," Ali confirmed.

Bob nodded. "Nobody makes too big a deal about it. He just goes by, picks it up, loads it into the Bronco, and drops it off. The food's still usable. This way it doesn't go to waste and people who would otherwise go hungry have something to eat. He takes along any blankets and clothing that have come in during the week. That was what was on the schedule for today—your credenza and his run up the mountain."

Ali nodded. "I had expected him this morning, but he didn't drop off the credenza until after lunch. I told him I thought he did a beautiful job, by the way."

"He did," Bob agreed. "Fat lot of good it does any of us, though," he added bleakly. "I taught him a useful skill, but if he's back on the sauce it'll all go to waste."

Ali shivered against the cold. "What did Triple A say?" she asked.

"They're sending a truck. Should be here in less than an hour. You don't have to wait with me. Go on back," Bob said. "I'll be fine."

"No," Ali told him. "You won't be fine. I'll wait, too. We both will—in the car. It's too cold to stand around out here. If you catch pneumonia, Mom will come looking for me with a club and a skinning knife."

Knowing she was right, Bob headed toward the Cayenne without further argument. Ali had unlocked the doors and was about to climb inside when she heard the sound of a helicopter passing overhead. Months earlier, a low-flying helicopter had played a pivotal and almost fatal part in a Palm Springs area shoot-out. Before that, helicopters had come and gone overhead without Ali's ever paying the slightest attention. Since then, however, the noise of approaching helicopter rotors sliced into her consciousness with hair-raising clarity.

Ali stopped dead and stared up into the star-studded sky until she located the flashing lights of the chopper. It was headed south, flying fairly low and fast, following the general path of the freeway and moving toward Phoenix. Bob paused with one foot in the Cayenne and followed his daughter's troubled gaze.

"Medevac," he explained. "Probably taking some poor sick bastard to one of the big hospitals in Phoenix."

Despite her father's reassurances, Ali noticed that when she reached to turn the key in the ignition, her hand was trembling. She knew for a fact that her involuntary tremor had nothing to do with the icy temperatures. Not looking at Bob, she quickly turned up the heater and switched on the heated seats.

"Where would Kip go?" Ali asked, more to take her mind off the rapidly disappearing helicopter than because she wanted to know the answer.

"You mean if he isn't timed out in a bar someplace?" Clearly Bob Larson was still bent out of shape by his missing handyman. Just because his precious Bronco wasn't irretrievably broken didn't mean he was prepared to let Kip Hogan off the hook.

"I mean where did he come from before he ended up in that homeless encampment up on the Rim?" Ali asked. "He must have family somewhere."

"Probably," Bob agreed. "But I have no idea where. All in all I'd have to say Kip was a pretty close-mouthed son of a bitch."

"But everybody's from somewhere," Ali objected.

Her father gave her a disparaging look. "You don't understand, Ali. If you're going to work with certain kinds of people—with the Kip Hogans of the world—you have to get used to taking them at face value. You have to go with what they tell you—with what they want to tell you. You can assume whatever they say is a bunch of baloney, but you have to treat it like it's the truth, otherwise you lose them. Understand?"

"I think so," Ali said, but she wasn't at all sure she did.

They sat in the car in an extended period of silence while the heater gradually warmed up the SUV's interior. "I'm going to miss him," Bob said at last. "He was a big help around the place. Your mother can call me an old fool until hell freezes over, but even she would have to agree with me on that one. Kip Hogan was an excellent worker, and right up until today he was totally dependable."

"At least you didn't lose the Bronco," Ali commented, hoping to lift his spirits.

It took a little over an hour for the tow truck to show up and another hour after that to get the Bronco hauled to the secured area of a local garage. By the time Ali dropped her father off at her parents', it was after one in the morning. Back home, Ali parked next to Chris's Prius. Glad he was there, she was happy to creep into her own room and tumble into bed, where she fell asleep immediately. It seemed as though she'd been sleeping for only a matter of minutes when the phone rang again. As she fumbled to answer it, the clock on her bedside radio showed it was four-fifteen.

"Hello."

"Ali," Dave Holman said quickly. "I'm so sorry to wake you, but you said I should call you day or night."

Ali switched on her bedside lamp and sat up. "Where are you, and did you find Crystal?" she asked. "Is she okay?"

"I'm in Vegas," Dave said. "I just checked into the hotel, and we sort of found Crystal. That's why I'm calling you."

"Sort of?" Ali repeated. "How can you sort of find her? Either you have or you haven't."

"She called me on my cell a little while ago and wanted me to come get her."

"Great!" Ali exclaimed. "That's wonderful!"

"Except she's in Mund's Park and I'm in Vegas," Dave returned.

Mund's Park was a way station on I-17, a few miles south of Flagstaff. It was forty miles and an hour's drive from Sedona.

"It would take hours for me to get back to where she is," Dave continued. "I offered to have the sheriff's department send a patrol car to pick her up, and she totally freaked—like I was trying to have her arrested or something. And that's why I'm calling you. Would you go pick her up, Ali? If you could take her to your place long enough for me to get back there . . ."

"I'll be glad to," Ali responded. "Where is she again?"

"That's the thing," Dave answered. "She called on her cell phone. She said she's all right, but she wouldn't tell me exactly where she was until I promised I wouldn't send a cop car for her. We finally settled on my calling you. She said you should call on her cell and she'll give you directions about where to come to get her. Jeez, Ali! The idea that she's out there in the dark and the cold all by herself . . ."

Dave's final sentence faded away, but Ali had heard the hard edge of anger in his voice—anger and relief and frustration all mixed together. By then she was already scrambling out of bed.

"I'm on my way," Ali said. "Just let me find a pencil so I can write down the number." While Ali searched frantically through the debris on her bedside desk, a concerned Chris appeared in her doorway.

"Mom," he said. "I heard the phone. Is something the matter?"

"It's Dave," Ali said, waving him aside. "Everything's fine. Go back to sleep."

Giving his mother a disapproving shake of his head, Chris disappeared back down the hallway.

"Okay," Ali said. "I've got a pencil finally. Give me the number."

She took it down. "All right," she said. "I'll call her as soon as you hang up."

"I really appreciate this, Ali," Dave said. "You have no idea how much."

"Let's just say it's a little bit of payback," she said with a laugh.

"I'm not going to cancel the Amber Alert or tell Roxie what's happened until after I hear back from you and know for sure she's in your car," Dave continued. "Is that all right with you?"

"Sure," Ali said. "That's fine."

"Thanks again," Dave said. Then he hung up.

Ali immediately dialed the number he had given her. "Hello." Ali could tell it was the voice of a young girl. "Who is this?"

"My name is Ali Reynolds. I'm a friend of Dave Holman's. Is this Crystal?"

"Are you a cop?" the girl asked without answering.

"No, I'm not a cop," Ali replied. "I'm a friend of Dave's. Now tell me, is this Crystal Holman or not?"

"Yes," a small voice answered.

"Where are you?"

"Mund's Park."

"I know you're in Mund's Park," Ali said. "Your father already told me that much. Where in Mund's Park?"

"The restaurant is closed right now," Crystal said. "Just pull into the parking lot and wait there. I'll come to you. What kind of a car will you be driving?"

"It's an SUV," Ali said. "A blue SUV."

"Okay. Just pull into the restaurant parking lot and turn your lights off and on," Crystal said. "I'll be able to see them and come to you."

Mund's Park, a natural clearing in the forest of the Mogollon Rim, had once been the summer headquarters for a major cattle-grazing operation homesteaded by a guy named James Mund, but the cattle were long gone. Now Mund's Park's wintertime major claim to fame was as the only gas station stop on I-17 between Verde Valley and Flagstaff. There were a few hardy souls who lived there year-round, but many of the residents were of the "summer only" variety. That meant that during the winter months a lot of cabins and campers sat empty, and Ali knew that unoccupied homes were often attractive to certain segments of society.

"Did you break into someone's house?" Ali asked.

Crystal said nothing, and that was answer enough. No wonder she didn't want her father to send a cop car to pick her up.

"I'll be there as soon as I can," Ali told her.

Ending that call, she redialed Dave's number. "Okay," she said. "I've talked to Crystal. She told me where to meet her."

"Thank God," Dave breathed.

The relief in his voice was heart-wrenchingly apparent. Ali could find no good reason to mention the breaking-and-entering part of the equation. As a law enforcement professional, Dave would probably figure that out on his own soon enough.

"Drive carefully," he urged.

"Don't worry," Ali said. "I will."

Before Ali left the house, though, she stopped in the hallway closet long enough to strap on her holstered Glock. Ali had a license to carry a concealed weapon. If she was going to go driving around by herself in the middle of the night, she was going to have her nine millimeter along—just in case.

Better to have it with her and not need it than the other way around.

## { CHAPTER 6 }

Out in her frigid car, Ali turned on her heated seat and once again headed for I-17. This time she merged into the northbound lanes rather than the southbound. She actively disliked doing nighttime driving on that particular stretch of the freeway. For one thing, during the winter, it was often icy in spots—icy or snowy or both. This time snow wasn't the issue. There had been a single big blizzard just before Christmas, but by now most of that had melted away. All that was left lingered along the highway in murky gray strips or lay in a patchwork of shady spots off in the woods. The real danger that particular night consisted of wandering herds of elk who liked to make leisurely nighttime crossings of the highway, meandering across the busy lanes with zero regard for oncoming vehicular traffic.

As she approached the Mund's Park exit, Ali saw flashing emergency lights. As she slowed for the turn, it was clear from the collection of vehicles that someone had come to grief on the far side of the southbound lanes. Tow trucks had probably removed the damaged vehicles, but a few cops were still in attendance busily completing paperwork.

Ali pulled into the deserted restaurant parking lot and flashed her lights. She was feeling tired and more than slightly resentful toward her teenaged charge. For the better part of five minutes, nothing happened, then a figure materialized out of the darkness on the far side of the Cayenne and tapped sharply on the window. Ali rolled it down.

"Crystal?"

"Yes."

"Are you alone?"

"Yes. Hurry. I'm freezing."

Ali unlocked the passenger door and a shivering Crystal Holman scrambled inside. "Are you all right?" Ali asked, switching on the interior light.

Crystal didn't answer. Her teeth were chattering. She was wearing jeans, tennis shoes with no socks, a rhinestone-decorated lightweight denim jacket, and a black T-shirt that didn't come close to covering her bare middle. No wonder she was cold. What might work as outerwear for school in wintertime Las Vegas wasn't nearly enough for wintertime Mund's Park.

Ali reached in the back and collected the featherweight wool shawl she kept there. When she handed it to Crystal, Ali caught a glimpse of the girl's face. In the tearstained remains of layers of makeup, Ali noticed the clear outline of a hand on Crystal's right cheek. "You're hurt," Ali said. "Who hit you?"

"I'm all right," Crystal said.

"If you've been assaulted, we should call and report it."

"No. We don't need to report anything. Can we please just get out of here?"

"Not until your father knows you're safe," Ali said.

"You call him, then," Crystal said, huddling in the far corner of the seat. "I don't want to talk to him right now."

Dave answered his cell the moment it rang. "Got her," Ali said.

She heard Dave's heartfelt sigh of relief. "She's okay?"

From what Ali could see, Crystal was a long way from okay. "Medium," she said.

"Put her on the phone," Dave said. "I want to talk to her."

Ali held the phone in Crystal's direction. She sat with her arms crossed, staring straight ahead, and refused to take it.

"That would be a no," Ali said into the phone.

"She won't talk to me? What the hell's going on with that girl?" Dave demanded.

"I'm not sure," Ali said. And she wasn't.

"I'll get in the car, head back down there, and straighten her out," Dave said.

Ali doubted Crystal was in any condition to be "straightened" just then.

"Don't be ridiculous," Ali told him. "You've already driven five hours tonight. We don't need you to crash and burn driving another five back to Sedona. Let Roxie and everyone else know that Crystal's safe. Get yourself a decent night's sleep. I'll take Crystal home with me. You can pick her up in the morning."

*Although it already is morning,* Ali thought.

"You're sure you don't mind?"

"Not at all."

Ali knew Crystal was frightened and upset. She had come to get the girl, and Ali was prepared to be sympathetic and understanding, but Crystal's adamant refusal to speak to her father was puzzling. Still, the warmth in the vehicle had worked its magic. At least Crystal's teeth were no longer chattering.

"You should have talked to him," Ali said. "You put your whole family through hell, Crystal. He just wanted to hear the sound of your voice so he could tell for himself that you were all right. Are you going to call your mom?"

"He'll call her," Crystal said defiantly. "Can't we just go? Do we have to sit here all night?"

"You need to fasten your seat belt," Ali reminded her.

"My mom doesn't make us wear seat belts," Crystal replied.

By then, Ali's sympathy was pretty much stretched to the breaking point. *I can't help it if your mom's an idiot,* Ali thought. "Either fasten your seat belt or get out and walk," Ali said firmly. "It's up to you."

"But you told my father you were taking me home," Crystal argued.

"Yes, I did, but seat belt use is required in this state, and it's nonnegotiable. I won't break the law by letting you ride in my vehicle without one. So you choose. It's either use your seat belt or get out. Which is it?"

With an exaggerated sigh, Crystal flung herself around in the seat, located the seat belt, fastened it, and then settled back into the seat. "Satisfied?" She scowled.

Ali shoved the Cayenne into reverse. Moments after exiting the deserted parking lot, they were back on the freeway. As they headed south, Ali wanted to know more about what Crystal had been up to, and since kindness didn't seem to work, maybe a touch of toughness would.

"Whose house did you break into?" Ali asked evenly.

"Who says I broke in?" Crystal returned.

"Do I look stupid to you?" Ali wanted to know. "You weren't standing around outside dressed like that the whole time you were waiting for me, and if you'd been loitering over by the gas station, somebody would have called the cops."

There was a pause. "I didn't hurt anything," Crystal said

finally. "I was cold and hungry, and I didn't have any money. Only there wasn't any food in the house. Not even crackers."

Since being tough was working, Ali didn't let up. "Well, boo-hoo-hoo," she said with zero sympathy in her voice "Everybody should leave some food lying around the house so whatever burglars happen to break in won't have to go hungry. Why did you run away?"

"You're not a cop. You can't ask me all these questions."

"No, I'm not a cop," Ali agreed. "I'm just the poor dope who's spending a couple of hours of her beauty sleep saving your butt from freezing to death. So consider this a replay of the seat belt situation. Answer the questions or I'll stop the car and let you out."

There was another long period of silence. Finally Crystal said, "I wanted to come see my dad. I wanted to come live with him."

"But you wouldn't talk to him on the phone just now."

"He's mad at me."

"If you wanted to come live with him, you should have asked; you should have discussed the custody situation with the adults in your life instead of running away."

"There wasn't any use in asking," Crystal said. "Mom wouldn't let me."

"How did you get here?" Ali asked. "It's a long way from Vegas to Mund's Park."

Again there was a pause before Crystal answered. "I hitch-hiked," she said at last.

Ali was appalled. "Do you have any idea how dangerous that is?"

"I didn't have enough money for a bus ticket," Crystal explained. "And the guys who gave me rides were mostly pretty nice. The one who gave me a ride from Boulder City even bought me lunch in Kingman."

"For free?" Ali asked.

"What do you mean?"

"He gave you lunch for free?"

Crystal shrugged. "Pretty much," she said.

"What does 'pretty much' mean?"

"All he wanted was a blow job," Crystal said.

Ali almost wrecked her car. "He what?"

"A blow job. You know what that is, don't you?"

"Yes," Ali replied grimly. "I do know what blow jobs are." *Why the hell do you?*

Crystal shrugged again. "So I gave him one. It wasn't a big deal."

"You gave him a blow job for what, a Subway sandwich?"

"No. KFC."

Ali could barely believe her ears, and she knew when or if Dave heard the full story, it would totally break his heart.

"I suppose you know what that makes you then," Ali said. "If you're selling sex for money or food, you're a prostitute."

"Blow jobs aren't sex," Crystal asserted. "That's what the boys at school say—that you can save your virginity for marriage and still do blow jobs now. Just 'friends with benefits.' No problem."

For a moment, Ali was beyond speechless. When she was finally able to reply, she measured her words very carefully. "Some boys will say anything to get what they want out of a girl. But if I were a nice man looking for someone equally nice to marry, a blow-job virgin wouldn't be first on my list."

Ali waited for Crystal's response. When none was forthcoming, Ali glanced in her direction. The enveloping warmth of the vehicle must have affected Crystal because she had nodded off in mid-conversation. With her body sagging against the car door, she sat there with her eyes closed and her mouth slightly open, breathing deeply. Ali realized that she probably hadn't even heard Ali's parting remark.

As Ali drove on through the cold winter night, her heart went out to Dave Holman. *He has no idea what he's up against.*

• • •

In the cold hard predawn darkness, a single vehicle, an SUV, slowed and then rolled to a stop in the middle of the Burro Creek Bridge on U.S. 60 north of Wickenburg. While the driver stayed behind the wheel, two people got out. For a few moments they milled indecisively around on the bridge deck. Finally they went to the rear of the vehicle and pulled something heavy from the luggage area.

They carried it over to the guard rail, hoisted it, and then shoved it over the side, letting it plummet to the floor of the canyon, hundreds of feet below.

The driver honked the horn impatiently. "Let's go!" he yelled. "Somebody's coming. We've got to get out of here."

• • •

By the time Ali drove back into Sedona, it was already after six. Ali started to drive straight home. Then, at the last minute, she pulled into the Sugarloaf parking lot instead. As soon as the car stopped, Crystal stirred, sat up, and looked around.

"What are we doing here?" she asked sleepily.

The tough-broad act seemed to be working, so Ali kept at it. "You said you were hungry earlier. I'm willing to buy you breakfast, but on one condition."

"What's that?"

"The people who own this place are my parents. They're also friends of your father's. So, when we walk in the front door, I want you to turn right just past the cash register, go straight into the restroom, and use soap and water to scrub that god-awful mess of makeup off your face."

For a moment it looked as though Crystal was getting ready to argue, but the air in the parking lot was heavy with the scent of Edie Larson's freshly baked sweet rolls. Eventually they carried the day.

"All right," Crystal allowed gracelessly. "I'll do it."

It was early yet. When they entered the Sugarloaf, only the corner booth was occupied, filled with a bunch of regulars, a crew of construction worker bees who had to be on shift by 7 A.M.

As soon as Ali slipped onto one of the stools at the counter, Edie Larson came over, bringing an empty mug and a steaming pot of coffee. "If you're not a sight for sore eyes," she said, pouring Ali's coffee. "An answer to a maiden's prayer. And who in the world is that with you, the person who just disappeared into the restroom? She looked like something the cat dragged in—or maybe not even that good."

"That's Crystal Holman," Ali answered. "Dave Holman's thirteen-year-old daughter. There was some kind of family altercation up in Vegas. Crystal came to see her dad. I picked her up over in Mund's Park about an hour ago."

"A family altercation," Edie repeated. "You mean she ran away from home?"

Edie always seemed to be two steps ahead of everyone else in any given conversation.

"More or less," Ali answered. "She looked like the wrath of God. I sent her into the restroom to wash several layers of dead makeup off her face."

"Looked like someone beat her up, too," Edie observed, then she examined her daughter. "You don't look so hot yourself," she added.

"Gee, Mom, thanks," Ali said. "But why am I the answer to a maiden's prayers?"

"It's your father," Edie said. "He left me a note. He was out half the night on some wild goose chase trying to locate that Bronco of his. I know it was after one before he ever got to bed, so when my alarm went off this morning, I turned his off. I thought it would be better for all concerned if he had a chance to sleep in. With me in the kitchen slinging hash, we're going to be short-handed out front. I was wondering if you could pitch in for an hour or two—just until your dad wakes up and can drag his tail over here."

Ali, too, was dead on her feet and ready to be in bed. And this was part of the good news/bad news dynamics of being back home in Sedona—she was always close enough to be called on to help her parents in an emergency—if only for a couple of hours.

"What do I do with Crystal?" Ali asked.

"Does she know how to bus tables or wash dishes?" Edie asked.

"I doubt it," Ali said.

"There's no time like the present to learn," Edie said. "You know where the sweatshirts are. Get one for you and one for her."

When Crystal emerged from the restroom, her face was scrubbed clean. Except for the still visible bruise on her cheek, she looked altogether better. By then Ali had donned a Sugarloaf Café signature sweatshirt and had another one lying on the counter.

"What's this?" Crystal asked, picking up the shirt as she slid onto her stool.

"Your uniform," Ali answered.

"Uniform? What for?"

"For working here," Ali replied. "If you want breakfast, you'd better be prepared to bus tables and wash dishes."

"No way," Crystal returned.

"No work, then no breakfast," Ali answered.

"But I'm too young to work in a restaurant," Crystal said.

"You're too young for hitchhiking and a lot of other things I could mention, but that didn't stop you," Ali replied. "Now, put on the sweatshirt."

Without another word, Crystal unfolded it and pulled it on over her head.

"What do you want to eat?"

"French toast. Bacon. And maybe one of the sweet rolls they have back there on the counter."

"She'll have French toast, bacon, and a sweet roll, please," Ali called to her mother, who had retreated to the kitchen to oversee the grill. Ali turned back to Crystal. "When you finish eating, please clear the dirty dishes off the counter and tables and put them in that plastic dishpan over there. Then please reset the tables with clean silverware and new place mats and napkins. When the dishpan is full, please take it back into the kitchen. My mother will show you how to run the dishwasher."

Several new customers and the Sugarloaf's other morning waitress, Jan Howard, entered at once, all of them talking and laughing. Leaving Crystal to wait for her breakfast, Ali stood up, collected an order pad and a coffeepot, and headed off down the counter.

In the next little while Crystal wolfed down an order of

French toast and bacon, two sweet rolls, a glass of orange juice, and a glass of milk. Then, pushing her plate aside, she gave Ali a single questioning look before she, too, went to work.

It turned out that, under Edie's and Jan Howard's tutelage, Crystal was a much quicker study than Ali would have anticipated. By the time Bob Larson turned up, a little before nine, she had learned to do a credible job of busing tables and running the dishwasher back in the kitchen.

As soon as Bob saw Ali working behind the counter, he came straight to her station. "What are you doing here?" he wanted to know.

"Pinch-hitting for Mr. Lazy Bones," Ali returned.

Just then Crystal pushed through the swinging door from the kitchen and emerged carrying a tray loaded with clean glasses.

"And who's that?" Bob wanted to know, nodding in her direction.

"You should probably ask Mom about her," Ali suggested. "She can tell you the whole story."

"If she's speaking to me, that is," Bob said mournfully.

"She turned off your alarm clock," Ali said. "She fixed it so you could sleep in. If that isn't love, I don't know what is."

Without another word, Bob turned and headed for the kitchen. "Have you heard anything from Kip?" Ali asked after him.

Bob stopped and shook his head. "Not a word," he said, then disappeared through the swinging door. A few minutes later Edie emerged. She had shed her cooking apron and had changed into a clean sweatshirt of her own. "You two go on home now and get some sleep," she said, collecting Ali's order pad. "I'll take over from here."

Shortly after that, Ali and Crystal headed out the door. Crystal was still wearing her uniform sweatshirt, a gift from Edie. As Ali climbed into the Cayenne, she felt as weary as she remembered feeling in years. Once they got to the house, Ali gave Crystal a stack of bedding and directed her to the sofa. Then she handed her one of Chris's T-shirts to use as a nightshirt. Ali was in the bedroom pulling on her own nightgown when her cell phone rang.

"I'm just coming into Flagstaff on I-40," Dave said. "How are things?"

"Well, I'm certainly glad to know you took my advice and slept overnight in Vegas," Ali said. She walked over to the alarm key pad and turned it on. "Crystal and I just finished up helping out with breakfast at the Sugarloaf. Now we're hoping to get some sleep."

"Crystal helped out at the restaurant?" Dave asked. "Are you kidding?"

"You'd be surprised how far hunger goes in producing willing compliance," Ali told him. "You can come by here a little later to pick her up, but give us a couple of hours before you do. Neither one of us has had much sleep."

"That makes three of us," Dave said. "I'll go home, then, too. Give me a call when you're ready. That way you can wake me up instead of the other way around."

"How's Roxie taking all this?"

"Long story," Dave said. "Let's not go into it right now."

"Sounds good to me."

Ali was asleep as soon as her head hit the pillow. Sometime later a ringing telephone jarred her awake. "Ms. Reynolds?" a stranger asked.

"Yes. Who is this?"

"Your EMS operator. Your system is alarming. Could you

please give me your password, and are you all right? Do you need us to summon some assistance? I see on my screen that someone has gained access to your home through the front door . . ."

Ali reeled off her password and scrambled out of bed, pulling on her robe as she went. She hurried out into the living room. Crystal's blankets and pillow lay abandoned on the sofa. Her clothes and shoes were nowhere to be seen. Obviously Crystal had taken off on her own. Where the hell had she gone?

"It wasn't someone coming in," Ali told the operator. "It was someone going out—a guest going out who had no idea that opening the door would set off the alarm."

"You're all right then?"

"I'm fine," Ali said. *Fine but pissed!*

"You'll key in the end-alarm code then?"

"Yes," Ali said. "Yes, I will." And she did. Then she threw on a tracksuit and a pair of tennies and raced outside to the Cayenne. She caught up with Crystal halfway down the hill and pulled up beside her. Seeing Crystal in one of Chris's ski jackets didn't improve Ali's frame of mind.

"There's nothing like being an ungrateful pain in the ass," Ali told her. "Just where do you think you're going?"

"To see my friends," Crystal returned.

"It's a school day," Ali said. "Your friends are all in school. At least they *should* be." *And you should be, too,* Ali thought. "Get in."

"I'll walk over and see my dad then," Crystal said. Defiance seemed to be the order of the day.

"Not in my son's ski jacket, you won't," Ali said. "Now, either get in the car or I call the cops and have you arrested for petty theft."

"You wouldn't," Crystal said.

"Yes, I would," Ali told her. "I don't know what makes you

think people don't mean what they say. Do you see the phone in my hand? Do you see me dialing nine-one-one?"

Crystal favored Ali with a long stare. Finally, with a disparaging shake of her head, she flounced around the front bumper to the Cayenne's passenger side door and climbed in.

"Take off the jacket," Ali said, once Crystal was inside.

"Why should I?"

"Because I told you to."

"But it's cold," Crystal objected.

"Too bad," Ali returned.

Crystal removed the jacket and then flung it into the backseat. "Besides," she added. "I was just borrowing it. It wasn't really stealing."

"You didn't have my son's permission to take it," Ali pointed out. "That makes it stealing the same way taking food or money for sex—even sex you don't think is sex—is called prostitution."

When Ali glanced in Crystal's direction again, she noticed that for the first time the girl's tough-as-nails demeanor seemed to have crumpled a little.

"Don't tell my father I took it," she whimpered suddenly as tears sprang to her eyes. "Please don't tell him about the other, either—about, you know, the hitchhiking."

Ali knew full well that Crystal's running away had been a cry for help. Something was definitely wrong in this young woman's life. But Ali also knew that she was dealing with a master manipulator, and she had no intention of being routed by this sudden case of deliberately staged waterworks. She didn't relish having to tell Dave what his darling daughter had been doing, but someone was going to have to tell him—and Ali's first choice for that job was Crystal herself. Things were never going to get better for Crystal unless she accepted some responsibility for her own actions.

"If you don't want me to tell him, then you'd better," Ali said.

"I can't," Crystal said softly.

"Why not?"

"Because when he finds out what I've done, he'll probably kill me."

"And most of the parents I know wouldn't blame him if he did," Ali returned. "Seat belt," she added.

This time Crystal fastened hers without a murmur of objection, so maybe they were making progress. "Where are we going?" she asked.

"Where you said you wanted to go," Ali countered. "To see your father." And they headed into town.

Forced to move out of his house in the aftermath of his divorce, Dave Holman had taken up residence in the basement apartment of an old house on Sky Mountain. His landlady, a well-to-do widow with a penchant for traveling, was happy to have a dependable tenant to look after the place while she was off on one of her year's several cruises or staying for months at her flat in London. Dave, on the other hand, was glad to rent from someone who was seldom around and who gave him very little grief.

Pulling up the steep driveway with its tricky turnaround, Ali was reminded of Arabella's place. This house was comparable to the Ashcroft's in size and elevation but the view from that one was three hundred and sixty degrees. This one, built into the hillside, was only one-eighty and looked off to the east.

When Ali stopped the car, Crystal reached for the door handle. "Are you coming in?" she asked.

"Not right now," Ali said. "Please tell your dad what's going on. He's a good man, Crystal, and he needs to know. Let him help you."

Crystal nodded. "Okay," she said.

Dave must have heard them drive up. The door to his downstairs apartment swung open and he came striding through it, walking with a cell phone pressed to his ear. As Crystal exited the car, Ali saw a storm of warring expressions distort Dave's handsome face. He was at once furious and grateful; angry and concerned. As he hurried forward to gather his daughter into his arms, gratitude won the day.

"Thank you," he mouthed silently to Ali over the top of Crystal's head.

Ali nodded.

"Will you come in?" he asked aloud.

"No, thanks," Ali said. "I'm sure you two have a lot to talk about. I'd just be in the way. I'll leave you to it."

*Good luck,* she thought. *You're going to need it.*

# { CHAPTER 7 }

Having had her whole day blown out of the water, Ali was eager to get back home. She had yet to make any of the cancer treatment calls she'd promised to make on Velma's behalf, and she had yet to touch Arabella Ashcroft's diary.

With Crystal safely in her father's keeping, a relieved Ali turned around and drove back down the mountain. It was early afternoon and almost time for the Sugarloaf to close for the day. Still as she started to drive past the restaurant, she was surprised to see several more vehicles in the parking lot than should have been there at that time of day, including a City of Sedona police car. Knowing that there was little love lost between her father and the local constabulary, Ali made a U-turn and then went back to the parking lot, where she pulled in beside the patrol car.

The CLOSED sign was in the window, but the door was unlocked. Ali let herself inside. Her father was seated in the corner booth along with two uniformed City of Sedona police officers. One of the officers was new to Ali. The other one, Kenny Harmon, she did know. As a rookie patrol officer, Kenny had given Bob Larson his one and only speeding ticket—for doing forty in a thirty-five. Kenny's presence accounted in large measure for the thunderous look on Ali's father's face. The fourth person in the booth was a woman. Her back was turned to Ali, but she seemed to be doing most of the talking.

"We're closed," Edie Larson called from the kitchen when the bell over the door announced Ali's entrance. Edie appeared in the swinging door, wielding a mop. "Oh," she said. "It's you."

"What's going on?"

Edie jerked her head in the direction of the only occupied booth. "That's Sandy—Sandy Mitchell. She's one of the clerks over at Basha's. She's also Kip Hogan's girlfriend. Your dad's helping her file a missing persons report."

Ali did know Sandy. She had been a grocery clerk at Basha's for years. The idea that she was involved with Kip—the idea that anyone was involved with Kip—was news to Ali. No wonder he'd gone to the trouble of having his teeth fixed.

"Kip was supposed to see her last night, only he didn't show up. She came by here after work today looking for him. That's when your father finally decided maybe it was time to call the cops. There's still a little coffee left. Want some?"

"Coffee would be great," Ali said, accepting her mother's offer and grabbing a seat at the counter.

"Have you had lunch?"

Ali shook her head. "I thought you were closed."

"We don't have to be open for me to make you a sandwich. Tuna? And I've got a container of stew for you to take home for dinner."

Ali nodded. "Thanks," she said. "A sandwich would be very nice, and Chris adores your stew."

Edie rolled her eyes. "Why do you think I made it?" she asked.

Seated at the counter in the almost deserted restaurant, it was easy for Ali to hear everything being said at the corner booth.

"So that's the last time you saw him," Kenny was saying. "When he came by the store late yesterday morning to give you some flowers."

Sandy nodded tearfully. "It was our two-month anniversary," she said.

"Did he mention anything about what his plans for the day might be? Did he mention where he was going or what he was going to do?"

"He said he needed to deliver some furniture. Then he was going up to the Rim, but he didn't have to say so," Sandy added. "He always goes up there on Tuesday afternoons. I was upset about what had happened with those kids earlier. He offered to put the trip off until today, but I told him he should go ahead. People were counting on him. I told him I'd be fine. I needed him to go so I could write up the incident report."

"What incident report?" Ali asked her mother.

"There were some college kids up for the day who came into Basha's yesterday expecting to buy booze. They came through Sandy's register and were all bent out of shape when she carded them and wouldn't let them buy," Edie explained. "They were still at the store and giving Sandy grief about it when Kip showed up and shut them down. Kip can be pretty intimidating on occasion."

Ali regarded that as a bit of an understatement. Even with new teeth and carrying a bouquet of flowers, Kip Hogan would have been scary as hell.

"We usually meet up at an AA meeting on Tuesday evenings,"

Sandy was saying. "That's where we met—Alcoholics Anonymous. He wasn't there, though, and he didn't come by later, either. I worried about it some overnight, but this morning, at work, when I heard about Mr. Larson's Bronco being found, that really scared me. Kip knows how much Mr. Larson loves that car. He'd never do anything to jeopardize it, especially not considering the way the Larsons have treated him. He told me once they were more like family than his own family."

"So Mr. Hogan does have family then?" the cop asked.

"I guess," Sandy answered.

"Any idea where we might find those family members?"

Sandy shook her head. "He never said."

Kenny, pen in hand, turned to Ali's father. "Did Mr. Hogan ever mention to you where he was from?"

"No," Bob answered. "Not to me, anyway."

"You think he had something to hide?"

"If we live long enough, we all have something to hide," Bob Larson said.

Ali could tell from her father's tone of voice that Bob was fast running out of patience.

"Where was his driver's license from?" Kenny asked.

Bob glanced guiltily at his wife before he answered. "He told me he had a driver's license," Bob said. "I guess I never actually saw it."

"You just took his word for it?"

Bob looked pained. "I had hurt my leg," he said. "I needed someone who could drive for me."

"Good lord!" Edie muttered under her breath, taking a seat next to her daughter. "There's no fool like an old fool."

"So you don't even know what state it would have been from or whether or not it had been suspended."

Bob shook his head.

The other cop seemed content to let that one go. "Forget it, Kenny. You told us he doesn't have a cell phone, Mr. Larson. Is there a chance that he might have made any long-distance calls that showed up on your bill—calls that might lead us to some other people who know him or who knew him in the past?"

"I don't remember that he did," Bob replied.

"Believe me, if there'd been an unexplained call on the phone bill, your father would have remembered," Edie told Ali in a pained whisper. "He goes over every line of every bill every month, but he couldn't be bothered with asking whether or not Kip had a driver's license? As soon as the cops leave, I think I'm gonna kill the man and be done with it."

By the time Edie's rant was over, the cops were ready to leave. "This doesn't give us a whole lot to go on, but we'll see what we can do," Kenny said. "You say your Bronco's still up at Franco's Garage?"

"It's still there," Bob answered. "Along with the goods Kip was supposed to drop off at the homeless encampment up on the Rim. They evidently weren't good enough for the creep who took my tools, gas can, and spare tire."

As the two cops left, Edie followed them to the door and locked it behind them. She went over to the booth where Bob was still sitting with Sandy, who had burst into tears. "Where could Kip be?" Sandy wailed. "Something terrible has happened to him. I'm sure of it."

Edie slipped into the booth next to her and put her arm around Sandy's shoulders. "I'm sure the cops will do everything they can to find him," she said kindly. "Won't they, Bob?"

"Absolutely," Bob agreed, but only after Edie nudged his ankle under the table. "Of course they will."

Sandy turned her tearstained face in his direction. "Do you think so?" she asked. "Really?"

"Definitely," Bob declared with what sounded like absolute confidence. "No doubt about it."

A few minutes later, when Bob stood up to walk Sandy out to her vehicle, Edie turned to her daughter. "So, where's your charge?" she asked.

"Dave's home now," Ali said. "I dropped her off with him."

"Does he know what she's been up to?" Edie asked.

"Crystal's supposed to tell him."

"What if she doesn't?" Edie asked.

"Then I'll probably have to," Ali allowed. "I don't want to be stuck in the middle of it, but I'll do it if I have to."

Edie clicked her tongue. "It's going to break Dave's heart when he has to take her to a doctor to have her tested for STDs."

Ali looked at her mother in surprise. She had always been baffled by her mother's uncanny ability to see everything and know everything, and the fact that Edie Larson was conversant on the subject of sexually transmitted diseases seemed to be another case in point.

"Crystal told you what she'd been up to?" Ali asked.

"She didn't have to tell me a thing," Edie Larson returned. "All I had to do was look at her. I wasn't born yesterday, you know."

• • •

By four that afternoon, Ali had made several calls to California. Then with Sam curled contentedly on the couch beside her, Ali was ready to reply to Velma Trimble's e-mail:

*Dear Velma,*
*I'm so sorry it's taken so long to get back to you. Things have been crazy around here. I've spoken to several doctors in your general area. The one that's getting the highest marks is a concierge medical practice in Costa Mesa called Cancer Resource Specialties. I guess you'd call them a cancer care clearinghouse.*

*You pay a set fee to join their practice, and none of that fee would be covered by either insurance carriers or by Medicare. Cancer Resource then provides routine medical care. After all, people with cancer still get the flu. On the cancer front, however, they arrange for referrals to appropriate specialists all over the country. They help organize appointments with oncologists, arrange for scans and MRIs, put patients in touch with surgeons, pain management specialists, and whatever else may be needed. In other words, you pay them to know all the stuff you need to find out right now when you don't have the time or the energy to track it all down on your own.*

*The woman who started Cancer Resource is an internist named Dr. Nancy Cooper. I met her several years ago at a luncheon and found her to be very impressive. She got involved when she realized how dealing with the ins and outs of a cancer diagnosis can simply overwhelm both the patient and the patient's family. Her whole focus is trying to coordinate care and smooth out some of those rough spots.*

*As I said at the beginning, this service is relatively*

*expensive, but I have no doubt it's well worth whatever she charges. Her fee scale is listed on her Web site. Check it out. If this is more than you can afford, let me know and I'll see what other options may be available.*

ALI

With that out of the way, it was only natural for Ali to turn to the blog. The cutloose mailbox was brimming over with comments, all of them dealing with her last post, the one she had written just after she had learned of Crystal's disappearance. Without knowing the girl had been found, Ali's readers were still hanging in limbo—still waiting to hear. Scanning through the outpouring of commentary, Ali was interested to see that responses often touched on opposite sides of the same story.

*Dear Babe,*
*My father was an abusive drunk. My mother was a doormat who would never say a word when he lit into us kids with a belt or a spoon or whatever else came readily to hand. I thought nothing could be worse than staying where I was, so when I was fifteen I ran away from home. How wrong I was. By the time I was eighteen I'd had three abortions and was strung out on heroin. I'm clean and sober now, but I also have hepatitis C and am HIV positive. My father sobered up years ago. My younger sister says he's a different person now. She thinks I should come home—that I should forgive him and let bygones be bygones. It's not fair. He got his life back. Mine is over. I hope your friend finds his daughter before it's too late. I hope it's not his fault that she ran away.*

DAWN

Ali studied that one for a long time. There was so much hurt in the words, she hardly knew where to begin in crafting a response:

*Dear Dawn,*
*The life you have is the life you have, and it isn't over until it's over. Don't give up too soon. And your sister may be right. Forgiving your father may make it possible for you to forgive the other person in your life who needs forgiveness—yourself.*

*I think your comment is an important one, and I'd like to post it on the blog, but I won't do so without your express permission. Please let me know.*

BABE

The next one came from the parent of a missing child.

*Dear Babe,*
*I'll be praying for the girl's safe return. My daughter Sally disappeared when she was twelve—on January 11, 1966—forty-one years to the day before your friend's daughter went missing. That's why, when I read your post, it made the hair stand up on the back of my neck. We still don't know what happened to our Sally or if she's dead or alive. Part of me knows that she's dead—has always known that she's dead. But another part of me still hopes that someday the front door will slam open and she'll be standing there saying, "Mama, I'm home."*

*Please let us know if your friend's daughter returns safely.*

LOUANN

Ali posted that comment and skimmed the rest. More comments came clicking in while she was reading. In the end, there were so many that it simply wasn't feasible to respond to them all individually. She replied in her post instead.

**CUTLOOSEBLOG.COM**

*Wednesday, January 11, 2006, supplemental*

The response to my last post about my friend's missing daughter has been absolutely overwhelming. Thank you all for your concern, for your prayers, and for your kind comments.

First and most important I want you all to know that what was lost has been found. My friend's daughter is home. She's safe. And, externally at least, she doesn't seem to have been harmed. However she did run away from home. Why she did that remains to be seen, and I'm sure she and her family will be addressing that and other issues in the course of the next few days—and most likely for sometime after that as well.

She was found and brought home last night, but things were so hectic today that I didn't get around to picking up my computer until just now. When I did so, I was utterly stunned by the huge number of messages I found there. As always, the thing that astonishes me is the number of people I've heard from who wrote to express their concerns, people who have dealt with similar problems in their own lives. Of the messages I've skimmed I've posted only the one from LouAnn.

> The sheer volume of mail on this topic precludes me from answering each of them on an individual basis. I'll be posting more and responding individually when appropriate and as time allows.
>
> *Babe, posted* 4:55 P.M.

By then it was late afternoon. When Chris came home after school, he went directly to the kitchen to dish up and zap a bowl of his grandmother's beef stew. "The last I knew you were heading out to find Dave Holman's missing daughter," Chris said while he waited for the microwave. "How did that work out?"

"Not all that well," Ali said. "I brought her home here, and while I was sleeping this morning, she tried to sneak off in one of your ski jackets."

"As in steal?" he asked.

"Exactly," Ali replied.

"So she wasn't particularly grateful."

"You could say that," Ali agreed. "Not particularly."

"How old is she again?"

"Thirteen."

"And you did get my jacket back?" Chris asked.

"Yes."

"So where is she now?"

"I dropped her off at her dad's."

Chris grinned. "So, now she's his problem." He pulled his bowl out of the microwave. "I don't remember ever being quite that difficult."

"I don't remember it either," Ali said. "Because I don't think you ever were that difficult—not even when you were sixteen, which, as I remember, wasn't a banner year."

"Does that mean the next time I leave the kitchen a mess, I've got some slack coming?" he wanted to know.

"Get out of here," Ali said. She plucked a small pillow off the couch and threw it at him. Sam, who disapproved of pillow fights, disappeared into the bedroom while Chris, bowl in hand, headed for the basement studio they had carved for him out of what had once been Aunt Evie's two-car garage. Later, Ali heard him head out for the evening. She didn't ask him where he was going, and he didn't offer to tell her.

In the deepening twilight, Ali helped herself to her own bowl of stew. Only after dinner had been eaten and cleared away and with the house quiet once more, did she realize that she no longer had any viable excuse for avoiding Arabella Ashcroft's diary. By agreeing to take the volume with her, she had tacitly agreed to read it—whether or not she wanted to—and it was time to start.

Ali adjusted the living room lights and turned on the gas log in the fireplace. Then, after retrieving the diary from her purse, she settled onto the leather sofa. She had no more than sat down when Sam joined her there, snuggling up against her leg and purring noisily. Comforted by the big cat's solid presence, Ali opened the gold-embossed book. Shuffling through the book, she found that the vast majority of the pages were blank, but the pages that had been used were covered in a blocky, immature cursive. Ali turned to the first one.

*Happy birthday to Me,*
*Happy birthday to Me,*
*Happy birthday dear Bella.*
*Happy birthday to me.*

*Because it is my birthday and I'm nine whole years old today. And I got just what I wanted for my birthday—a bright blue parakeet. I think I'm going to call him Blueboy, and I'm going to teach him to talk. Parakeets can talk, you know, almost as well as parrots, you just have to know how to teach them. I would have taken a parrot, but mother says they're a lot bigger and a lot more trouble.*

*I didn't really want a diary, but Miss Ponder gave it to me anyway. Miss Ponder hasn't been here very long, but she's the nicest governess I've ever had. The others were all stiff or mean or old, and they never gave me any presents. Miss Ponder isn't mean at all and the way she listens when I talk makes me want to tell her stuff I wouldn't tell anyone else. Like the fact that I want to be a writer when I grow up. That's why she gave me this diary. She says writers need lots of practice before they can actually write books and that lots of famous writers started out by keeping a journal. Or a diary. So that's what I'm doing. Starting out.*

That initial diary entry wasn't at all what Ali had expected. She had thought she'd encounter something terribly graphic or terribly grim or both, and she hadn't wanted to inflict those gory details on herself. She didn't really want to know exactly how little Arabella Ashcroft, incest survivor, had been victimized by her older brother. What Ali had discovered instead, was a profound and completely unexpected connection between herself and the nine-year-old child who had penned those innocently bittersweet words some six decades earlier.

Ali Larson had been around nine years old when she, like Arabella, had been bitten by a similar ambition. Ali Larson had decided in fourth grade that she wanted to be a writer. And through some combination of luck and determination, and with the timely help of Arabella's mother, Ali had done just exactly that—she had become a journalist. And now she was writing every day in her blog with people reading what she had written and, more important, responding to it in very personal ways

For whatever reason, Arabella's ambitions had never come to fruition. And maybe that's what this was all about. Maybe that was one of the reasons Ali had been put in touch with Arabella at this juncture in their lives. Maybe, even at this late date, Ali Reynolds could somehow help Arabella Ashcroft realize her long-buried dream. Or perhaps Ali was involved with Arabella, just as she was with Velma T, in order to sort things out between these two aging women and their interfering younger relatives—Velma's son and Arabella's nephew.

Before Ali managed to turn to the next entry in the diary, her phone rang. "What am I going to do with her?" Dave Holman asked.

He sounded exasperated beyond bearing. Having spent several long hours with Crystal Holman, Ali knew the girl came complete with a tangle of complications, none of them with easy answers. Before Ali tried to reply, though, she needed to know which one of Crystal's many thorny issues Dave's question addressed. Was it primarily due to Crystal's being a runaway? Was it about her precocious and generally blasé attitude toward sexual activity and the need to have her checked out for possible STDs? Maybe the real answer was all of the above.

"It's like I don't even know her anymore," Dave went on. "She's not the same kid she used to be. She won't look me in the eye. When I ask her questions, she won't give me a straight answer about anything."

"Did you ask her why she ran away?"

"Of course."

"What did she tell you?"

"All the usual BS," Dave replied. "She hates her new school. She doesn't have any friends. Her teachers are stupid. Gary Whitman is a jerk. Her mother likes Richey better than she likes her. It's all pretty typical teenage angst. My God, Ali. I know I wasn't the easiest kid to deal with when I was her age, but I never pulled anything like this."

Listening to Dave's recitation of what Crystal had told him, Ali couldn't help thinking about Arabella Ashcroft. She had been molested and had never told anyone, most especially her parents. Would things have been better for Arabella if she had told? And did anyone else have the right to tell Dave about what was going on with his daughter if Crystal couldn't bring herself to do it? Yes, Crystal was a child, but even children had a right to some privacy.

As for Dave? He was an experienced homicide cop, used to interrogating crooks and getting them to answer tough questions. Evidently his tried-and-true questioning techniques weren't working very well on his own daughter.

"Did you talk to her about hitchhiking?" Ali asked. "About how dangerous it is?"

"Are you kidding? I talked about that until I was blue in the face," Dave returned. "But I don't think she was listening. I tried to explain to her how lucky she was that something terrible hadn't happened to her on the way here."

*Something terrible did happen,* Ali thought. *She lost her innocence. She sold her body for a ride, and the damage to her self-respect will probably last a lifetime.*

"Did she tell you about the guy who hit her?" Ali asked.

"She said it was a boyfriend, and that she's broken up with him now," Dave continued. "But she's still threatening to run away, especially if I'm going to take her back to Vegas. So what happens when I have to go to work in the morning, Ali? I'm due to testify in court tomorrow or the next day. The county courthouse is in Prescott. That means I have to be in Prescott as well. What do I do with Crystal while I'm gone? Lock her up in the house? And if she were to let herself out, all she'd have to do is walk down to the bottom of the hill and stick out her thumb. She'll be long gone in a matter of minutes."

"You're right to be worried," Ali said. "But since you have to work, and since Roxie is the one with custody, couldn't she or Gary drive down from Vegas to pick Crystal up?"

"They have jobs, too," Dave replied. "Besides, Roxie has taken the position that this whole thing is somehow my fault, that I must have encouraged Crystal to run away. Now that Crystal's here, Roxie says it's my responsibility to get her back home. While I was talking to Roxie on the phone, I could hear Gary talking in the background, muttering something about 'custodial interference.'"

"You think they'll try to make some kind of official issue out of this?"

"I'd bet money on it," Dave said. "The sooner I can get it handled, the sooner it'll go away, but the earliest I'll be able to drive back up to Vegas will be Saturday morning—unless the court appearance finishes up earlier."

"Does Crystal want to go back?" Ali asked.

"What do you mean?" Dave asked.

"When I picked her up last night, I got the impression that she was hoping to come live with you on a permanent basis."

"Crystal's old enough to have some say in the matter, but not by pulling a stunt like this, and for right now the divorce decree is very clear. It specifies that Roxie gets full custody and I get to pay full child support. If Crystal were to come to live with me,

Gary and Roxie would have to lose some of the child support. Believe me, that's never going to happen.

"Besides," he added, "if it did, what would I do with her? Where would we go? This is only a one-bedroom place, but it's as much as I can afford. I'm fine here on my own, but it would never work for two people. Tonight, Crystal is in the bedroom, and I'm camping out on the couch. That's not feasible in the long run. If she was going to stay on here permanently, I'd have to find somewhere else to live. You take what I make, deduct what I pay in child support, and figure out how much is left. Not very much. Not enough to pay for a decent two-bedroom apartment. We'd end up in one of those trailer parks down by Oak Creek. They're probably okay, but they're not the kinds of places where I'd like to raise my daughter."

Ali could hear the distress in Dave's voice. Buffeted by indecision, he was unable to see his way clear in any one direction.

"Why don't you bring Crystal here tomorrow and let me look after her for the day?" Ali suggested finally. "Better yet, bring her along to the Sugarloaf when you come to breakfast tomorrow morning. I'll come down to the restaurant and pick her up. She can stay with me until you get back from Prescott. Ditto for Friday."

"Are you sure you wouldn't mind?" Dave asked. The relief in his voice was obvious. "I mean, you've already done so much . . ."

"Hey, Dave," Ali said. "Hello!!! It's Ali Reynolds, remember me? Remember everything you did for me when we were out in California? We're a long way from being even. Besides, isn't that what friends are for?"

"As long as you're sure you don't mind."

"I don't," Ali said. "See you in the morning."

Ali had planned on returning to Arabella's diary, but she changed her mind, closed the slim volume, and returned it to her purse.

*If I'm going to be dealing with Crystal Holman all day tomorrow,* Ali told herself firmly, *I'd better try to get some sleep.*

# { CHAPTER 8 }

For the second day in a row, Ali was at the Sugarloaf bright and early. Dave's aging Nissan was already parked outside, and he and Crystal were seated in one of the booths. Ali stopped off at the counter where her mother had just picked up a freshly filled coffeepot. She poured a cup for her daughter.

"Any word on Kip yet?" Ali asked.

Edie shook her head. "Not so far. Your father's worried sick about him. I'm still of the opinion that the man's off on a toot somewhere and he'll be back once he sobers up. Even Kip Hogan is smart enough to see he's got a good thing going here. If your dad's soft-headedness isn't a good thing, I don't know what is. Chicken-fried steak?"

Ali nodded. "Sounds great," she said. Then, taking her coffee, Ali walked over to Dave and Crystal's booth. "May I join you?" she asked.

Dave greeted her with a grateful smile. "Sure. Have a seat."

Crystal, looking like a clown in a pair of her father's oversize sweats, was anything but cordial.

"So I guess you're stuck babysitting me today?" she demanded, shoving her emptied plate and silverware aside. "Aren't I a little old for that?"

"Crystal!" Dave admonished. "Ali's a good friend of mine, and she's doing me a huge favor by looking after you today. There's no need to be rude."

*At this rate, it's going to be a very long day,* Ali thought. *Time to put on the tough-broad act again.* "That depends," she replied.

"On what?" Crystal wanted to know.

"On you," Ali said. "I can keep you company today or I can be your babysitter. If you insist on acting like a baby, then I suppose I'll be forced to treat you like a baby."

The slightest hint of a grin tweaked the corners of Dave's mouth. Meantime Crystal favored Ali with a sour stare before turning her attention fully on her father. "If you don't want to leave me at your place alone, why can't I go to Prescott with you?" she wheedled. "Why do I have to stay here with her?"

Having Ali there seemed to give Dave some much needed backbone where his headstrong daughter was concerned. "Because I said so," he answered. "Because I'm going to Prescott on official police business in an official county vehicle. I'm not allowed to bring along passengers."

"But . . ."

"No buts," Dave said.

"Crystal," Ali said cheerfully. "I'm not nearly as bad as you think I am. Besides, since your dad's paying for breakfast, you won't even have to wash dishes."

Crystal pulled a face. Out of her line of sight Dave winked at Ali and then glanced at his watch. "If I'm going to be on time, I need to go collect my wheels and head out." He stood up and extracted his wallet from his pocket. "See you later."

Crystal crossed her arms. "Whatever," she said.

After Dave left, Ali and Crystal sat silently in the booth with Ali sipping her coffee and with Crystal staring out the window. Crystal was the one who finally broke the silence.

"Are you his girlfriend or what?" she asked.

"Your father and I are friends," Ali said. "Good friends. Ever since high school."

"Dad made fun of Mom for living in a trailer, but now he's hanging out with someone who does, too, and who works in a café. I can hardly wait to tell Richey and Cassie that Dad is dating a waitress."

"Helping my parents out on occasion doesn't necessarily make me a waitress—but what would it matter if I was?" Ali asked. "There's nothing wrong with being a waitress. On the other hand, behaving like a spoiled three-year-old and insulting people isn't a good way of showing you don't need a babysitter," Ali said.

"But I *don't need* a babysitter," Crystal insisted. "And you can't keep me here against my will. Isn't that like false imprisonment or something?"

"Maybe you'd prefer real imprisonment," Ali replied. "If you run away while your father has left you in my care, I'll have an Amber Alert posted on you so fast that you'll never make it to the freeway. When the cops catch up with you, you'll be in trouble and so will whoever's giving you a ride. By the way, did you happen to tell your father what you used for bus tokens to get here?"

Crystal turned away and didn't answer. Meantime, Edie showed up with Ali's breakfast.

"How are you doing?" Edie asked Crystal. "Do you want anything more?"

"Maybe another sweet roll," Crystal said.

"So what are we going to do then?" Crystal wanted to know once Edie left their table. "Sit around in this stupid place all day?"

"Get you some decent clothes maybe?" Ali asked. "Your father's don't exactly suit you."

"Where from?" Crystal asked sarcastically. "Wal-Mart?"

Obviously Wal-Mart didn't measure up, but Ali pretended cluelessness. "Sure," she said. "If Wal-Mart's okay with you, it's fine with me."

Ali had almost finished her chicken-fried steak and Crystal had mowed through her second sweet roll when the front door crashed open and a distraught Sandy Mitchell staggered inside. Dodging around the counter, Sandy pushed her way into the kitchen and fell into Bob Larson's arms.

"They think they found Kip," she sobbed. "He's in Phoenix at St. Francis Hospital. He may not make it."

Leading Sandy by the arm, Bob brought her back out of the kitchen and eased her onto one of the stools at the counter. Everyone else in the restaurant fell silent, listening.

"Where?" he asked. "Where did they find him?"

"Up by Flagstaff somewhere," Sandy said. "They said it looked like someone had beaten him with a baseball bat and left him for dead along I-17. They airlifted him to Phoenix to the trauma center at St. Francis. They've brought in a surgeon from the Hyde Neurological Institute. They've already done one round of brain surgery. They may have to do another one today."

Ali remembered being at Sunset Point to retrieve her father's crippled Bronco and hearing the low-flying helicopter pass overhead. But that had been the night before last. How could it have taken this long to connect the dots between the Sedona missing persons report and a severely beaten trauma victim?

"Can you drive down there with me?" Sandy continued. "I'm not sure I can do this by myself. I'm so upset right now that I almost wrecked the car twice just getting here."

Bob glanced around the crowded restaurant. It was already full and more customers were clustered near the door waiting to be seated. With Bob out front, Edie had ducked back into the kitchen.

"I can't go right now," Bob said. "Later on today, yes, but not right now."

"I'll take her," Ali offered. "Crystal and I can give her a ride down to Phoenix, and you can bring her back home this evening."

"Is that all right with you, Sandy?" Bob asked.

Sandy nodded. "If Ali doesn't mind."

"Crystal and I were planning on doing some shopping today, and the shopping is definitely better in Phoenix," Ali said. "We'll be happy to give you a ride."

Crystal rolled her eyes.

"All right," Bob said. "It's settled then. You go with Ali. I'll come down this afternoon as soon as the restaurant closes."

With that, he returned to the kitchen and resumed possession of his spatula. Once Edie returned to the counter, she went straight to Sandy.

"Have you had anything to eat today?" she asked.

"No," Sandy said, shaking her head. "Not yet."

"Have something then," Edie urged. "You need to keep up your strength, and you know what hospital cafeterias are like. They're expensive and the food stinks."

Sandy left the restaurant a little while later with a fully stocked care package of food. Ali took Crystal and stopped by her own place long enough to make sure Sam had food and water and to straighten up.

If Ali was going out in public in Phoenix, she was determined to look reasonably decent. In the privacy of her bedroom, she applied her makeup. Then she changed out of her casual around-Sedona sweats in favor of a pair of tight-fitting jeans and a bright magenta long-sleeved T-shirt, both of which looked terrific on her newly Mr. Bowflexed figure, thank you very much.

With Ali's recent history in mind, she no longer left home without taking her Glock. To finish off her outfit she slipped on her small-of-back holster and topped that with a hip-length denim jacket. At the last moment, thinking her computer might come in handy for keeping Crystal entertained, Ali dragged that along out to the car. Then they drove to Sandy's place in Oak Creek RV Haven, a low-rent trailer park that had almost washed away in the previous summer's severe flooding.

While they waited for Sandy to emerge from a camper trailer that made Kip's LazyDaze seem spacious by comparison, Ali called Chris's cell phone. She knew he was in class and couldn't answer, but she left him a message so he'd know what was going on. Then she turned to Crystal. "How about if you ride in back?"

"Do I have to?"

Ali had to bite back a sarcastic reply. *Crystal's a child,* Ali reminded herself. *A very troubled child.*

"You don't *have* to ride in back, but I'd appreciate it if you would," Ali said. "I know you think your life sucks at the moment, and I'm not saying it doesn't. But so does Sandy Mitchell's. The man she loves is in the hospital and may be dying. She's really upset right now and may need to talk."

"All right," Crystal agreed grudgingly. She got out of the front seat and into the back one, slamming both doors as she went.

"Seat belt," Ali said.

With an exaggerated sigh, Crystal complied. Once she was belted in, she pulled an iPod from the pocket of her father's oversize sweats, plugged in her earphones, and went away. Ali couldn't help being struck by the fact that Crystal had run away from home with no clothes but with plenty of electronic gear—both a cell phone and an iPod.

A few minutes later, Sandy emerged from her trailer carrying a small suitcase. "I decided to bring some extra clothes along in case I end up having to stay over."

And that, Ali decided, was the difference between a child of the twenty-first century and a grown-up from the twentieth.

"Good thinking," she said. "You'll probably need them."

• • •

Intent on making their next-of-kin notification, Detectives Larry Marsh and Hank Mendoza stepped up onto the flagstone porch and rang the bell.

The bell was answered by a man wearing a white jacket who was anything but friendly. "Yes," he said. "May I help you?"

"We're looking for Ms. Ashcroft," Larry said. "Ms. Arabella Ashcroft."

"And who might I say is calling?"

Larry produced his ID wallet and passed it inside. "I'm Detective Larry Marsh and this is my partner, Hank Mendoza. We're with the Phoenix Police Department. Homicide."

Larry heard a woman's voice calling out from somewhere deep inside the house. "Was that the doorbell, Mr. Brooks? Is someone here?"

"One moment, please," the man said. "Let me check and see if now would be a convenient time for Madam to see you."

He closed the door quietly but very firmly in their faces.

"Madam," Hank repeated. "Was that what I think it was—a real live butler?"

"So it would seem," Larry replied. "And I don't think we passed the approved visitor test."

Several minutes elapsed, leaving the cops with little to do but admire the view. "How much do you think a place like this is worth?" Hank asked.

Larry was always perusing the real estate sections of newspapers in hopes of finding someplace cooler to go when he retired. He had researched the Sedona market and had learned that his pension would come up short when it came to retirement housing in that particular area.

"With a view like this and with as much property? I'm guessing the place is worth a bundle."

The cops were about to give up and go away when the door opened once again. "Sorry for the delay," the butler said, with a stiff half bow. "Madam will see you now. This way."

The two officers followed the butler into a spacious living room where a hint of morning wood smoke from the fireplace still lingered in the air. A woman with a halo of silvery hair stood next to the cooling fireplace.

"Good morning," she said, while the butler hovered attentively nearby. "I'm Arabella Ashcroft. You wanted to see me?"

"Yes, ma'am," Larry said solicitously. "I'm afraid we have some bad news for you."

"What kind of bad news?" Arabella asked. "Mr. Brooks said you're with Homicide. Does that mean someone has been murdered?"

"Yes," Larry said. "It does. Your nephew, William Ashcroft, was found murdered Tuesday morning in the South Mountain Preserve."

Arabella staggered slightly and raised her hand to her chest. "Oh, my goodness," she said, making her way to a nearby chair. "This is dreadful. Billy's dead? How can that be? He was here just the other day, and he was fine then, perfectly fine. What day was that when he was here, Mr. Brooks? Do you remember?"

"It was Sunday," the butler replied. "Sunday afternoon."

"As far as we can ascertain, Ms. Ashcroft, you're his only living relative," Detective Marsh continued. "We understand he has an ex-wife, somewhere, but so far we've been unable to locate her. We found you through Mr. Ashcroft's phone records."

"Oh, dear," Arabella said. "I'm forgetting my manners. Do sit down. Make yourselves comfortable. And would you care for something to drink—coffee, tea?"

"Coffee would be great," Hank said, settling onto a couch.

Detective Marsh nodded in agreement. "I'd like coffee, too, if it's not too much trouble."

"No trouble at all, is it, Mr. Brooks," she said. "Do bring them some. And while you're at it, you might bring me something a bit stronger. This has been a terrible shock."

• • •

"I think it was those kids," Sandy Mitchell said as they headed south on I-17. "And that means that everything that happened is all my fault."

"Which kids?" Ali asked.

"You know. The ones I carded at the store. The one was especially obnoxious. He was making a scene and giving me all kinds of grief. And then, all of a sudden, out of nowhere, there's Kip, standing there holding a bouquet of flowers and looking sweet and funny and fierce all at the same time. At first the kid just ignored him. I think he thought it was some kind of joke. Then

Kip grabbed his sleeve, lifted him off the ground—Kip's very strong you know—and told him to get out or he'd . . ." Sandy looked uncomfortable, and gestured with her head toward the backseat where Crystal was sitting.

"Or he'd what?" Ali asked.

"You know. Shove those flowers up his . . ." Sandy stopped then continued, "That's when the kids finally got it—that Kip meant what he was saying. So they left. Didn't even finish buying the rest of their groceries. Just left them there on my check stand."

Somehow Ali doubted that the phrase *shove up your ass* was something that would offend Crystal Holman's thirteen-year-old, none-too-tender sensibilities, but it was nice that Sandy Mitchell thought it might. Besides, Crystal appeared to be lost in her music and was paying no attention to anything being said in the front seat.

"It was really wonderful," Sandy continued wistfully. "When he chased them off like that, I felt like I'd been rescued by a knight in shining armor."

Sandra Mitchell was sixty-something if she was a day. She'd put on some hard miles. She was a dumpy plain jane, yet Kip Hogan—the very scary Kip Hogan—had made her feel like some latter-day Guinevere. To Ali's way of thinking, that was nothing short of astonishing.

"I know the kids left the store then, but I don't know if they left the parking lot. I'm wondering if they didn't follow Kip when he left the store. I'm betting they waited around until he was alone and then they beat the crap out of him. Three to one isn't a fair fight."

"And where exactly did the cops find Kip?" Ali asked. "You never did say."

"Just off the freeway at Mund's Park," Sandy said. "Around eleven somebody called nine-one-one from the gas station on the other side of the interstate and reported a fight in progress. Cops were dispatched to the scene. That's where they found him. He was in such bad shape that they took him out in a helicopter."

Yes, Ali definitely remembered seeing the helicopter when she'd been with her father at the rest area. She also remembered seeing emergency vehicles still assembled around Mund's Park when she had gone there to pick up Crystal. She had assumed she was seeing the tail-end of some traffic mishap. Now it seemed otherwise.

Using the rearview mirror, Ali glanced into the backseat. For some reason, Crystal had removed her earphones. She was sitting with her arms folded across her chest, staring out the window. She seemed to be hearing none of the conversation, but something about her bearing put Ali on edge. She was listening, all right, listening with avid attention, but without wanting anyone to know what she was doing. Ali wasn't her mother's daughter for nothing.

"Crystal," Ali said. "Did you see anything out of line that night?"

Crystal jumped and feigned ignorance. "What?" she asked.

"You were at Mund's Park that same night Kip Hogan was attacked. Did you see any of that?"

"No," Crystal answered without hesitation. "I didn't see a thing."

Ali knew for a fact that the girl was lying, but if Crystal had witnessed some of the horrific attack on Kip, it was possible she was lying for good reason—because she was petrified.

Sandy was quiet for a long time. When she spoke again, she

seemed not to have noticed any of the byplay between Ali and Crystal.

"I didn't want to tell your dad about this because I didn't want to upset him," Sandy said. "But the person at the hospital told me that Kip is in very serious condition. Critical condition. What if they're trying to locate his next of kin in case they need to pull the plug?"

"What do you know about his family?" Ali returned.

"Not much," Sandy admitted. "All he said was that they were estranged—that he hadn't spoken to his mother in years."

"Did he tell you why?" Ali asked.

"No."

"And he never gave you any kind of a hint as to where he was from?"

"No. I'm pretty sure he grew up somewhere here in Arizona. I picked that up from little comments he made now and then, but he never said where exactly."

As a journalist, Ali knew that the Internet had, at the click of a mouse, made searches available to a lot of non-law-enforcement people who would never have been able to access the information before. And Ali did have her trusty computer along, but in order to begin a search, she needed to have a snippet of information.

"We could probably find out," Ali said. "Is Kip his real name, or is it short for something?"

"I don't know," Sandy answered. "We never really talked about that, either."

It occurred to Ali that there was a lot Sandy and Kip had never discussed, and maybe that was all right. Maybe at some point, it was best just to disregard the past and move on. Sometimes that was the only way to move on.

Ali reached over and engaged the Cayenne's hands-free cell phone. A moment later, Dave Holman's voice came through the speakerphone.

"Just hanging out in the courthouse lobby," he replied in answer to Ali's question about what he was doing. "We're all waiting to find out if the case is going to go to trial today. I was about to give you a call."

Quickly Ali explained where they were going, what they were doing, and why. "Since you've got a spare moment, could you maybe check with the department of licensing and see if Kip Hogan has a valid driver's license?"

"He must," Dave said. "He's been driving your dad's Bronco all over hell and gone for months now."

"Those would be my mother's sentiments exactly," Ali said. "It would also be nice to know who, if anyone, is listed as next of kin, and if Kip is his given name or if it's a nickname."

"Wait a minute," Dave said. "Why are you asking about next of kin? Since the assault took place in Coconino County, they'll probably want to have their people handle that end of things."

"We're on our way to the hospital, and someone there asked Sandy. They need the information, too."

"All right," Dave agreed. "I'll see what I can do. In the meantime, how's it going?"

*As in how's it going with your daughter from hell?* Ali thought.

"You're on speakerphone, Dave," Ali told him. "Crystal's right here. Why don't you ask her yourself?"

"Crystal?" Dave asked.

"I'm fine!" Crystal answered abruptly.

In the annals of woman-speak, it was a cold, two-raised-eyebrows *fine*—the most dangerous kind. Ali knew that things between her and Dave's temperamental daughter were anything but fine. Unfortunately Dave Holman was totally oblivious to the reality of the situation.

"Excellent," he said enthusiastically. "I'm delighted to know that two of my favorite people are spending some quality time together."

The speakerphone didn't come close to transmitting the sneer Crystal Holman leveled at the back of Ali's head. The rearview mirror did.

"I'll see what I can do about Kip, though," Dave added. "Since I'm right here in the courthouse, I should be able to get someone to help me. I don't know how long it'll take, and if my case gets called . . ."

"Check if you can; don't if you can't," Ali said. It was her way of letting Dave off the hook.

"Thanks so much, Detective Holman," Sandy said. "I really appreciate anything you can do."

As they approached the hospital, Sandy grew more and more apprehensive. Ali didn't blame her. Hospitals affected her that same way.

"How much do you think all this is going to cost?" Sandy asked. "I mean, I know for sure that Kip doesn't have any insurance. What if they ask me to pay his bill?"

After dealing with her first husband's glioblastoma, Ali happened to have more than a passing knowledge of how much brain surgery had cost twenty or so years ago. It was far more expensive than that now. Combine that with ICU care and medevac costs, and there could be little doubt that the price tag on Kip's injuries already amounted to a budget-busting sum.

By then they had pulled up next to the hospital entrance.

"Don't sign anything at all," Ali cautioned. "If that means you don't get any information on his condition right away, we'll just have to live with it. But remember; sign nothing."

"Aren't you coming up?" Sandy asked.

"In a little while," Ali said. "Write down my cell phone number so you can call if you need to, but first Crystal and I have a couple of errands we need to run."

As soon as Sandy exited the Cayenne, so did Crystal, slamming her way out of the backseat and into the front one. "What errands?" she said. "Is this when we go to Wal-Mart and buy me some different clothes?"

"No," Ali said. "This would be where the two of us have a little heart-to-heart chat. I want you to tell me everything you know about what happened in Mund's Park."

"There's nothing to tell," Crystal said. "I didn't see anything." But the sullen look she shot back in Ali's direction was a dead giveaway.

"Let's not play games," Ali said. "I know you saw something. You can either tell me the truth, or I'll find a cop who will ask you the same questions. In fact, I'm sure the homicide detectives from Coconino County will be delighted to talk to you."

"Why do you keep threatening me with stuff?" Crystal asked. "Why don't you just leave me alone?"

"Crystal," Ali urged. "This is an attempted homicide. If Kip Hogan dies it'll be more than attempted. Don't you want to help?"

"Why should I?" Crystal returned. "It's none of my business."

Ali's phone rang then. It was Dave. Since they were still parked, Ali answered the call without putting it on speaker.

"You're not going to believe this," Dave said. "Rudyard Kipling Hogan."

"That's his name?" Ali asked.

"Yup. No wonder no one's ever seen his driver's license. With a handle like that, I wouldn't show it to anyone, either."

"What about a home address?"

"I checked on that. He listed a homeless shelter in Phoenix as his permanent address."

"And next of kin?"

"None listed. He's an organ donor, though. I told the person in records what the deal was. She's faxing the information to both Coconino County and to the hospital down in Phoenix as well."

"Thanks," Ali said. "You've been a huge help."

"Are you there yet?" Dave asked. "It sounds pretty grim. Any word on how he is?"

"When we know something, I'll call," Ali said.

Behind her, a cabdriver laid on the horn and motioned for her to move out of the way.

"Gotta go," Ali said. "I'm blocking traffic."

She hung up the phone, drove forward far enough to turn onto Thomas, and then looked across at Crystal. "Well?" Ali demanded. "What's it going to be?"

"I already told you," Crystal said. "I didn't actually see anything, not really."

"You must have seen something," Ali returned.

Driving West on Thomas, Ali turned off onto a side street and then threaded her way through a neighborhood until she reached an almost deserted parking lot at Encanto Park. Once she turned off the engine, she focused her attention on Crystal.

"Please tell me," Ali said.

Crystal gave a resigned shrug. "Well, the guy who gave me a ride from Flagstaff pulled over there at Mund's Park so we could . . . well, you know . . . do it. And we were, or at least I was, when all of a sudden he started cussing and said, 'We have to get the hell out of here. Something's wrong.' By the time I sat up, he was already hauling ass. I thought there were cops coming or something, but when we drove away, all I saw were three guys standing there in the headlights. They were sort of standing in a circle, and one of them was holding something. It looked like a baseball bat, but I'm not sure. Then I realized there was someone else there, too, a fourth guy, only he was lying on the ground. I could see he was covered with something that looked like tar, but it was probably blood."

Ali nodded. "What happened then?" she prompted.

"I was scared," Crystal said. "I just wanted to take off and get as far away from there as possible. Curt said we had to call nine-one-one."

"Curt?" Ali asked.

Crystal nodded. "That's his name, Curt. I had a cell phone and so did he, but Curt said we shouldn't use them. Instead, we drove across the freeway to a gas station. There was a phone booth out back. While Curt made the call, I went inside and hid in the restroom. I was afraid they'd seen me when we drove past and that they'd come there looking for me—for us. When I came out, Curt was gone and so was his car. I didn't see the guys with the bat, but they could have been there. I knew I couldn't hang around the gas station any longer without people asking questions, so the minute I could, I made a run for it. That's when I broke into the house. I stayed there for a while, but it was cold and I was hungry, so I finally called my dad."

"Could you identify the vehicle the bad guys were driving?" Ali asked.

"No."

"So you don't know how they left Mund's Park or which way they went?"

Crystal shook her head. "While I was still in the restroom, I heard the sirens. I knew Curt must have gotten through because the cops were already there. And a little later, while I was hiding in the house, I saw the helicopter land and take off."

"If you knew the cops were there, why didn't you talk to them?" Ali asked. "Why didn't you tell them what you'd seen?"

"Because I knew they'd want to know who I was and what I was doing there." Crystal's voice cracked. "And because I knew they'd tell my dad," she said with a sob. "You won't tell him about me, will you? Please?"

The tough-talking, smart-mouthed Crystal seemed to have disappeared completely, leaving behind a girl who was little more than a child—a scared, lost child. She broke Ali's heart.

"Somebody needs to tell him," Ali said softly. "But I won't if you don't want me to."

# { CHAPTER 9 }

Ali put the Cayenne in gear and pulled out of the parking space.

"Where are we going now?" Crystal wanted to know.

"Back to the hospital," Ali said.

"Do we have to?" Crystal asked.

"Yes, we have to," Ali returned. "In case Sandy needs us. Now tell me again about the guys you saw at Mund's Park—the ones with the bat. Would you recognize their faces?"

Crystal hesitated before she answered. "Probably not," she said finally. "We were driving pretty fast when we went past them. I only saw them for a second or two."

Crystal's momentary pause had already alerted Ali's natural lie-detecting system. She suspected that everything Crystal had said after that pause was a fib, but for the moment Ali seemed prepared to let that statement go unchallenged.

"From what you did see, would you say they were older or younger?" she asked.

"Older, I guess," Crystal returned. "Maybe a couple of years older than my brother Richey."

*You did see them well enough after all,* Ali thought. She said, "So they might have been in high school then, or maybe even in college?"

Crystal nodded.

"What about Curt, the guy who gave you a ride?" Ali asked.

"What about him?"

"Is it possible that he saw the attackers better than you did?"

"I suppose," Crystal agreed reluctantly.

"We need to find him," Ali said.

Crystal stiffened in her seat. This time there was no hesitation at all. "Why?" she demanded. "Why do you need to find him?"

"Because Curt is a witness to a crime," Ali responded firmly. "An eyewitness to an attempted homicide, and so are you. Maybe Curt got a better look at the bad guys' faces than you did. Maybe he'd be able to recognize them. In any event, the cops working the case are going to want to talk to both of you. In order to find the men who tried to kill Kip Hogan, the detectives will need your help."

By then they had arrived once more at the hospital garage.

"I can't," Crystal insisted. "I know Curt's first name, but that's all. And I don't know how to find him, either."

"What kind of a car does he drive?"

It was almost as though Ali's questioning had toggled some kind of switch. Crystal immediately retreated into her shell. She shrugged and didn't answer. While they'd been at the park, Ali had felt she was making progress with Crystal—as though she was getting somewhere. Now she wasn't.

"What kind of car?" Ali insisted.

"I don't know," Crystal answered angrily. "And I wouldn't tell you if I did. I mean, he could get in trouble, too, couldn't he—for being with me like that?"

"Yes, he could be in trouble—and most likely would be," Ali conceded. *Big trouble,* she thought. "No matter what the boys at your school may say, having oral sex with a minor—and you are a minor, by the way—is a crime. What you and Curt did together, even if it was consensual, makes him a sexual predator. I'm sure he knew it was wrong, and so did you. Otherwise you wouldn't be so worried about your father finding out."

She glanced at Crystal, who stared straight ahead and didn't reply.

"Even so," Ali continued, "let's give the guy some credit. Curt was still willing to do the right thing—at least as far as calling in and reporting the assault on Kip was concerned. He went to the trouble of driving across the freeway to that gas station and placing the nine-one-one call. What we need for him to do now is come forward and tell the cops anything else he might know. And regardless of whether or not your father finds out about what you and Curt were doing, you need to do the same thing, Crystal. You need to talk to the investigators and tell them what you saw."

"No," Crystal insisted. "I won't talk to them. I don't have to. And I don't want to go into the hospital, either. You go see Sandy. I'll just wait for you in the car."

Ali couldn't help but marvel at the fact that in the space of a few minutes—the time it had taken to drive several city blocks—Crystal Holman had managed to do another one-eighty, from a tearful little girl to a recalcitrant, hostile teenager.

"No," Ali replied simply. "You're not waiting in the car." Ali climbed out of the Cayenne and then reached into the backseat to collect her purse and computer bag, both of which she slung over her shoulder. Then she walked around to the far side of the car and opened the passenger door for Crystal. "You're coming with me," she said.

"You're not my mother. You can't make me do anything if I don't want to," Crystal returned.

Ali was unimpressed. "Oh?" she said. "Watch me. All I have to do is call the cops and report you as a truant. Children your age are supposed to be in school, you know."

"You wouldn't do that," Crystal objected. "Besides, you told my dad you'd look after me."

"I am looking after you, honey lamb," Ali returned in a tone that brooked no further argument. "Which is why you're getting your sorry butt out of my car right now and coming into the hospital with me. Move it!"

There was a long pause, during which Ali wondered what would happen if the confrontation turned physical and she had to reach into the car and bodily drag Crystal out of the passenger seat. Would someone see her and call the cops, reporting the incident as child abuse or an assault or both? At that point, she didn't much care.

Finally Crystal reluctantly complied, slamming the car door behind her and flouncing off through the parking garage with Ali hurrying after her.

Ali remembered visiting St. Francis Hospital years before when she had been a little girl. Back then it had been a single stand-alone building. Now the medical center was a whole campus of buildings complete with multiple parking garages and a valet parking stand. Ali found Sandy waiting alone in the main hospital lobby. While she sat down next to Sandy, Crystal stalked off to the far side of the room, where she found a chair that allowed her to sit with her back to them.

"What's going on?" Ali asked.

"Kip's still in surgery," Sandy answered. "That's all they'll tell me, and I guess I'm lucky to know that." She subsided into silence and blew her nose into an already soggy tissue. "It's not fair," she added. "I mean, just because Kip and I aren't married they treat me like I'm nothing. Like I have no right to know anything about what's going on."

The new hospital privacy rules may have been news to Sandy Mitchell, but Ali had already stubbed her toe on them on more than one occasion. Before Ali could respond, her phone rang.

"I'm still hanging fire at the courthouse here in Prescott," Dave said. "And I still don't know if I'm going to get called as a witness today or not, but I've talked to Lee Farris. You remember him, don't you?"

Homicide Detective Farris was Coconino County's counterpart to Yavapai County's Detective Dave Holman. Farris had been part of the joint investigation into the death of Ali's best friend from high school, Reenie Bernard.

"Yes," Ali said. "I remember him."

"Now that Kip's case has turned into an attempted homicide, the missing persons interview Sandy did with the City of Sedona just isn't going to cut it. Lee is on his way down to Phoenix right now. He's coming to the hospital in hopes of reinterviewing Sandy and gleaning some additional information. I told him she'd probably be there at the hospital most of the day. I didn't have a cell phone number for her, so I gave him yours. Hope that's okay with you."

"It's fine," Ali said.

"Lee had heard about the confrontation that happened at Basha's the other day, the one between Kip and those kids who were hassling Sandy. He's hoping Sandy will be able to do sketches of them. Coconino County contracts with a composite artist based in Phoenix. Lee is trying to make arrangements to have the artist meet up with Sandy there in Phoenix at the hospital rather than having her drive up to Sedona and back."

"Okay," Ali said. "I'll let Sandy know."

"And how are things with Crystal?" Dave asked.

Ali glanced warily across the room to where Crystal sat with her shoulders hunched and her back still turned to Ali and Sandy.

"We're doing okay," Ali said guardedly. "Not great but okay."

"She's not giving you any trouble, is she?"

"Nothing I can't handle," Ali told him.

• • •

When Crystal's cell phone buzzed with the IM announcement, she almost jumped out of her skin. And she checked behind her to make sure no one was watching. When she saw Curt's initials in the sender's window, her heart skipped a beat. She had been scared something bad might have happened to him. She was glad to know he was safe, and she wanted to warn him about what was going on—about Kip Hogan and the fact that the cops might be looking for Curt.

"RUOK?" she typed.

"Y"

"WRU?" Where are you?

"FNX"

"CNICU?" Can I see you?

"Y"

"WN?" When?

"W8" Wait. "WN I CN" After a while, she added a plaintive request. "CNUTAKMEHOME?"

"EZ" Curt told her. "NO PROB"

• • •

Only a few minutes after Joanna was warned about the impending arrival of the composite artist, the woman herself appeared on the scene. She was stocky with short gray hair and dragging a heavy-duty roll-aboard computer case behind her. She spoke briefly to the receptionist, who nodded and then pointed in Sandy's direction. Ali stepped forward to intercept her.

"Ms. Mitchell?" the woman asked.

"No. I'm Ali Reynolds, a friend of Sandy's. That's her over there."

But the woman was focused on Ali. "Ali Reynolds? Wait a minute," she said. "Don't tell me you're Alison Reynolds. I remember you. Weren't you on the news over in L.A.?"

Ali nodded.

"Madeline Havens with Composite Systems," the woman said, holding out her hand. "I used to live there, too—in L.A. Did someone tell you I was coming?"

"They didn't mention you by name," Ali said, "but for some reason Madeline Havens sounds familiar. I seem to remember that I did a story on you once, but the details escape me."

Madeline grinned. "You did do a story on me. In fact, you did several, and it's ironic, because what happened to me isn't all that different from what I understand happened to you a little later on. For years I was an in-house composite artist for LAPD. Then, when the new chief came along, all of a sudden and despite glowing performance reviews, they let me go and replaced me with a whole bevy of private contractors.

"So I did the same thing you did—filed suit for wrongful dismissal—and went freelance. It turns out I'm an EEOC triple threat: age—fifty-one; sexual orientation—lesbian; and race—

Indian—Paiute, not East Indian. Took the bastards to court and won big-time. Now I'm a private contractor myself—I do composites for smaller jurisdictions, the ones that don't have budgets big enough to support in-house artists. Our company has even been able to undercut the guys who replaced me at LAPD on occasion. That felt particularly good. So, what are you up to these days?"

Ali thought about that. It didn't seem like she was doing much. "Some blogging," she said. "And I'm trying to decide what I want to be when I grow up."

"No sense in rushing," Madeline said. "Fifty's the new forty, you know."

With that, Madeline turned her attention to Sandy. Once they had been introduced, she took the seat next to her. Within minutes, armed with both a laptop computer and an old-fashioned sketchbook, Madeline had engaged Sandy in conversation and gone to work. Her computer was stocked with images of hundreds of individual physical features—eyebrows, eyes, hairlines, hairstyles, chins, noses, lips. Once Sandy selected individual features, Madeline incorporated those into a handmade sketch.

Ali found the process fascinating. With Sandy providing the details and with Madeline Havens skillfully combining them, the image of a young man gradually emerged on paper. He was in his early to mid-twenties with wide-set eyes, a long crooked nose, and a brush-cut hairstyle. In the drawing there was an odd disconnectedness in his expression that reminded Ali of photos she had seen of Timothy McVeigh, the Oklahoma City Bomber. There was something about his angry, dead-eyed expression that made Ali's blood run cold.

As Ali watched the image materialize she realized that, good as it might be, the information Sandy was providing merely placed the guy at the confrontation in Basha's. Crystal, however, had been at the scene of the almost fatal attack in Mund's Park. Would she recognize the subject of the drawing as one of the toughs she had seen there?

Enthralled by the sketching process, Ali had momentarily stopped paying attention to Crystal. Now, though, wanting to show the drawing to Crystal, Ali discovered to her dismay that the girl was no longer there. While Ali had been otherwise occupied, Crystal had simply vanished.

• • •

When Crystal reached the park, Curt's car still wasn't there. She stood there for a moment, undecided. What if Ali came looking for her?

Looking around for a place to hide, Crystal spotted a thick clump of sharp-leaved dusty bushes close to the parking lot. She ducked into them. The ground underneath was dirty and dusty and strewn with garbage—dead drink containers and empty grease-covered McDonald's wrappers—that had been totally invisible from the outside. But the fact that the trash had been invisible from the outside meant that Crystal was, too. As she settled in, her nose began to run. Her eyes itched like fire. She was grateful to have her father's long-sleeved and oversize sweats protecting her from the smelly, prickly leaves while she waited—seeing without being seen.

The parking lot was full of people. Two vans with signs that read SUNSHINE DAYCARE pulled up and parked in the two spots closest to Crystal. Several women and seven little kids clambered out of them. While the attendants pulled out a series of multiple-child strollers and began loading children into them, Crystal caught sight of the Explorer. It pulled into the lot and stopped a few parking places beyond the vans.

The women and kids and strollers were right there in front of Crystal—only a few feet away. If she popped out of the bushes right then, Crystal knew she'd startle them and draw way too much attention to herself. So she waited, willing them to move on; willing her itchy nose not to sneeze. But then, just as the crowd started moving out of the way, something happened in one of the middle strollers—one containing three toddlers. The middle child began howling and whacking away with one little fist at the child on his right. The whole parade came to a stop, while the lady pushing the stroller tried to figure out what was going on.

*Come on,* Crystal urged silently. *Get out of the way.*

But they were still there, milling in front of her, when beyond them, Crystal saw the door of the Explorer come open. A man stepped out. Crystal could barely believe her eyes. It wasn't Curt—it wasn't him at all. But the man driving Curt's truck was someone Crystal recognized. She had seen him once before as a frightening figure caught in the Explorer's headlights—someone wielding a baseball bat.

Crystal gave a sharp intake of breath. One of the women seemed to notice. She looked around, frowning, but then her charges drew her attention once again, and she turned back to the kids in her stroller. Moments later the whole group moved on, clearing the way between Crystal and the Explorer.

Shaking with dread and afraid of being seen, Crystal stayed where she was and waited. While she watched, the man who wasn't Curt pulled a phone out of his pocket and began pressing buttons. A moment later, Crystal's cell phone buzzed, announcing a text message. The vibration startled her so much that she could barely pull the phone out of her pocket. With her breath coming in short, shallow gasps and with her fingers trembling so much she almost dropped the phone, Crystal read the message:

"WRU?" Where are you? CU wanted to know.

CU was Curt's handle, but he wasn't the one who had been sending Crystal messages. The man in the parking lot, the man driving Curt's Explorer, was the one who had offered to give Crystal a ride back home to Sedona. So what did all this mean? If Curt wasn't here—if he wasn't the one driving his truck or using his phone, Crystal wondered, where was he? Was he dead? Had those awful men from Mund's Park used a baseball bat on Curt the same way they had on Kip Hogan? She had seen two of them get Curt's SUV. Had they found Curt while Crystal was hiding in the restroom and taken him away? If they had killed Curt and almost killed Kip, what would they do to Crystal if they ever found her?

Without ever emerging from the bushes, Crystal used her trembling fingers to key in her response.

"UHA." Under house arrest. "SRY."

Over in the parking lot, the man who wasn't Curt muttered something under his breath and kicked the tire. Then he jumped into the Explorer, slammed the door behind him, and drove away.

Watching him go, Crystal Holman was smart enough to know that one thing and only one thing had saved her—that howling little boy who had been so intent on beating up his seatmate. If it hadn't been for him, Crystal knew she would have been a goner.

• • •

When Ali first noticed Crystal was gone, she wasn't all that concerned. Thinking she might have simply responded to a call of nature, Ali got up and went across the lobby to the women's restroom. Unfortunately it was empty. Crystal wasn't there and no one else was, either. With rising apprehension, Ali hurried over to the lobby entrance where a uniformed security guard was stationed just outside.

"Excuse me," she said. "Did you see a girl come out this door in the last few minutes? She was wearing a pair of oversize sweats."

"Blue sweats? Long blond hair in a ponytail?"

Ali nodded. "That's the one."

"Sure, I saw her," the security guard said. "Just a couple of minutes ago." He pointed. "Headed off toward Thomas on foot."

Ali headed that way, too. As she did so, she pulled out her cell phone and scrolled through the call history until she found a number that had to be Crystal's. When she reached Thomas, she paused on the sidewalk and looked in both directions. Nothing, and when Ali called Crystal's cell phone, there was no answer on that, either.

She had ended the call and was hurrying back toward the parking garage when her phone rang. Hating the idea of having to tell Dave what was really going on and that his runaway daughter was once again on the lam, Ali was relieved to see her son's name in the caller ID window.

"Hey, Mom," Chris said. "I'm at lunch. I thought I'd call and see how things are going down there. How's Kip?"

"Still in surgery," Ali told him. "And everything else is a disaster. Believe it or not, Crystal just took off again."

"You mean she ran away?"

"Evidently. There's a woman here working with Sandy on a set of composite drawings. I got caught up in that. Crystal must have realized I wasn't paying attention and made her getaway. I never expected her to pull a stunt like that."

"You should have," Chris counseled. "She's a teenager after all."

"You never did any of this stuff," Ali countered.

"Don't be so sure, Mom," Chris said with a laugh. "Most of the time I was lucky and didn't get caught."

By then, Ali was back at her car. "I'm hanging up now," she said. "I'm going to drive over to the freeway and see if I can spot her between here and there. Maybe Crystal's trying to hitch a ride back home."

Once in her Cayenne, Ali drove straight to I-17. Heading north, she checked entrance and exit ramps as far as Bethany Home Road, all to no avail. Frustrated beyond bearing but still stalling on making the necessary call to Dave, Ali was on her way back to the hospital when her phone rang again.

Ali was almost sick with relief when she heard the missing girl's voice. "Crystal!" she exclaimed. "Where are you?"

"I'm scared. Can you come get me, please?"

"Where are you?"

"At the park where we went earlier this morning. The parking lot by that little lake."

"What are you doing there?"

"It doesn't matter. Just come get me," Crystal insisted. "Please."

There were dozens of questions Ali wanted to ask, but Crystal sounded so upset—so desperate—that Ali stifled all of them. "I'm on my way," she said grimly. "I'll be there in a few minutes."

More furious than she was relieved, Ali swung into the parking lot with a squeal of tires. At first Crystal wasn't visible, but as soon as Ali stopped the car, the girl emerged from beneath some oleanders and came sprinting toward the Cayenne. Once inside, she fastened her seat belt without having to be reminded.

"What in the world were you thinking?" Ali demanded. "Why did you leave the hospital? What are you doing here?"

But whatever was going on with Crystal and no matter how scared she was, she wasn't prepared to give a straight answer. "I don't want to talk about it," she half-sobbed. "Can't we just go back to the hospital?" she begged. "Please. I won't do it ever again. I promise."

For two days Ali had done her best to be understanding and sympathetic toward this troubled child. Now she was in no mood for Crystal Holman's latest set of drama-queen histrionics.

"I should hope not," Ali said.

Crystal sat huddled miserably on the far side of the car, but instead of watching where they were going, she seemed to be concentrating on traffic in the rearview mirror. Her verbal response, when it finally came, was the last thing Ali expected.

"Thank you," Crystal said.

*For what?* Ali wondered. *For picking you up or for giving you hell?*

"Are you going to tell me what you were up to?" she asked.

"I just needed to get out of the hospital for a while," Crystal said. "I needed to be by myself."

"That's probably a lie," Ali said. She held out her hand. "Now give me your cell phone."

"My cell phone?" Crystal repeated with a gasp. "Why?"

"Give it to me," Ali repeated.

"You're taking my cell phone away? How come?"

"Because having a cell phone is a privilege, not a right," Ali replied. "At the moment, as the person who's supposed to be looking after you, I'm declaring that your behavior doesn't warrant any privileges."

After a long moment's hesitation, Crystal sighed, plucked her cell phone out of the pocket of her sweats, and dropped it into Ali's open palm.

"Are you happy now?" Crystal wanted to know.

"Hardly," Ali answered. "I'm not going to be happy until I can hand you back over to your father and turn you into his problem instead of mine."

• • •

Back in the hospital lobby, Detective Lee Farris had arrived on the scene and taken charge of the situation. He had moved Sandy Mitchell and Madeline Havens to the far corner of the room and had commandeered both a small table and a power outlet for Madeline's computer. By then all three sketches had been completed. While Lee began questioning Sandy, Madeline used a tiny portable scanner/printer to run off copies of the composite drawings.

With no one paying particular attention to her, Crystal wandered over to the printer and picked up one of the sketches. She looked at it for only a moment. Then, turning deathly pale, she let the paper slip from her hand. "I've gotta go to the restroom. I'm gonna be sick."

As she raced away, Ali picked up the fallen sketch, which turned out to be the one of the empty-eyed man she had seen earlier. Crystal may not have picked the sketch out from a law-enforcement-approved montage, but her reaction was enough to convince Ali that for Crystal Holman, the chilling likeness was of someone she recognized.

Ali followed Crystal as far as the restroom door, where the very convincing sound of retching made it clear that Crystal really was sick. Before Ali could storm inside and confront her about any of it, however, Crystal's cell phone vibrated in her pocket. When Ali went to answer, she discovered it was a text message rather than a voice call, a message from someone called CU. *Does that C stand for Curt?* Ali wondered.

"WHERE R U?" the message read. "WENT TO PARK. U DIDNT SHOW."

The words confirmed Ali's worst suspicions. Crystal hadn't gone to the park just to get away from the hospital. She had gone there to meet this person who was now text-messaging her. And wasn't it possible that this was also the same guy Crystal claimed she couldn't contact, Curt with no last name? And why was he so eager to be in touch with Crystal now? Ali was reasonably sure he was looking for a second helping of whatever sexual favors Crystal Holman had been offering.

Staring at the screen, Ali wanted to reach through the phone and grab CU by the neck. Much as she would have enjoyed strangling him, she also knew someone needed to convince him to come forward and tell the authorities whatever he knew about Kip Hogan's attackers. Since Detective Farris was fully occupied with interviewing Sandy Mitchell at the moment, Ali decided to take matters into her own hands. And fingers.

Ali and Chris had been sending text messages for years. When she had been working late hours at the station, text messaging had afforded her the simplest means of staying in touch with her son. And because she had been considered "in the know" on that topic, she had done a series of stories designed to help clueless parents have some idea of what their kids were doing and saying with their now ubiquitous cell phones.

Ali hesitated for a moment. Would she be able to reply without letting CU know that someone other than Crystal was responding? *What's there to lose?* she wondered.

"WENT," Ali said, keying in her response. "CAUGHT." Ali had had to think a minute. "UHA." She was pretty sure that meant under house arrest, but she had no way of knowing if CU understood what she was saying.

"WAYN?" That one was easy. Where are you now?

"HOSPITAL"

"ST FRANCIS?"

"Y" YES.

Inside the restroom the toilet flushed. That meant Crystal would be coming out soon. "L8R," Ali wrote. "PAW" Ali knew that was universal teen speak for "parents are watching."

Ali shoved the phone back into her pocket just as Crystal emerged from the restroom. "Better?" Ali asked.

Crystal nodded wanly. Either the girl really was sick, or she was doing an excellent job of faking it. She went over to a love seat and lay down on it, covering her eyes with her arm. Meanwhile, the phone was once again vibrating in Ali's pocket, announcing the arrival of another message.

Just then Bob Larson bounded into the hospital lobby. Ali hadn't expected him until much later—not until after the restaurant closed in the early afternoon and he had a chance to drive down.

"My Bronco's still in the shop," Bob explained. "Franco gave me a loaner and your mother let me off early, so here I am. What's happening?"

Crystal's phone vibrated impatiently. "Detective Farris from Flagstaff is here interviewing Sandy," Ali told him. "And we now have a set of composite drawings of the guys Kip confronted the other day."

"Are they the same ones who beat him up?" Bob asked.

"Could be," Ali answered. "We don't know that for sure."

Bob glanced at Crystal, who was still sprawled on the love seat. "What's going on with her?" he asked. "Is she okay?"

"She claims to be sick," Ali said. "But I'm not sure I believe her." With that, Ali walked over to the love seat.

"Sit up, Crystal," she ordered. "I need to talk to you."

Crystal uncovered her eyes, but she didn't move. "What?" she asked.

"I have errands to run," Ali told her. "My dad's here. He's your babysitter for the moment, and he's going to watch you like a hawk. If you know what's good for you, by the time I get back, you'll have spilled your guts to Detective Farris. Otherwise I'll tell him you've been withholding information in a homicide investigation. I believe that qualifies as a felony, by the way."

With that Ali turned and headed toward the door with the phone still vibrating in her pocket and with her father padding along after her.

"Aren't you being a little tough on her?" Bob Larson asked.

"Not nearly tough enough," Ali replied. "And I'm serious. Keep an eye on her. She's already run off once today, and she'll do it again if you give her half a chance."

"But where are you going?" Bob wanted to know.

"Out," Ali said. "There's something I need to do."

"When will you be back?"

"When I can." Realizing that she, too, was sounding like a rebellious teenager, Ali hurried outside and extracted Crystal's vibrating telephone.

"RUOK?" CU wanted to know. "IWSN"

Ali's stomach tightened into a knot. IWSN was a parental red flag for I want sex now.

*You turd,* she thought. "ME2," Ali wrote.

"WAW" That translated into where and when?

Headed for her car in the garage, Ali scrambled for an answer. She needed a place with enough vehicle traffic that her Cayenne would blend in. She also needed a spot where, conceivably, Crystal could arrive on foot.

"CFEE SHP ON THOMAS," Ali wrote.

"CUT" That would be IM-speak for see you there.

*And I will see you there, you worthless jerk,* Ali thought grimly. *I just won't be the thirteen-year-old you're expecting.*

# { CHAPTER 10 }

It took less than three minutes for Ali to exit the parking garage and make it to the parking lot of the dingy coffee shop across from the hospital. She pulled into a space next to a uniform store and waited. Minutes later, and even though she was expecting it—waiting for it—she was shocked when a white Ford Explorer nosed slowly through the parking lot without stopping.

Suddenly meeting up with CU was no longer a remote possibility. It was all too real. What would she say to Curt? Apprehensive about the coming confrontation, a combination of fear and rage swept through her. Ali's heart sped up. Her hands began to cramp.

A few minutes later, the Explorer was back. Again it didn't stop, but the second time through the lot, Ali managed to jot down the license number. The third time it pulled into a space directly in front of the restaurant and stayed there for several minutes with the engine idling. No one got in or out, and the tint-darkened windows made it impossible for Ali to see inside.

With her palms wet with sweat, Ali gripped the steering wheel. She had managed to lure CU out into the open, but she had no idea what his next move would be or hers, either.

With her full attention focused on the Explorer, Ali jumped involuntarily when Crystal's phone sprang to life and buzzed again.

"HERE," CU wrote. "WAU?" Where are you?

"TRYING TGTHOOH," Ali added. Trying to get the hell out of here.

"TRY HARDER," CU wrote back. "TYPO." Take your panties off.

The idea that he was trying to lure someone as young as Crystal out of the hospital for quickie sex made Ali furious. Stymied by the tinted windows, Ali was almost to the point of exiting the Cayenne to see if she could get a better look inside the Explorer. That's when her own phone rang. She had to put Crystal's phone down before she could answer.

"Ali?" a woman said. "Arabella Ashcroft here. Have you read it yet?"

"Read what?" Ali asked.

"The diary," Arabella answered impatiently.

Guiltily Ali realized that the mostly unread diary was still where she had left it the night before—in her purse.

"No," Ali admitted. "I've been caught up in a crisis. I haven't had a chance."

"That's probably just as well," Arabella replied. "Things have changed on my end, too. I don't need you to read it after all. If you'd be so kind as to just drop it off here when you have a chance."

Crystal's phone was buzzed again. "CNT W8 ALL DAY. MYB." Move your butt. Clearly CU was running out of patience.

"I'll have to get back to you on this," Ali said to Arabella. "I'm in Phoenix right now and busy."

"Certainly," Arabella said. "At your convenience. There's no rush."

"PLS," Ali wrote. Please. But by then the Explorer was already backing out of the parking place. As it eased south on Third, Ali made a split-second decision. She put the Cayenne in gear and followed. Traffic was a mess. It was all she could do to keep the Explorer in view while at the same time trying to remain unobtrusive. There was sweat on her face now, slipping down her forehead and dripping into her eyes; soaking the back of her shirt.

Despite CU's apparent impatience with Crystal—or at least with the person he thought was Crystal—the man didn't seem to be in that big of a rush to leave the neighborhood. Ali's frantic reality slipped into a strange slow motion. Time seemed to stand still. She followed the SUV as the driver made his way back across Thomas and cruised around the hospital grounds, probably checking to see if Crystal was actually on her way. He stopped briefly at a passenger loading zone right next to the hospital entrance. For a heart-stopping moment, Ali was afraid he was going to leave the Explorer with the valet and go inside looking for Crystal. Finally, though, he drove away and headed west on Thomas. Hoping to stay out of sight, Ali delayed as long as she could before turning onto Thomas several car lengths back and following him into what was fast turning into afternoon gridlock.

Intent on her pursuit, Ali was startled when her phone rang while she was stopped at the light at 19th and Thomas. Grabbing it up, she was relieved to see Dave's number in the readout.

"Court just recessed for today," he told her. "I didn't get called, which means I'll have to be back here tomorrow. So where are you? Should I head for Phoenix or back home to Sedona?"

Ali was in full crisis mode, and the very sound of Dave's calm, unruffled voice helped her get a grip.

"You should probably come on down to Phoenix—to the hospital," she said.

"Fine," he said. "I'll be there as soon as I can, but you sound funny. Are you all right?"

Ali was a long way from all right. The light changed and traffic inched toward the freeway, but the Explorer didn't make it through on that cycle, and neither did Ali.

"I'm stuck in traffic," she said. "And I need your help."

"Name it."

"I need you to run a plate for me."

"Run a plate?" Dave repeated. "Have you switched over to cop lingo now?"

Ali read off the letters and number. "Please," she added when she finished. "Just run it."

"You realize it's against regulations to run a plate for private use?"

Ali took a deep breath. "It's about Crystal," she said.

"Why didn't you say so?"

Ali hung up. The Explorer turned onto the eastbound I-10 entrance ramp at Thomas and waited for the metered traffic light to allow it to merge onto the crowded freeway. Ali followed suit. Once on the freeway, the Explorer cut in and out of traffic, forcing Ali to do the same. Even so, it took the better part of an anxiety-ridden hour of nail-biting to travel from there to where the Explorer exited onto eastbound U.S. 60.

While she waited for Dave to call back, Ali worried about what she would tell him. She had used a possible connection to

Crystal to galvanize him to action. Ali knew that sooner or later she would have to tell him what was really going on with his wayward daughter. Crystal wasn't ever going to tell him. That would be up to Ali. Between worrying about telling Dave about Crystal's issues and dreading the coming confrontation with the driver of the Explorer, Ali's stress level was off the charts.

"Got it," Dave said when he finally called back. "The 2001 Ford Explorer belongs to Curtis Wilson Uttley of 101 Blue Spruce Circle, Flagstaff, Arizona. Who is he? What's going on?"

So CU was Curtis Uttley. That made sense, but before Ali could answer, she realized that the Explorer was headed for the exit ramp at McClintock. With traffic the way it was, Ali realized she could either drive or talk. She couldn't do both.

"Thanks, Dave," she said. "I'll have to get back to you."

At the light, the Explorer turned right on the red and headed south. Unfortunately, the vehicle two cars in front of Ali decided to go straight through the intersection. Ali was forced to wait interminably until the light finally turned green. By the time she made the corner, the Explorer had vanished.

For the next several minutes, Ali cruised the neighborhood streets, hoping to catch a glimpse of where the Explorer had gone. A Roto-Rooter truck was parked in front of one of the houses, but that was the only sign of life. Ali saw no pedestrians on the street, no joggers or kids out riding bikes, no people she could have asked for help in tracking down exactly where the missing SUV had gone.

Shaking with a combination of frayed nerves, letdown, and frustration, Ali eventually had to give it up and head back to Phoenix. On the way, she picked up her phone and called Dave back.

He answered right away. "What's going on? Are you okay?"

"I was driving," she said. "Traffic was bad."

"Tell me about Curtis Uttley's vehicle. Where did you spot it? Was he driving it or was somebody else?"

"I was following it, but I lost it over in Tempe," Ali said. "And I have no idea who was driving it. I couldn't see inside. Why?"

"Because that vehicle is listed on a BOLO, a be-on-the-lookout-for, in a missing persons case out of Flagstaff," Dave said. "Curtis Uttley reportedly left there on Tuesday night, supposedly to visit one of the casinos down in Scottsdale. He evidently has a bit of a gambling problem. His wife didn't bother reporting him missing until today. Now tell me," Dave added. "What's going on?"

Ali felt her heart constrict as she found herself wondering if the CU who had been sending text messages to Crystal's phone had been someone else and not the real Curtis Uttley at all. She had been pretending to be Crystal. Maybe someone else had been pretending to be Curtis Uttley. Clearly turnabout was fair play.

"I'm afraid this particular missing person may have far more serious problems than gambling," Ali said.

"Why?" Dave asked. "What makes you say that?"

Ali didn't answer directly. "Are you on your way here now?"

"As a matter of fact I am," Dave said. "Why?"

"Because," Ali told him. "We need to talk."

• • •

Ali returned to the hospital to find Madeline Havens gone. Crystal was closeted with Detective Farris in a small conference room just off the lobby, and Bob Larson was still commiserating with Sandy Mitchell. If there had been any change in Kip's situation, no one had bothered to come let Sandy know. That was where things stood when Edie Larson appeared on the scene.

Bob seemed surprised to see his wife. "What are you doing here?" he wanted to know.

"I had to come," Edie declared. "No one's exactly burning up the phone lines between here and Sedona letting me know what's going on."

"That's because we don't know. They're not telling us anything," Bob returned. "If he's out of surgery, they may have taken him to the ICU."

"Why don't we find out then?" Edie asked. "Which way is the ICU? Let me go rattle a few cages."

"I'll go with you," Bob offered, and off they went.

Once they were gone, Ali walked over to the conference room door and pushed it open. To Detective Farris's obvious annoyance, Ali let herself into the room and placed Crystal's cell phone on the table between them.

"What's this?" Farris demanded. "Can't you see we're busy here?"

"Let me guess," Ali said. "Crystal has told you that she was with some guy the other night but that she has no idea who he was or how to get in touch with him, right?"

Farris studied Ali somberly for a moment then nodded. Ali, in turn, directed her remarks to Crystal. "A woman from Flagstaff reported her husband missing this morning," Ali continued. "His name is Curtis Uttley. Sound familiar, Crystal? And it happens that somebody using the name CU has been sending you text messages all afternoon. He's been trying to be in touch; wanting to meet up with you in person. In fact, he came here to the hospital a little while ago, looking for you. He was driving a white Ford Explorer. Does that ring any bells?"

Crystal's cheeks paled. "He, like, actually came here?" she asked.

Ali nodded. "He actually did," she returned. "You didn't happen to have your phone in your possession, but I did. So I've been texting him back for you. And because you weren't straight with me and didn't tell me what I was really dealing with, I followed him all the way to Tempe before I lost him. What do you think would have happened to me if I'd caught up with him?"

Refusing to meet Ali's gaze, Crystal studied her hands and said nothing. "So what's the deal, Crystal?" Ali prodded. "Did you tell Detective Farris exactly what you and Curtis Uttley were doing there in Mund's Park the other night?"

"Making out," Detective Farris supplied.

"I thought that's what she'd say," Ali said. "Actually they were doing quite a bit more than that, Detective Farris. So maybe it's time you started the interview over again from scratch. And maybe this time Crystal will be kind enough to tell you what was really going on up there at Mund's Park—and I do mean all of it. Like how she got there from Vegas and how she hooked up with Mr. Uttley. And don't bother telling Detective Farris that you didn't get a look at Mr. Hogan's attackers. I know from hearing you barf your guts out in the ladies' room that you recognized at least one of them. I'm guessing Curtis Uttley did, too, and that's why he's gone missing. He's hiding out."

Ali waited to see if Crystal would say anything. She didn't.

"You might want to move along with that interview," Ali continued. "With any luck, you'll be finished before your father gets here."

"Dad's coming?" Crystal asked faintly.

"Yes, he is," Ali said. "And believe me, he's going to get an earful."

With that, Ali left the conference room. Out in the lobby, Bob and Edie were nowhere to be seen. Sandy sat alone, deeply immersed in reading what seemed to be a Bible. Rather than interrupting her, Ali found a chair in a relatively quiet corner and turned on her computer. She planned to check for cutloose correspondence. Instead, on a whim, she logged on to the Internet and Googled Curtis Uttley. It turned out there were any number of listings, most of them talking about Curtis's reputation as a trophy-winning coach of girls' softball and soccer teams. The most recent mentions came as a result of coaching teams in the Flagstaff area. Previous items came from towns in Texas, Kansas, and California.

*A rolling stone gathering no moss,* Ali concluded. *And with an endless supply of adolescent girls. What more could a pedophile want?*

Edie Larson emerged from the elevator and went straight over to Sandy. She placed one hand on her shoulder. After a whispered conversation, Sandy stowed her Bible, stood, and accompanied Edie back to the elevator. Ali rose and made as if to follow them. From the back of the elevator, Edie discouraged her doing so with a single shake of her head. Feeling a little rejected and still angry with Crystal, Ali returned to her computer screen.

She had scanned the first list and was halfway through the second when she found the Web site, AskCoachCurt.com. Coach Curtis Uttley answers your team sports questions. Ali immediately logged on to the site and scrolled through a series of essays. How to Be a Team Player; Get Off the Bench and Get on the Field; Winning Isn't Everything; It's Never Too Early to Look for a Scholarship. There at the bottom of the page was one final note. For individual questions or coaching advice, feel free to write to *CoachCurt@askcoachcurt.com.*

*So this is how he meets girls,* Ali thought. *Then he reels them in with text messages that never show up on computer screens that parents might actually see.*

Going back to the original list, Ali made a note of each town mentioned in the coaching articles. It would probably be worthwhile to contact school and recreation folks in each of those areas to see why a teacher who was also a winning coach had suddenly moved on. Ali had a feeling that Crystal Holman wasn't Coach Uttley's first teenage conquest and that, rather than confronting him, the authorities in the other towns had simply passed him along and turned him into someone else's problem.

*And now he's mine,* Ali thought.

She wrote and posted the next blog entry while sitting in the hospital lobby.

**CUTLOOSEBLOG.COM**
*Thursday, January 12, 2006*

It's been a long day. I'm in a hospital lobby, waiting for a friend whose loved one is hovering between life and death. Sitting here is giving me some time to reflect on some of the things I've learned today, and they aren't pretty.

What I want to do is speak to every parent with an adolescent or pre-adolescent child and say to those parents: WAKE UP!!! If your child has a computer, check it out. Find out what chat rooms he or she visits, and find out what's going on there. Find out who's on your child's buddy list. Who sends e-mails to your child's address and what do those e-mails say? And what does your child say back? Does this sound like an invasion of your precious offspring's privacy? You bet it is. It's also called parenting.

The same rules apply to your child's cell phone. What comes and goes on your son or daughter's text messages is private. It's also possibly deadly. Today I've caught glimpses of some of the people out there, evil people—who are trolling the cyber-ether for innocent children to victimize—your children. And yes, you should be very afraid for your children.

And if looking over your son or daughter's shoulder when they're online annoys them? Fine. You can tell them from me that being a parent is a dirty job, but somebody has to do it.

*Babe,*
*posted 6:07 P.M. January 12, 2006*

• • •

Dave Holman arrived at the hospital a few minutes later. "Where's Crystal?" he wanted to know.

"In a conference room talking to Detective Farris," Ali told him.

"Lee is interviewing her? How come? She's involved in this?"

Wrestling with how much to tell and when to tell it, Ali nodded. "Before I picked her up the other night in Mund's Park, she may have seen something."

"What?"

"She was in the car with Curt Uttley," Ali said. "They were there at the time of the attack."

"What were they doing there?" Dave asked. "Car trouble? How is Kip, by the way?" he continued without waiting for Ali to answer. "And where's Sandy?"

Ali knew it was only a matter of time before she'd have to tell Dave the whole story, but right that moment she was grateful for any delay that spared her from doing so.

"Kip's out of surgery and back in the ICU," Ali said. "That's where Sandy is, too, along with my folks. They're all up in ICU."

"I need to let Sandy know that we've finally got a lead on Kip's family. He has a daughter named Jane Eyre Hogan. Her married name is Braeton. She was born April 1, 1974. Her mother's name was Amy Sue Laughton Hogan. Jane was raised by her grandmother, Elizabeth Hogan, a retired Kingman High School English teacher."

"Raised by her and most likely named by her, too, I'll bet," Ali offered. "Anyone who would stick a poor little boy with a name like Rudyard Kipling wouldn't hesitate at naming a baby girl Jane Eyre. Elizabeth Hogan must be quite unusual, though. Mostly it's maternal grandmothers who pick up the child-raising responsibilities when the parents take a hike."

"But I ran into a brick wall trying to find her," Dave continued. "Elizabeth Hogan left Kingman long enough ago that there's no longer a valid forwarding address. She may actually be dead by now, although there's no sign of a death certificate anywhere I could find. The records clerk over in Coconino County had better luck with the daughter—Jane Hogan Braeton. I have an address for her here in Phoenix—down in Chandler, actually. The clerk tried to call the information in to Detective Farris, but his phone is turned off, probably because he's doing the interview. I told her I'd pass it along as soon as I saw him."

Dave looked expectantly toward the conference room door. Ali's first instinct had always been to leave the tale telling to Crystal, but she seemed incapable of telling the truth to anyone about anything. Now, with a few minutes of relative privacy, Ali knew it was time to come clean.

She took his hand and led him toward the room's most distant seating. "Listen, Dave," she said, changing the subject. "We need to talk about your daughter, and you're not going to like what I have to say."

"What has she done now?" Dave asked.

"It turns out she's been doing lots of things."

By the time Ali finished giving him her account of what had been going on, Dave was crushed—crushed, livid, and irate all at the same time.

"You mean to tell me she's been screwing around like this right under Roxie's nose?" he demanded. "How's that possible? And she calls herself a blow-job virgin? I can't believe it. She's only thirteen, for God's sake!"

"I know," Ali agreed.

"And where do I find this worthless son of a bitch Curt Uttley so I can put him out of his misery?" Dave demanded. "He's probably hiding out in Tempe somewhere near the same place where you lost whoever was driving that Explorer. Take me there. I'll find him if I have to take the neighborhood apart brick by brick. What's the address?"

"I never saw exactly where he went, so I can't give you an address," Ali said. "The Explorer turned onto a residential street and disappeared—probably into an attached garage. Once the door was shut, there was no way to tell which one it was."

"I'll figure it out," Dave said determinedly.

Just then Lee Farris left the conference room and came over to where Ali and Dave were sitting. "Did you tell him?" Lee asked. "About what she was doing in Mund's Park?"

Ali nodded.

"Sorry about that, Dave," Farris said. "She claims she met the guy over the Internet."

"At askcoachcurt.com?" Ali asked.

Frowning, Farris gave Ali an appraising look. "How did you know that?" he asked.

"Lucky guess," she said.

Farris turned back to Dave. "According to what Crystal told me just now, while she and Uttley were parked there, they witnessed part of the attack on Kip Hogan. Uttley drove across the freeway to report the incident. Crystal thinks Mr. Hogan's assailants came there looking for Uttley and Crystal both. When Crystal came out of the restroom, she broke into a house, looking for a place to hide. She was afraid the assailants might come after her, too. And it turns out one of them did—earlier today. She saw him."

"Today?" Ali asked.

"Crystal said she heard from Uttley late this morning—at least she thought it was him. He offered to give her a ride back to Sedona. She went to a park down the street to meet him, but he didn't show. Crystal was being cautious and was keeping out of sight because she was afraid you might come there looking for her as well. The Explorer parked, but the guy who got out of it wasn't Uttley. The driver turned out to be one of Mr. Hogan's attackers."

"She recognized the guy?"

Farris nodded. "And it scared her to death." He held out one of Madeline Haven's composite sketches. "This one," he added. "She says this is the guy."

Ali recognized the sketch, too. It was the same one Crystal had dropped earlier. Looking at it and seeing the man's dead-eyed stare, a cold chill ran down Ali's spine. If this was the man who had come looking for Crystal, he was most likely also the man Ali had followed. For miles. Only being caught at that stoplight had kept her from catching him—or him from catching her. When Ali glanced in Dave's direction, he was staring at her.

"If Crystal hadn't been hiding from you at the park, the guy probably would have caught up with her. And if you hadn't confiscated her phone, he definitely would have caught her the second time. Thank you, Ali," he said, crushing her in a bear hug. "Thank you so much."

"Taking the phone was pure luck," Ali said with a laugh. "I wanted to get her attention. Since spanking her wasn't an option, I did the next best thing—I took away her lifeline."

"Thank you," he said again.

"I saw you come in, Dave," Lee Farris said. "I told Crystal you were here, but she wouldn't come out to talk to you. You should probably go talk to her."

"What the hell am I going to say?" Dave asked despairingly as he stood up. "Any suggestions about what a father should say to a sexually active thirteen-year-old?"

"That's easy," Lee said with a sympathetic chuckle. "You could always threaten to lock her up for the next four years. That's what I told my daughter when she went off the rails in middle school. It's not fatal. And eventually Gina figured out I was right."

Dave started toward the conference room moving like a death-row inmate taking his last walk.

"Crystal sees herself as a drama queen," Ali called after him. "Don't fall for it. You don't have to be mad, but you do need to give her a dose of reality. Tell her the first order of business will be taking her to a doctor to be checked for STDs. Maybe that will get her attention. She's operating under the idiotic notion that oral sex isn't really sex. Somebody has to get the truth through to her."

Dave stopped and looked back at Ali, his haggard face full of regret. "You always wonder how you'll do the birds-and-bees talk with your kids," he said. "I never imagined it would turn out like this."

*Crystal's a long way beyond birds and bees talking,* Ali thought. *She's into birds and bees doing.*

"I know you didn't," Ali told him kindly. "All you can do now is play the hand you've been dealt and hope for the best."

Nodding, Dave started away and then stopped once more. "I almost forgot, Lee. You need to turn your phone on and check with your records clerk. They believe they've got a line on Kip's family."

While Dave headed into the conference room to talk with his daughter, Farris plucked his phone out of his pocket and dialed. "But first we need to get a line on whoever's driving Curtis Uttley's Explorer. So tell me again, Ms. Reynolds. Where were you exactly when you lost him?"

Ali started to tell him, but by then someone had answered his call. "Okay," Farris said. "I'm still down in Phoenix, but I'm going to need you to put out a BOLO on a white Explorer registered to one Curtis Uttley of . . ."

"He was?" Farris resumed. "Really? When did this happen?" He listened for a moment more and then added, "And they've got detectives headed here? All right. Give them my number so we can coordinate. Yeah, I'll keep my phone on. I was doing interviews and didn't want to be interrupted. And Mojave County will be following up on tracking down his cell phone? That's probably the best way to pinpoint the location of whoever has it. The problem is, that could take some time."

There was another pause before Farris continued. "Yes, Detective Holman's still here in Phoenix, and yes, he did mention something about that, but he didn't have a chance to go into any details. Okay, shoot." For the next several minutes, Farris jotted lines into a notebook. Finally he closed it and put it away. "Okay," he said. "I've got all that. Tell the sheriff that with everything happening down here right now, I'll probably have to stay over tonight."

Farris closed his phone and turned to Ali. "So much for Curtis Uttley," he said.

"What do you mean?" Ali asked.

"I mean he's over," Farris said. "Dead as a doornail. One of the construction workers on the new Burro Creek Bridge found what everybody thought was an unidentified jumper down in the bottom of the canyon yesterday morning. Except when they got around to doing the autopsy this afternoon, it turns out he wasn't a jumper at all. Signs of restraints on his ankles and wrists, and the guy was dead before he ever hit the ground. The ME says his injuries are mostly blunt force trauma. So somebody beat the crap out of him the same way they did Kip Hogan. And tonight when the Mojave County ME finally got around to running the dead guy's fingerprints through AFIS, guess what? Curtis Uttley's name came up because of the thumbprint on his California driver's license, which he hadn't bothered to change."

"They killed him?" Ali asked.

Farris nodded.

"And they took his vehicle," Ali added. "Just like they took my dad's truck after they attacked Kip."

"Looks like," Lee Farris agreed. "Luckily for your dad, they blew a tire on that Bronco of his or it would still be gone. It also looks like you're real lucky you didn't catch up with this creepo today. His losing you was the best thing that could have happened. Otherwise we'd probably be looking for you now, too."

Half sick to her stomach, Ali knew it was true. She hadn't been following Curt Uttley—she had been following Curt Uttley's killer, and if she had managed to catch him, no doubt she'd be dead as well. So far both she and Crystal had been incredibly lucky.

*There's only one question,* Ali thought. *Will the killers give up or will they come back and try again?*

# { CHAPTER 11 }

The door to the conference room opened. Dave Holman emerged from the room. His daughter did not.

"We've had our little father/daughter chat," he said. "Crystal says she's too embarrassed to come out, and maybe that's a good thing."

Folding a piece of paper and stuffing it in his jacket pocket, Dave looked from Lee's face to Ali's. "What's up?" he asked.

"Uttley's dead," Farris said without preamble. "Somebody killed him and threw him over the guardrail where they're building that new bridge at Burro Creek."

Dave took a few seconds to process that. "Thank God for small blessings," he said. "Saves me the trouble."

Farris nodded. "I'm on my way to Tempe right now to see what I can do about tracking down our bad guys."

"Me, too," Dave Holman said.

"No," Farris objected. "Absolutely not."

"What do you mean, no?" Dave argued. "At this stage of the investigation, the more feet on the ground the better."

"Not your feet," Farris returned. "We need uninvolved feet,

Dave. We need people with no ax to grind. Uttley's murder happened in Mojave County. They've got a pair of detectives headed this way. We'll be able to use them. The attack on Mr. Hogan happened in my jurisdiction, and I'll be working the case as well. What I want you to do is walk away and let us handle this."

"I'm supposed to ignore that one of these guys was hanging around here looking for my daughter?"

"That's all the more reason for you *not* to be involved," Farris returned.

"I'm off duty," Dave pointed out. "What I do on my own time is none of your business."

For a long tense moment, the two men squared off, staring eye to eye. Afraid punches might be thrown, Ali held her breath. Lee Farris was the first to blink.

"Look," he said with a conciliatory sigh. "You know you're too close to this part of the investigation to be unbiased, but there is something you could do. How about if you head down to Chandler and see if you can locate Mr. Hogan's daughter? You're a cop, but you're also one of his friends. It would be a big help to me, Dave. That would mean one less thing I'd have to worry about."

Dave thought about that for a time. "All right," he said at last. "Fine."

"Good," Farris said. "Thanks. You have all the information you need?"

Dave nodded. "I've got it," he said.

With that, Detective Farris strode off. As soon as he was out of sight, Dave, too, headed for the lobby door, with Ali trailing behind. "Where are you going?" she asked. "Chandler?"

Dave shook his head. "Tempe," he said grimly.

"But I thought you said . . ."

"I lied," Dave said. "Besides, I still have these." He reached into his pocket and unfolded the three composite sketches. "I'll stop by a Kinko's on my way and make a bunch of copies, then I'll start canvassing gas stations and grocery stores in the area. Even bad guys have to eat and buy gas. If the driver of that Explorer could access a garage door with an opener, chances are he lives somewhere around there. Somebody is going to recognize him."

"What about contacting Kip's daughter?" Ali objected.

"I'm sorry," Dave said. "Getting these guys off the street is a hell of a lot more important than doing a next-of-kin notification." He opened a small notebook, tore out a page, and handed it to Ali. "If it's so important to you, you do the notification. You're Kip's friend every bit as much as I am.Or maybe your father can do it. We're dealing with a bunch of cold-blooded killers, Ali. They're out there looking for Crystal. Right now, finding them is my first priority."

"What about Crystal?" Ali asked.

"What about her?"

Dave, suddenly focused on the hunt, was prepared to head out without uttering a word to his daughter. "You can't just walk away and leave her here," Ali said.

"I can't very well take her with me, either," Dave said. "Could I leave her with you awhile longer?"

As Dave's friend, Ali had listened sympathetically to his version of how the wheels had come off his marriage. The way he told it, Roxanne had been largely to blame. In that instant though, as he prepared to walk away without a word, Ali understood the end of the marriage wasn't all Roxie's fault. Whenever duty called—whatever kind of duty—Dave would have been off and running, leaving Roxie holding the bag, juggling the three kids and trying to keep the home fires burning.

In two days, Ali had had more than a bellyful of Crystal Holman, and she wasn't eager to sign on for more. "Did you make any progress when you talked to her?" Ali asked.

"Some I suppose," Dave said with a shrug. "We called her mother from the conference room and talked to her together. Roxie says she and Richey will drive down tomorrow and take Crystal home. But that's tomorrow. Tonight I can't very well take her along to Tempe with me. It's too dangerous. What if something were to happen to her?"

*What if something happens to you?* Ali wondered, but by then, Ali knew she was stuck. "All right," she agreed. "I'll keep Crystal with me for the time being, and when I go back to Sedona, I'll take her to my house."

"Thank you," Dave said. "Thanks for everything."

"You're welcome," Ali said. "But you're not leaving without telling her what's going on. You're her father, Dave. She needs to hear it from you, not from me."

"All right," he agreed reluctantly. "I'll tell her."

When Ali and Dave turned back toward the conference room, they were both surprised to see that Crystal, looking isolated and resentful, was standing silently in the doorway. There was no telling how long she had been there or how much she had heard.

While Ali watched, Dave hurried over to her. Crystal greeted everything he had to say with a temper tantrum of stormy objections. Eventually he wore her down.

"Please, Crystal," Dave begged. "I need to help catch these guys."

"All right," Crystal said, relenting. "But it's just for tonight.

She treats me like I'm a baby or something. I'm glad she's not my mother."

*And that,* Ali thought with genuine gratitude, *makes two of us.*

• • •

Jason Gustavson could hardly believe that the crazy bitch had followed him all the way home from Phoenix, but now, watching the evening news, he was putting it all together. It was terrible luck that the girl was somehow connected to the guy from the store, but that was the problem with small towns. Everybody knew everybody. Everyone was connected to everyone else.

Thanks to the eager news reporter standing in front of St. Francis Hospital, he knew the man they hadn't quite managed to kill was being treated there. Jason fully intended to go there and finish the job. He'd take care of him and of the others, too—the girl who had somehow gotten away and the crazy broad in the blue Cayenne, who had driven like a maniac to keep up with him.

After a lifetime of keeping his urges bottled up, Jason had finally given himself permission to be real. He wasn't appalled by what he'd done. He was proud of it. He'd finally stood up for himself. All his life he had talked about doing something spectacular. Time after time, he'd laid out plans and then given them up. This time, he was moving forward. This time he was really doing it. The other guys were petrified, of course. They were scared shitless of the cops and of Jason, too, and they weren't wrong.

On his way to the bathroom, Jason felt the slightest twinge of guilt for the Roto-Rooter guy. After all, he was just a poor jerk out doing a dirty job to support his family, but he was also in the wrong place at the wrong time. Because of that, he would be the first to die.

Jason found Tom Melman on his knees in the bathroom, replacing the broken toilet. When the door opened behind him, he didn't look up. "I'll be done in a few minutes," he said, "then I'll get your water turned back on."

He may have heard a click because he started to turn around, but the bullet from the silenced .38 plowed into the back of his head and exploded out the front. He fell face-first into the uninstalled Toto. If it hadn't been for the blood splatter all over the room, he might have been a frat boy who'd had way too much to drink.

Clint Homewood was next. He was sprawled on the beanbag chair in his room, totally engrossed in his PlayStation game and listening to his tunes. "How's it going, Jas," he asked as the door opened. "Want to play?"

But Jason Gustavson no longer had any interest in virtual bullets. He'd become enamored with the real thing. "Not right now," he said, and he pulled the trigger. Again, shooting from mere inches away, there was no question of missing, and he didn't. The PlayStation fell to the filthy, pizza-box- and beer-can-littered floor and so did Clint. Something about seeing him lying there with his shattered head next to a half-eaten pepperoni made Jason smile.

"Hey," Mitch Warren called from out in the hall. "What's going on? Did you hear a funny noise?"

Jason had planned to take Mitch in his room, lying on his bed. Instead, Jason confronted his second roommate in the hallway. When he pulled the trigger, Mitch clutched his gut and crumpled to the floor, moaning. Jason was tempted to leave him there, but he was tired of loose ends, so he pulled the trigger again and put Mitch out of his misery. Then, stepping over the body, he left his roommates' wing and headed for his own room in the master suite on the far side of the house.

Jason Gustavson had a few last-minute items to pull together before he could finish this. It might very well be his last evening on earth, and he planned to make it memorable.

• • •

"Come on," Ali said, once Dave had disappeared through the lobby door.

"Where?" Crystal asked.

"Your father has work to do, and so do we."

"Like what?" Crystal wanted to know. "What do we have to do?"

"First we have to go upstairs and talk to my parents and tell them where we're going. Then we need to track down Mr. Hogan's daughter and let her know what's happened to him."

"Why?" Crystal asked.

"Because your father asked us to for starters, and we're going to tell my parents because that's what responsible people do—they let other people—people who love them—know where they're going and when they'll be back."

"But I'm hungry. Can't we have something to eat first?"

Ali reminded herself that this was a child who could mow her way through two Sugarloaf sweet rolls at one sitting. "Sure," Ali said. "We'll find something on the way."

They took the elevator up to the ICU floor, where they found Bob and Edie Larson seated side by side in a small waiting room. Sandy wasn't visible.

"They let her in to see him?" Ali asked.

"Thanks to your mother," Bob said.

"How's Kip doing?"

Bob shook his head wordlessly and swiped at his eyes with a pair of balled fists. Edie reached over and patted his knee. "Not very well," she said. "He's on a ventilator. I don't think he's going to make it."

Ali never remembered seeing her father quite so broken up. Kip had worked for the Larsons, but he and Bob had become good friends as well—and Kip was a friend Bob didn't want to lose.

"Dave found out that Kip has a daughter," Ali said.

"A daughter?" Bob asked incredulously. "Are you serious? He never once mentioned having kids."

"I have her address," Ali continued. "She lives down in Chandler. Dave asked me . . . us actually," she revised, motioning toward Crystal, "to contact her and let her know what's going on."

Bob nodded. "If she's going to get here before it's too late, you should probably just call her."

Ali shook her head. "Dave wanted her to be notified in person, and I think he's right." She motioned to Crystal. "Let's go."

Edie got up and followed them as far as the elevator. "We won't be able to stay much longer," she told her daughter. "Sandy's brother is supposed to be coming a little later, but if we have to go back home . . ."

"It's all right," Ali said. "I'll make sure Sandy isn't left here by herself."

"Good," Edie said.

Moments later, Ali and Crystal descended to the lobby and walked out into the unexpected chill of a cold desert night. They stopped at a Jack in the Box just shy of the freeway.

"Did your father tell you why he was going to Tempe?" Ali asked while they waited for their to-go order.

Crystal shrugged. "He just said he was going. He didn't say why. When he's working on a case, he never does."

"Curt Uttley is dead," Ali said quietly.

Crystal gave a small involuntary gasp. "He's what?"

"He's dead, Crystal. Someone trussed him up with rope or duct tape. Then they beat him to death and dropped him off the Burro Creek Bridge between Wickenburg and Kingman. That's who your father is looking for in Tempe. The people who did that. He's afraid they're looking for you, too."

Crystal was uncharacteristically silent, and in that bit of quiet, Ali had a sudden stroke of inspiration. Crystal Holman had been lying to everyone all along, and she probably still was. "Did you see them?" Ali asked quietly.

"See who?"

"Did you see those men, the ones with the bats, meet up with Curt Uttley at the gas station?" Ali asked. "Did you actually see what happened?"

Once again Crystal didn't answer, but a brief grimace passed across the girl's features and a vehement denial followed.

"Why do people keep asking me stuff like that?" Crystal declared. "I'm telling you, I didn't see anything!"

"Excuse me, Crystal, I already know you're a liar, and I happen to think you're lying about this, too. But if your father is going to put his life and his job on the line trying to track these guys down, don't you think somebody deserves to know the truth about what went on?"

Another long period of silence followed as they drove through the relatively light nighttime traffic with the computer-generated voice of the dashboard GPS issuing its bland directions as they went.

Finally Crystal let out a long breath. "Curt had finished making the call and was going back to his SUV when all of a sudden three guys came rushing at him out of nowhere. I saw the whole thing. It looked like they were arguing or something. And then Curt and two of the three got into Curt's car and drove away. Another car followed them."

"Willingly?" Ali asked. "Did Curt Uttley get into the car because he wanted to or because they forced him to?"

Crystal didn't respond.

"Well?" Ali prodded.

"I think they made him go," Crystal admitted at last.

"And you saw the other car? What kind? What make and model?"

"I don't know," Crystal said. "I don't really know all that much about cars."

"Why didn't you tell someone about this at the time?" Ali asked. "Why didn't you report it? Curt Uttley may have been a pedophile and a worthless excuse for a human being, but if you had called the cops right then and told them what you knew, maybe they could have done something about it. Maybe they could have saved him."

"I was scared," Crystal whimpered. "I was afraid they'd come after me, too. I mean, I saw what they were doing to that other guy. They were hitting him with a bat. I didn't want to get hit. And I was afraid to have my dad find out what was going on. But then, this morning, when I got the text message from Curt, I was really happy to hear from him and know he was okay."

"He isn't okay," Ali pointed out. "He's dead, and he might not have been if you'd reported what happened in a timely manner."

"Don't you think I know that now?" Crystal whispered. "I knew it this afternoon as soon as that guy got out of Curt's car. I knew it right then. I'll never be able to think of anything else."

Ali knew Crystal had been scared, and that she still was. No wonder she'd been so difficult. Still, now that they were moving forward, Ali kept up the questions.

"Did you tell Detective Farris any of this?"

"No," Crystal admitted. "But that's why I don't want to go back to Vegas. Daddy's a cop. He won't let anything bad happen to me. My stepfather . . ." Again her voice faded away.

"What about your stepfather?"

Crystal shrugged. "He's pretty much useless. He wouldn't be able to keep me safe if they came there looking for me. Not ever."

Ali wasn't sure Dave could keep his daughter safe, either. She wasn't sure anyone could.

By then they had finally arrived at the address listed on Dave Holman's piece of notebook paper. It turned out to be in a golf course development on the far east side of Chandler. Par 5 Drive was a quiet cul de sac that evidently backed up to a fairway on the Desert Steppes Golf Course. In the glow of neatly spaced streetlamps the houses themselves seemed spacious and commanding, but it appeared that only a few feet separated one house from its next-door neighbor. The distinctly California-like density led Ali to believe this was a relatively new development.

She pulled up to a curb and stopped in front of the house. "Here we are," Ali said.

"Do I have to come in?" Crystal asked. "Can't I just wait in the car?"

"We've already been over this once today, and I think you know the answer," Ali told her. "Yes, you're upset, but you've proved to be untrustworthy. Come on."

Caught up in the conversation with Crystal, Ali had given no thought to what she would say to Kip Hogan's long-lost daughter. Ali was still scrambling for ideas when she pressed the doorbell. In the far reaches of the house the drone of a television set was abruptly silenced. A few minutes later, the porch light flipped on, the door opened a crack, and a tall black man peered out at them.

"Yes?" he asked cautiously.

"Is this the Braeton residence?" Ali asked.

"It is," he said. "And I'm Jonathan Braeton. Who are you and what can I do for you?"

His voice was wary, but it was also cultured and smooth. His response to unexpected late evening visitors wasn't rude, but it wasn't especially cordial, either.

*And why would he be?* Ali wondered. After all, it was eight-thirty at night, and the man was faced with a pair of complete strangers who had appeared unannounced on his doorstep. Police officers doing this kind of thing at least had official ID to offer. Ali had nothing.

"I'm sorry to intrude," she stammered. "My name is Alison Reynolds from Sedona, and this is Crystal Holman. We're looking for a Jane Hogan Braeton. I'm a friend of her father's."

"Really," the man said. "You don't say."

He stepped back from the door then, but he didn't open it. Instead, he engaged the security chain. "Janie," he called. "You may want to come hear this."

A woman's voice called from somewhere in the background. "What?"

"There's someone here who claims she's a friend of your father's."

"A friend of my father's?" the woman repeated. "I don't have a father. Is she nuts?"

"You'd better come see for yourself," he told her.

Ali hadn't been particularly surprised when a black man had

answered the door. After all, interracial marriages had been on the scene for a long time. What she hadn't expected at all, however, was that Kip Hogan's daughter would also turn out to be an African American. Because she was. Her skin was several shades lighter than her husband's, but she was still clearly black.

*If Kip Hogan is her father, her mother was or is black,* Ali decided. *Or else she's adopted.*

Not the least intimidated, Jane Braeton refused to hide behind the half-open door. Instead, she disengaged the security chain and flung the inside door wide open. For a moment she stood framed in the doorway with her husband directly behind her.

Jonathan Braeton was tall and rangy and in his early to mid-forties. Jane was short and stout and looked to be ten years younger than her husband. The top of her head barely reached the height of her husband's broad shoulders. He was wearing a sweatsuit with a towel casually draped around his neck and looked as though he had just finished a workout. She was still dressed for work in a skirt, blouse, blazer, and stockings. But no shoes.

"Who are you?" she demanded. "What do you want, and what kind of a scam are you trying to pull?"

"It's about Kip Hogan," Ali offered. "That's how we know him. Or, as he's listed on your birth certificate, Rudyard Kipling Hogan."

"Words on a birth certificate do not a father make," Jane returned. "Mr. Hogan has been out of my life for a very long time, and I want him to stay that way."

"He's been hurt," Ali said. "Gravely injured in fact. A gang of thugs beat him up with a baseball bat. He's in the ICU at St. Francis Hospital. That's why we came to let you know, so you could go visit him."

Jane Braeton crossed her arms. "What makes you think I'd want to? You claim you know Kip Hogan?" she asked.

"Yes," Ali said.

"And does it look to you like he could possibly be my father?"

"Well, no," Ali admitted. "It doesn't, but . . ."

"You're right. He isn't. And how badly hurt is he?"

"Very," Ali said. "He had brain surgery this morning. He's on a ventilator. According to what my mother was able to learn, he may not make it."

"What was this, some kind of barroom brawl?"

"It didn't happen in a bar. It happened along I-17 south of Flagstaff. A couple of days ago three young punks came to the grocery store in Sedona where Kip's girlfriend, Sandy Mitchell, works as a check-out clerk. They were underage and tried to buy booze. When she carded them, they started hassling her. Kip showed up in the middle of it, stuck up for Sandy, and put a stop to it. Afterward, the kids evidently lay in wait for Kip and took a baseball bat to him."

"I've wanted to take a bat to him myself," Jane Braeton said. "Let's let sleeping dogs lie."

"Janie," Jonathan Braeton admonished. "Remember, what goes around comes around. We owe Elizabeth more than that. You can't just turn your back on the man."

"Why not?" Janie returned. "That's what he did to us, didn't he? He walked away from his own mother, for heaven's sake! He never looked back and never lifted a finger to help her. As far as I can see, he never gave a damn about anyone but himself, and I don't see why we should care about him, either."

"Janie . . ."

"Don't you start with me about it," Jane said fiercely. "You weren't there. You don't know what it was like. You don't have any idea."

"Still," Jonathan said calmly after a short pause, "let's remember our manners. We don't need to broadcast this discussion to the whole neighborhood. How about if we invite these nice ladies in out of the cold, offer them something warm to drink, and have this discussion in a civilized fashion?"

Jane Braeton looked as though inviting Ali and Crystal into her home was the last thing she wanted to do, but eventually she acquiesced. Stepping back, she motioned them inside. "Won't you come in," she rasped. She might just as well have been eating glass.

Jonathan, on the other hand, was far more welcoming. "Have a seat," he said, leading Ali and Crystal into a spacious, comfortably furnished living room. "Now, what can I get you?" he asked. "Hot tea? Cocoa?"

Ali and Crystal settled on matching chintz-covered easy chairs. "Cocoa," Crystal said at once. After a pointed look from Ali, she added a tardy, "Please."

"Thank you," Ali said. "Cocoa sounds nice. I'll have some of that, too."

Jane took a seat on a nearby sofa and leveled her questioning gaze on Crystal. "I suppose you're a friend of Mr. Hogan's as well?" she asked.

Crystal shook her head. "Not really," she said.

"She's with me," Ali said. "I apologize for bringing her along, but I didn't have anywhere to leave her."

"Oh," Jane said.

After that an uneasy silence enveloped the room. It took only a few minutes for Jonathan to return, bringing with him a tray laden with two cups and saucers. He handed one to Crystal. She held it nervously, with the bottom of the delicate china cup clattering on the saucer. For a moment Ali was reminded of herself, all those years ago, nervously sipping her first cup of Anna Lee Ashcroft's tea.

Jonathan sat down next to his wife. "Call her," he said.

Jane looked at her watch. "It's too late," she said. "She's probably already asleep."

"Call her," he urged again. "Wake her up. He's her son after all. What if this turns out to be Elizabeth's last chance to see him? You wouldn't want to be responsible for her missing that opportunity."

With an angry shrug, Jane Braeton rose abruptly and stalked off to another room, slamming the door shut behind her.

"I had no idea Kip's mother was still alive," Ali said. "No one was able to sort out where she went after she left Kingman."

"She's in her nineties," Jonathan explained. "She lives in an assisted living facility down in Queen Creek. She has macular degeneration, Parkinson's, you name it. Having to put Elizabeth there almost broke Janie's heart, but eventually it reached a point where it was too much. We could no longer have her here at home, not even with live-in help."

He stopped and steepled his fingers in front of his chin before adding thoughtfully, "I suppose you can see that Janie's family situation is a bit . . . shall we say . . . problematic. I won't presume to go into all that. It's Janie's story and it's entirely up to her whether or not she decides to share it. But tell me more about Mr. Hogan. How did you come to know him?"

For the next several minutes Ali explained about how Kip Hogan had come into her parents' lives straight from the homeless camp on the Mogollon Rim; how Kip had helped care for Bob Larson in the aftermath of his snowboarding accident; and how he had stayed on and continued to work around the place long after Bob was back on his feet. She ended by telling him about the refinished bird's-eye maple credenza—the last job Kip had completed before he had been assaulted.

"So he was trying to straighten himself out then," Jonathan said.

"Yes," Ali said. "Very much so. He's been attending AA regularly and he has a steady girlfriend, Sandra Mitchell. She's been at the hospital all day. She'll be devastated if she loses him. My parents will be as well."

Ali had known for sure how much Bob was affected. Her mother might not admit it, but the very fact that Edie had jumped into her Alero and driven down to the hospital was a strong indication that she, too, cared about Kip Hogan and what happened to him.

Just then the door came open down the hall and Jane Braeton marched back into the living room. She was wearing shoes now—a pair of stylish black pumps. She had a purse in one hand and a coat slung over the other arm.

"You're right," she said grudgingly to her husband. "She wants to go. The night supervisor said it'll take forty-five minutes or so for an attendant to get Elizabeth out of bed and dressed. They'll bring her down to the front entrance."

Jane paused and gave Jonathan a searching look. Then she turned to Ali. "I suppose my husband has been running off at the mouth and giving you my whole life history?"

"I did no such thing," Jonathan protested. "I told them that was up to you."

Jane sighed. She tossed her purse onto the coffee table and then sat down on the couch. "I could just as well, I suppose," she said. "My version will be mercifully shorter than Elizabeth's will be. Do you mind getting me a cup of tea, Jon? I think I'm going to need it. And maybe our guests would like some more cocoa."

"Would you care to help me?" Jonathan asked Crystal.

To Ali's surprise, Crystal leaped willingly to her feet and followed Jonathan into the kitchen.

# { CHAPTER 12 }

Jane waited until the door swung shut behind them. She sighed again. "I suppose you can tell I don't much like talking about this," she said. "It's painful to have to acknowledge that you were unwanted. Not entirely unwanted. Elizabeth Hogan wanted me, and I bless her for it, but she was the only one who did."

Puzzled, Ali nodded but said nothing.

"The man you know as my father, Kip Hogan, was a native of Kingman. Both his father's people and his mother's, the Brownings, came from there as well. Kip's father and grandfather both worked for the railroad. His dad was a brakeman who died in a train accident when Kip was only three. As for his mother? Since the family name was Browning, when their first child turned out to be a girl, they decided to name her Elizabeth Barrett. It was supposed to be a joke, but Elizabeth ended up having the last laugh. She was the first girl in her family ever to go to college. She went to Flagstaff back when Northern Arizona University was still the Northern Arizona State Teacher's College. She graduated from there with a teaching certificate and eventually a full-fledged degree in English. She went back home and taught English at Kingman High School for her entire career."

"Hence Rudyard Kipling Hogan," Ali offered.

Jane nodded and smiled apologetically. "Exactly. So Kip grew up there. He was a typical teacher's kid, which is to say he was a born hell-raiser. He never even finished high school. Instead, he dropped out and volunteered for the army, then got shipped to Vietnam. Elizabeth always told me he was different when he came back—different—but at first he seemed to be okay. He came back home and hired on with the fire department. That's where he was working when he met my mother."

"Amy Sue," Ali said.

Jane gave her a shrewd look. "Yes," she said. "Amy Sue Laughton Hogan. She said she was from Virginia, but that was probably a lie. Everything else she said was a lie, so why would that be any different? She showed up in town on a Greyhound bus with nothing but a couple of suitcases. She rented herself a room, went to work in one of the local dives, and set her cap for Kip Hogan. And voilà, next thing you know, she tells him she's pregnant. By then, he's trying to be the man, so he trades shifts, takes two days off from work, and off they go to Vegas to get married. That was July fourth, 1973."

The kitchen door swung open. Jonathan came in with his tray, two cups and saucers—a new one for Ali and one for his wife, and no Crystal.

"That poor little girl is starving," he said to Ali. "I'm making her some toast and cheese. I hope you don't mind."

Having fed her one meal on the way here, Ali wondered if Crystal had a hollow leg. Jane Braeton, on the other hand, sent a grateful smile in her husband's direction. Seeing it, Ali realized that keeping Crystal in the kitchen was a ploy on Jonathan's part, a way of giving his wife some privacy in order to tell a story she most likely wouldn't want to relate in front of a thirteen-year-old girl.

Jane waited until Jonathan returned to the kitchen before she continued. "They were in Vegas on their honeymoon when a train derailed coming through Kingman. A tanker loaded with liquid propane was involved, and the resulting BLEVE was huge."

"The what?" Ali asked.

"A boiling liquid expanding vapor explosion," Jane explained. "On July fifth a rail car loaded with liquid propane caught fire and blew up. It was Kingman, Arizona's darkest day. Eleven firemen and one civilian were killed. Several others—firemen and police officers—were seriously injured, and ninety-some-odd civilian bystanders also suffered burns."

Ali remembered the story now but only vaguely. She had been in junior high when it happened. For days the fire had been headline news all over Arizona. Geographically Sedona was a long way away from Kingman. Eventually the story had faded, but Ali understood that for a small town like Kingman, one which had suddenly lost a whole troop of its finest young men, the fire had to be a tragedy whose tentacles still held.

"So, when all hell broke loose, Rudyard Kipling Hogan was off in Vegas honeymooning with his brand-new wife," Jane went on. "They headed back as soon as they heard the news and arrived while the fire was still burning. Kip went to the site and looked at the damage, but he never even suited up. Instead, he left again without a word and without even bothering to unpack his suitcase. He didn't give a damn if Amy Sue was pregnant or not. He left her that very day and never came back. Elizabeth always said it was because of the guilt—that he couldn't stand the idea that he was alive when his friends were dead."

"So your parents were married for two days?" Ali asked.

"Let's just say that Kip and Amy Sue were married for two days," Jane allowed. "Elizabeth told me that she was shocked and disappointed when her son took off like that. He left Amy Sue with nothing—no money for rent, no place to stay, no car, nothing. Even though Kip wasn't prepared to do the right thing, Elizabeth was. She let Amy Sue move in with her, and everything was peachy keen until I was born a good month or so earlier than anyone except Amy Sue expected. Once I was there in the hospital nursery for all to see, it was pretty clear that Rudyard Kipling Hogan wasn't my father."

"So your mother was white then?" Ali asked.

Jane paused, sipped her tea, and then nodded. "Apparently," she said. "I did some checking after the fact. I'm pretty sure Amy Sue was already pregnant on the day she arrived in Kingman. She targeted Kip to be her fall guy, her baby's daddy. The problem was, he was the wrong color, and by the time she figured that out, it was too late. She stayed in the hospital for three days after I was born and didn't even bother giving me a name. She came home to Elizabeth's house long enough to drop me off. She left the house in the middle of the night that first night without saying good-bye to anyone. I've never heard from her since. I have no idea if she's dead or alive."

Tears welled in the corners of Jane Braeton's eyes. "I'm sorry," Ali murmured.

Jane shook her head as if shaking off the momentary sadness that had overtaken her. Then she continued. "For the longest time, Elizabeth didn't even let on to anyone that Amy Sue had bailed. She was afraid if people found out, some busybody from social services would decide she was too old to be raising a baby and take me away."

"And she's the one who named you?" Ali asked.

Jane allowed herself a bleak smile. "Right. Jane Eyre Hogan. Who else but an Elizabeth Barrett Browning would name me that? Elizabeth hired a former student of hers, a Mexican lady named Roseann Duarte, to look after me. And those are the people who raised me, Elizabeth Hogan and Roseann. Elizabeth was never my mother, but she's the only mother I've ever known. She took care of me, loved me, and saw to it that I got a good education. My husband is right. I do owe her, and that's why we're doing this. That's why we're going to the hospital tonight, and that's the only reason—not because some stranger's name is on my birth certificate."

Jane looked at her watch and stood up. "We should probably get going."

Crystal emerged from the kitchen with Jonathan right behind her. "Do you want me to come with you?" he asked. "I can help with the wheelchair, whatever."

Jane shook her head. "No," she said. "We'll be fine."

"All right," Jonathan agreed. "You and Elizabeth do what you have to do, but drive carefully."

"I will," Jane said. "I always do,"

• • •

Crystal was strangely subdued on the drive back to the hospital. Lost in her own thoughts, Ali let her be. Having heard Kip's story through Jane Braeton's point of view, Ali felt a whole lot more empathy for the man. He had come home from Vietnam damaged. Even without knowing that Amy Sue was playing him for a fool with her shotgun wedding routine, the added trauma of surviving the fire in which so many of his buddies had perished had been more than Kip could handle. His fragile ego had shattered, and he had spent decades wandering in the wilderness until Bob Larson had offered him a way out.

"They're nice people," Crystal said.

At first Ali thought she meant Bob and Edie Larson.

"I mean, they asked us in and gave us food and everything. While we were out in the kitchen, he was asking me about school. Did you know Jane is a teacher?"

"No," Ali said. "I didn't."

"English," Crystal said. "Junior high."

*That figures,* Ali thought. *What else would someone named Jane Eyre do?*

"Kip Hogan ran away, too, didn't he?" Crystal said thoughtfully.

"Yes."

"How old was he?"

"I'm not sure," Ali said. "I don't know how old he is now. He was probably in his twenties or thirties."

"So grown-ups run away sometimes, too."

"Yes."

"And his family is still mad at him about it."

"Mad and hurt both," Ali said.

"How come?"

"How come they're mad?" Ali asked.

"I mean how come he ran away?"

Since Jonathan Braeton had respected his wife's right to privacy, Ali could hardly do less.

"There was an accident," she said. "An accident and a huge fire and lots of firemen died. Kip was working in the fire department at the time, and a lot of the people who died were friends of his."

"So he was mad at himself for not dying, too?" Crystal asked.

Coming from someone Ali had dismissed as being totally self-absorbed, it was a very perceptive question.

"Pretty much," Ali said.

"But nobody did anything to him? Nobody hurt him?"

"I don't think so," Ali said. "You heard what happened. Even after all these years, his mother's on her way to the hospital right now to see him."

"So, she still loves him."

"So it would seem."

"Oh," Crystal said.

Ali's phone rang. A glance at the readout told her it was Dave Holman. She tossed the phone to Crystal. "It's your dad,"Ali said. "Why don't you talk to him."

"Hi, Daddy," Crystal said. "We're on our way back to the hospital. We just finished talking to Kip Hogan's daughter."

*Not exactly,* Ali thought. *But close enough.*

"She was nice," Crystal said. "And so was her husband. She's going to pick up Kip's mother from somewhere and take her to the hospital so she can see him. Where are you? Really? A big fire? Will it be on the news?"

"What's on the news?" Ali asked.

Crystal waved her hand for Ali to be quiet.

"Are you coming back to the hospital then?" There was a pause followed by Crystal's disappointed, "Oh. Okay. Here she is." Crystal shoved the phone in Ali's direction. "He wants to talk to you."

"What fire?" Ali demanded.

Crystal didn't answer. Dave did. "We managed to locate Curt Uttley's Explorer, or what's left of it anyway, but I'm afraid we were a day late and a dollar short. The Explorer was parked in the garage of a house that burned to the ground late this afternoon."

"Whose house?" Ali asked.

"The house belongs to some well-to-do guy from Minneapolis named Karl Gustavson. He bought it for his son, Jason, who's going to school at ASU. According to the neighbors, the kid lives there with two roommates."

"What happened?"

"Gas leak. At least that was what the Tempe Fire Department had said on a preliminary basis. Now they're saying that there could have been some explosives involved as well."

"Does Lee Farris know you're there?"

"He wasn't happy about it when I turned up a few minutes after he did, but he's over it now."

"How bad a fire?" Ali asked.

"Very," Dave said. "The home is gutted, a complete loss. One of the firefighters told me they know of at least one fatality. We're waiting for someone to go inside and check. Right this minute, what's left is still so hot and so unstable that no one can get near it."

"If no one's been inside, how do they know there's a fatality?"

Dave sighed. "Believe me," he said, "there are ways to tell. I had planned on coming back to the hospital, but right now, I don't know when I'll get away. Depending on the time, I'll either come there or else go straight back to Prescott."

"Don't worry about it," Ali said. "Crystal is with me, and we've got it covered." She closed the phone.

"He always does that," Crystal said. "The cases he's working on are always more important than we are."

Ali couldn't help leaping to Dave's defense. "I'm sure that's not true," she said.

"Yes, it is," Crystal replied. "Coach Curt is dead. If Dad doesn't care about me either, I could just as well go back to Vegas."

Ali had no idea how to respond to that. If Coach Curt was a preferred alternative to going home to Vegas, Crystal's family life back home with her mother had to be far worse than anyone knew.

• • •

It was almost ten by the time they returned to St. Francis Hospital, where they discovered that getting inside the facility at night was a lot more difficult than it had been during the day. A seemingly humorless security guard had set up a check-in stand just inside the sliding lobby doors. All visitors arriving between the hours of 10 P.M. and 6 A.M. had to present valid identification, sign in, list the name of the patient they intended to visit, and be issued a visitor's pass. Since Crystal was only thirteen, she had no photo ID available.

Ali was still trying to argue her way past the gatekeeper when Jane Braeton showed up pushing a wheelchair. In it sat a tiny, white-haired woman who had to be Kip's mother, Elizabeth Barrett Browning Hogan.

"What's the problem?" Jane stopped the chair directly behind Ali.

"Crystal doesn't have any ID," Ali explained. "They're not going to let her in."

"Who are these people?" Elizabeth wanted to know, turning her head back and forth in the direction of each of their voices. "What's wrong?"

"These are the people I told you about, Nana," Jane said. "The ones who drove down this evening to let us know what had happened to Kip. This is . . ." She paused, having forgotten Ali's name.

"Alison Reynolds," Ali supplied, reaching out and taking

Elizabeth's trembling and icy-cold hand. "And this is my friend, Crystal. The problem is, she's thirteen and, as a consequence, doesn't have any photo ID. They won't let her into the hospital without it, so I guess we can't go up."

"Who won't let her go up?" Elizabeth asked.

"The security guard here," Jane said. "The one who issues the visitor's passes."

"Where?"

Jane had maneuvered the chair so it was parked directly in front of the desk and then began searching for her own ID. Elizabeth, in the meantime, moved her head around until she found a spot where her macular degeneration still allowed her some degree of sight.

"Young man," she said briskly. "You are a young man, aren't you?"

"Yes," he said with an uncomfortable grin. "Yes, ma'am, I suppose I am."

"And these people here, the woman and the girl with no photo ID, are people I've only just met. They drove all the way from here down to Chandler to let me know that my son has been injured and is in your hospital. Do you have any children?"

"Yes, I do," he replied.

"And how old are they?"

The guard looked ill at ease, as though he was uncertain whether or not he should answer his pint-size wheelchair-bound inquisitor. Finally he did. "One is four and the other is six months," he said.

"And you," she said. "When were you born?"

The security guard turned to Jane, hoping for assistance. Aside from holding up both her own and her mother's photo IDs, she wasn't giving him any.

"Well?" Elizabeth prodded. "When?"

She may have been old and blind, but she was still sharp. Evidently her years of practice in herding high school students had made Elizabeth Hogan more than a match for the hapless security guard.

"Nineteen seventy-seven," he said.

"See there?" she crowed. "I haven't seen my son since July the fifth, nineteen seventy-three. That was before you were born—longer ago than you are old. Until today, that is. Today I have a chance to see him again, and that wouldn't be happening if it weren't for these very kind people. These women aren't criminals—as you can plainly see—especially this young girl here. And they're not here to harm anyone, either. I can vouch for that personally. Now, are you going to let them come into the hospital or not? Because if you don't, I'm afraid I'm going to have to take this matter up with your superiors."

Since keeping unwanted visitors out was the security guard's primary function, reporting him to his superiors for actually doing his job seemed like an idle threat. Much to Ali's surprise, the man caved.

"Who is it you ladies are going to be visiting?" he asked.

Elizabeth beamed at him. "My son," she said. "Rudyard Kipling Hogan. I call him Rudy, but you may have him listed as Kip. He always hated his given name."

"And what's this young lady's name again?" he asked, peering across the desk.

"Crystal," Ali supplied quickly. "Crystal Holman."

The guard took the other names off the sign-in sheet. "Mr. Hogan is up in the third floor ICU," he said as he finished filling out the set of four stick-on badges. "There you go."

With Ali leading the way, they headed for the elevators.

The downstairs lobby had clearly received a recent upgrade that made it seem more like an upscale hotel lobby than a hospital. Renovations had not yet made their way to the ICU waiting room. It was as small and unremittingly grim as all the other hospital waiting rooms in Ali's experience. It was also surprisingly chilly.

There were only three people gathered in the room, no doubt prepared to maintain a long, overnight vigil. The first, Sandy, sat at a small table in the middle of the room. A Bible lay open on the table in front of her, but her chin rested in her hand and she appeared to be dozing. The second was a middle-aged woman, a few years older than Ali, who sat in the farthest corner of the room, knitting frenetically. The only sound in the room came from the industrious click of her needles. The third occupant, a balding, potbellied man, sat on a stiff-backed chair staring up at a wall-mounted television. The set was on and tuned to CNN, but the volume was muted. The lips of the broadcasters moved but nothing emerged. The only news available was whatever scrolled silently and with endless repetition across the bottom of the screen. Still, the man watched it with avid attention, as though his very life depended on what he saw there.

Something alerted Sandy to the newcomers' arrival. She blinked awake and made as if to rise, then glanced down at her watch and subsided back into the chair.

"Hi, Ali," she said wearily. "Thanks for coming back. I must have dropped off for a couple of minutes. It's too soon to go back in. They only allow visitors in to see patients for ten minutes at a time once every hour."

Ali looked around the room. "Where's your brother?" she asked. "I thought he was coming to be with you."

"Phil's heart's in the right place," Sandy said, excusing him. "But he's never been very dependable."

"Is this her?" Elizabeth Hogan asked from behind Ali. "Is this Rudy's girlfriend? Move me closer, please, Jane. I want to get a look at her."

While Jane Braeton obliged, Sandy sat up straighter in her chair and tried to smooth her hair. "Rudy?" she asked.

"This is Elizabeth Hogan," Ali explained. "Kip's mother, and Jane Braeton."

"So you're Kip's daughter?" Sandy asked, looking questioningly at Jane Braeton.

Jane glanced in Ali's direction and shook her head. "Not really," she replied.

She had parked Elizabeth's chair so the old woman's knees were almost touching Sandy's. Elizabeth leaned forward. Once again she moved her head from side to side as if trying to find a place where Sandy's face would be in focus.

"Has Rudy been good to you?" she asked.

"You mean Kip?"

"My son, yes."

Sandy's eyes filled with tears. "Yes, he's been very good to me, Mrs. Hogan. And he wouldn't have gotten hurt and wouldn't be here if he hadn't been defending me. That's why those punk kids attacked him. I feel like this is all my fault."

Elizabeth reached out and touched Sandy's knee. "I'm sure that's not true," Elizabeth said kindly. "These things happen and they're nobody's fault. What do the doctors say?"

"To me, very little," Sandy replied. "After he came out of the OR, Ali's mother talked them into letting me come up here to wait. They've let me go in to see him, but since I'm not a blood relative or his wife, they won't tell me anything about his condition. What I do know is he hasn't regained consciousness yet, and that's probably a bad sign."

Elizabeth nodded. "You may be right," she agreed. "It isn't a good sign, but let's go see about getting some real information, Janie. Which way is the nurses' station?"

Sandy pointed. Watching Jane and Elizabeth's progress toward a glassed-in window, Ali noticed the red-lettered sign posted above it: NO CELL PHONES NO EXCEPTIONS. Since Ali's computer air card was essentially a cell phone, technically that meant no Internet access, either.

Crystal plucked an extra blanket from a stack on a table by the doorway. Then, stuffing her earphones in her ears and turning on her iPod, she curled up in a chair as far from everyone else as she could manage.

Meanwhile Sandy studied the two women who were speaking in low tones to the woman stationed behind the glass partition. "She's the charge nurse," Sandy explained. "What about the one pushing Elizabeth's chair? Is she a nurse, too?"

Ali simply shook her head and didn't really answer. "Long story," she said.

The other woman in the waiting room checked her watch, put down her knitting, and went over to the swinging door that led back to the unit. She paused. "Are you coming?" she asked the man in front of the silent television set.

"Not right now," he said. "You go ahead. But you need to think about what the doctor said," he added. "You need to think about letting him go."

A look of absolute fury washed across the woman's face. "No," she said. And then again, more fiercely. "No!"

Abruptly she turned and disappeared behind the swinging doors. The man stayed where he was and as he was, still gazing up at the TV, oblivious to the fact that the discord between him and his wife had been witnessed by a roomful of strangers.

"They're divorced," Sandy whispered to Ali. "It's their son. Motorcycle accident. He and Kip had the same surgeon."

Jane Braeton turned away from the window and gestured for Sandy to join them. As Sandy left the table, Ali sat down next to where she'd been sitting. Part of a discarded *Arizona Reporter* lay there. Out of a lifetime's habit, she picked up the local news section and scanned the headlines. A small article near the bottom of the page caught her eye: DRAGGING VICTIM REMAINS IDENTIFIED.

A homicide victim who had been dragged behind a vehicle and whose body was found on a deserted roadside in South Mountain Park on Tuesday morning has been identified by the Maricopa Medical Examiner's officer as California real estate developer William Cowan Ashcroft, III.

The familiar name leaped out at Ali from the printed page. William Ashcroft? As in Arabella's nephew, William Ashcroft, the one she had called Billy? Instinctively Ali reached for her phone, but then, mindful of both the cell-phone-use prohibition and the lateness of the hour, she left the phone where it was and returned to the article.

Phoenix Police Department spokesman Shannon Willis said that Mr. Ashcroft had been visiting the area on business for a number of weeks prior to his death. So far detectives working on the homicide have acquired few leads.

Mr. Ashcroft was reported missing by his business partner on Wednesday after he had failed to appear at a meeting scheduled for Tuesday afternoon. Anyone with knowledge of the victim's activities in the days prior to his death is asked to contact the Phoenix Police Department.

The words brought back Arabella's mysterious phone call from earlier in the afternoon, the one where she had suggested things had changed and it was no longer necessary for Ali to read the diary she had entrusted to Ali two days earlier. Billy—the nephew who had tried to extort Arabella's money—was dead. Was that what had changed Arabella's mind?

Without a moment's hesitation, Ali reached into her bag and extracted the small, leather-bound volume.

Since so much had happened between the time Ali had read the first entry, and now she reread it. She expected that other entries would deal with the incest situation in detail. They did not. Going on, Ali was surprised to discover that most of the month's worth of entries that existed in an otherwise blank book dealt primarily with Arabella's birthday present, her prized parakeet, Blueboy.

Evidently Miss Ponder, the governess, had been enlisted to help in the process of teaching Blueboy to talk. She had also encouraged Arabella to do some research into the proper care and feeding of parakeets—covering their cages at night, making sure that their water and feed were fresh, cleaning the cages—something Arabella had clearly prided herself in doing on her own. The Ashcroft household Arabella had grown up in appeared to be long on servants and short on loving familial connections. In that world of old-fashioned educated-at-home wealth, the arrival of a blue-feathered parakeet had been a cause for celebration in the life of what must have been a very lonely little girl.

*Miss P says that in order to teach Blueboy to talk, we have to start with something simple, but it also has to be something that keeps his interest. She said a whistle might be easier than a word to begin with, so she suggested I whistle first—you know the kind of wolf whistle that boys give pretty girls—and follow that with one or two words, and always the same words. Pretty Baby is what I chose. A whistle and Pretty Baby.*

*And I think she's right. The first time I tried it, Blueboy was just sitting in his cage, but as soon as I whistled at him, he cocked his head to one side like he was really listening to me. Like he was interested. Miss P says that when I whistle first, it lets Blueboy know that I'm really talking to him. It's like when Mother rings the bell, that means the butler is supposed to come or the maid.*

*I've never had a pet before. Ever. Father has his horses but those are racehorses so they're not pets at all, and the only people who get to be around them are the grooms and the jockeys and the trainers. Regular people never get to ride them or even touch them.*

The next two entries were full of harmless chatter about Miss Ponder and the parakeet. In the one after that, however, Arabella's diary took a turn that hinted something was amiss.

*Mother told me this afternoon that Bill is coming home for Thanksgiving. This week. I loved it when he went away to school in September and everyone said he wouldn't be back until Christmas. But Father wants him here, so he's coming home anyway. He'll be here in two days. I already know Christmas will be ruined. Now Thanksgiving will be too. I hate him. HATE HIM. Why couldn't he just stay where he was?*

*Maybe it won't happen again. Maybe I should tell Miss P. I can talk to her about things I can't tell anybody else, but she probably wouldn't believe me. She really likes Bill. She told me once that she thinks my brother is very handsome. She wouldn't think that if she knew what he's really like.*

*Maybe I should run away, but I don't have any money and I don't know where I'd go. And if I do run away, what will happen to Blueboy? I can't carry a suitcase and a birdcage at the same time. I guess I have to stay.*

The final entries were short and scribbled so hurriedly that it was hard to decipher them.

*Father fired Miss P. I don't know why. She just left in a taxi.*

Followed by:

*Blueboy is dead. He killed him.*

And that was it. End of story. *He who?* Ali wondered. Arabella's faulty pronoun reference left the parakeet's killer's identity a mystery, but Ali suspected that she knew who was responsible. Had there been something going on between the now ex-governess and the stepbrother she had previously referred to as "handsome?" That was unmentioned, but it was certainly a possibility.

The diary had contained far less damning information than Ali had expected. And it had stopped almost in mid-entry, coming to an end without coming to a conclusion. Dissatisfied, Ali closed the book and returned it to her purse. Days earlier she hadn't understood why Arabella wanted her to read it. Now that Ali had read it, she still didn't know why, but she was reasonably sure why Arabella had changed her mind on that subject and why she wanted the diary back.

*It's because Billy's dead,* Ali told herself. *And I'm wondering if Arabella had something to do with it.*

# { CHAPTER 13 }

Emerging from being caught up in the diary, Ali glanced around the waiting room and realized that things had changed. The once-hourly ICU visitation schedule had evidently ended. Sandy Mitchell was again seated at the table. So was Kip's mother. She sat with her wheelchair pulled up close to Sandy's knees, and the two of them seemed lost in a low-toned conversation. Jane Braeton sat off to one side, absently thumbing through a dog-eared magazine. The other woman in the room, the mother of the injured motorcyclist, was back at her station, knitting away with single-minded concentration. Her husband—her ex-husband—continued his stolid vigil in front of the silenced television news. Crystal, with her earphones still attached, was curled up in a chair and appeared to be sound asleep.

The atmosphere in the room was so quiet and subdued that when Ali's cell phone rang it startled everybody, including the nurse who said nothing but gestured pointedly toward the overhead sign that prohibited the use of cell phones. Leaping to her feet, Ali hurried out of the room and down the corridor. She didn't answer until she was standing in the elevator lobby and well out of earshot of the charge nurse.

"I just wanted to set your mind at ease," Dave Holman told her. "I think it's over."

"What do you mean?" Ali asked.

"One of the Tempe Fire Department guys just came out of the burned-out house. He's located three separate sets of scorched human remains of gunshot victims along with one weapon. So we think we're looking at a double homicide/suicide."

"You're sure one of the dead guys is the one who was after Crystal?" Ali asked.

"Reasonably sure," Dave replied. "Right now it's all tentative, pending positive ID of the remains, of course, but that's where we are right now. I thought you'd be relieved to hear it."

Three people were dead, but if one of them was the guy who had attacked Kip and had tried to lure Crystal out of the hospital, Dave was right. Ali was glad to hear it. She didn't let herself think about how close she herself had come to tangling with him, and she was glad Dave didn't mention it.

"Who are they?" she asked.

"Students at ASU. A kid named Jason Gustavson and his two roommates. The house actually belongs to Jason's father. Daddy is on his way here tonight, flying by private jet from Minneapolis, so I'd say the family's probably loaded. The thing is, you can have all the money in the world and your kid may still turn out to be a total screw-up."

"And a killer besides," Ali added.

"That, too," Dave agreed.

The elevator door opened. A man in a wheelchair with a canvas computer case perched on his lap rolled out of the elevator and into the corridor where Ali was pacing with the phone to her ear. The man paused to study the signage then turned toward the ICU. In that split second when his face was no longer averted, Ali recognized him. First she noticed his brush-cut blond hair and crooked nose. Then the eyes. For an electric moment their gazes met, and Ali felt herself being scrutinized by that peculiar dead-eyed stare she had found so chilling in Madeline Havens's hand-drawn likeness. Finally he shrugged, looked away, and continued down the hallway.

Too shocked to speak or move, Ali struggled to suppress an involuntary gasp. Dave had just finished telling her that three people were dead in Jason Gustavson's home in Tempe, but if this was Jason, he was definitely back among the living and looking far too hale and hearty to have survived a horrendous house fire.

"Ali?" Dave asked into the suddenly silent phone. "Are you there? Did I lose you?"

The man was still well within earshot, and Ali barely trusted herself to speak. "I think he's here," she managed to croak.

"What?" Dave asked.

"Which one's Jason?" she asked. "Which one of the drawings?"

"The one with the crooked nose and the funny eyes . . ."

"He's not dead," Ali whispered. "He's here."

"Where?" Dave demanded. "At the hospital?"

"Here on the floor. On the ICU."

"What?"

"Call the cops," Ali urged. "I've gotta go."

By then Gustavson was rolling purposefully down the hall, and Ali understood his intentions. If there were weapons in the computer bag, Crystal, Sandy, and Kip himself were all in mortal danger. And no officers Dave could summon now would arrive in time to help—unless Ali could somehow manage to stall him. The only good thing about that was that although she knew who he was, the reverse was not true. At least she hoped so.

Ali shoved the phone in her pocket and started down the hallway. She needed a way to slow him down without sparking a confrontation. "Hey," she called after him. "Hey, you. Did anyone ever tell you that you look like John Denver?"

It was the lamest of ploys because, of course, Jason Gustavson looked nothing at all like John Denver, but it was enough to cause him to hesitate.

The chair stopped moving, and he turned to face her. "Are you talking to me?" he asked. He was wearing a clean, freshly pressed blue denim shirt with the words ROTO-ROOTER embroidered across the pocket, a spare he'd found in the Roto-Rooter van.

As Ali hurried to catch up, her phone rang. She ignored it.

"Yes," she said. "Yes. Has anyone told you that?"

But by the time she reached the wheelchair Gustavson had shifted the computer bag on his lap. He picked up the .38 semiautomatic that had been concealed beneath it and pointed it at her. Compared to Ali's little Glock, the gun looked enormous, and it put her at a distinct disadvantage. Her Glock was still holstered. The .38 was in Jason Gustavson's hand and pointed directly at her.

At sight of the weapon, Ali stopped short and took two quick steps backward, instinctively placing her own body between the wheelchair and the entrance into the ICU waiting room.

"No, lady," he said with a sneer. "I don't believe anybody ever told me that before. If they had, I wouldn't have believed it for a minute. And I don't think you believe it, either. Now, get out of my way."

"What do you want?" Ali demanded loudly. This was a man who had already killed at least three people—probably four—and Ali was all that was standing between him and several more innocent victims. She needed to raise an alarm that would alert the unsuspecting people in the waiting room and at least warn them that trouble was coming.

The sound of her own voice surprised her. She was scared to death—petrified—yet her voice was steady and, considering the circumstances, amazingly calm.

"Move it," he said.

Ali didn't budge. Mere seconds ticked by, but Ali's mind was racing. *What will it feel like when the bullet smashes into me? How much of a mess will I leave on the wall? How much on the floor? Will it hurt when I fall down? At least I'll already be in the hospital.*

"I know who you are," Gustavson was saying. "You're the dumb broad who followed me home this afternoon in that blue Cayenne. You're also the one who kept poor little Crystal on such a tight leash all day long. That doesn't matter, though. I wanted her, and I'm still going to get her. As for that other woman, that busybody old hag from the grocery store? I didn't see her name on the sign-in list, but since her boyfriend's still here, I'll bet she is, too."

So much for thinking Jason didn't know who Ali was. He must have followed her and the others in through the lobby.

Ali knew she needed to keep him talking. She tried to imagine how the authorities would respond to Dave Holman's request for help. She couldn't hear any sirens, but surely cops were on their way. There were ceiling-mounted video surveillance cameras throughout the hospital. Once help arrived, Ali knew the responding officers would be able to see what was going on. They'd probably try to treat this as a standard hostage situation by shutting down the hospital elevator system and trying to localize the problem on a single floor before attempting any kind of negotiation, SWAT team action, or rescue maneuver. But Ali already knew this was no ordinary hostage event. Jason Gustavson wasn't interested in hostages. He was a spree killer out shopping for victims—the more the better.

"Why?" Ali asked. "Why are you doing this?"

"Because I'm sick and tired of having human scum tell me what to do," he explained. "Gustavsons aren't raised to take orders or to have lowlifes like that jerk in the store bossing me around. Do you know who I am? Do you have any idea who my father is?"

Somewhere in the background the hospital PA system crackled to life with a series of incomprehensibly coded announcements. Ali's phone continued to ring intermittently—stopping now and then only to resume seconds later. And there were other phones ringing as well, landline phones in the waiting room and at the nurses' station. But those sounds might just as well have been coming from a distant planet. Shutting them all out, Ali remained focused on Jason Gustavson—and on his gun.

"I have no idea who your father is," she returned coldly. "And I don't care. What I do know is that there are innocent people on this floor—doctors, nurses, patients, and visitors. They've done nothing to you, Jason. They don't deserve to die."

The fact that she knew his name seemed to startle him. "And who's going to stop me?" he asked after a short pause. "You?"

"If she doesn't, then I will," a male voice said from behind Ali.

Without turning to look Ali knew at once that the man who had been watching the muted TV news—the man whose son was about to be taken off life support—had heard the uproar out in the hallway and had come to Ali's aid.

"This man's a killer," she announced matter-of-factly to her newly arrived ally. "Two of the people in the waiting room and one of the patients in the ICU witnessed what he did. That's why he's here—he came after them." Then to Jason she added, "I've called the police. They're already on their way. You won't get away with this."

"You don't get it, do you?" he returned. "I don't *care* if I don't get away with it. That's not the point. In fact, I'd rather be dead than have to live in a place where inmates like you are put in charge of the asylum. Let's go."

"My son's in there," the older man said quietly but firmly. "The only way you're getting inside the ICU is through me."

Jason laughed, stood up, and shoved the wheelchair out of the way. He had used it as a prop to give him credibility inside the hospital hallways. Now it was no longer needed. The visitor badge clipped to his shirt said he was visiting Kip Hogan, 3rd floor, ICU.

"Oh, really?" Jason returned, waving the gun menacingly. "Hey, old man. I don't give a rat's ass about you or your son, but if you want to die a hero, that's up to you."

Jason was no longer paying any attention to Ali. Dismissing her as a possible threat, he was focused instead on the man behind her, trying to assess what he might or might not do. In typical male fashion, it didn't occur to him that Ali, too, might be armed and dangerous. All she needed was a chance to unholster her weapon.

Ali stepped aside and turned to face her would-be rescuer. He wasn't a particularly impressive specimen. About her father's age or maybe a little older, he was sallow-faced, paunchy, and visibly out of shape. His thin, sandy, comb-over hair was standing straight up. But out of shape or not, he stood there in the hallway, calm and determined, helping Ali face down an armed assailant. It took only a second or two for Ali to realize that his presence offered the momentary diversion she needed.

"I said get going," Jason growled.

Keeping her left hand out of sight, Ali made a slight movement with her fingers, hoping to let her ad hoc partner know that she needed to pass in front of him. She couldn't be sure if he understood or not, but he nodded slightly.

"All right," Ali said. "I'm going."

She ducked into the waiting room. As soon as she was inside, she stationed herself behind the wall just inside the doorway and managed to extract her Glock from its holster.

Ali had expected to find the waiting room full of people, but to her astonishment and immense relief the place was empty. Completely empty. The glass partition into the nurses' station was blacked out, blocked by something Ali would later learn was a mattress. Windows in the swinging doors that led into the ICU itself were also darkened, as though someone had lowered a set of shutters. With any luck they were barricaded as well.

The wave of gratitude Ali felt was almost overwhelming, but she couldn't afford to give in to it; couldn't afford to let down her guard. With the gun clutched tightly in a two-handed grip, she stood just out of sight, holding her breath and waiting to see what would happen.

Again she became aware of the cacophony of sound. Her cell phone was still ringing somewhere, but she was no longer holding her purse. The sound seemed to be coming from somewhere out in the hallway. A new announcement blared over the PA system. This one came in plain English rather than hospital Newspeak.

"Mr. Gustavson, we have you surrounded. Put down your weapon."

Whatever Jason Gustavson had in mind, he had no intention of it happening in the hallway. Ali heard the sound of something sliding along the smooth tiled surface of the hallway. "There, old man," Jason said. "Help me out. You carry the bag. Now!"

Out in the hallway, Ali caught a glimpse of the older man stooping down to pick up the computer bag. As he straightened and started into the waiting room, Ali held her breath. She knew she would have one chance only—one shot. She was reasonably proficient with her weapon. In recent months, once she had finally wrested her Glock from the authorities in California, she had put in hours of target practice at a shooting range outside Sedona. Ali knew instinctively she couldn't afford a shot that would simply disarm her assailant. This was a survival-of-the-fittest moment, a time to kill or be killed.

Ali's helper stepped into the waiting room, carrying Jason's bag. The killer's gun, at the end of a fully extended arm, appeared next. Taking aim from that, Ali waited for one more fraction of a second before squeezing off a shot. The bullet hit Jason square in the chest. He grunted with surprise but he didn't go down. The force of the blow knocked the wind out of him. He dropped the .38. It went spinning away from him and came to rest under the chair where Crystal had been sleeping minutes earlier.

After what seemed like only a moment, Jason seemed to catch his balance. He came roaring back into the waiting room, pausing in the doorway, clutching his chest, and looking for his weapon—looking for any weapon.

*I hit him!* Ali thought desperately. *Why the hell isn't he dead?*

That's when she realized that he had come to the hospital

fully prepared for a shoot-out, carrying weapons and wearing a Kevlar vest.

He turned on her then, holding out his hand. "Give it to me," he demanded. "Give me that gun."

There were noises out in the hallway now, running footsteps, voices shouting. But before any of the arriving cops made it to the doorway, something else happened. Moving faster than Ali would have thought possible, the old man—the paunchy, out-of-shape old man—turned on Jason Gustavson and head-butted him back out into the hallway where he came to rest against the far wall.

"Get down," one of the cops shouted unnecessarily. "On your stomach. Hands behind your head."

Ali hurried over to her rescuer who, still gripping Jason's computer bag, stood in the doorway and stared out into the hall. Then he limped across the room and put the bag down on what had been Crystal's chair.

His face was bright red. He was breathing heavily, and his hair was still standing on end, but he was grinning from ear to ear.

"Are you all right?" Ali asked.

"Hurt my leg when I tackled him," he muttered. "But damned straight I'm all right! Those vests may be bulletproof, but they sure as hell ain't headproof. Not by a long shot!"

With chaos still reigning in the hallway behind him, the man wrapped his pudgy arms around Ali's body and held her close. Hugging him back, Ali realized that right that moment, this unassuming, quiet man with his dying son had become her greatest hero. He had come to her rescue when there was no one else to step up. Ali had no doubt that his actions had saved her life and probably several others as well—and she didn't even know his name.

"Thank you," she said. "Thank you so much."

He gave her another squeeze. "You're welcome," he said. "It's nice to do something useful for a change."

The next several minutes were frenetic. While the cops handcuffed Jason, someone removed the makeshift barricade that had temporarily barred the way into the ICU. When the swinging doors opened, the lady with the knitting needles shot out through them. She bodily booted Ali out of the way and fell into her ex-husband's arms.

"Bernie, Bernie, Bernie," she murmured. "How could you do something so stupid and wonderful at the same time? How could you? There's a security monitor in the nurse's station. We saw the whole thing. It's a miracle you weren't killed."

When Crystal emerged, she was crying. "Thank you," she said, giving Ali a shy hug. "If it hadn't been for you . . ." She shuddered and fell silent.

"It's all right," Ali said. "They've got him now. He won't be able to come after you again."

Except it turned out that wasn't true.

A uniformed cop had just approached Bernie and, with a latex glove-covered hand, tapped him on the shoulder. "Excuse me, Mr. Bernstein," the cop said, pointing. "Is that Mr. Gustavson's suitcase . . . computer case?"

Bernstein. That was the first Ali remembered hearing Bernie's last name, but it was one she would never forget.

With some difficulty, Bernie extricated himself from his former wife's fierce embrace long enough to nod in the direction of the chair. "That's it," he said. "I put it down over there to keep it out of the way."

From the moment Jason Gustavson had moved the computer case to reveal his .38, Ali had assumed the case had held an arsenal of reserve weapons. It seemed likely the cops were of the same opinion. Ali watched as the young uniformed officer went over to the chair, picked up the computer case, and opened the zipper. She also saw the look of horror that washed across his face when he saw what was inside. Moments later the whole east wing of St. Francis Hospital was being evacuated.

As they were hustled out of the waiting room toward the emergency exit, Ali managed to grab her own computer from the chair where she'd left it earlier. On the way down the hallway, she heard her cell phone ringing. The phone was still in her purse, which she had inadvertently dropped in the hallway during the confrontation. She made no effort to retrieve either the purse or the phone. Those as well as her Glock were now part of a crime scene investigation. She knew from past experience that it could take weeks if not months to regain her property from evidence impounds.

As patients, visitors, and workers alike were being herded outside and away from the building, the bomb squad van arrived along with a phalanx of ambulances and aid cars. Those were lined up outside the ER doors and were used to transport the hospital's most seriously ill patients—Kip Hogan and Danny Bernstein among them—to other facilities. Meanwhile everyone else gathered in anxious groups where, dazed and shivering from fear as much as cold, they tried to make sense of what had happened while a collection of news helicopters clattered noisily overhead.

For more than an hour, they stood outside, waiting for an explosion that never came. Finally the bomb squad, still wearing protective gear, emerged from the hospital and put something in their armor-plated van. As they drove away, the people outside applauded ecstatically.

Caught up in the emergency evacuation, there had been no time for investigators to take statements from anyone. Instead, they placed Ali and the others under the watchful eye of uniformed officers.

Standing in the dazed crowd, waiting to be interviewed, Ali knew that sooner or later someone from the media would pick up on her involvement in the situation. When that happened, there would be all kinds of unwanted attention. The same would be true for Bernie Bernstein as well. For the moment, Ali reveled in her anonymity. She wasn't dead. Neither was Crystal or anyone else for that matter, and for that Ali Reynolds was incredibly grateful.

Jane Braeton came by and sought Ali out. "They've transported Kip to Phoenix Providence," she said. "I have Elizabeth and Sandy in my car. I'm going to drop Sandy off with Kip and take Elizabeth back home. This has been a very long night for her. She's tired. It's all been too much."

Ali nodded. "I'm sure it has."

"But she needed to be here," Jane added. "She wanted to be here. It's an answer to thirty years of prayers. So, thank you, Ali. Thank you for everything. You go, girl."

With that Jane Braeton disappeared into the crowd. Watching her walk away, Ali was amazed by the difference those few critical hours had made.

Moments later, Crystal sidled up to Ali. "Can we go sit in the car, please?" she asked. "I'm freezing."

Ali put one arm around the girl's shoulder. She was shaking convulsively. Her teeth were chattering.

"Of course," Ali said. "Come on."

After telling the watching cop where investigators could find them, Ali and Crystal made their way through the crowd to the parking structure, where they walked up the stairs to the Cayenne parked on the second level. With her shoulder aching from the added weight, Ali was happy to unload her laptop. Once in the car, she started the engine and activated the heated seats.

"You saved all of us tonight," Crystal said thoughtfully a short while later. "If it hadn't been for you and that old man, I'd probably be dead by now. So would Kip and Sandy."

"Bernie," Ali interjected. "The old man's name is Bernie Bernstein, and you're probably right. What he did made all the difference."

"I heard two of the nurses talking," Crystal mused. "Bernie's son, Danny—the one who was in the motorcycle wreck?"

Ali nodded.

"They said Danny probably isn't going to make it, but his father helped us anyway. He helped you. How come?"

Ali shrugged. "Because he wanted to, I guess," she said. "He thought it was important, thought it would make a difference."

"And why did you do it?" Crystal asked.

Ali considered for a moment before she answered. "Because I could," she said finally. "Because I didn't think anyone else would."

"When I was watching, when he was pointing the gun at you, I kept thinking that if you died, it would be my fault, just like it's my fault Coach Curt is dead."

The events of the evening seemed to have made an impression on the girl. She was far more subdued. As a consequence, Ali hoped that Crystal might be in a place where she'd be willing to listen to reason.

"What happened isn't your fault," Ali told her. "Yes, you and Curt Uttley were both in the wrong place at the wrong time and for all the wrong reasons, but Jason is the one who murdered Curt, not you. And I'm sorry Curt's dead, but since he was a pedophile who went prowling the Internet looking for young women to prey upon, he wasn't exactly blameless."

"But he didn't deserve to die," Crystal protested.

"You're right. If he'd been arrested for child molestation or statutory rape, he probably would have gone to prison. What he did to you wasn't a capital offense, but men like that do deserve to be in jail, Crystal. It's against the law," Ali added.

Crystal's phone rang. "Hi, Daddy," she said in a voice that was choked with emotion. "Yes, I'm okay. I'm with Ali. It was cold, so we're sitting in her car in the parking garage. Yes, I love you, too. Do you want to talk to her? Here she is."

Crystal handed the phone to Ali. "Thank God you're both safe!" Dave exclaimed. "I've been worried sick. I've been trying to get through to you, but the circuits are busy. Why don't you answer your damned phone? You need to call your parents. Your dad managed to get through to me. He heard about what happened at the hospital and he's frantic."

"I can't call anyone," Ali said. "I lost my phone."

"Lost it. Where?"

"It was in my purse. I dropped it during the struggle out in the hallway—a hallway that's now a crime scene. My purse and phone—and my driver's license, most likely—are all in some crime scene investigator's evidence bag. At least I had my car keys in my pocket and not in my purse. Where are you?"

"Seventh and Thomas," Dave said. "I've been on my way for the better part of an hour—ever since you hung up on me. But with all the emergency vehicles, traffic's a mess. I could probably get there faster if I just parked the car and got out and walked. Have they interviewed you yet?"

"Not so far. They're too busy with the bomb squad."

"And you shot the guy?"

"Tried to," Ali replied. "He was wearing a vest."

"More's the pity," Dave said.

"If the third victim in that house fire wasn't Jason, who was it?" Ali asked.

"We still don't know about that," Dave answered. "Since Jason's vehicle was there and so was Uttley's we assumed . . ."

"Did Jason have a job?" Ali asked.

"A job? Are you kidding? Not as far as I know. He's a playboy kind of student who was born with a silver spoon in his mouth and goes through life with a Platinum AmEx in his pocket. I doubt he's ever done an honest day's work in his life. Why?"

"Because when I saw him, Jason was wearing a Roto-Rooter shirt—a uniform shirt."

"You say Roto-Rooter—as in stopped drains? Let me get back to you on that," Dave said.

Ali closed the phone and gave it to Crystal.

"Is my dad coming?" Crystal asked.

"He's trying to," Ali said. "He'll be here soon, but traffic's not helping."

"At least he's coming," Crystal murmured. "I'm glad."

"I need to call Chris and my parents," Ali said. "Can I use your phone for a few minutes?"

"Sure," Crystal said, handing it back. "They're probably really worried."

Crystal Holman had done yet another about-face. When it came to dealing with teenagers, it was getting harder and harder for Ali Reynolds to keep score.

# { CHAPTER 14 }

It was almost 4 A.M. before Ali finally left the grounds and headed home. By then many of the displaced patients were being readmitted to St. Francis.

She should have been sleepy, but she wasn't. After everything that had happened, Ali wasn't sure she'd ever sleep again. The preliminary interview had lasted until well after three, but the detectives had cautioned that there'd probably be more to come at a later date.

For Ali, the best part about leaving the scene at that late hour meant that the crisis was pretty much over and most of the media folks had disappeared hours earlier. In other words, although Ali Reynolds's name would no doubt be mentioned in reporting on the incident, her photo would be mercifully absent.

On the drive back to Sedona, Ali mulled over everything she had learned. Yes, she had shot a man—she had tried to shoot him, that is. And yes, if he hadn't been wearing a bullet-resistant vest, she probably would have killed Jason Gustavson. If that had happened, maybe Ali would have been sorry, but she doubted it. At this moment, instead of being dead, he was now being held in the Maricopa County jail, where he was expected to be charged with several counts of homicide and several more of attempted homicide.

It was chilling to think that this privileged young man had somehow turned into a murderous monster who had taken the lives of both friends and strangers with zero compunction. One of his presumed victims was a Roto-Rooter plumber named Tom Melman, now declared missing. The married father of two had been dispatched to Gustavson's Tempe house earlier that afternoon to install a new toilet. His missing company van had been traced to the parking garage at St. Francis Hospital, where it had been found in a space only a few slots away from Ali's Cayenne.

"So you're saying he followed me here?" Ali had asked the detective.

He nodded. "Looks that way—followed you into the garage at least."

"But how did he know it was me? How did he know I was driving a Cayenne?"

"Jason has a girlfriend who works Records for Maricopa County. When she heard he was possibly involved in the hospital situation, she came forward and spoke to her supervisor, and believe me, she will be dealt with. He evidently called her earlier this afternoon requesting information about you. He claimed it was for a friend who had seen you and was hoping to hook up."

"How did he get my name?"

"He didn't have your name. We're theorizing he must have noticed you following him home from Phoenix earlier. All he had when he called in was a partial plate number."

That was the whole problem with living in the information age, Ali decided. If critical information ended up in the wrong hands, it could do incredible damage. But of course, she and Dave had been doing exactly the same thing—trying to locate Curtis Uttley. It seemed best not to mention that.

By the time Ali turned off I-17 and headed toward Sedona, she was back to thinking about Arabella Ashcroft's diary. Nothing in it had been even obliquely worthy of blackmail, yet Ali was convinced that there was some connection between what had been written in the book and the fact that Billy Ashcroft was now dead. But what was Ali's responsibility in this regard? She had raised hell with Crystal for not stepping forward and sharing vital information with the authorities after the vicious attack on Kip and the kidnapping of Curt Uttley. If Ali had reason to believe Billy's failed extortion scheme had something to do with his death, didn't she have a moral obligation to come forward as well?

But for the time being, the whole question was moot since Arabella's diary had been collected along with all the other hallway debris as part of a major crime scene investigation.

Once back home Ali entered her bedroom and found Sam curled in regal splendor on her pillow. When the bedside lamp came on, the cat decamped at once, however, hopping off the bed with an annoyed huff and stalking away as if to say Ali had been out past her curfew and was now persona non grata in her own bed.

"Hey," Ali called after her. "Come back. It isn't my fault I'm so late."

But Sam wasn't interested in doling out forgiveness. Giving up on the cat, Ali crawled into bed, where she fell into a deep, dreamless slumber. It was after eleven when she finally staggered out to the kitchen the next morning. Even in its thermal carafe, the coffee Chris had made before he left for school was dead cold when Ali tasted it. She'd had nothing at all to drink the night before—except for far too much coffee and cocoa, which hadn't kept her awake. Even so she felt groggy and tired and nowhere near ready for the onslaught of attention she knew was likely once her connection to the St. Francis Hospital incident was made public.

Determined to have a robe day, Ali went to make a new pot of coffee. There she found the note Chris had left for her on the counter.

"Welcome home. I know you got in very late. I pulled the phone jack out of the wall so you could sleep. Love, Chris."

Grateful that her son was so thoughtful, Ali plugged in the phone. Immediately it began to ring.

"You're awake then," Edie Larson said. "I've been trying to call you off and on all morning."

"What's going on?"

"Kip didn't make it," Edie said. "Sandy Mitchell just called. She and Kip's mother . . . How did they ever find his mother, by the way? Anyway, the two of them were both there with him a little while ago this morning when they took him off life support."

"I'm so sorry," Ali murmured.

"I am, too," Edie agreed. "And your father's really broken up about it. It gave Dad a lot of satisfaction to think he had helped Kip back from the edge. Now it's all for nothing."

Ali thought about the look on Elizabeth Hogan's face as Jane Braeton had wheeled her into the ICU.

*Not for nothing*, Ali thought. *But too little too late.*

"Anyway," Edie continued, "Bobby just went home to shower, then he'll head down to Phoenix to bring Sandy home. Did Dave reach you?"

"No."

"He called here a little while ago. He was on his way back to Prescott to testify in that trial. He said to tell you that Crystal's at home sleeping, and Roxie's supposedly coming down from Vegas later today to pick her up. Crystal wasn't a problem when she was here at the restaurant, but from what I'm hearing about everything that's gone on the past few days, it sounds like she's a kid who could use some serious counseling."

Edie Lawson's instinctive diagnosis of Crystal Holman's mental issues had Ali's wholesale agreement, although she had no intention of going into any of the particulars. All Ali said was, "Yes, I think counseling is definitely in order."

During their conversation Ali's call-waiting signal had buzzed several times. Those had been easy to ignore. Now though, when someone rang the doorbell, Ali ended the call. While Sam scampered for the nearest hiding place, Ali pulled her robe tight around her and went to answer. Arabella Ashcroft's butler, Leland Brooks, stood on Ali's front porch while the yellow Rolls-Royce idled in the driveway.

"So sorry to disturb you, madam," Mr. Brooks said through the screen when Ali opened the inside door. "Miss Arabella was most interested in being in touch with you this morning. Something about a borrowed book, I believe. She's been calling to ask about it, but your telephone seems to be out of order and your cell phone keeps going to voice mail."

On the way home from Phoenix Ali had struggled with what she should do. She knew she would most likely call someone down in Phoenix to report her suspicions, but not until after she'd had at least one cup of coffee.

"I'm so sorry," Ali told the waiting butler. "I don't have access to Miss Ashcroft's book right now. I can't answer my cell phone since I had to leave it down in Phoenix last night."

Mr. Brooks glanced warily over his shoulder in the direction of the Rolls.

"Is she with you?" Ali asked.

He nodded. "I'm afraid so," he said. "As I said, she's rather upset about this. I'll be glad to relay the information, however."

Clad in only a bathrobe with her hair a mess and no makeup on, Ali was hardly in any condition to receive guests—especially guests who were accustomed to entertaining in the manner Arabella Ashcroft did. Still, Ali felt an obligation to give the woman the bad news about the missing diary in person.

"No," Ali said. "I'm not exactly prepared for company, but I'm the one who should tell her what happened to it. Please ask her to come in, Mr. Brooks."

The butler bowed. "Of course, madam," he said. "I shall extend your invitation."

While he was gone, Ali hurriedly swiped all the loose papers off both the dining room table and the coffee table. She stowed those and the computer in her bedroom. By the time she emerged, Mr. Brooks had ushered Arabella to the front door. She didn't look nearly as put together as she had the other day. She seemed anxious and ill at ease. The butler handed her off to Ali and then returned to the waiting Rolls. Arabella allowed herself to be led inside. When she spoke, though, she sounded like her old self.

"You're most gracious to invite me in this way," Arabella said. "I shouldn't have come. It's quite rude to show up unannounced like this. I've never done it before—ever."

"It's fine," Ali assured her. "Please do come in. I'm sorry you weren't able to reach me by phone. As I told Mr. Brooks, I ended up leaving my cell phone down in Phoenix last night. My landline is back in service now, but it was temporarily out of order."

Once seated on the couch, Arabella glanced curiously around

the room. "Evie always said she was going to buy a mobile home," she remarked. "I must say, it looks quite solid and not the least bit mobile."

Ali laughed. "Mobile homes should probably just be called manufactured homes. Most are only mobile until they're delivered," she explained. "Once they've been set up on a slab or a foundation, they usually stay put."

"Barring tornadoes or hurricanes," Arabella said.

"Yes," Ali agreed. "Barring those. Now how do you take your coffee—black, cream and sugar?"

"Black by all means," Arabella said.

Ali went out into the kitchen. As she filled coffee mugs and set them on a tray, she wrestled with how best to break the bad news. In the end Arabella beat her to the punch.

"Where is my diary?" she asked as Ali carried the coffee into the living room. "I must have it back."

"Arabella," Ali said. "I'm so sorry. I don't have it."

"You don't have it!" Arabella exclaimed. "What do you mean? Surely you haven't lost it!"

Ali set the tray on the table. "It isn't lost," she said soothingly. "But I don't have it here. There was a problem in Phoenix last night—at one of the hospitals. You may have seen it on the news. I was there, and, as it happens, so was the diary. It was in my purse. I lost my purse in all the confusion. I'm sure the police have the purse and the diary, too."

"How could you be so careless!" Arabella declared angrily. "I want it back, and I want it back today!"

Arabella's abrupt change of mood took Ali by surprise. Surely this wasn't that big a deal. The diary had been under wraps for more than half a century. Why was it so essential that she have it back immediately?

"Please, Arabella," Ali continued hurriedly. "I didn't do it on purpose. My purse, my cell phone, and your diary were picked up during the evidence sweep. I'm sure they'll all be returned in good time. Besides, when you gave it to me the other day, it didn't seem like you were in that big a hurry. I was under the impression that I could read it at my leisure."

"Did you read it?" Arabella asked sharply.

"Yes."

"I hoped you wouldn't. I told you not to."

"I thought I was supposed to read it so I could help you decide about the book you're writing."

"I'm not writing a book," Arabella said at once. "I've changed my mind about that, too."

"Why?" Ali asked. "What changed your mind? What's going on?"

"I want my diary back. How can that be so difficult to understand?"

"Have the police talked to you about what happened to your nephew?"

"Two very nice detectives from Phoenix came to notify me that Billy was dead," Arabella said, softening a little. "Yesterday, I think it was, or maybe the day before."

"And did you tell them what was going on between the two of you?"

"I told them Billy wanted to do a reverse mortgage for me. Once I had time to think it over, it didn't seem like such a bad idea."

"Wait a minute," Ali objected. "You told me the other day that Billy threatened you; that he was going to try to have you declared incompetent and put away somewhere."

"He wouldn't have," Arabella said. "He'd never do such a dreadful thing."

*Of course not,* Ali thought. *Especially if he's dead.*

"The cops need to know what was going on between the two of you," Ali said aloud. "And I'm going to tell them."

Arabella looked at Ali in dismay. "The things I said to you were relayed in the strictest confidence."

"You may have thought it was in confidence, but I'm not an attorney," Ali said. "There's no attorney/client privilege when you talk to me, and no expectation of privacy, either. Concealing information in a homicide investigation is a felony."

"Surely you don't think I had something to do with Billy's death."

"Did you?" Ali asked.

Arabella stared at her and didn't answer.

"Did you?" Ali prodded again.

"You wouldn't really go to the police, would you?" Arabella asked.

"Yes, I'm afraid I would. I've just spent two days giving my friend's teenage daughter hell for not coming forward and giving pertinent information in another set of homicides. It would be hypocritical for me to keep quiet in this one."

"Even after everything Mother and I did for you?"

"I'm sorry, but yes. Even after all that. Not because I want to; because I have to. And no matter how much it costs, you need to find yourself an attorney."

Leaving her coffee untouched on the table, Arabella surged to her feet. She stood and straightened her sweater, the same mended cardigan she had worn on the previous occasion. Ali reached out to help her, but Arabella would have none of it.

"Leave me alone," she said, drawing away as if Ali's very touch was poisonous. "If you're determined to go to the authorities, we have nothing further to discuss."

She walked unassisted as far as the door. At the entryway table, she turned and looked back. "I know something about killing," she said. "I tried to kill my brother Bill once, you know. He came into my room, grabbed Blueboy out of his cage, and squashed him flat. Squeezed my poor little bird in his fist until he was dead. He told me if I ever told anyone, he'd do the same thing to me—squeeze me until I was dead, and he put his hand around my throat to show me he could do it. So I stole a knife from the kitchen and hid it under my pillow. That night, when he came to my bedroom the way I knew he would, I pulled out the knife and stabbed him. I was just a kid, and I think it surprised the hell out of him. He went to the hospital, but the son of a bitch didn't die. Damn him anyway, he didn't die."

Arabella's unsolicited confession was as chilling as it was fierce.

"What about Billy?" Ali asked. "What about your nephew?"

"What about him? Believe me, if I had wanted to kill him, I would have."

*But did you?* Ali wondered.

Arabella turned and stormed out the door. Ali watched through the sidelights as Leland Brooks hurried forward, offered Arabella his arm, and then carefully led her back to the waiting Rolls. They might have been an old married couple making their way together across treacherous terrain. Once he closed the car door, he turned and looked back toward where Ali was standing. Then, with a shake of his head, he climbed into the driver's seat.

As they drove out of sight, Ali couldn't help wondering if Arabella Ashcroft was capable of murder. Certainly she was capable of *attempted* murder. She had said as much herself. And what about Arabella's lies? Either she had lied to Ali when she said Billy had threatened her or she had lied to the cops when she said he had not. And since Billy Ashcroft was definitely dead, the cops needed to get to the bottom of the situation one way or the other.

For a long time after Arabella left, Ali struggled with what she should do. Yes, she owed her education to Anna Lee and Arabella Ashcroft. And yes, her whole career had come about as a result of their generosity. But if Arabella had murdered her nephew in cold blood—dragged him behind a car until he was dead—Ali couldn't just keep quiet. She couldn't.

She tried calling Dave, but he was probably in court. His phone went straight to voice mail. Instead of leaving a message, Ali went into her bedroom and located everything she'd emptied out of her jacket pocket the night before. There, along with her car keys, she found a collection of business cards that belonged to a series of Phoenix PD detectives. She picked one at random—Detective Mike Ryan. She dialed his number hoping he'd be able to put her in touch with whichever investigators had been assigned to the William Ashcroft homicide.

*It's a homicide investigation,* she told herself firmly as Ryan's extension began to ring. *I don't have a choice.*

• • •

While Ali waited for someone to call her back, she turned her attention to the blog. The situation at the hospital was an ongoing investigation. That meant there was little she could say, but she felt obliged to say *something.*

**CUTLOOSEBLOG.COM**
*Friday, January 13, 2006*

**I know my name is showing up in the news in reference to what happened last night at St. Francis**

Hospital down in Phoenix. I know many of you are worried about me. My mailbox is brimming with e-mails asking me if I'm okay and letting me know that the blog stopped opening earlier this morning due to too many hits on the server. So I'm posting this and hoping you'll be able to read it sometime soon.

I'm fine and I'm very grateful to be alive. My friend's daughter, who was targeted in the attack, is also safe and back home with her family.

Yes, it's true. I'm the same Ali Reynolds who was involved in the hostage situation at the hospital, but because of the nature of the ongoing investigation, I've been advised to say nothing more on that topic. If you're connected to one of the media outlets and you're reading this post, please understand that if you do happen to reach me, all you'll be given for the trouble is the usual "no comment."

I know that readers of my blog are accustomed to more information than this, but for right now this will have to do. Once again, let me say thank you for your concern, your prayers, and your e-mails. More on all of this later. With the way investigations of this magnitude go, however, I expect that means MUCH later.

*Babe, posted 1:05* P.M.

Evidently the server was still having difficulties. It took a very long time for Ali's post to upload. When it finally did, she turned to answering some of her voluminous e-mail. It was relatively mindless work that kept her from watching the telephone and waiting for it to ring. Detective Ryan had told her that someone involved in the Ashcroft investigation would get back to her, but she wondered how long that would take.

One at a time she made her way through the long list of received mail, discarding the spam and answering most with a brief one- or two-sentence response. Halfway to the bottom, she found a message from Velma. As she scanned down the list she saw it was only the most recent of three from the same address.

*Dear Babe,*
*I'm thinking about all this. Waiting is hard.*

VELMA

Closing that one, Ali scrolled down to the first of Velma's e-mails and opened that.

*Dear Babe,*
*I can't thank you enough for putting me in touch with those very nice people at Cancer Resource. As you said, it was quite expensive, but I was able to sign up over the Internet and I've been assigned a case-worker. She sent me the documents needed to request all my medical records and test results from my primary physician so I could be transferred over to them. She said once I had signed the various releases, they would make arrangements to have my records sent or delivered to one of their consulting oncologists. Once they have them, they'll make an appointment for me to have a second opinion.*

*Considering the way things have worked in the past, I expected it would take several weeks to accomplish all this, but the caseworker told me that the whole idea is to streamline the process, not slow it down. So the biggest variable will be how long it takes my primary physician to release the records. I just called him and told his office manager that I expect things to be expedited on their end. We'll see.*

*Anyway, thank you for sending me to someone who seems to understand that people facing a cancer diagnosis don't have all the time in the world.*

Velma T in Laguna

That was something Ali remembered from her experience with her first husband, Dean. It seemed as though it had taken forever to get lined up for the various tests and then it took even longer to get the results back, especially if the news was bad. In fact, the worse the news, the longer it took to get it.

She scrolled up the list and read Velma's next note, one that had been sent on Thursday.

*Dear Babe,*

*I'm still waiting. A courier is supposed to pick up my records today. Maybe I'm just being paranoid, but it seems like there's a new lump that's right next to where they did the needle biopsy. And maybe one on the other side, too. If that's the case, if these damned things are growing that fast, maybe the first doctor was right and there's nothing to be done. But if I'm sick, shouldn't I feel sick? If I opt for treatment—surgery or surgeries, chemo, or radiation—I know I'll for sure feel sick then.*

*I talked to my caseworker about this. She said*

*the best thing to do is to do nothing until we have the information. She's nice enough, and I know she means well, but it isn't her body. It isn't her life. I hate waiting.*

VELMA T

After several minutes of thought, Ali finally replied:

*Dear Velma,*
*Waiting is the hardest part. Please keep me posted.*

ALI

She had just pushed SEND when her phone rang again.

"Ms. Reynolds?" a male voice asked. "My name's Larry Marsh, Detective Larry Marsh, with the Phoenix Police Department. This is about the William Ashcroft homicide. Detective Ryan suggested we give you a call. You have some information for us?"

Ali took a deep breath. "Yes, I believe so."

"And that would be?"

"You've spoken to Billy Ashcroft's aunt, Arabella? Is she under suspicion?"

"I'm sorry. This is an ongoing investigation, Ms. Reynolds. I can't comment on what we're doing one way or the other. At this point the field of suspects is wide open. Do you have specific information for us?"

Trying to be helpful, Ali also wanted to be diplomatic. "Did Arabella mention that she wasn't on the best of terms with her nephew?"

"She didn't indicate there was any particular problem," Detective Marsh replied.

"She probably told you he came around offering her a reverse mortgage."

"Correct," Marsh said. "Come to think of it, she did mention a reverse mortgage."

"But I think there was more to it than that," Ali continued. "I believe Billy was trying to extort money from her and threatened to have her put away in a home somewhere if she didn't hand it over."

"Ms. Ashcroft mentioned something to the effect that she and Mr. Ashcroft had discussed her future living arrangements," Detective Marsh allowed. "Beyond that, however, she didn't seem upset, and she certainly didn't mention being threatened."

"She mentioned it to me," Ali asserted quietly.

"Were you privy to some kind of interaction between the two of them?" Marsh asked. "Did you actually hear what was said?"

"No," Ali answered. "Arabella told me about it, and it sounded serious."

"And what's the nature of your relationship with Ms. Ashcroft?"

"Mine?" Ali returned. "We're friends. We've been friends for years."

"So you wouldn't be in a position to benefit from Ms. Ashcroft's financial arrangements one way or the other?" Marsh asked.

"Absolutely not."

"And what about Mr. Ashcroft? Do you know him?"

"I've never met him," Ali said. "And I don't believe Arabella had either, prior to this week. What I do know is that there had been bad blood between Arabella and Billy's father. Years ago she actually tried to kill him."

"Arabella tried to kill Billy?" Marsh asked.

"No," Ali answered. "She tried to kill Billy's father—William Ashcroft Junior. He was her stepbrother. He'd been cruel to her, abused her, and killed her pet bird. She got even by stabbing him."

"And this was when?" Marsh asked.

"November of 1944."

"I see," the detective said. "And you know about this how?"

"Because Arabella told me about it, some of it just today."

"Let me get this straight," Marsh said. "The two of you must be exceptionally good friends. Not only does she clue you in on her nephew's current threat, but she also confesses to the long-ago attempted homicide of her brother?"

"Her stepbrother," Ali said. "Bill Junior was ten or so years older than she was, and he had been molesting her for years. What finally pushed her over the edge was the death of her pet parakeet. Her stepbrother killed Blueboy right in front of her. A matter of hours later, she took after him with the knife."

"I take it the brother—the stepbrother—didn't die as a result of her attack?"

"No. He died several years later in an automobile accident."

"I'm a homicide detective, Ms. Reynolds. I generally don't deal with cases concerning dead birds—past or present. And you already told me that the stepbrother didn't die. This ancient history is all very interesting, of course, but can you explain to me how any of it applies to what's happening in the here and now?"

Ali had contacted the authorities with the intention of letting them know about Arabella's diary and how she thought it might somehow be connected to Billy Ashcroft's death. In the face of Detective Marsh's outright derision, it wasn't easy to plunge on, but Ali did so.

"I believe Billy Ashcroft's murder may be connected to Arabella's diary," she said.

"What diary?" Marsh asked. "She's keeping a diary?"

"Was keeping a diary," Ali corrected. "Back when she was nine, back when this all happened. And when she found out it was missing a little while ago, she was very upset. That's when she blurted out the story of trying to kill her brother. If you managed to read it yourself . . ."

Marsh was losing patience. "You said a moment ago that the diary is missing. How could I possibly read it?"

"It's missing from my house here in Sedona," Ali said. "It's not missing from there in Phoenix. It was in my purse last night during that whole mess at St. Francis Hospital. I'm sure it was picked up in the evidence sweep along with my purse and cell phone. It's probably locked away in an evidence locker somewhere at your department."

"And you're asking me to read it?"

"Yes," Ali said.

"Is there anything else?"

Ali, too, was losing patience. It sounded as though Marsh's ears were closed and his mind was made up.

"No," she said. "I can't think of anything else."

"Good then," he told her. "I want to thank you for coming forward, Ms. Reynolds, but I also feel obliged to give you a word of caution. While we appreciate your interest in the case, it's usually not a good idea for civilians to insert themselves into one police investigation after another . . ."

"Wait a minute," Ali interrupted. "If you're talking about last night, let me remind you that that particular 'investigation,' as you call it, came to me."

"Be that as it may, Ms. Reynolds. My advice is the same. You might want to take a step back from all this and leave it to the professionals. Of course, just in case you happen to come across any additional information, let me give you my numbers. . . ."

"Don't bother," Ali said. "I believe I've already got your number. That came through loud and clear."

# { CHAPTER 15 }

In their office cubicle at Phoenix PD, Larry Marsh sat staring at his telephone receiver.

"She hung up on you?" Hank asked.

"Pretty much," Larry said. "So, where are we?"

"I'm working on tracing the Silver Star that was found under the floor mat in Mr. Ashcroft's vehicle. The name A. Reed is engraved on the back, but so far no luck tracing Mr. Reed. While Ms. Reynolds was hanging up on you, I was being bitched out by some battle-ax at the VA who read me the riot act and let me know in no uncertain terms that we're breaking the law."

"Breaking what law?"

"It turns out that found military medals are supposed to be returned directly to the Defense Department. We're to make no effort to locate either the serviceman in question or his surviving family."

"But this is a homicide investigation," Marsh objected.

"Wouldn't you think," Hank agreed. "Which is why I plan on working my way up the chain of command. What about you?"

Marsh stood up. "I think I'm going to take a walk down to the evidence room."

"How come?"

"Evidently we have Arabella Ashcroft's diary down there under lock and key. Something weird about a dead parakeet. Ali Reynolds seems to be of the opinion that we should take a look at it, and I guess I will."

• • •

Ali was still fuming long after she put down the phone. She had done her civic duty by reporting her concerns and had felt like a traitor for doing so. Detective Marsh had mocked her suggestion that Arabella's dead parakeet might somehow be connected to everything that had happened, even though Ali had no idea what that connection might be. Marsh's attitude had been nothing short of galling. Ali Reynolds wasn't accustomed to being dismissed as some kind of meddling wacko.

"Leave it to the professionals," she groused aloud, mimicking Detective Marsh's snide delivery. "Don't insert yourself into the investigation."

But she had already been inserted—by none other than Arabella Ashcroft herself. All her life Ali Reynolds had responded poorly to being told to sit down and shut up, and this time was no exception. Her immediate response to Detective Marsh's back-off suggestion was to want more information.

To track down the general history of the Ashcroft clan, Ali knew she could spend the next several hours combing through computerized searches. With those, she would come away with the bare-bones outline of what had gone on through the years. Over the weekend and with Chris's help, she could probably flesh out those reports into something reasonably comprehensive, but what she was looking for right then was a way to jump-start her investigation. To do that, she turned to her computer, all right, but to her address book rather than Google. A few minutes later she was dialing the number for Deborah Springer.

In the realm of female journalists, Mrs. Deborah Springer was legendary. A World War Two widow who never allowed anyone to refer to her as Ms., Deb Springer had gone to work in the L.A. *Times* secretarial pool to support her three small children. She had gradually boosted herself into doing actual reporting and had spent several years writing the obligatory society postings on the women's pages. Eventually, though, Deb had beaten the odds and snagged herself a business beat. At a time when "women's libbers" were just starting to burn their bras, Deb's hard-nosed reporting had landed her a coveted editorial position. Retired since the mid-1980s, no one knew more about southern California's movers and shakers than Deb Springer.

Ali had done an interview with the woman on the occasion of Mrs. Springer's ninetieth birthday. The filming had been done in the lobby area of the assisted living facility in LaJolla where Deb and her now deceased third husband had taken up residence. Ali and Deb Springer had liked each other instantly, and Ali had come away from the interview with a deep respect for this sharp-witted woman who, years after leaving the newspaper business, had lost none of her encyclopedic knowledge of the California business community.

When the interview had ended, Mrs. Springer had given Ali her direct telephone number and invited her to call if she ever wanted to chat. But at least three years had passed since then, and Ali had been away from California and out of the loop for part of that time. As she dialed the number, she worried that she'd hear a recorded message saying that the number had been disconnected. She did not.

"Hello. Hello," Deb Springer's cracked voice announced. "Just a minute. Hold on until I get my hearing aid out. There now. Who's calling, please?"

"Alison Reynolds," Ali answered. "I used to be on TV in L.A. I did an interview with you."

"Oh, yes. For my ninetieth. Ali, how good of you to call. I understand they put you out to pasture, too. When is the world going to figure out that women don't wear out nearly as soon as the old boys think we do? Of course, a lot of very smart men are turned out before their time as well. It's all very shortsighted, if you ask me, so don't get me started."

At the time of the Springer taping, Ali had just passed forty. It hadn't remotely occurred to her that she was already on the slippery slope of ageism. No doubt Deb Springer had known that even then.

"What can I do for you?" Deb asked.

"I'm working on a research project," Ali answered. "I was hoping you could help me out."

"What kind of research?"

"William Cowan Ashcroft," Ali returned.

"Which William Cowan Ashcroft?" Deb wanted to know. "Number one, two, or three? I know more about Senior than I do two and three."

Not only was Mrs. Deborah Springer not dead, she was still as bright as she had ever been.

"All of the above," Ali said. "For argument's sake let's start with number one."

Just then call waiting buzzed. Ali checked and saw the number of the Sugarloaf Café. That meant it was her mother calling. Edie Larson would have to wait.

"I've seen pictures of him from back in the early days. You probably would have called him a hunk," Deb Springer said. "He was good-looking. In fact, he was movie-star handsome—a widowed father with a young son, a single struggling car dealership in San Diego, and a reputation for being something of a bounder when Amelia Askins tapped him to marry her daughter, Anna Lee."

"Tapped him?" Ali asked. "As in picked him out for an arranged marriage?"

"Exactly," Deb answered. "A necessary marriage. A hurry-up marriage. Anna Lee was in a family way, you see, and a suitable husband was needed in short order. Bill Ashcroft was a very eligible bachelor who was about to go bust and needed an infusion of cash in order to keep going. Amelia Askins came from old East Coast shipping money, and Anna Lee was her only heir. I'm not at all sure the match was a very good deal for Anna Lee, but for her husband, it was a whale of a bargain. As the Depression deepened and car dealerships were going belly up left and right, Ashcroft was able to buy like crazy. And when World War Two came along, he had diversified enough that he was able to weather that storm as well."

"And the baby?"

"Her name was Arabella."

"So Arabella Ashcroft is an Ashcroft in name only?" Ali asked.

"Pretty much. Rumor had it that she was never quite right somehow, and neither was her parents' marriage. Anna Lee moved to Arizona sometime in the fifties. She and Bill Senior never divorced, but they didn't live together most of the time they were married, either. I assumed he didn't divorce her because she might have taken her fortune with her and that would have left him high and dry. As for why Anna Lee didn't divorce him? I can't imagine. I certainly would have. She was an attractive woman who deserved better."

"So it was a marriage of convenience then?" Ali asked.

"On both sides," Deb said. "Come to think of it, she may have had a few outside interests as well. Sauce for the goose and all that, but right this minute I can't dredge up any details. Everyone knew what was going on but nobody reported on that back then. It wasn't considered proper in a family newspaper."

Bearing in mind what had happened with Ali's own philandering husband, it seemed as though nothing had changed in the intervening years. Lots of people had known about Paul's carrying on. No one had mentioned his numerous affairs to Ali.

"Do you know if Bill Ashcroft number one had a sister?" Ali asked.

Deb paused. "I seem to remember he did, a younger sister maybe. I believe she died tragically and at a very young age. I don't remember if it was an illness, an accident, or what."

*Suicide is tragic, all right,* Ali thought. *It's definitely not an accident.*

"Tell me about Bill Ashcroft number two," she prompted.

"People called him The Hand." Deb Springer returned. "I never met him, but everybody who knew him said he was a piece of work. Nowadays they'd call him an arrogant asshole who was conveniently 4-F and didn't have to go off to fight in World War Two. Everyone pretty well figured Bill Senior had paid off the doctor."

"They called him The Hand?" Ali repeated. "Where did that come from?"

"Mostly because he didn't have one," Deb replied. "A hand that is. He lost it early on in some kind of accident. Injured it badly enough that the doctors had to amputate. After the operation, he insisted on keeping it. Pickled it in formaldehyde and took it with him when he left the hospital.

"The name came along a few years later. He was running several of his father's car dealerships, and it came time to fire one of the managers. Bill Junior called the poor guy into his office and told him, 'You may have been expecting a gold watch, but here's what you're getting instead—a wave.' Then he opened his briefcase, pulled out the jar with his hand in it, and set it on the desk. I was told the poor guy who got fired puked the whole way out the door."

"Nice," Ali said.

"Not," Deb returned. "There was nothing nice about him. He was a wart. From then on, Bill Junior always kept the jar with him, just in case he needed to fire somebody. But he was also a show-off and a drinker. Even with only one hand, he bought himself a Corvette when he shouldn't have. He had it specially equipped with some kind of leather cuff so he could steer with his left wrist, but nobody was really surprised when he drove himself off a cliff just north of the Golden Gate Bridge. As I recall, nobody was particularly sorry about it, either, including his relatively new wife of less than a year who was already separated from him at the time he died."

"Less than a year? That was quick," Ali said.

Deb Springer laughed. "I'll say. There were rumors at the time that he had a thing for little girls, but as far as I know that's all they ever were—just rumors."

*Not to hear Arabella tell it,* Ali thought.

"Which brings us to number three."

"After Junior died, Grandpa held his daughter-in-law's feet to the fire. There was an ugly custody battle. When the legal maneuvering was over, Senior got custody of the baby and raised him himself. After the old man died in the mid-eighties, number three wasn't much interested in cars. He sold off the car dealership empire his grandfather and father had built and set about squandering the money—something he was evidently very good at. What's he doing these days? I heard he was caught up in some shady real estate dealings."

"He's dead," Ali said. "Someone murdered him."

Call waiting buzzed again. Again Ali ignored it.

"There you go," Deb Springer said. "Good riddance."

"What about Arabella?" Ali asked. "Do you know anything about her?"

"I seem to remember she had mental problems of some kind. Growing up in a dysfunctional family like that, why wouldn't she? I believe she was institutionalized for a number of years somewhere up in the Bay Area or maybe in Arizona. I'm not sure which. That's what prominent families did with troubled children back in those days—they locked them up and threw away the key. I don't know what became of Arabella once she got out. Or even if she got out. I seem to remember something about a fire at one of those places, but you'll have to forgive me. I'm not at all clear on the details."

"You've been very clear on the details," Ali said. "You've been a huge help."

"And what about you, Alison?" Deb Springer asked. "What are you doing with yourself these days?"

It was much the same question Madeline Havens had asked

in the lobby of St. Francis Hospital. In terms of elapsed time, an entire day had yet to pass, but it seemed more like years. Ali Reynolds had almost died. So had any number of other people.

"This and that," Ali said with a laugh. "Trying to stay out of trouble."

"Don't," Deb Springer advised. "Nobody ever accomplished anything worthwhile by staying out of trouble. You need to decide what it is you want to do and then set about doing it."

*Good advice,* Ali thought. *Remind me to pass it along to Detective Marsh the next time I speak to him. If ever.*

The doorbell rang. "I'm sorry, Mrs. Springer," Ali said. "Someone's at the door."

"You go answer it," Deb said. "But feel free to call me back anytime. It's fun dredging up all this ancient history. And give me your number. If anything more comes to mind on those appalling Ashcroft boys, I'll call you back."

• • •

For the second time that day Ali's robe day was interrupted by the arrival of unexpected visitors. Looking out through the peephole, she saw a young man standing there—an older teenager. Only when he turned his face in her direction did Ali see the family resemblance. The boy looked so much like Dave Holman it was downright spooky. Ali had never met Rich Holman, but this had to be Dave's son.

Ali opened the inside door. "Richey?" she asked uncertainly through the screen.

He nodded and raised his hand in a halfhearted greeting. "Oh," he said. "You're home." He sounded disappointed to see her.

*If you didn't want me to be home,* Ali thought, *why are you ringing my bell?* "What are you doing here?" she asked.

Rich shuffled his feet uneasily. "It's my mom," he murmured. "She's the one who wants to see you. She's out in the car. We stopped off down at the Sugarloaf and got directions. Is it okay if she comes in?"

Suddenly Ali understood why Edie Larson had been trying to call so urgently—she must have been hoping to give her daughter a heads-up that Roxanne and Richey were on their way.

"Sure," Ali said. "Just wait here in the living room. I'll go get dressed."

Spooked by the company, Sam beat Ali to the bedroom, but only just. Hurriedly Ali slipped out of the robe, put on a pair of sweats, and smoothed her hair into a slipshod ponytail. Examining herself critically in the mirror, she paused long enough to powder her nose and apply some lipstick.

When Ali returned to the living room, the woman she assumed to be Roxanne Whitman was seated on the couch. Rich was standing in front of the entryway credenza, running an admiring finger over the satiny-smooth wood finish.

"I'm taking a woodworking course," Richey said to Ali. "This is really a nice piece."

"Thank you," Ali said. "A friend refinished it for me." *A friend who's gone now,* she thought.

Richey went to the couch, where he took a seat next to his mother. Although Ali knew of Roxanne Holman Whitman, she had never met the woman in person. Roxie might have been pretty in a garish sort of way, but she was wearing too much makeup, all of it inexpertly applied.

"I'm sorry to barge in on you like this," Roxie said nervously as her hands fidgeted in her lap. "I hope you don't mind."

"It's fine," Ali said. "Can I get you something?"

Roxie shook her head. "No, nothing for me. We can't stay

long. Dave would kill me if he knew I was horning into his personal life this way. And he'd really be upset if he knew I'd dragged Richey into it as well, but with everything that's happened the last few days, I just couldn't drive myself down here to bring Crystal home and leave town without talking to you first. I wanted to say thank you—thank you for everything you've done the last few days, and thank you for saving Crystal's life last night."

"You're welcome," Ali said. "I was happy to help out. But as far as horning in on Dave's personal life? I'm not sure what you mean."

"Of course you do," Roxanne said, beaming. "Dave seems to think I'm a bit dim, but I understand some things well enough. You never would have done what you did for Crystal—saving her from that killer the way you did—if you and Dave weren't involved."

"Mom!" Richey objected, horrified.

"Well, it's true," Roxie declared. She was getting into her groove now. Sounding more confident, she was totally undaunted by her son's squirming embarrassment.

"Since Crystal wants to stay here so much, I thought I should see for myself who the competition is," Roxie continued. "Dave's already met Gary, you see. Gary's my new husband. Fortunately he's crazy about my kids. It seems only fair, then, that I should meet whoever Dave is lining up to be my kids' wicked stepmother. That's a joke. I can see you already care about Crystal a lot, just like my Gary does."

Ali was dumbfounded. "Excuse me, Mrs. Whitman," she objected. "You're mistaken. I'm not being 'lined up,' as you say, to be anybody's stepmother!"

Roxanne was undeterred. "Call me Roxie," she said with a

smile. "Everybody does. Since we're practically going to be relatives, we should probably be on a first-name basis. And I can certainly see why Crystal liked it here so much. Your place is beautiful, by the way. It doesn't even look like a mobile home, but then ours is only a single-wide, a fourteen-by-seventy."

Roxanne's comment about Ali's house echoed what Arabella Ashcroft had said earlier, only from the opposite end of the spectrum. While Roxie cast an admiring glance around the room, Richey sat next to her looking as though he hoped a hole would somehow open in the floor and swallow him.

"Mom," he pleaded. "Can't we just go?"

"No," Roxie said. "Since Ali's such an important part of your father's life, it's high time the two of us met."

"Look," Ali said forcefully. "I'm afraid you're mistaken. Dave and I are good friends—we've always been friends. He asked me to look after Crystal because it was an emergency situation with work, and he didn't have anyone else to ask. I was glad to do it, by the way, but believe me, Dave and I are not involved. And the fact that Crystal's life got saved last night has as much to do with a guy named Bernie Bernstein as it does with me. I can assure you that Bernie isn't romantically involved with Dave Holman, either."

For the first time, Roxanne seemed uncertain. "But I know he was over there in California with you a few months ago when there was all that trouble," she objected. "And from what Crystal said . . ."

That was true, Ali and Dave had been in California together—when Dave had come to help *her.* But they hadn't been staying in the same hotel room. They hadn't even been in the same hotel.

"What exactly *did* Crystal say?" Ali asked.

Roxie shrugged. "Just that you were an incredibly wonderful person, smart, and brave, too."

At first Ali felt flattered by Crystal's unlikely praise. Then she remembered. *Crystal Holman is a chronic liar.*

"She also said that you and Dave are going to get married soon and move in together here," Roxie continued. "She says the way your mobile is situated on this hill, it has a big basement carved out downstairs. She says there'll be plenty of room for all three kids to come live with you if they want to. That way they could even go back to their old schools."

Having spent several days dealing with the spin-meister Ali had come to know as Crystal Holman, Ali suddenly saw this for what it was—Crystal claiming that what she wanted to be true was true, or simply working one parent against the other in typical child-of-divorce fashion. For a moment Ali felt sorry for Roxanne Whitman—and for her daughter as well.

"Only none of it is going to happen," Ali said. "I'm not sure why Crystal is so dead-set against living in Las Vegas. Maybe you should ask her, but I can assure you her being determined to stay here in Sedona has nothing to do with me."

It was Roxanne's turn to be thunderstruck. "You mean you and Dave aren't . . . ?"

"That's exactly what I mean—we definitely aren't!"

"See there?" Richey said. "I tried to tell you that you shouldn't listen to her. Crystal's always telling stories like that. You can't believe a word she says."

For the first time Ali wondered how much Rich knew about his sister's secret life.

"Did she ever mention someone named Coach Curt to you?" Ali asked him.

Rich scowled. "Sure," he replied. "She said he was like this world-famous soccer coach or something and that he was going to turn her into a soccer star and help her win a scholarship to college. Right. I'll bet she made him up just like she makes up everything else. He probably doesn't even exist."

World famous or not, Coach Curt had existed once. Ali was shocked to realize that so far no one—including Dave—had evidently mentioned any of that inconvenient part of the story to Crystal's mother. No doubt the Coach Curt saga would come out eventually—if and when Crystal was called to testify in court against Jason Gustavson. Ali could imagine that at some point a sleazy defense attorney would find it necessary to ask Crystal exactly what activities she and Coach Curt had been engaged in at the time they witnessed the fatal attack on Kip Hogan.

For right now, though, Roxanne Whitman was blissfully ignorant about her daughter's unsavory behavior, and Ali Reynolds sure as hell didn't want to be the one to tell her. Instead, she changed the subject.

"When are you heading back?" Ali asked.

"Crystal's doing laundry," Roxanne said. "She didn't bring much with her when she took off like that. As soon as her jeans are dry, we'll get going. I usually have to work on Friday. I traded with someone so we could come here today."

"The earlier you head north the better," Ali said, meaning every word and wanting them out of town sooner rather than later. "I understand driving from here to Vegas on a Friday afternoon can be a real bear."

Ali's phone was ringing again as Roxanne and Richey took their leaves. Ali didn't answer the phone until after she closed the door behind them.

"Ali," Edie said. "Where've you been? I've been calling and calling."

"I've been right here," Ali began. "I was on the phone. Thanks for trying to warn me."

"So Roxanne Whitman already stopped by?"

"You'd better believe it," Ali said. "She came to give me the once-over. She thinks Dave and I are going together—that we're practically engaged."

"Well?" Edie returned. "Are you?"

"Am I what?"

"Are you dating Dave Holman?"

"No," Ali answered, exasperated. "Absolutely not."

"Too bad," Edie said. "Sorry to hear it. He's one of my favorite people. Now, what are you doing tonight?"

"I don't know. Why?"

"Your father called a few minutes ago. He and Sandy Mitchell are just now leaving Phoenix to come back to Sedona. Considering everything that's happened the past few days, Sandy probably shouldn't be left on her own tonight. Her brother, Phil, will be here, but he's not worth the powder it would take to blow him up. So I told Dad I'd make dinner for them. Dave should be back from Prescott by then. What with the three of them, the two of us, you, Chris, and Athena, it'll be a tight fit in our little dining room, but the more the merrier. You'll come, too, right?"

"Dave is coming?" Ali asked.

"Yes. I just talked to him. You don't mind, do you?"

"No. Of course not," Ali said. "But who's Athena?"

Edie took a deep breath. "You don't know about Athena? Chris hasn't told you about her?"

"Who's Athena?" Ali repeated.

"Oops," Edie said cheerfully. "Me and my big mouth. Well, you didn't hear it from me. You'd best ask Chris. So there'll be eight of us for dinner, and we'll eat around six. I'd better get cracking."

"Mother!" Ali objected. She was still holding the telephone receiver, but Edie Larson was long gone.

Astonished, Ali put down the phone. Chris had a girlfriend, one Ali knew nothing about? And this mystery girlfriend, this Athena, was coming to dinner at Bob and Edie's house that very night? How dare Chris not tell her? Ali glanced at her watch. It was an hour at least before Chris would be home from school. She fully intended to corner him on this, but it wasn't something that could or should be done over the phone.

Frustrated and needing something to take the edge off, Ali did the only thing that made sense—she grabbed Aunt Evie's old Oreck out of the entryway closet and vacuumed like mad. Vacuumed and fumed.

Later though, once she'd run out of steam, Ali picked up her computer. Arabella had threatened to write a family saga, and from what Deb Springer had said, there were probably enough skeletons in the Ashcroft family closet to fill several volumes. Working alone and with one eye on the clock, Ali set about creating her own Ashcroft history.

She came up with mountains of material, whitewashed in the journalese of the time, but Ali was able to see through it to the uglier ramifications—the corporate takeovers that littered the business pages contrasted with the glowing charitable outreach that was chronicled in the society sections. Ali found a splashy article detailing William Senior's marriage to Anna Lee Askins. In among the descriptions of the designer bridal dress and the sumptuous reception, Ali unearthed enough code words about the various attendees to make it clear that this was a hastily arranged affair. And the timing of the wedding, juxtaposed with Arabella's birth date seven short months later, seemed to validate Deb's claim that Anna Lee had been pregnant at the time she made her vows. That meant that the blue blood running in Arabella's veins came from Anna Lee's side of the family rather than William Ashcroft's.

As far as information was concerned, there was plenty more where that came from, and Ali would have been glad to keep plowing through it, but her phone rang. Caller ID identified Dave Holman's home number, but since Dave was still in Prescott at the county courthouse, it seemed unlikely that he was the person calling. Ali braced herself for another dose of Roxie Whitman.

"Ali?" Crystal said.

"Yes. Hi, Crystal. How are you?"

"Tired. I slept all morning."

*I wish I had,* Ali thought.

"My mom's here and my brother. We're getting ready to go," Crystal said. "Getting ready to go back to Vegas."

"I know," Ali said. "Richey and your mother came by earlier and told me you were heading back."

There was a pause. "They did? They came by your house?"

Crystal sounded almost as surprised and offended as her brother had been.

"Your mother was somehow under the impression that wedding bells were about to ring for your father and me."

"I'm sorry," Crystal said. "She shouldn't have done that."

"As I told you the other day, your father and I aren't in that kind of a relationship. I told your mother as much. How are you?"

"They all ganged up on me and they're making me go back home," Crystal said. "Even though I don't want to. Even though I hate it."

"Why?" Ali asked. "Why do you hate it so much?"

"It doesn't matter."

"But it does matter, Crystal," Ali told her. "Your parents both care about you, and I'm sure they want you to be happy. I don't know what the laws are in Nevada. You may be old enough to have some say in your custodial arrangements. But if you're fighting with all the adults in your life, if you're not going to school, and if you're running away every time you get a chance, people aren't going to pay attention. Your parents won't, and neither will a judge."

"You think a judge might listen to me, really?" Crystal asked. "That he'd let me come stay with my dad?"

*Or she,* Ali thought. "A judge might," she said, "but only if you meet them halfway."

"You mean only if I behave."

"Well, yes," Ali said. "Arrangements like this don't happen overnight, and you'd better behave. For your sake and everyone else's."

"I'll try," Crystal said finally.

"Has anyone told your mother what's been going on?" Ali asked. "As in what's really been going on?"

There was dead silence on the other end of the phone.

"You need to tell her," Ali said.

"It's bad enough that my dad knows," Crystal whispered. "Do I really have to tell my mother?"

"Yes, you really do,"Ali insisted. "She loves you. She'll want to protect you. She'll want to protect you from yourself."

"I've gotta go," Crystal said abruptly. "Thank you for everything."

"You're welcome . . ."

But Crystal was already gone.

"Good-bye," Ali murmured into her empty receiver. "Travel

safe." Before she could put the phone down, though, it rang again.

"Ali?" her new caller announced. "It's Deb Springer again. Is this a bad time?"

"No," Ali told her. "It's fine."

"I've been racking my brain ever since we got off the phone, and I finally came up with it. The Mosberg Institute."

"What's that?"

"The name of the place where they sent Arabella Ashcroft. And it wasn't the Bay Area, it was located in Paso Robles. I believe it started out as a home for the criminally insane. By the time Arabella went there, it had become a bit more upscale, but it was still a dreadful place. I can't imagine sending a child of mine into a world of electroshock therapy, ice baths, and God knows what else. I'm sure it wasn't at all like those posh rehab places they have up and down Malibu these days. But about the Mosberg, I'm fuzzy on the details. I believe it's closed now, but I seem to remember there was some kind of fire there, and I think several people died."

The very mention of ice baths and shock treatments caused Ali to shiver. If that had been Arabella Ashcroft's reality at age nine, no wonder she would have objected to Billy Ashcroft threatening to have her locked up again.

Ali thanked Deb for her help, ended her phone call, and was about to enter Mosberg Institute into her search engine, when she heard Chris's Prius pull up outside. She closed her computer with a snap.

It was time to turn away from some of the Ashcroft family carrying-ons and pay attention to her own.

# { CHAPTER 16 }

Larry Marsh returned from the evidence room to find Hank on the phone, apparently on interminable hold.

"So where are we?" he asked.

Hank impatiently waved him to silence. "Okay," he said. "Thanks so much. If he could call me back with that information, I'd really appreciate it." Hank put down the phone. "Still tracking with the VA," he explained. "What about you?"

"I read the diary," Larry Marsh answered. "It could be Ali Reynolds is right and there is something there."

"What do we do about it?" Hank asked.

"Let's order up everything available on the other two Ashcroft characters. You take Senior. I'll take Junior, and we'll see what gives. We should probably do the same thing for Arabella while we're at it."

For the better part of the next two hours the only sounds coming from their cubicle were the click of computer keys and the whir of their printer. It didn't take long for Larry to hit pay dirt.

"Look at this," he said. "It's from a column in the L.A. *Times*. It squares with what Ali Reynolds said and also with what was in the diary: 'We are saddened to report that over the holiday weekend, Bill Cowan Ashcroft Junior's hand was severely injured as a result of a tree-cutting accident at his father's Brentwood Estate. He was taken by ambulance to the hospital, where he underwent emergency surgery. No further details about his condition are forthcoming at this time, but we certainly wish Bill and his family well.'"

"A tree-trimming accident?" Hank repeated. "With a father richer than God he has his son out cutting trees instead of a gardener? Sounds bogus to me."

"Right. They came up with the tree story so no one would hear the real one, as in I was messing with my baby sister and she came after me with a knife. When it comes to having the story show up on the news, having a close encounter with an ax is a lot more palatable than the baby-sister angle."

By then, Hank had finished with Bill Senior and had moved on to Arabella. "What are you finding on her?" Larry asked.

"Not much at all," Hank told him. "No driver's license that I can find. No marriage. No kids. No divorces, and almost zero press. The Ashcroft menfolk were publicity hounds. And Arabella's mother, Anna Lee Askins Ashcroft, was a big deal in her own right. There are articles about her participation in museum galas and plenty of opera and symphony events. Once she moved to Arizona, she was even a big-time supporter of Barry Goldwater's presidential campaign. Compared to the rest of the family, Arabella's interaction with the public is damned near nonexistent."

"If she doesn't have a valid operator's license, who drives that Silver Cloud we saw in her garage?" Larry asked.

"Arabella Ashcroft is the registered owner all right, but the insurance company lists Leland Brooks as the only driver."

"That would be the butler?" Larry asked.

Hank nodded. "The butler/chauffeur. He's been with the

family for years. The mother, Anna Lee, died in 1995 after outliving Bill Senior by a dozen years. Since then it's just been Arabella and the butler."

• • •

Ali had always valued her close relationship with Chris, and the idea that she had been kept in the dark about a potentially serious girlfriend came as a shock. Ali had raised her son alone and had prided herself on the fact they had remained close through those difficult years of teenage angst when many mother/son relationships had run aground. As Chris came into the house and paused to hang up his jacket, it struck Ali as totally unfair that at the moment she knew far more about the details of Crystal Holman's tempestuous life and intimate relations than she did about what was going on with her very own son.

"Hey, Mom," he said. "How's it going?"

There was no sense in attempting to play coy. "Tell me about Athena," Ali returned.

Chris's handsome face fell. "Who blabbed?" he asked. "Grandma?"

"Who's Athena?" Ali insisted. "And what's wrong with her?"

Chris picked Sam up off the couch and then sat down in the same spot with the cat ensconced in his lap. "What makes you think something's wrong with her?"

"Because you didn't tell me about her."

"I wanted you to meet her first so you could make up your own mind," Chris said. "I didn't want you to have any preconceived ideas about her. Besides, you've been so busy with Crystal Holman and everything . . ."

*Not that busy!* Ali thought. "But Grandpa and Grandma have already met her?" she asked.

Chris shrugged. "We went to the Sugarloaf for breakfast the other morning," Chris said. "She loves the sweet rolls."

"But since we're all meeting for dinner tonight, you also knew that you couldn't keep her a secret forever. Tell me. Tell me everything."

"She's older," Chris said guardedly.

"How much older?"

"Six years."

Ali was relieved. It could have been a lot worse. "That's not so bad," she said. "Where did you meet her?"

"At school. She teaches math—algebra, geometry, trig, calculus."

That was a surprise. Chris had fallen for a math major? Ali's idea of advanced mathematics was balancing her checkbook.

"What else?"

"Mom, what do you mean 'what else?' Why the third degree?"

For the first time Ali realized that she had been blessed—or maybe cursed—with some of her mother's abilities at discernment.

"Because there's more you're not telling me."

"She's divorced," Chris admitted. "But that was finalized last summer, before I even met her."

"Kids?"

"No kids."

Ali sighed. "That's a relief."

"But she'd make a great mother," Chris put in quickly.

"I'm sure she would," Ali agreed. "So that's it? That's everything?"

Chris paused. "Not exactly," he admitted finally.

Ali had tried to raise her son to be open-minded. She had welcomed friends of all shapes, sizes, and races into their home.

*That's it,* she thought. *I'm about to have my very own* Guess Who's Coming to Dinner? *moment.*

"What exactly?" Ali prompted.

For a long moment Chris sat stroking Sam's silky fur saying nothing. "She was in Iraq," he said finally. "She went there with the Minnesota National Guard."

"She's a soldier, then?"

"Was a soldier," Chris said. "Her Humvee got hit by an IED while she was riding shotgun. She's a double amputee. She lost her right leg above the knee and her right arm above the elbow."

That was *not* what Ali had been expecting—not even close. For a moment Ali said nothing. She had hoped that Chris would somehow avoid her checkered marital experience and find his way to the perfect suburban life with a lovely wife, a couple of cute kids, and even a dog or cat or two. But this didn't sound lovely at all. She couldn't dodge the unwelcome juxtaposition between this and what Deb Springer had told her about Bill Ashcroft Junior's amputated hand.

"But you wouldn't know it," Chris continued cheerfully. "She's terrific, Mom. I know you'll like her. She bowls better than I do—left-handed, and she's hoping to play basketball again, but that's a lot harder."

Ali looked at Chris. As he talked about the girl, his face glowed with excitement. And happiness.

"You're really serious about her, aren't you?"

Chris paused. "I didn't mean to be," he said. "It's just that she's different from the other girls I've dated. A lot more . . . I don't know. A lot more grown up, I guess."

"What happened to her husband?"

"He was in the National Guard, too. That's where they met—

basic training. She got sent to Iraq; he didn't. He got involved with someone else while she was deployed. Dumped her with a Dear Jane letter while she was still recovering at Walter Reed. That's why she left Minnesota and came here. Her ex still lives there with his new wife."

Ali looked at Chris as though he was a stranger. In the blink of an eye, he had gone from being a boy to being a man—a man whose mind was made up.

"When did you know?" Ali asked.

"Know what?"

"That she was the one."

"The first time I saw her," Chris said. "At the very first faculty meeting back in August. She walked in the door, and I knew. It took me a while to work up the nerve to ask her out."

*Love at first sight,* Ali thought. That was what had happened to her with Dean, and with Dean it had worked. That instant attraction had sustained them both through all the tough times that had come along later.

"Why didn't you tell me about her?" Ali asked. "Why have you kept it under wraps all this time?"

Chris chewed on his lower lip before he answered. "To begin with, you were going through that whole divorce mess," he said. "Then, after Paul died and you were, well, upset, it just didn't seem fair for me to be falling in love when your life was in the toilet."

Hearing that made Ali's heart wince. He had kept Athena a secret from her because he was trying to protect her. That was Chris, all right—thoughtful to a fault.

"It sounds as though you're taking on a lot," Ali said.

Chris nodded. "But wait 'til you meet her, Mom. You're going to love her as much as I do."

Ali reached over and patted her son's knee. "I'm sure you're right," she said. "And I'm sure I will."

Eager to change the subject, Chris glanced at Ali's computer. "Working on cutloose?" he asked.

"I'm actually doing some research on Arabella Ashcroft and her family," Ali said.

"How come?"

"Her nephew was murdered down in Phoenix this week. I think he was threatening to blow the lid off some long-buried family secret, and I think that's why he's dead. So I'm looking into the Ashcroft archives. The problem is, they were prominent members of the California business establishment for decades. I have a feeling there's going to be tons of material. The trick will be boiling it down and figuring out if any of it is relevant."

"Want some help?"

"Please," Ali said. "I'd really appreciate it."

"Hang on," Chris said. "I'll go get my laptop."

In a little less than an hour of working on the project, Chris had amassed an astonishing amount of material on the Ashcroft clan—their various businesses, charitable events, and forays into southern California's high society. He gathered the articles from various sources, printed them, and handed them over to Ali, who read through them one at a time.

For ease of study, Ali sorted the assembled articles into stacks, one for each person involved. It didn't take long for Ali to realize that the Ashcroft menfolk were definitely front and center in all this while the women faded into the background. There was far more information about Anna Lee Askins Ashcroft after she had moved to Sedona than there had been while she was still in California. It was as though she had been forced to move to another state in order to come into her own right.

It was in one of the Anna Lee articles where Ali found a first mention of the Mosberg Institute. Anna Lee was cited several times as a leading benefactress for the Mosberg Institute. Later she was quoted briefly in a much longer article from the *Paso Robles Herald,* dated March 20, 1956, which discussed the previous week's fatal fire:

> **"This is an unspeakable tragedy," said Mrs. Anna Lee Ashcroft, a longtime Mosberg Institute supporter. "These are vulnerable people and we're fortunate more lives weren't lost. And the idea that someone actually set the fire is absolutely appalling."**

Ali was still reading the whole article when Chris closed his computer. "We can do more of this later," he said. "Right now, I need to go pick up Athena. I promised Grandma we'd come by to help move furniture and set the table."

The Larsons' tiny home contained a kitchen and a living room but no formal dining room. To accommodate groups larger than four, it was necessary to move the kitchen table into the living room and drag in seating from elsewhere in the house.

"You go on ahead," Ali said. "As soon as I finish reading this one article, I'll shower and dress and be there, too."

She was about to shut her own computer when a click announced the arrival of an incoming e-mail. Thinking the message might be from Velma T, Ali clicked over to her e-mail account. The address line on her newest message was disturbingly familiar—uttley, t.uttley.

*Some relation to Coach Curt?* Ali wondered and pressed OPEN.

*So your friend's runaway "daughter is safe at home," the little slut? I'm sure you didn't post her name in your blog because you're protecting her privacy. How can you? She's a wicked temptress who led a good man into sin. Why should she be protected? Who's going to protect my two boys? What about their privacy? Their father is dead, and it's all because of her. My husband's name is being dragged through the mud in the paper and on the news. That means my boys' name is there, too.*

*Curtis and I had our troubles, but we got counseling for them. He came back to church with me and the boys. We were doing fine until she came along, got her hooks into him, and led him astray. And if you don't believe she's evil, maybe you'll want to check out this Web site. I found it on Curt's computer and couldn't believe I was seeing such filth. Maybe you should post it on your blog so the people who read it will know the kind of company you keep.*

*The Good Book says we should pray for our enemies. I am praying for her all right. I am praying that girl will rot in hell.*

*Sincerely,*
THERESA UTTLEY

*Here's the link.*

Ali could hardly argue with the idea that the sins of the father ought not to be visited on the children. Coach Curt's sons were in no way responsible for what their father had done, but the suggestion that Crystal was somehow solely to blame for Curt's going astray was preposterous.

Shaking her head, Ali hit the link and waited for the URL to load and open. When the image first came on the screen, it was so poorly lit that it was difficult to make any sense of what was there. Ali decided that the filming was being done by someone with very limited know-how using computerized podcast equipment. Eventually, though, the images clarified themselves, and then it was all too clear. A middle-aged man's sagging, naked body complete with nonsagging equipment stood directly in front of the camera. And a girl—a very familiar girl—was being pulled toward him. "Come to Daddy," he was saying. "Come to Daddy."

Filled with revulsion, Ali slammed shut the lid of her laptop, breaking her Internet connection and shutting off the video. She sat there for a very long time feeling sick to her stomach. Gradually she was able to remember what Theresa Uttley had said. Something about Crystal being a temptress and leading Curt Uttley astray. Only someone totally blinded by her own grief and despair could fail to see that Crystal was anything but a temptress here. She was a victim, too—a manipulated, helpless victim.

*Who the hell is this jerk?* Ali wondered. *Gary Whitman, maybe? And once I know who he is, how do I keep Dave from killing him?*

The phone rang. Ali had to take a deep breath before she was able to answer. What if it was Dave? What would she say to him? How would she tell him?

"Am I still in the doghouse?" Ali's mother wanted to know.

Ali was still so shaken by what she'd just seen that it was difficult to get a fix on what Edie was saying. "No," Ali answered at last. "You're out of it. Chris and I had a chance to talk. Everything is fine."

"You're sure?" Edie asked. "You don't sound fine."

"I'm sure," Ali said more forcefully.

"All right then. I was going to ask Chris to bring along a couple of bottles of wine from that wine cellar of yours, but then I realized Kip and Sandy met in AA, so probably no wine, right?"

"Right," Ali agreed. "And Chris is already on his way. He's off picking up Athena right now."

"Fair enough," Edie said. "See you in a little. I've fallen a bit behind. I know I told you we'd be eating at six, but it'll probably be closer to six-thirty."

Wanting to wash the ugly images of Crystal's victimization from her mind, Ali stood under the shower and let the water fall full on her face. *Who is Daddy?* she wondered. It was a common enough phrase. Ali knew enough about Dave's trim physique to recognize his wasn't the body featured in the offending video, and the man could have been anyone. Vegas was full of men looking for sex with runaways, prostitutes, whatever. Then again the problem could be much closer to home. Ali had never met Gary Whitman in person, so she had no idea what he looked like, but Ali was left with the sinking feeling that Crystal's stepfather wasn't in the running for Father of the Year.

And what if that turned out to be the case? Hadn't Ali just counseled Crystal to go back home to Las Vegas and make a sincere effort to get along with her elders, Gary Whitman included? If Gary was at fault, it was likely Ali had made things worse instead of better. And what would Dave do once he learned about the offending Web site—however Ali managed to tell him about that? Was there something else she could do instead?

What if she called the cops in Las Vegas? What would they

do? How would they proceed? Or would they? Ali's last interaction with cops certainly hadn't gone very well. What made her think officers in Vegas would be any different? And what would happen to Dave's kids, all three of them, if their new family situation was blown apart? But then again, if what Ali suspected was going on, hadn't that already happened?

Still awash in indecision, Ali stepped out of the shower and reached for a towel.

# { CHAPTER 17 }

Larry Marsh was on the phone to the Marin County Sheriff's Department. Yes, someone would get back to him on the William Cowan Ashcroft situation, but it wasn't likely to be that day, especially since it would take time to locate the record as well as any remaining evidence of that fatal car wreck. Would tomorrow work, or maybe the next day?

In the background, Hank's phone rang and soon he was busily taking notes.

"What do you have?" Larry asked.

"My mole in the VA came through with two possibilities," Hank answered. "Alan Dale Reed of Birmingham, Alabama, got his Silver Star in Vietnam, 1965. The problem is, he died in 2004. Arthur Reed is from Red Bluff, California. His Silver Star came from Korea, circa 1953. As far as I can tell, he's still alive and kicking and driving."

"Address?" Larry asked.

"And phone number."

"Let's give him a call."

They used a phone in the conference room and put it on

speaker. The way investigations went, Larry expected that they'd run into a nonworking number or that Arthur Reed would also be deceased or unavailable. But he wasn't. The woman who answered the phone said only, "Just a minute." Then, "Dad, it's for you."

"This is Detective Larry Marsh with the Phoenix Police Department."

"Wait a minute. You're not supposed to be calling me. I already told you to take me off your goddamned call list. These police guild and fire department calls are just a ripoff. I've got half a mind to report you to the attorney general's office."

"Wait, wait, Mr. Reed," Hank said. "This isn't a solicitation call."

"What is it then?"

"It's a homicide investigation," Marsh said. "Detective Mendoza and I are homicide detectives with the Phoenix Police Department."

"You think I killed somebody in Arizona? I've never even been to Arizona. You've got the wrong guy. I'm hanging up now."

"No, wait," Marsh said. "Please, Mr. Reed. Don't hang up. We're just looking for information. Maybe you can help us."

"What kind of information? If this is some kind of trick . . ."

"It's no trick. As I said, we're investigating a homicide . . ."

"Who died?"

"William Cowan Ashcroft the third."

"Never heard of him. Wouldn't know him from a hole in the ground. What does this have to do with me?"

"It's about your Silver Star, the one you were awarded for service in Korea?"

"What about it?"

"A Silver Star with your name engraved on it was found in the floorwell of Mr. Ashcroft's vehicle after he was killed. We were wondering if you had any idea how it might have gotten there."

In the background they could hear a woman's voice. "Who is it, Dad? What do they want?"

"It's the cops," he said. "Somebody else calling about my medals."

"I thought you got rid of those," the woman said.

"I did," he said impatiently. "I told you I would and I did."

"Somebody else called you about your medal?" Hank asked.

"Yeah, some guy who's writing a book on Silver Star recipients," Reed said. "I have no idea how he got my name. Julie here found out I'd talked to him and pitched a fit."

"Julie?"

"My daughter. If you must know, she and my granddaughter both are certified peace activists. They're not just against this war; they're against all wars. So when I had to move in with her a couple of years ago, she wanted me to get rid of all that wartime crap—didn't want it in her house. Julie's mother and I had saved them through the years—my medals, uniforms, and all that other stuff—kept them up in the attic. Once a Marine always a Marine, but Connie was gone by then, and since I was moving into Julie's house, I had to respect her wishes. I got rid of everything."

"What did you do with them?"

"Took 'em to Goodwill mostly."

"Even the medals?"

"Except for the Silver Star."

"What did you do with that one?"

"I gave it away."

"Who did you give it to?" Larry asked.

"What do you know about the Korean War?" Arthur Reed asked.

"Not much. It was a little before my time."

"Ever get to Red Bluff? If you do, come by for a beer. If Julie's not home, I'll tell you all about it."

"The Silver Star . . ." Larry prompted.

"Right. You probably never heard of Hagaru?"

"No."

"What about Koto-ri?"

"Never heard of that, either."

"Korean hellholes both of them, ten miles apart. Early December. Cold as hell. Took thirty-eight hours to move that ten miles. They called it 'advance to the south' in those days, but that was all bullshit. Nobody wanted to say the word *retreat,* but that's what we were doing. Getting the hell out of Dodge because those Chinese were coming at us like crazy. We were all freezing our butts off, but that morning, before we set off, those crazy Brits did a full unit inspection—polished, shaved, everything. We thought they were nuts."

"What crazy Brits?" Larry asked.

"From the Forty-first Commando. Royal Marine Corps. There weren't very many of 'em, not more than a hundred or so, but we were glad as hell to have 'em. Especially that day. I was with the Marine Five and we, along with Forty-one Commando, were supposed to bring up the rear. We were, too. Our truck got hit. It went off the road and crashed into an icy river. Ice on top—water cold as hell underneath. Would have drowned for sure, but these two Brits showed up and dragged us out of the drink. Cooks. Not munitions guys. Not signalmen. A pair of dumb-ass cooks. Put us in the back of their truck, dried us out, and saved our sorry lives. And then, when we made it to Koto-ri, they saved us again. Invited us to their damned Christmas party. They had booze. We didn't. Hell of a party, too."

Reed's story seemed to have traveled very far afield. "The Silver Star," Larry Marsh reminded him again.

"Oh, right. I won that, later. In a firefight in January, but I wouldn't have been alive to do it if it hadn't been for those two Brits. So I tracked the one guy down and sent it to him. I sent my Silver Star to him as a thank-you. I figured he'd earned it, too. If it hadn't been for him, I never would have lived long enough for someone to pin it on my chest.

"In December 2001, we had this reunion—a fiftieth. It was supposed to be a big deal but it got downsized by 9/11. The reunion was held down in Bakersfield. Didn't even have to go all the way into L.A., and I was able to drive instead of fly. Told Julie I was going to meet an old girlfriend whose husband had just died. That she didn't mind. So I went. A few of the Forty-one Commando guys made it, and I kept asking everybody who showed whatever became of those two cooks. I finally ran into somebody who knew. He said one of them went back home and opened a restaurant in a place called Brighton. The other one—who turned out to be queer as a three-dollar bill—had immigrated to this country right after the war and had gone to work as a butler for some rich old lady. I kept hoping he'd turn up, but he never did."

"A butler? Did this butler have a name?"

"Sure," Arthur Reed said. "It was Brooks—Leland Brooks. Funny little guy, no bigger 'an a minute. He's not the one who's dead, is he?"

"No, that man's name is Ashcroft."

"Oh, good," Reed said. "Glad to hear it."

Larry Marsh, trying to hang up, was already on his feet and headed for the door. "Thank you, Mr. Reed. Thank you so much."

"You don't need anything else? I've got lots of stories."

"Appreciate your help," Hank said. "But I believe we've got everything we need." He slammed the phone down and turned to face his partner. "There you go. Aunt Arabella decides to off her troublesome nephew? Conveniently enough, she just happens to have a trained ex-commando on staff to help her do it."

"Amazing," Larry agreed as they headed for the elevator. "I've been in homicide for a dozen years. For the first time ever, it looks like the butler did it. Where's Agatha Christie when you need her?"

• • •

By ten after six, Ali was standing in the bathroom fully dressed. Her hair was dry and she was applying the last of her makeup, when the doorbell sounded.

*Who is it this time?* she wondered. The quiet, recuperative day she had wanted to spend at home had turned out to be anything but quiet or restful.

Ali checked the peephole and was amazed to find that, for the second time that day, Arabella Ashcroft had arrived on her doorstep. She stood on Ali's front porch wrapped in an old-fashioned but still lush fur coat that appeared to be two sizes too large for her. She was holding a battered briefcase that seemed to have long outlived its expected life span.

Ali opened the door. "Hello, Arabella. What are you doing here?"

"I hope you'll forgive me for dropping by unannounced again," Arabella said with a bright smile. "It's actually rather fun. I may start making a habit of it."

Ali looked around, expecting to see Mr. Brooks and the Rolls lingering in the background. The yellow Rolls was exactly where she expected it to be. Mr. Brooks was nowhere in evidence.

"I'm sorry," Ali said. "I'm on my way out. I've been invited to dinner."

"This won't take long," Arabella returned. "I wanted to show you something."

Good manners trumped good sense. Ali stepped back and motioned Arabella into the house. As she wafted in, so did a cloud of gin.

"Where's Mr. Brooks?" Ali asked.

"I'm afraid he's otherwise engaged at the moment," Arabella said.

"You drove here yourself?"

When Arabella set the briefcase down on the coffee table, there was a distinct rattle as though loose contents were rolling around inside. Apparently unconcerned by possible breakage, Arabella smiled conspiratorially in Ali's direction. "Oh, yes," she said. "I do drive occasionally. It's a lot like riding a bicycle. I'm sure I could still do that, too."

*She's drunk,* Ali thought, but there was a singular glitter in Arabella's eyes that made Ali wonder if Arabella was operating on something more powerful than booze.

"Are you going to offer me a drink?" Arabella asked. "I know you had a martini with me the other day. I find teetotalers very annoying, don't you?"

*The same goes for drunks,* Ali thought. It seemed to her that Arabella had already had plenty. "Sorry," Ali said. "I believe you've had enough."

Arabella sighed and shook her head. "You sound just like Mr. Brooks, but that's all right. Not to worry." Popping open the lid of the briefcase, she pulled out an old-fashioned silver flask, unscrewed the lid, and took a drink. "BYOB," she added. "A premixed martini. Not chilled, but definitely shaken, and better than doing without. I believe in being prepared."

Ali was losing patience. "Arabella, I don't want to be inhospitable but as I told you, I was just leaving. What is it you wanted to show me?"

"Evie always said you were smart," Arabella said. "And, of course, the only way to help you without giving away the game was to help others, too. So all those other scholarship winners have you to thank, but you're not being smart now. You have no idea who you're dealing with. Neither did Billy."

"What are you talking about?"

"Come on, Ali. Didn't you just finish telling me to go to the cops and confess all my sins or you'd do it for me?"

"I tried," Ali said. "They didn't seem particularly interested."

"But they will be," Arabella said.

Once again she lifted the lid on the briefcase. When she pulled out a bag with a Crown Royale insignia on it, Ali thought she was about to help herself to another drink. But the bag didn't hold a bottle of booze. Instead, Ali found herself staring at a lidded jar—a wide-mouthed canning jar filled with a not quite clear liquid. In the dusky light of the living room it took a moment or two for Ali to make sense of the pallid shape suspended inside the glass.

"My God!" she exclaimed. "Your brother's hand!"

"Right you are," Arabella agreed. "Give the girl a gold star. So you know all about that then?"

Ali wasn't sure she knew "all" about anything. But she knew enough. And she remembered Deb Springer saying that Bill Junior had kept his amputated hand with him—at all times.

"How did you get it?" Ali asked.

"Maybe he gave it to me," Arabella said. "Or maybe I took it. But does it really matter? Come on, Ali. If that worthless nephew of mine was bright enough to figure it out, surely you can, too."

"Are you saying you were there when Bill Junior died? When he went off the cliff?"

"Was I?" Arabella laughed. "Maybe I was. Maybe I wasn't." Clearly she regarded this as some kind of game, and she appeared to be enjoying herself immensely.

"But you told me the other day you had nothing to do with his death; that you were out of the country at the time he died."

"I've said a lot of things over the years," Arabella admitted. "The older I get the harder it is to keep all those stories straight."

"Like passing off your years of treatment at the Mosberg Institute by saying you were going to finishing school?"

Arabella gave Ali an appraising look and then took another hit from her flask. "So you know about the Mosberg?" she said. "Yes, I was there. As for treatment? There wasn't a lot of that going on in those days. My father sent me there because he thought I was psychotic. He was probably right about that, by the way. I was psychotic, but just because someone's crazy doesn't mean she's stupid, too. It didn't take long for me to figure out how the system worked."

"What system?" Ali asked.

"Sex was the coin of the realm at the Mosberg. Thanks to my big brother, sex was something I knew a whole lot about. All I had to do was spread my legs and I could have whatever I wanted. 'You don't want electroshock therapy today, little lady. What would you like instead?' Or how about, 'You want a weekend pass? What have you got to trade?' And it turned out, I had plenty to trade. There were guys lining up to take the crazy girl into town. I was a hot date. Of course, that was long before the arrival of birth control pills. Much to the director's chagrin, I'd had to have three abortions by the time I was eighteen. That's when they finally fixed me."

"Fixed you?" Ali asked.

"With a hysterectomy," Arabella replied.

Ali was aghast. "At age eighteen?"

Arabella shrugged. "They did me a favor. After that I could do whatever I wanted. It was a lot easier not to get caught."

The story was appalling; so was Arabella's nonchalant delivery. The problem was, Ali couldn't figure out if Arabella was telling the truth this time or if she was simply spinning yet another web of lies.

"Where was this place?" Ali asked. "When was it?"

Arabella shrugged. "In California," she said. "Outside a town called Paso Robles. After the fire, Mother brought me here to Arizona—to a facility near where Carefree is now. That one was a lot nicer, but it closed. The people who owned it sold it to someone who turned the place into a resort—very posh, I understand."

Ali had already learned a good deal about the fatal fire at the Mosberg Institute, but she wanted to hear the story in Arabella's words. "There was a fire?" Ali asked.

"Oh, yes," Arabella said. "At the Mosberg. A terrible fire. A nurse died in it and one of the patients. I knew the nurse. I never met the patient."

Something about the way Arabella said the words sent a chill of recognition through Ali's body. "Did you have anything to do with the fire?" Ali asked.

"Me?" Arabella responded. "Why would you ask such a thing?"

"Did you?" Ali pressed.

"I suppose it's possible. I might have had something to do with it."

"And what about Billy?" Ali asked. "Did you have anything to do with what happened to him?"

Arabella sighed. "If only he hadn't looked so much like his father. That was a real shock to the system."

"He looked like Bill Junior?"

"Amazingly so. When Mr. Brooks brought the man into the living room, seeing him took my breath away. For a moment I thought Bill Junior had come back to life and that his hand had grown back, too." She unscrewed the lid on her flask, took another sip, and giggled. "That would have been something, wouldn't it? If his hand had grown back, but of course it hadn't—it was still safe and sound and put away right where I've kept it all these years." She patted the briefcase affectionately.

For the first time Ali understood that in addition to being drunk, Arabella Ashcroft was also nuts—totally, completely, and certifiably crackers.

Ali had been standing in the middle of the living room. Now she took a tentative step toward the kitchen counter—and the telephone.

"Where are you going?" Arabella asked.

"I need to call someone," Ali said. "You need help, Arabella. Maybe Mr. Brooks could come get you."

"No, no calls. Mr. Brooks has helped me quite enough through the years. That's why my mother hired him, of course—to look after me and to keep me out of trouble. I have to say, he's done a splendid job of it most of the time, but he's always been at a bit of a disadvantage since he never knew the full story."

Ali glanced at her watch. It was twenty past six. If she was late to dinner, someone was bound to notice. Dinner was scheduled for six-thirty, and Edie Larson expected people to be present and accounted for when food was served. All Ali had to do was stall for time. Eventually her mother would call. Edie might even dispatch a search party.

"What is the full story?" Ali asked.

"About Bill Junior? No one would believe what he was doing to me," Arabella said. "Even my mother didn't believe it. The one person who did was Miss Ponder."

The only clue that the conversation had taken a sudden six-decade detour was the mention of Arabella's old governess. "Wait a minute," Ali said. "You told me the other day that you hadn't told your mother."

Arabella looked puzzled. "Did I? Of course. Why wouldn't I? That's what I told myself over the years, too—that she must not have known. When you tell people and they don't believe you, it hurts too much, so I convinced myself otherwise and didn't think about it very much. I just ignored it. When Miss Ponder went away, Mother told me at the time that she'd been fired because Father caught her stealing something. She said Miss Ponder went back home to New Jersey. I didn't find out until years later that she was dead. Murdered."

"And you think your brother was somehow responsible for her death?"

"I know it," Arabella said fiercely.

"You know it how?" Ali asked. "Did he tell you himself?"

"No."

"Was he ever arrested or questioned in regard to that case?"

"I doubt it," Arabella said. "Not by the police. There wasn't time. When Mother told me Miss Ponder's body had been found, I wrote Bill Junior a letter. He and my father were both flying high in those days. They had a number of big deals on the table.

When I told Bill Junior I knew what he had done and that I was going to find a way to go public, he didn't like it at all."

"You were going to blackmail him?"

"After what he'd done to me, why not? He came to see me to try to talk me out of it. That's when he went off the cliff."

"He came to the Mosberg?"

"Not officially. I had gone AWOL and hitched my way to San Francisco. I had Bill Junior meet me there. He was taking me for a little ride when he went off that cliff."

"You somehow sent him over the edge?" Ali asked.

"Absolutely. Who else was going to do it? I took care of him once and for all."

"How?"

"I'm not sure. We'd both been drinking. People who are drunk do a lot of stupid things."

"How did you get back to the hospital?"

"I don't know. I hitchhiked, probably. Someone must have given me a ride. Dropped me off outside the gate. When questions were asked, the hospital covered for me—covered for themselves actually. They didn't want anyone knowing I'd been off wandering about on my own when Bill Junior died. But somehow, after all these years, Billy finally figured it out."

"And when he came to you looking for money, you took care of him, too," Ali said.

"In more or less the same way. I was waiting for him when he came to his apartment in Scottsdale. He'd been out jogging. I held a gun on him and had him drive out to South Mountain Park. He didn't have either a cell phone or a wallet with him and I thought that way the cops might have a harder time identifying him. He was convinced I was going to shoot him. I thought so, too, but then he somehow managed to get the gun away from me. When he tried to drag me out of the car, I slammed the door on his hand, put it in gear, and drove until he shut the hell up."

*Drunk, crazy, and dangerous as hell,* Ali thought.

"So why are you telling me this, Arabella?" she asked. "Are you planning on taking care of me, too?"

As Ali asked the question, she wondered if she shouldn't try to make a run for it. The front door was only a few feet away, and Arabella Ashcroft was no spring chicken. If Ali could make it out the door and down the hill to one of the neighbor's, maybe she'd be able to duck inside and use a phone to summon help. On the other hand, there was always a chance that running might prove more dangerous than staying where she was.

"I guess I hoped that if I told you the whole story, maybe you'd help me," Arabella continued. "I really do admire cutloose. At one time I thought I could do some good by sharing my story with others. I've been working on writing it down for months, but that's not going to happen now. What Bill Junior did to me didn't just destroy my childhood, Ali. It destroyed my whole life. By the time he was done with me, sex was all I was good for—sex and revenge. Once those were gone, I wasn't good for anything."

In Arabella's despairing words, Ali was afraid she was catching a glimpse of what might be Crystal Holman's grim future, as well—unless someone did something to change it.

"How do you expect me to help you?" Ali asked.

Arabella frowned. "After you talked to me this afternoon, I thought I'd come here and have you help me locate an attorney so I could turn myself in, but now I've changed my mind. There's something else I need to do first."

"What?" Ali asked.

The phone rang. Ali jumped and so did Arabella. Before Ali could move toward the phone, Arabella had reached into the still-opened briefcase and retrieved a handgun that she pointed in Ali's direction.

"Answer it," Arabella ordered.

"Hello," Ali managed.

"Why are you still at home?" Chris wanted to know. "You should be here. Everybody else is. Grandma and Athena are dishing up."

"I'm on my way," Ali managed. "I'll be there in a little while." She put down the phone.

"Good girl," Arabella said with a smile. "You are on your way. In fact, I think the two of us are on our way."

"On our way where?" Ali asked.

"Just a little trip together," Arabella said. "We'll know when we get there. As you have so kindly pointed out, I've had a bit too much to drink. That being the case, you should probably drive."

• • •

Holding the gun with one hand, Arabella tucked the flask into her bra. Then she used the other hand to return the jar to the briefcase, which she clicked shut.

"Shouldn't you have wrapped that?" Ali asked.

Arabella picked up the briefcase and rattled the contents. "I don't think so," she said. "It'll be fine. Let's go. We'll take the Rolls. Get in on the passenger side and then slide over. I'll sit in the back."

As they moved toward the front door, Ali once again considered making a break for it. When she opened the door, though, her ears were assailed by the pneumatic *blat, blat, blat* of a bouncing basketball. That meant that Gabe, the eighth-grader who lived down the street, was out in the driveway dribbling endlessly and shooting baskets. Ali couldn't do anything that would endanger him or anyone else. And once behind the wheel, Ali realized she wouldn't be able to risk driving erratically and provoking a traffic stop, either. No telling what Arabella would do if an officer approached the vehicle. Without a cell phone or any way to summon help, all Ali could do was play a waiting game and hope that eventually the booze would do its work.

Ali complied wth her marching orders while Arabella, puffing slightly, clambered into the back. Ali cringed as the briefcase landed heavily on the floor behind her with the jar rattling loosely around inside it.

"Here," Arabella said. "Put this on. It'll look better." She dropped Leland Brooks's short-billed cap into the front seat. "And the key is there in the ignition."

*Only someone who wasn't used to driving would make that kind of mistake with a Rolls,* Ali thought. When she turned the key, the perfectly tuned engine purred to life. It took a moment to fasten her belt, adjust the seat, and locate the headlight switch. Nothing was familiar.

"Where to?" Ali said finally, pulling out of the driveway.

She caught a hint of gin as Arabella took another hit from the flask. "When you get to the bottom, turn left."

As soon as Ali turned onto the highway, she saw the Sugarloaf Rock and below it the café. The lights were out, but there were several cars still in the parking lot. She caught a glimpse of her father's Bronco, somehow repaired and returned from the garage in a surprisingly timely fashion. She saw her mother's Alero, Chris's silver Prius, Dave's battered Nissan, and two more vehicles Ali couldn't quite identify. Earlier she had dreaded going there and having to tell Dave the latest piece of Crystal's bad news.

Now, though, Ali could easily imagine the crowded living room of her parents' cramped house, and that was exactly where Ali Reynolds wanted to be, seated along with everyone else in a humble living room masquerading as a dining room and breaking bread with people she loved. That wasn't to be. Instead of being there and being able to meet the young woman who might become Chris's wife, Ali was stuck in a bright yellow Rolls-Royce, being held captive by an armed old woman who was certifiably crazy.

*Just like Detective Marsh said,* she thought ruefully. *Definitely inserted and definitely in danger.*

"Where are we going?" Ali said.

"Just drive out to the freeway," Arabella told her. "I'll tell you what to do once we get there."

• • •

When the two detectives arrived in Sedona, it was well after dark. There were lights on deep in the interior of Arabella Ashcroft's house, but no one was home.

"What do we do now?" Hank asked.

Larry Marsh sighed. "I hate to mention it, but I guess we'd better look up Ali Reynolds after all."

"Do we know where she lives?"

Larry was already pulling the cell phone out of his pocket. "We will in a minute."

Twenty minutes later they arrived at a mobile home at the top of Sedona's Andante Drive. There were several vehicles parked in the driveway with people milling around inside and out. Somewhere in the background the slap of a basketball pounded on pavement.

"What's going on?" Larry asked an older woman standing outside, talking animatedly on her phone.

"It's my daughter, Ali," she said. "She's missing. Are you cops? Dave was just now calling. How did you get here so fast?"

"We are cops," Larry said, pulling out his badge. "But probably not the ones who were called. Your daughter is Alison Reynolds? What's your name, and how long has she been gone?"

"Edie, Edie Larson. My grandson talked to his mother right at six-thirty. We were putting dinner on the table, and she was already supposed to be there by then. She told him she was on her way, but she never showed. Finally we came up the hill to check. Her car is here and so are her keys, but no purse and no cell phone. I've tried calling that—but she doesn't answer."

Larry Marsh knew exactly where the missing phone and purse were—back in Phoenix in the evidence room. No wonder she hadn't answered.

A man showed up and looked anxiously from Edie to Larry. "Who's this?" he asked.

"Detective Marsh," Edie told him. "From Phoenix."

The guy held out his hand. "I'm Dave Holman," he said. "Detective Dave Holman, Yavapai County Sheriff's Department. What brings you here?"

"We're investigating the death of a man named William Ashcroft. We wanted to speak to Ms. Reynolds about Mr. Ashcroft's aunt, Arabella."

Just then a young man came jogging back up the hill. "I talked to Gabe down the street," he said. "He was out shooting baskets and saw Mom leave. She was driving a big old yellow car. He didn't know what kind exactly, and he said there was someone sitting in the backseat."

"That would be Arabella Ashcroft's Rolls," Larry Marsh said.

"Why would Ali be driving Arabella's Rolls?" Dave asked. "Where's her driver—what's his name?"

"Brooks," Larry supplied. "Leland Brooks."

A pair of squad cars nosed their way up the street and stopped behind the Phoenix PD Crown Victoria. As uniformed officers converged on the scene and began trying to assess the situation, Larry pulled his partner aside.

"Once we get an APB put out on that Rolls, we'll leave the locals to work this scene," Larry said. "And while they're busy with that, we'll head back over to Arabella's house. Maybe we missed them in transit."

## { CHAPTER 18 }

"Which way?" Ali asked when they reached the freeway. Her hands were sticky with sweat. She knew now that Arabella Ashcroft was completely nuts. She was also armed and dangerous.

"South," Arabella said. "Get off again at Camp Verde."

*Make conversation,* Ali counseled herself. *Try to make things seem normal.* "You still haven't said where we're going," she added.

"I'm going to say good-bye," Arabella said.

"Good-bye to what?"

"We're going to a place I loved," Arabella explained. "Mother called it her 'cabin in the woods.' It's on a piece of private land in the middle of the wilderness. It's very peaceful there. Once they lock me up, I'll never see it again. And when I die, they'll knock it down and turn it back into wilderness. It'll be gone forever."

Back at the house Arabella had seemed defiant—giggly and almost gleeful. Now her mood shifted. She sounded morose and brooding. Ali sensed that this subtle change, booze induced or not, made Arabella more dangerous to deal with rather than less.

And if her intention was to go somewhere to say good-bye, what were the chances that she intended to take Ali with her?

"Did you do what I told you?" Ali asked. "Did you contact a defense attorney?"

In the course of their long, rambling conversation, Arabella Ashcroft had admitted to committing two homicides. She had also hinted that she might be involved in two more. It occurred to Ali that if and when the woman was taken into custody, even the most effective representation might not be enough to save her. Arabella seemed to have arrived at the same conclusion.

"No," she said. "I didn't see any point. Why waste the money? They're going to send me to jail or somewhere else. Either way, I'm not coming back here. This is over."

"What's over?" Ali asked in an effort to keep Arabella talking.

"Everything," Arabella said. "I've lived my whole life, and I've never done anything worthwhile."

"What about those little girls you wanted to help? Did you mean what you said about helping them?"

"Yes, I meant it. Of course I meant it!" Arabella's anger briefly resurfaced. "But once everything that's happened is made public no one is going to pay any attention to anything I say."

"I know a girl like that," Ali said quietly.

"A girl like what?"

"One like you were, only she's a couple of years older. She's someone who has been abused and who has decided to use her body for whatever it'll buy."

"Your friend's daughter?" Arabella asked. "The one who ran away?"

*Of course,* Ali thought. *Arabella reads cutloose.* "What would you say to her?" Ali returned, without answering Arabella's question one way or the other.

They were approaching Camp Verde by then. "Turn here," Arabella said. "I'm hungry. Stop at the McDonald's—at the drive-up."

"I don't have any money," Ali said. "I didn't bring my purse." *Or my driver's license,* she thought.

"I have money," Arabella said. "Stop with the back window at the drive-up. I'll take care of it. And don't try anything."

"Don't worry," Ali said. "I won't."

• • •

Back at Arabella Ashcroft's house for the second time, Larry and Hank found an older 4 x 4 Mazda pickup truck parked in the driveway. A man, bent under the weight of a heavy box, was hurrying from the truck toward the front door.

Hank stopped the car and Larry jumped out. "Mr. Brooks? Mr. Leland Brooks?"

With his white hair glowing in the headlights, the man turned to look at them. He was dressed in full rhinestone cowboy regalia, from the sequined cowboy shirt to the tips of his snakeskin boots. The box in his arms, full to the brim, was one of the three-side produce boxes used to pack groceries at Costco.

"Yes, I'm Leland Brooks," he said. "Who are you? What's going on?"

"Police," Larry said. "We need to talk to you. Put down the box and then get on the ground."

"Get on the ground? Are you joking?"

"Not at all. Get on the ground."

With some difficulty Brooks tried to comply. He stooped over and let go of the box. Groceries spilled out through the opening, rolling in all directions. He dropped stiffly onto one knee, groaning with pain. "My knees aren't what they used to be," he said. "If you want me on the ground, you're going to have to help me."

*He's an old man for Chrissake,* Larry thought guiltily. *Give the guy a break.*

By then, Hank was out of the car. Instead of pushing Brooks to the ground, Larry grabbed him by his upper arm and hauled him to his feet. "Hands behind your back, then."

"Behind my back? You're handcuffing me? What have I done? I had two beers in Prescott, but that was hours ago. If you want a sobriety test . . ."

"You're wanted for questioning in the murder of William Cowan Ashcroft the third." As Larry fastened the cuffs, he automatically recited the Miranda warning.

"Wait a minute," Brooks said when Larry finished. "You think I murdered Billy? Are you kidding? Why would I? Where did you get such a crazy idea?"

"Where's Arabella?" Larry asked.

"Where would she be? Inside and asleep, I'm sure. I gave her all her medication before I left. She should be sleeping through the night. Why? What's wrong?"

"Because she's taken off somewhere, and she's taken a woman named Alison Reynolds with her."

"Ms. Reynolds is missing?" Brooks asked. "Whatever may have happened, I can't imagine that Miss Arabella has anything to do with it, and I'm sure you'll find the Rolls is right here in the garage where it belongs."

"Do you mind showing us?"

"Of course not. The clicker's in my pocket. You'll have to get it out."

"Which pocket?"

"The front one."

"Do you have anything dangerous in here—anything that will hurt me?"

"You mean like a needle or something? Certainly not!" Brooks said. "I'm not some kind of druggie, if that's what you're implying."

With some difficulty Hank emptied Brooks's pockets, extracting a wallet, a set of keys, and a small plastic clicker. When he punched the button the heavy garage door rolled up and a light came on revealing an expanse of shiny concrete polished to a high gloss.

"It is gone," Brooks said, confirming the obvious. "But someone else must have taken it. I'm sure Miss Arabella is asleep in her room exactly where I left her."

"Do you mind if we check?" Larry asked.

"Of course not. Go into the kitchen, through the swinging doors, and then down the hall. Her room is the first one on the left, but I can tell you for sure. Miss Arabella wouldn't be driving the car. She doesn't even have a license."

"That doesn't stop some people," Larry observed.

Hank set off without further urging. He was back in less than a minute. "No one's there," he said. "The place is empty."

"Oh, my," Brooks said. Sounding genuinely dismayed, he staggered over to the front porch where, unassisted, he sank down on the top step. "How can this be?"

"We thought maybe you could tell us something about that, Mr. Brooks," Larry said. "When was the last time . . ."

"Wait a minute," Brooks interrupted. "You've read me my rights? Don't tell me you think I had something to do with Mr. Ashcroft's death. I can't imagine why you'd think such a thing. It's outrageous."

"Have you ever heard of someone named Arthur Reed?"

Larry asked. "I believe he served in Korea about the same time you did?"

"Of course, I remember Art Reed. United States Marine Corps. Why wouldn't I?"

"And he gave you his Silver Star?"

"Yes, he did. I was really honored and touched. I saved his life once. Later when he was awarded a Silver Star, he decided to share the honor with me."

"What became of it?"

"Of the star itself? I'm not sure. It wasn't mine to wear, of course, since I hadn't earned it. I treasured it, but I lost track of it years ago, shortly after it was given to me. How do you know about it, and why are you asking?"

"How do you suppose your Silver Star would have turned up in William Ashcroft's vehicle?" Larry asked. "Our CSI team found it under the floor mat after he was murdered."

"I have no idea where it's been all this time or how it got there."

"You must."

Larry's phone rang. "Detective Marsh? Dave Holman here. Your people down in Phoenix have brought us into the loop. I thought you'd want to know that when we put out the APB on that Rolls, we got a hit."

"You already found her then?"

"No," Holman answered, "but the Rolls was caught by a red-light camera making an illegal left turn in Scottsdale at Scottsdale and Camelback, just before midnight, Monday night. The citation went out in the mail today. Your records folks were able to scan through the video record and come up with the actual photo. It would appear that Arabella Ashcroft was at the wheel, and she was alone in the vehicle."

Larry closed his phone. "So where were you on Monday night, Mr. Brooks?" he asked.

The butler shook his head. "I know that's the night Mr. Ashcroft died," he said. "But I was out the whole evening, from late afternoon on. It's my day off."

"Where did you go?"

"Prescott."

"What did you do there?"

"If you don't mind, I'd rather not say."

"You might want to reconsider," Larry suggested. "I've just received word that the Rolls was cited for running a red light in Scottsdale on Monday night and the insurance company has you listed as the sole driver. We also know that property directly traceable to you was found at the scene of the crime. So if you happen to have a verifiable alibi for the time in question, Mr. Brooks, now might be a good time to mention it."

Leland Brooks sighed. "I was at Paddy's," he said after a pause. "Paddy O'Toole's."

"Where's that?" Hank asked. "One of those bars on Prescott's famed Whiskey Row?"

Leland shook his head. "It's a world away from Whiskey Row. It's a private club. A gay private club out in the valley. Some of the people I saw there might not want to be connected to a homicide investigation."

"Name one," Larry said.

"There's the bartender," Brooks said reluctantly. "His name is Barry—Barry Stone."

"Anyone else?"

"Can you be discreet?" Leland asked.

"That depends."

"Patrick Macey," Leland said. "Judge Patrick Macey."

"What kind of judge?"

Leland Brooks sighed. "Superior court. We've been involved for a dozen years. He's married. His wife's an Alzheimer's patient. His kids don't know about him. They don't know about us."

"Phone numbers, please," Larry said.

Brooks reeled them off from memory, and Hank keyed the first one into his phone.

"Please," Brooks begged. "It's cold out here. I'm freezing. Can't we go inside?"

With Detective Mendoza outside on the phone, Larry took Brooks into the kitchen and seated him at a table. The kitchen was surprising cold as well. At Brooks's direction, Larry switched on the baseboard heat. The room was starting to warm up when Hank came inside several minutes later, carrying the scattered groceries.

"His story checks out," Hank said, setting the box down on the counter. "Both Stone and Macey say he was there, from late afternoon until closing."

Brooks heaved a sigh of relief. "I told you," he said. "I told you I had nothing to do with it."

"What about Mr. Ashcroft's visit here on Sunday?" Larry said. He came across the room and removed the cuffs. "Were you privy to their conversation? Do you know what was said?"

"Thank you," Leland said, rubbing his wrists. "As to your question, I maintain certain professional standards. That means there are some lines that are never crossed. In other words, I don't listen outside doors, if that's what you're implying. Yes, I was aware of Mr. Ashcroft's visit. I showed him in and I showed him out. I was curious, of course, but all Miss Arabella told me was that he had asked her for money. He would have been better served asking me about that since I'm the one who handles the finances, but he didn't."

"She didn't go into any further detail?"

"Not until you were here on Tuesday. That was the first I heard anything about Mr. Ashcroft's bizarre reverse mortgage proposal. I would never have let that one fly."

"What happened after he left?" Larry asked.

"I'd have to say Miss Arabella seemed anxious and distressed, enough so that I was afraid it might trigger another one of her episodes . . ."

"What kind of episode?" Marsh asked.

"She has debilitating emotional episodes from time to time—has had her whole life," Brooks replied. "A good deal of the time she stays on an even keel, but she goes a bit haywire on occasion, can't sleep, suffers from delusions, talks to people who aren't there. That sort of thing. At times like those I'm especially careful that she takes all her medications, and I did that this time, too. Even when you came to tell us Mr. Ashcroft had died, it just never occurred to me that she might have done something that drastic."

"Could she have?" Larry Marsh asked.

Brooks didn't answer for some time.

"Well?" Larry pressed.

"Perhaps," Brooks admitted at last.

"How?"

"There was a problem with the mileage."

"What kind of problem?" Larry Marsh asked.

"On the Rolls. I keep track of the mileage each time I get gas. On Thursday, when I went to fill up, I noticed there was a two-hundred-plus-mile discrepancy between what I had written down last week and what was showing on the odometer. I thought I'd just forgotten to make the proper notation. It never crossed my mind that she might have taken the car out and driven somewhere herself."

"What about weapons?" Hank Mendoza put in. "Do you have any handguns in the house?"

Brooks stiffened and seemed to get a grip. "Several," he said at once. "Mrs. Ashcroft was a very talented markswoman. And Miss Arabella is a fair shot, as well. We've done target practice, but only under strict supervision. And you don't need to worry about the weapons. They're all locked away in the safe in the library. I can show them to you if you like."

"Lead the way."

They followed Brooks through the house, through a dining room and living room and into a spacious library. "The light switch is over there," he said, nodding. "And I can tell you how to move the panel, but it would be ever so much easier if you'd allow me to do it."

"Be our guest," Larry Marsh said. Brooks moved forward, touched a place on the wall, and a whole section of bookcase swung open, revealing a massive safe. Brooks expertly worked the combination lock then pressed the handle. The door swung wide and a light came on inside, revealing an interior as large as a laundry room. One side was hung with wall-to-wall fur coats.

Brooks frowned. "Where's the mink?" he asked.

Walking over to a tall cabinet, he pulled out one drawer, slammed that one shut, and opened another and another and another. "Damn!" he muttered. "They're gone—all of them. But how's that possible? I'm the only one with the combination to the safe."

"Evidently not," Larry Marsh said. "So what kinds of guns are we talking about, and how many?"

• • •

"Where is she?"

"Who?" Ali asked.

"The girl," Arabella said. "The one you told me about."

When Ali had tried to bring up the subject of Crystal earlier, Arabella had shut down so thoroughly, Ali wasn't even sure she had heard her mention it. Now though, with their Big Macs gone and with the Rolls back under way and driving through the forested night, Ali was surprised when the conversation returned to that topic as though there'd been no interruption.

"She's back home," Ali said. "Back with her family. So how would you advise her? If you could talk to her and give her the benefit of your experience, what would you say?"

"Does her mother love her?"

"Of course."

"Don't say that like it's always the case," Arabella cautioned. "It isn't always true, you know."

"Are you trying to say your mother didn't love you?" Ali asked. "I met her, you know. I saw how she was."

"There's a difference between love and duty," Arabella said. "Mother had a duty to take care of me, especially since, as people like to say, 'I wasn't quite right in the head.' I give her credit. She did that; she's still doing that. That's why Mr. Brooks is still looking after me. Mother arranged all that long before she died. But don't kid yourself. I don't think Mother ever really loved me."

"Why wouldn't she?"

"Because I was the reason she had to get married."

"But your father . . ."

"Bill Ashcroft Senior gave me my name, but he was definitely not my father," Arabella said flatly. "It was like I was dropped into a family of strangers. So what about this girl? What's her family like, and does her mother love her?"

Ali thought about Roxanne Whitman. "Yes," she said. "I think she does."

"And the father?"

"He loves her, too. There's a stepfather in the picture, though," Ali said. "I'm worried about him."

"The girl should tell her mother, then," Arabella declared. "She should definitely tell her mother."

"And what if the same thing happens to her that happened to you? What if her mother doesn't believe her?"

"Well," Arabella said thoughtfully, after a pause. "In that case, don't let her have any knives."

• • •

When the three men returned to the spacious kitchen, Brooks offered to make coffee. While Hank hurried outside to notify the other jurisdictions of the changed dynamics in the situation, Larry Marsh sat at the kitchen table and watched while the butler bustled about, starting a pot of coffee and making a platter of sandwiches. By the time Hank came back inside, the coffee was ready. He picked up one of the sandwiches, which had been cut into small pieces and stacked three deep on a delicately flowered china platter.

When Hank bit into the first tiny morsel, a broad smile lit up his face. "Damn," he muttered. "If this doesn't beat the roach coach all hollow."

Brooks handed each of the cops stiff white napkins that had been starched and pressed with military precision. The coffee was excellent, but it was served in tiny white cups with handles much too small for Detective Marsh's somewhat meaty fingers.

"So tell us about the guns," Larry Marsh said, munching another piece of sandwich. "How many are missing?"

"Three," Brooks said. "All of them handguns. Mine was a thirty-eight—an old Chief's Special. I bought it new in 1955 when Mrs. Ashcroft hired me. She was interested in having both a butler and a bodyguard. Since I was a former commando who had been trained as a cook, she decided I filled her bill. She actually sent me back to England to attend butler school."

"So this thirty-eight. What was it?" Larry asked. "A Smith and Wesson Airweight?"

Brooks frowned. "Yes, it was, but how would you know that?"

"Because we found one just like that," Larry said. "At the crime scene."

"You didn't mention Mr. Ashcroft was shot," Brooks said.

"He wasn't, but that's still where we found the gun. What were the others?"

"Mrs. Ashcroft had a pair of pearl-handled first model Ladysmiths, both small-frame revolvers chambered for seven twenty-two-caliber long rounds. Those are missing as well, but those are mostly used for target practice. Less dangerous than the thirty eight."

"Not at close range," Marsh returned. "So wherever she is, we have to assume she's armed and dangerous. Is she a good shot?"

"Unfortunately, yes," Brooks said. "I suppose she is. I trained her myself."

"But you said she was nuts," Marsh objected. "Why would you do such a thing?"

"I didn't say she was nuts, sir," Brooks said. "Miss Arabella is prone to moods, and I did it because I was asked to. Besides, we only did target shooting. The rest of the time the guns were safely under lock and key."

"Right," Hank Mendoza said. "You mean like they are right now."

Brooks nodded and said nothing.

"What do you know about the death of Mr. Ashcroft's father?" Larry asked.

"That would be Bill Junior. That's how Mrs. Ashcroft always referred to him. But I thought this was all about Billy. Bill Junior died in an automobile accident in 1956. He was a notorious drinker. He went off the side of a mountain and that was the end of him."

"Was Arabella ever questioned in conjunction with that death?" Larry asked.

"No one was questioned that I know of. But there would have been no reason at all to question Miss Arabella. She was miles away at the time, hospitalized at a facility in Paso Robles."

"Yes," Larry Marsh said. "The Mosberg Institute. We know that's where she was supposed to be. We also know that the charge nurse who was primarily responsible for Arabella's care at the time died in a tragic fire at the Mosberg a few days after Mr. Ashcroft's death."

"I seem to remember that, too," Leland Brooks said. "And a patient died as well. I believe he was something of a firebug—a serial arsonist. The fire was laid at his door, metaphorically speaking, but Mrs. Ashcroft was of the opinion that there was a good deal of covering up about that incident. It was one of the reasons she took Miss Arabella out of there and moved her to the Bancroft House, a place down in what's now part of Carefree. It was after Miss Arabella came to Arizona that Mrs. Ashcroft decided to buy this place."

"You were already working for the Ashcrofts at that time?"

"I worked for Mrs. Ashcroft from 1955 on," Leland Brooks said stiffly. "I never worked for Mr. Ashcroft Senior, and I never had anything to do with him, either." The butler shuddered. "He was a perfectly dreadful man. So was his son. Mrs. Ashcroft, on the other hand, was a wonderful human being and very generous. At the time of her death, she saw to it that I'd be taken care of so that her daughter, in turn, would be taken care of. I look after the house and the vehicles, manage the household accounts, make sure Miss Arabella sees her doctors and takes her medications. I also drive her wherever she wants to go."

"It sounds pretty all-encompassing," Larry Marsh said.

"Of course it is," Leland Brooks returned with a smile. "I'm a butler."

• • •

As the Rolls turned off the highway onto a small, single lane road that wound through the West Clear Creek Wilderness, Ali was beginning to wonder if they should have bought gas at the same time they stopped for those Big Macs. But at least here, in the middle of nowhere, if she decided to overpower Arabella and take her down, no one else could possibly be hurt. She was still hoping that, at some point, Arabella would simply fall asleep.

"Punishment," Arabella announced from the backseat. "That's what's important. If your friend's abuser gets punished, that helps. A little. You see, I took care of what Bill Junior did to me. And I took care of what he did to Miss Ponder. But what about the others?"

"What others?"

"The ones I don't know about," Arabella said. "There must have been others. Those are the ones I think about when I can't sleep. He was never punished for any of those. But that's also why he kept his hand, you see. I think that was his way of trying to punish my mother for what I had done to him. That's why I have it. I did it for her."

"Did your mother know you had Bill Junior's hand?"

"I doubt it," Arabella said.

"When it comes to punishment, what about you?" Ali asked, glancing at Arabella in the rearview mirror. "Should you be punished for what you did?"

"I suppose," Arabella said. "But I don't want to be locked up again. Mother promised me that I never would be."

"Did she know what you had done?"

"Maybe," Arabella said. "Probably."

"Your mother wasn't a judge and jury," Ali said. "She had no right to make that promise."

"But she did," Arabella insisted. "And I believed her. Here we are."

They entered a small clearing. Ali looked around, expecting to see a small, snug cabin, but she saw nothing. No outline of a building; no flashes of headlights off windowpanes. But then there was something—a gleam in the dark. She pulled closer. What she saw was her headlights reflecting back off what remained of half a wall.

"There's nothing here," Ali explained. "There's no cabin."

"I know," Arabella said. "It burned down last summer. Vandals."

"Then what are we doing here?"

"We're going to sit here for a while," Arabella said. "We're going to sit here and let me think. Then I'm going to say good-bye."

*Good-bye!* Ali thought. *Good-bye? She's going to kill me. What the hell am I supposed to do now?*

# { CHAPTER 19 }

It was after ten by the time the two detectives left Arabella's house and headed back to Phoenix.

"Damn," Larry Marsh complained. "It annoys the hell out of me to think that Arabella snowed us completely."

"Sounds like she snowed everybody, Mr Brooks included. And don't forget Alison Reynolds and Billy Ashcroft. She told Billy she was dead broke. According to Brooks, that's not the case at all. The money may not be liquid, but it's there. She told Ali Reynolds all about this mysterious diary of hers, one you've even seen, but her butler never saw it. How can that be? My guess is we could hook Arabella up to a lie detector, ask her questions all day long, and have her come up with two or more contradictory answers to every question without ever having any of them register as a lie. If she's crazy, she probably doesn't know the difference between fact and fiction, to say nothing of right or wrong."

"Which will make her damned hard to convict."

"In my book she's a person of interest in four different homicides—Billy and Bill Junior as well as the firebug and the nurse at the Mosberg. What's kept her from knifing poor old Brooks in his sleep all this time?"

"Enlightened self-interest," Larry said with a mirthless chuckle. "If she did that, who would bring her her morning coffee?"

As Larry drove south on I-17, Hank called Dave Holman to check on the APB. "Still no word?"

"None," Dave said. "As long ago as they left, they could be anywhere by now—through Phoenix or Flagstaff and halfway to California or New Mexico. If they're still on the move, we should have found them."

"How's Ali's family holding up?" Hank asked.

"About how you'd expect. I'm here at the house with her son and his girlfriend. Her parents went home to go to bed. After what went on at the hospital last night, everybody's pretty much strung out," Dave said. "But she saved my daughter's life, and now we've got to save hers."

• • •

Ali and Arabella sat in the Rolls with the engine running for the better part of the next half hour. Several times, when Ali tried to say something, Arabella insisted on silence. "I told you," she said. "I need to think."

Ali was thinking, too. With the sweat trickling down her sides and with her stomach in a knot, she was appalled by their complete isolation. They had seen no lights on the way down the narrow road, no other signs of habitation.

*We're completely alone,* Ali thought. *No one on earth knows we're here. Arabella will shoot me and then herself and it'll be weeks before anyone finds us.*

Last night, in the hospital, she hadn't had time to be scared.

Jason had been there—a mortal threat to everyone he met—and Ali had simply reacted. This was different. As the minutes crept by, one by one, Ali thought she understood how condemned prisoners must feel on the night they're due to be executed.

*I don't want to be dead,* Ali told herself. *I'm not ready.*

"All right then," Arabella said finally, emerging from her trancelike silence. "Here."

Ali turned to look as Arabella held up the jar. "I told you I came to say good-bye. Now get out of the car and take this over there to where the porch used to be."

Ali was shocked to see Arabella was handing her the jar.

"No," Ali said. "I won't touch it."

"Yes, you will," Arabella insisted. "Have you forgotten I have a gun?"

Ali hadn't forgotten about the gun, not for a single moment.

"All right."

Leaving the headlights on and the engine still running, Ali took the jar and got out of the car. Her legs seemed ready to collapse under her and the jar was surprisingly heavy, but she held it to her breast. She didn't want to drop it; didn't want to be splattered by the awfulness inside.

Picking her way across uneven ground, she made her way toward the nonexistent cabin. On either side of the clearing she could make out patches of snow. Ahead of her the denuded concrete pad of the house glowed against the surrounding blackness. Shivering with cold and revulsion both, Ali walked as far as what looked like the footprint of a porch.

"Set it down," Arabella ordered. "Set it down right there and step away."

Ali did as she was told. As she moved toward the Rolls, she saw Arabella assume a military stance, holding the tiny pistol in a two-handed grip. Petrified, Ali plunged to the ground. She was already facedown in the dirt when the sound of the gunfire pierced the silence of the bitterly cold night.

Behind her, the glass jar exploded into a million pieces. For a long moment, Ali huddled on the ground while the sound of that single gunshot reverberated in her ears. She lay there holding her breath, wondering if she'd been hurt by any of the flying glass and waiting for the next shot—which didn't come. Finally she looked up to find Arabella still standing calmly beside the Rolls and holding the gun at her side as if nothing out of the ordinary had happened.

"There," she said, casually waving the gun in Ali's direction. "I've said my good-byes. Come on now," she added. "I'm done here. Get in and let's go home."

Ali's knees were quaking and her hands shook as she resumed her place behind the wheel. She knew something about firearms. It was clear to her that Arabella Ashcroft was one hell of a shot. Ali knew, too, that if Arabella had really intended to kill her there was no question that she would be dead.

*Thank God I didn't try to run earlier,* Ali thought. *She would have plugged me full of holes.*

"What kind of gun is that?" Ali asked, trying to normalize the tension in the car with conversation.

"A Smith and Wesson Ladysmith," Arabella said. "It's a genuine antique. Belonged to my mother. Fires seven rounds."

*Which means there are probably six shots left.*

"Where did you learn to shoot?" Ali asked.

"I was trained by a former Royal Marine commando," Arabella answered.

In the darkness, Ali rolled her eyes. *Sure you were,* she thought. *And I'm a monkey's uncle.*

"He tells me I'm a very good shot," Arabella added.

Arabella Ashcroft may have been a liar, but that last statement was indisputably true. She was an excellent shot. She was also a cold-blooded killer.

As they headed away from the burned-out cabin, Ali tried to come to grips with how to deal with someone who was clearly a pathological liar. The same had been true for Arabella's mother, Anna Lee. Their checks had been good when they had offered Ali her scholarship, but was anything else she knew about them true?

Arabella claimed to be broke, and the mending on that old cardigan—Brooks's workmanship most likely—was real enough, but the coat Arabella was wearing right that minute was probably worth several thousand dollars. Arabella had implied that she'd had something to do with several murders. She had coyly refrained from coming right out and admitting to any of them, but the jar had been real enough.

"Where did you keep it?" Ali asked.

"Keep what?"

"The jar. With your brother's hand. You said you got it from Bill Junior. If you were locked up at the time, surely you weren't allowed to keep it in your room."

"You'd be surprised," Arabella said. "You've never been locked up anywhere, have you?"

"No."

"I had both the jar and the briefcase," Arabella said. "The briefcase with the jar inside it. Someone I was nice to there took it home and kept it for me, kept it until I was ready to have it again."

"How long?"

"Eight years. From 1956 until 1964, when they shut down Bancroft House."

"What's Bancroft House?" Ali asked. "I thought you were at the Mosberg Institute."

"Bancroft came later," Arabella said. "After the Mosberg."

"And somebody was willing to keep it for you for that long, with no questions asked?"

"That all depends," Arabella answered coyly.

"On what?"

"On what you have to trade."

On the drive back to Sedona, Ali kept hoping eventually Arabella would fall asleep, but she didn't. Ali prayed that somewhere along the way they'd see a patrol car of some kind. That didn't happen, either. By midnight, as they made their way up the hill to Arabella's house, there was almost no traffic of any kind. But when they pulled into the yard at Arabella's house, the garage door was wide open and a stack of suitcases stood barring the spot where Arabella expected Ali to park the Rolls.

"What is all that stuff?" Arabella demanded. "Honk the horn. Get Mr. Brooks out here to move it."

"Arabella, it's the middle of the night. People are asleep. I can't be honking the horn."

Just then the whole discussion became moot when Leland Brooks, lugging another pair of suitcases, entered the garage through the kitchen door. He set them down with the rest of the luggage then straightened slowly and started toward the Rolls.

Ali didn't know what to do. Should she warn him away? Let him come ahead on and hope that, between the two of them, they could somehow wrestle the loaded weapon from Arabella's hand? Before Ali could respond one way or the other, Brooks made straight for the back door and opened it. "Good evening, madam," he said to Arabella. "I'm glad you're home."

He reached in and took the briefcase. Without objection,

Arabella allowed herself to be helped from the car. "Get all that junk out of the way so she can pull into the garage," Arabella ordered. "And what on earth are you doing in that god-awful outfit?"

That was the first Ali actually noticed how Brooks was dressed—in a bright blue sequined cowboy shirt, narrow-legged jeans, and cowboy boots.

"Don't you like it?" he asked.

"Of course I don't like it," Arabella said irritably. "You look like you're about to go out trick-or-treating. And what is all this mess?"

"It's my luggage," Brooks replied. "My ride should be here in a while."

"Ride?" Arabella repeated. "You're going someplace? You're taking a trip?"

"Yes, madam," Brooks said. "I'm afraid I'm leaving."

"Leaving! You can't do that. You can't be serious."

"I'm entirely serious," Brooks returned. "I know I promised your mother that I'd look after you, but I'm afraid I can't do that anymore. You're far too dangerous—to yourself and others—including Madam Reynolds here. You are all right, aren't you Ms. Reynolds?"

His manner was as calm and unruffled as if he were inquiring about whether she wanted one lump or two in her tea.

"Yes," Ali managed with some difficulty. "I'm fine."

"Good," he said. "Very good." Then he turned back to Arabella. "I have reason to believe you've somehow managed to get into the safe and remove the guns. I'm sure that must be how you convinced Madam Reynolds to accompany you on this little jaunt tonight. Is that true?"

Arabella stared at him as if he were speaking some incomprehensible foreign language.

"Well?" he prompted. She said nothing and he held out his hand. "Give it to me," he said. "Give me the gun."

And to Ali's utter astonishment, Arabella complied.

"Where's the other one?" he asked.

"In the briefcase."

"Very well, then. Let's go inside. It's cold out here. I took the liberty of starting a fire in the living room in hopes you'd come to your senses and come home. We can talk there. You're welcome, too, Ms. Reynolds, if you wish. You might want to phone your family and let them know you're safe, but if you don't mind, I'd like to make a call or two first."

With Arabella leaning on his arm, Leland led her into the house. With him in his cowboy duds and her in her fur-coated finery, the two of them made an incongruous but somehow dignified pair. Seeing them together reminded Ali of pictures of the queen mum being escorted in some royal processional. They went in through the laundry room and kitchen—through parts of the house Ali had never seen before—where appliances that looked as though they should have been genuine antiques consigned to museums seemed to be still functional. They walked through the chilly dining room with its massive polished wood table and matching sideboard.

As promised, a cheerful fire was burning in the living room. Brooks deftly relieved Arabella of her coat and then deposited her in one of the chairs facing the fire.

"I notice your computer is missing," he said. "I'm assuming it hasn't been stolen."

"It's in the trunk of the Rolls," she said. "I was going to get rid of it, but then I forgot."

"Very well, madam," Brooks said. "I'll bring it back inside later. Now would you care for something to drink?"

"Oh my, yes. I'd love one of your martinis about now, Mr. Brooks. Wouldn't you, Ali? As cold as you can make them, of course, but do change out of those ridiculous clothes before you serve us."

Ali's head was spinning. By force of sheer willpower Leland Brooks had somehow managed to create a sense of normalcy out of chaos. His steadfast calm in the face of Arabella's erratic frenzy seemed to have dragged Arabella back into the real world as well. Was this how he had handled her all these years?

"Is that what you would like, Madam Reynolds?" Brooks asked. "A martini?"

"Yes, please," Ali said. "That would be fine. And a telephone."

"Very well. Please have a seat here by the fire. I'll be right back."

He took the coat and draped it over the back of a nearby chair and then exited the room, taking the briefcase with him. Arabella leaned into her chair, closed her eyes briefly, and sighed with contentment. She seemed happy to be home. *Maybe she's finally running out of steam,* Ali thought.

Facedown on the table between the two chairs lay a well-thumbed paperback copy of Louis Lamour's *High Lonesome.* Ali picked it up and looked at the cover. The two-dollar price tag printed on the cover probably meant that it had been around for a long time.

Arabella opened her eyes. "That's Mr. Brooks's book," she said. "He likes westerns. He reads to me sometimes when I can't sleep. Since my memory's shot a lot of the time, it doesn't matter if he reads the same story over and over."

*What a good man,* Ali thought.

When Brooks returned to the living room, he brought with

him a tray laden with shakers and glasses along with a thick stack of papers and a telephone. He put the tray on a side table, then he handed the phone to Ali, and approached Arabella with the collection of papers.

"Before I pour the drinks," he said, "there are a few items that must be attended to."

"Like what?" Arabella asked. "And why haven't you changed clothes?"

"This is a listing agreement," he replied, ignoring her question. "I finished signing it just a few minutes before you arrived. The real estate agent was more than happy to make an after-hours visit."

"A listing agreement for what?"

"To sell the house, of course," he answered. "Since I have your power of attorney, I've already signed it, but I wanted you to have an opportunity to review the documents."

Arabella seemed totally dismayed. "We're selling the house?" she asked. "But why? Where are we going to live?"

Ali's first phone call was to the sheriff's department, where she told the dispatcher what was going on and left a message asking Dave to come get her. Next she dialed her home number.

"Mom," Chris said anxiously. "Is that you? Thank God. Where are you? Are you all right?"

"I'm fine," she said. "I'm at Arabella's house."

"Athena and I can pick you up."

"No. I just talked to the sheriff's department. Dave's most likely already on his way here. This is going to take time. Dave will be glad to give me a ride home when things are sorted out."

By the time Ali was off the phone, the martinis were poured, but Arabella was once again in a towering rage. "You can't do that to me," she screeched at Leland Brooks. "You can't sell the house right out from under me. It's not fair. Why are you doing this?"

"Because you're going to need the money," Brooks explained patiently. "We don't have enough ready cash available to pay for the defense attorney. This is the best way to handle that."

"Like hell it is," Arabella returned. With that, she heaved the papers into the fire and smiled with grim satisfaction as they caught fire and turned into sheets of flying ash.

Brooks shook his head. "Those are merely copies of the original documents," he said. "Burning them will do no good at all. Now, please, settle down and have your drink."

"I won't settle down. And you can't do this to me. I won't stand for it. You're fired, do you hear? Fired. I want you out of the house now."

"All in good time, madam. All in good time. As I told you earlier, I'm waiting for my ride." Brooks turned to Ali. "I believe you've summoned the authorities?"

Ali nodded. "Dave Holman is on his way, too."

"I thought as much," Leland said.

"Why are you doing this?" Arabella asked again.

Brooks turned to look at her. "I suppose you've heard of the straw that broke the camel's back? In this case, we're talking about a star."

"A star?" Arabella asked.

"A Silver Star," Brooks replied.

"Oh, that," Arabella said.

Now it was Ali who thought they were speaking a foreign language. *What Silver Star?* she wondered.

"How do you suppose Mr. Ashcroft ended up with my Silver Star?" Brooks asked. "I used to keep it in my wallet back when I first started driving your mother back and forth to Paso Robles, and I never noticed when it disappeared. I thought it had just fallen out somewhere along the line, but you stole it from me, didn't you?"

Shrugging, Arabella picked up her drink and took an unconcerned sip. While Ali watched, she slipped back into the bizarre game-playing persona she had exhibited on their long drive together.

"What if I did?" she asked coyly. Somehow, trapped in that seventy-year-old voice, Ali heard the sound of a terribly disturbed nine-year-old girl determined to have her own way. No matter what.

"Did you plant it in Mr. Ashcroft Junior's car?" Brooks asked.

"Maybe I did," Arabella said. "Maybe I was hoping if the cops came around asking questions, they'd find the star and think you and mother were responsible for what had happened to him. I mean, you were just Mother's driver back then, but luckily no one ever asked any questions, either. Bill Junior was a drunk, he died, no big deal."

"Until Billy started asking questions," Brooks said.

"Yes. He finally had to clear out Bill Senior's storage unit where Bill Junior's personal effects from the crash scene had been kept. I'm sure he was looking for something else, but what he found was the star. He hadn't quite put the whole story together, though," Arabella added. "He thought the two of us were in on it as a team. I don't think he had any idea I was capable of doing something that drastic completely on my own. He found out, though, didn't he?"

The doorbell rang. Brooks glanced at his watch. "Good," he said. "Right on time."

"It's the middle of the night," Arabella muttered as Brooks went to answer the summons. "Who on earth could that be?"

A few moments later, Brooks escorted a newcomer into the room. Ali expected to see Dave Holman or one of the local Sedona uniforms. Instead, she saw a tall, sallow-faced stranger, carrying a briefcase of his own. Despite the lateness of the hour, he came dressed in a full suit and tie. His costume alone was enough for Ali to realize he had to be a lawyer.

"I'm not too late, am I?" the newcomer was asking.

"No, not at all," Brooks assured him. "No one else is here yet, although the police have been summoned. They'll be here momentarily."

"Good."

"What kind of strangers are you inviting in now?" Arabella wanted to know.

"Madam Ashcroft," Brooks said. "This is Morgan Hatfield, your criminal defense attorney. He's just now driven up from Phoenix."

"Send him back," Arabella insisted. "I already told you, I don't need a defense attorney. I don't want one."

"But you do need one," Brooks said. "And now you have one."

"And since the police are no doubt on their way," Hatfield said, "I should probably have a moment alone with my client."

"Very well," Brooks said. "Would you care for some coffee?"

"I'd like that very much, Mr. Brooks," the attorney said. "It's likely to be a very long night."

The butler turned to Ali. "If you don't mind, Ms. Reynolds, perhaps you would be so kind as to join me in the kitchen. I'll bring your drink along."

• • •

Not surprisingly, Dave Holman was the first to arrive. When the car came up the drive, Brooks hurried outside and brought Dave into the house through the garage.

"Goddamnit, Ali!" he exclaimed when he saw her. "When are you going to stop scaring me to death?" And then, without another word, he pulled her off her chair and gathered her into a smothering bear hug. Ali was surprised by how good it felt to have his arms around her and by how comfortable it was to lean into his shoulder.

"Is Friday the thirteenth over yet?" she asked.

Dave raised his hand behind her shoulder so he could get a look at his watch. "A long time ago," he said.

"Great."

In the meantime, Leland Brooks, the soul of discretion, busied himself at the counter, setting out cups, plates, and napkins. "How many officers do you think will be coming?" he asked.

"Several," Dave said. "From several different jurisdictions."

Brooks switched on the coffeepot and then turned to beam at them. "In that case," he said, "I'll make some more sandwiches. It's a good thing I bought groceries tonight."

• • •

The interviews with Ali were conducted in the kitchen while interviews with Arabella took place in the living room. A signed search warrant was produced. Brooks opened the trunk so they could retrieve Arabella's computer. He also handed over a battered Hartmann briefcase.

Sometime after three, Ali saw a pair of uniformed officers lead a handcuffed Arabella outside and place her in the back of a waiting patrol car. As they held her head to keep her from bumping it, Dave Holman was there watching the procedure. So was Leland Brooks.

*It's probably the first time he's ever watched her pull out of the driveway when he hasn't held the door for her,* Ali thought.

When Brooks returned to the kitchen a few minutes later, he kept his head averted and wiped at his eyes with the back of his sleeve. When he caught Ali watching him, he shrugged. "Time for a stiff upper lip," he said.

A few minutes after that, Dave stuck his head in the door from the garage.

"Judge Macey is here," he said. "He wants to know if the stuff that's here in the garage is what you want loaded."

"Yes, it is. Tell him I need to finish straightening up in here. I'll be out to help him in a few minutes."

"Don't rush," Dave said. "I can give him a hand."

Brooks set off into the living room with a tray, gathering plates, napkins, cups, and saucers as he went. Ali followed him. When he came to the chair where he had deposited Arabella's coat much earlier, he stopped and set down the tray. Then he picked up the coat and stood there for a long time, silently stroking the long, soft fur.

"You did the best you could for her," Ali said.

Brooks shook his head. "I'm afraid my best wasn't nearly good enough," he said. "When Mrs. Ashcroft was dying, I told her—I promised her—that I'd see to it Miss Arabella was never locked up again. But you saw what just happened. They took her away in handcuffs. They've arrested her and are taking her to jail. One way or the other, she won't be back. I've failed completely."

"Arabella Ashcroft killed people," Ali said. "She told me so herself. She's a murderess, Mr. Brooks. You've looked after her for years. When you saw what was happening tonight, you made sure she had legal representation. What more could you have done?"

"I could have put her in the Rolls, turned on the engine, and locked her in the garage," he said. "At least that way she wouldn't be under arrest."

"But you would be," Ali said. "What good would that do? How many years of your life have you devoted to this woman, who deliberately tried to pin one of her own murders on you?"

Brooks sighed. "Too many to count," he said.

"You've done enough for her," Ali said. "Far more than most people would."

"What I can't understand is how she could be so devious," he went on.

"Don't be so hard on yourself," Ali said. "It's tough to deal with people who never tell the truth. I should know," she added wryly. "I was married to one of them. Besides, it's clear that Arabella is mentally ill."

But Ali's comment did nothing to dissuade Brooks from his barrage of self-recrimination. "I always prided myself in knowing exactly what she was up to," he said. "But now it turns out I was wrong—completely wrong. The guns in particular, Ms. Reynolds. I have no idea how she gained access to the combination for the safe. I hold myself entirely responsible for that. And as for poor Mr. Ashcroft. I gave Miss Arabella her medication that night before I ever left for Prescott. She should have been asleep until morning."

"I believe Arabella Ashcroft learned to fake taking her medications a very long time ago," Ali said. "Long before you came into the picture."

He nodded. "I suppose you're right."

Out of long habit, he smoothed the coat and returned it to

the back of a chair while Ali picked up the tray and carried it into the kitchen. There was a dishwasher there, but it seemed to get little use. Brooks relieved her of the tray and then set about washing up the delicate bone china in a sink full of hot, soapy water.

"Where will you go?" Ali asked. "What will you do?"

"For the time being, I'll probably live in an apartment in Prescott. I'll need to stay around here long enough to handle the sale of the house. It's a shame. It was state-of-the-art when Mrs. Ashcroft had it built, but it'll probably end up being sold as a tear down. The real estate agent advised me to leave it furnished while it's being shown, but once it's sold I'll need to dispose of the contents—the furniture and the artwork, and the vehicles, as well. Once that's all handled, I'll stay long enough to see what happens to Miss Arabella. After that, I may do some traveling. I haven't been back home to England—to Dorset—in decades, not since Mrs. Ashcroft sent me there to school. I'm sure it's changed quite a lot."

"What about money?" Ali asked.

"Oh, I'm fine as far as money is concerned," Brooks said reassuringly. "That won't be a problem. Before Mrs. Ashcroft died, she set up an annuity for me—a generous annuity. And then there's my social security. Living here, I've had almost no expenses through the years, and I've been able to put aside most of what I've had coming in. It's built up into quite a sizable nest egg."

"And what about this house," Ali asked. "You've lived here a long time. Won't you mind leaving it?"

Brooks pulled his hands out of the dishwater, dried them on a towel, and looked around the room with its antiquated cabinetry and appliances. "I don't think so," he said at last. "I'm getting on in years, and taking care of this house has been a lot of work."

A man Ali had never seen before came in from the garage. The newcomer came over to the sink, stood beside Brooks, and put a comforting arm around the butler's shoulder. "Hey, Lee," he said. "How's it going?"

"Not too well," Leland Brooks said, with an audible catch in his throat. "Not well at all."

Something about the familiarity of the gesture and the way the men stood side by side in front of the sink told Ali more than she would have thought possible. Without another word being exchanged, she understood that they were far more than friends and that they had been together for years.

It was the same way Edie Larson knew things about people. She knew, too, that in his moment of grief, Leland Brooks deserved some privacy.

"I believe I'll go see what Dave is doing," Ali said. With that she abandoned the kitchen in favor of the garage, leaving the two men alone in the kitchen, but as she closed the door behind her, it seemed unlikely that either of them would notice.

## { CHAPTER 20 }

The sun was high in the sky that morning when Ali awakened to the tantalizing smell of coffee and to the guilty knowledge that when Dave had finally brought her home from Arabella's house, she had told him nothing about the Crystal video. It wasn't as if there hadn't been an opportunity. That would have been when he had walked Ali up to her door, but then other considerations had taken precedence.

"Sorry about Roxie," Dave said. "I talked to Richey earlier. He told me Roxanne had stopped by to give you the third degree."

"Crystal has her convinced that you and I have something going."

"Don't we?" Dave asked with a grin.

That was when Ali could have told him; should have told him, but she was too tired. "You tell me," Ali returned.

And that was when, to Ali's utter astonishment, Dave had leaned down and kissed her squarely on the lips. He kissed her as though he really meant it in a way that said Crystal and Roxie and even Edie Larson were absolutely right in their assumptions.

When Dave finally turned Ali loose, she had staggered into the house. She lay in bed for a while, wondering if the kiss had really happened or if, in a delirium of weariness, she had merely imagined it. Finally she fell asleep and slept without dreaming or moving. She knew about the latter because she had slept on one hand, which was now alive with needles and pins. Lying there waiting for the tingling to subside, she once again wondered about that phantom kiss. Was it real or had she made it up? And if she hadn't made it up, what did it mean?

Once Ali's hand was capable of movement, she put on her robe and headed into the living room, expecting to find Chris somewhere in the house. Instead, she was surprised to see an unfamiliar young woman seated on her couch with Sam draped contentedly in her lap.

"You must be Athena," Ali said.

Athena Carlson was a diminutive blonde with blue eyes and a ready smile. Her shoulder-length hair was pulled back and held in place by a clipped comb. She wore a vivid red-and-white tracksuit and a pair of Velcroed tennis shoes. A metal rod peeked out from under the bottom of the right leg of the tracksuit. The end of a complicated plastic-and-metal device that functioned in place of her right hand and arm rested on the couch beside her. If Sam noticed the difference, it apparently didn't bother her.

"Yes, I am," Athena said. "And you must be Chris's mom." Athena made as if to rise and started to move the sleeping cat off her lap.

"Don't get up," Ali told her. "Stay where you are. Sam looks like she died and went to heaven."

Athena settled back onto the couch. Sam opened her one good eye briefly, glanced around the room, and then closed it again and resumed her nap. Ali was impressed. Sam was notoriously picky—and spooky—when it came to visitors.

"I hope we didn't wake you, Ms. Reynolds," Athena continued nervously. "Edie called. She told Chris that she had set aside some sweet rolls for us and that he'd better come down and get them before she threw them out."

If Ali's mother was already being called Edie, if she was reserving some precious Saturday morning sweet rolls for them, and if Sam, who didn't like anybody, had already surrendered unconditionally to Athena Carlson's charms, then Ali was way behind the times. Not only had she missed dinner, she had missed a whole lot of other stuff, too.

The last of the hot water sizzled out of the reserve tank on the Krups coffeemaker, announcing that the brewing cycle was over.

"Coffee?" Ali asked.

"Please."

"How do you take it?"

"Black."

*Good answers,* Ali thought.

She brought the coffee and set one cup down on the end table next to Athena. "Call me Ali," she said. "Everyone else does."

"I'm glad to finally get a chance to meet you," Athena said. "I was afraid Chris was going to keep me hidden under a rock forever."

Ali would have preferred for Chris to be there running interference at this initial meeting, but he wasn't, so they would have to make do on their own. "I'm glad to meet you, too," she said. "I suppose after all this time you were expecting some kind of dragon lady?"

"No, not at all," Athena said with a smile. "Chris kept telling me that you were a wonderful person and that he was sure we'd get along like gangbusters. And if you're anything like your mother—who reminds me of my grandmother back in Bemidji, Minnesota, by the way—I'm sure that's true. I had a great time with your parents last night."

"I'm sorry I wasn't there," Ali said. "I planned to be there."

"Well," Athena said, "there's nothing like having somebody hold a gun on you to change your mind."

*So the word is out,* Ali thought.

Chris's Prius pulled up outside and he bounded into the living room carrying a plate of sweet rolls in one hand. He stopped short when he saw his mother and then looked anxiously back and forth between the two women. "You two have already met?"

"Yes, we have," Athena said. "And nothing bad happened. Worlds did not collide. Everything's fine."

Chris put the rolls on the counter, then came back to the couch, where he sat down next to Athena. Ali thought he still looked anxious, more so than introducing his mother to his girlfriend should have warranted.

"Did you tell her?" he asked Athena.

Athena shook her head. "Not yet. I didn't think it was my place."

Ali's motherly antennae were already up and operating. Now they went on high alert. *Tell me what?* she wondered. *What's going on here? Are they pregnant? Is that what this is all about? Am I about to be the mother of the groom at a shotgun wedding?*

"It's about your computer," Chris said.

Ali was so relieved, she almost laughed aloud. "My computer," she repeated. "What about it?"

"When you didn't show up at Grandma's and Grandpa's for dinner last night, we came back here looking for you. Later on in the evening when you still weren't back, I started thinking about that stalker who came after you last year. I wondered if maybe there was something on your computer that would let us know what had happened or where you had gone. So I logged on to your computer and read your files."

"Chris," Ali said. "That's no big deal. I don't know why you're so upset. It's not like what I do on my computer is top secret or anything."

"We saw the video," Athena said. "The video with Dave Holman's daughter."

"Oh," Ali said. "Oh, that." *Maybe there are some secrets on my computer after all.* "Did you tell Dave?"

"That's the thing, Ms. Reynolds," Athena said. "From what Mr. Holman had said at dinner, it was clear he had no idea about any of this. Unless you told him. Did you?"

"Please call me Ali," she reminded Athena. "But no, I didn't tell him either. I didn't want to show it to him until I could figure out what to say."

"We know who it is," Chris said.

Ali was stunned. "You do?" she asked. "How's that possible?"

"His name is on the video," Athena answered. "We saw it."

"I saw the video," Ali said. "There wasn't any name."

"Show her," Athena said.

"I'll go get my computer," Chris said. He brought it from the bedroom, set it up on the dining room table, and turned it on. Once it booted up, he logged on and then clicked on a link as Ali and Athena gathered around the table to watch. Moments later the disgusting video began playing on the screen. "Look behind them," Chris said. "On the wall."

It was difficult to ignore what was going on with Crystal and the man, but Ali did as she was told. "It looks like a piece of artwork," Ali said. "Something in a frame."

"Right," Chris said. "Now look at this." He clicked over to another file that showed a single frame from the video and then clicked on that image several times in rapid succession. With each click, what was happening in the foreground slipped further out of focus while the background became clearer and clearer. It reminded Ali of an optometrist doing a vision test.

"It's a diploma of some kind," Ali said at last.

"Exactly!" Athena said. "From a seminary in Weed, California, awarded to someone named Richard Masters."

"When I first saw the video, I thought Crystal's stepfather might be responsible for this awful stuff, but his name is Whitman, Gary Whitman. So, who is this guy, and how did you do this?"

"Sonja, my geeky best friend from college," Athena explained. "She's spent years working on an image-enhancement project. That program is now being used by law enforcement agencies all over the country to help decipher video-recorded images of license plates."

"When we first turned this on, Athena noticed there was something on the wall in the background," Chris continued. "We e-mailed this frame to Sonja. You're seeing what she sent back."

"Amazing," Ali said.

"And through the magic of the Internet,"Athena added, "we can now tell you that Pastor Richard Masters is the youth minister for a small congregation of disaffected ex-Baptists called Back Door Apostles who operate out of a very modest strip mall in North Las Vegas. That's where Crystal's family lives, isn't it?"

"Yes," Ali said. "In a trailer park somewhere in North Las Vegas."

"And if Crystal was having difficulty adjusting to her new

school situation," Athena said, "what are the chances that her family sent her to this jerk for counseling? My family moved twice when I was in junior high," she added. "It was hell. My mother sent me to a counselor, too. A good one though, not a creep like this."

"So, what do we do?" Chris asked. "Call Dave? Have him come take a look at this?"

Ali turned away from the computer screen, walked over to the counter, and poured herself a cup of coffee while she searched for an answer to those questions.

Dave had already admitted to Ali that he didn't necessarily have good sense when it came to dealing with Roxanne and her second husband. She seemed to remember his even making a threat of some kind toward Gary Whitman. That was one of the reasons Richey hadn't wanted him to come to Vegas when Crystal first disappeared. Now Ali worried that if Dave saw what she had seen on the video it would send the man completely around the bend.

"I'm going to go shower," she said. "That's where I do some of my best thinking. When I come out, we'll figure out what to do."

With hot water cascading over her tired body, Ali tried to imagine the best way to proceed. She knew without question that if they showed the images to Dave, he'd be on his way to Vegas in a matter of minutes—pissed as hell and armed to the teeth. If he charged into the good pastor's office and raised Cain about it, ordinary people would see him as a justifiably outraged father doing what fathers do. A defense attorney, on the other hand, would see him as an out-of-control police officer and would claim that any evidence resulting from Dave's actions, damning though it might be, would nonetheless be ruled inadmissable.

Ali knew someone needed to beard Richard Masters in his den, but Dave Holman was exactly the wrong person for the job.

Ali emerged from the shower and dressed. She returned to the kitchen, where Chris was just finishing frying bacon and eggs and Athena was setting the table. "You said you wanted to do some thinking, so we're having protein with our sweet rolls."

"Well?" Athena asked.

"How would the two of you like to take a day trip up to Vegas?"

"Cool," Athena said. "Sounds like fun."

"Great," Chris said. "Athena's never ridden in a Porsche."

"There's one problem," Ali said. "Since I don't have my driver's license back, one of you will have to drive."

Chris burst out laughing. "We'll manage," he said.

As they prepared to leave for Vegas, Ali was waylaid for twenty minutes while she searched for the scrap of paper—the back of a gas station receipt actually—on which she had jotted Crystal's cell phone number all those nights earlier. If she'd had her cell phone, it would have been simple to look up the information in her call history. And she could, she supposed, call Detective Marsh and have him look it up for her, but doing that would put her at risk of having to endure another "insert" lecture. Since she was obviously doing it again—not minding her own business—she didn't want to hear it. She was thrilled when she finally found the missing note in the bottom of her bathroom trash can.

But even though she had the number, she didn't want to call it. She didn't want to talk to Crystal until she was good and ready—until she and Chris and Athena had all their ducks in a row.

While Ali searched for the missing phone number, Chris downloaded the video and the file of photo enhancements onto a CD. Well after noon when they finally set out, Chris was at the wheel of the Cayenne and Athena rode shotgun. Ali, sitting in the backseat, mostly wanted to close her eyes and doze, but Chris had other ideas.

"Okay, Mom," he said. "It's a long drive from here to there. I want you to tell us about last night. All of it."

"It's not just last night," Ali said. Over the course of the next hour or so, Ali told Chris and Athena about her dealings with Arabella Ashcroft and how what had happened to her as a child led inevitably to what was going on with Crystal Holman. Athena got it with no problem.

"After Arabella's brother molested Arabella and when nobody believed her, she ended up taking the law into her own hands, and that screwed up her entire life."

"That's it in a nutshell," Ali agreed. "And that's why we're going to Vegas."

"To take the law into our own hands?" Chris asked.

"No, silly," Athena said. "To make sure Crystal doesn't take it into hers and wreck her life, and to make sure Dave Holman doesn't, either."

"Oh," Chris said.

*Yes,* Ali thought. *This girl is growing on me by the minute.*

"So what's the plan?" Athena asked.

"I've been thinking about that. Once we're there, I'll talk to Crystal. I'm hoping I'll be able to make her see that she needs to go to the cops and turn this dirtbag in. I'm worried about calling her in advance because I don't want to give her a lot of time to think it over. She took off more than once already this week, and it wouldn't surprise me if she did it again."

"What about this?" Chris said. "Don't give Crystal any advance warning at all. Why don't we bring the cops to her instead of having her go to them?"

"That might work," Ali said. "But the cops are another problem. What if they give us the runaround? The diploma on the wall is the one piece of solid evidence we have that ties Richard Masters to all this. But what if he tumbles to what's happening and while we're trying to convince the cops to get a search warrant and move on him, he takes off or has brains enough to ditch the diploma? I wish there was some way of verifying that the diploma is still there."

"How about trying for a photo op?" Athena asked brightly.

"What kind of a photo op?" Ali asked.

"We have the address of the church," Athena said. "What say we program it into the GPS. We can stop by there and see if the good pastor happens to be in. Maybe I can talk my way into his office. If the diploma's there, I'll take a photo of it with my cell phone. That way we can document that it was there at some other time besides just when the video was being filmed. With any luck I might even be able to get pictures of his computer equipment."

"That's taking a bit of a risk, isn't it?" Ali asked.

Athena laughed outright at that. "Riding in a Humvee in Iraq is taking a risk," she said. "Besides, I know the type. I may be a little too old to qualify for a youth ministry, but I'm betting Pastor Masters will turn out to be one of those smarmy goody-two-shoes guys who won't be able to see anything about me except what he thinks is a hopeless cripple. He'll fall all over himself trying to help me."

"As long as his help doesn't include anything more than talking," Chris said with a laugh. "You may be short an arm and a leg, but I'm guessing you'd still be able to clean his clock."

Ali fell asleep shortly after that and didn't wake up again until Chris slowed to exit the freeway. "Where are we?" she asked.

"Headed up Civic Center Drive toward North Las Vegas."

"Time to call Crystal," Ali said. "Let me use your phone."

Chris passed his to the backseat. "When are you going to get your own phone back?"

"Good question," Ali said.

She put in Crystal's number, pressed SEND, and was dismayed when a male voice answered.

"Is Crystal there?" Ali asked.

"She's busy. Who's asking?"

Ali wasn't eager to reveal her name. "A friend of hers," she said.

"Oh, yeah? Call back when you have a name." With that the man hung up.

Ali pressed REDIAL.

"Do you have a name now?" the same voice asked. He sounded surly and argumentative.

"My name is Alison Reynolds," Ali said. "I'm a friend of Crystal's and of her dad's."

"Oh," the man said. "Why didn't you say so? This is Gary Whitman, Crystal's stepdad. After what we've been through this week, no calls go through this phone without being screened first."

*A little late,* Ali thought. *But better than nothing.*

"Can I talk to her? I'm in town and would like to see her."

"We're at soccer practice right now," Whitman said. "It'll be over in about an hour. Is Dave with you?"

"No," Ali said. "Just my son and his girlfriend."

"Do you want to stop by the house then?" Gary sounded relieved, as though having Dave in tow might have been a problem. "Roxie's still at work," he added. "She won't be home until after five."

*Good,* Ali thought. *By then, maybe we'll be ready.*

"Do you have our address?" Whitman asked. "We live in Jackpot Dunes. It's a trailer park just south of Nellis."

"We'll find it," Ali said.

When they found the strip mall location of Back Door Apostles, Ali was a little surprised to see that, on a Saturday afternoon, it was a very busy place. There were several cars in the parking lot and a whole group of teens and preteens hanging around outside a door marked YOUTH MINISTRY.

When Athena started to get out of the car, Chris did, too. "We'll both go in," he said. "You can talk to the pastor, if he's in. I'll see what else is going on."

After the better part of an hour, Chris was the first to emerge. "You wouldn't believe it, Mom. This place is a regular kid magnet. They've got everything in there—a pool table, video games, computers, comics. My guess is that Masters uses the place to bring in all kinds of kids, then he finds the most vulnerable one and cuts her from the herd."

That was Ali's guess, too.

Athena returned to the Cayenne a few minutes later looking downright radiant. "Got him," she said triumphantly. "Masters was called out of the room for a couple of minutes. The diploma was still there. I got several pictures of that. I also got photos of his Web-casting equipment and his computer, serial numbers included."

"That's my girl," Chris said. "Where to now?"

"North Las Vegas PD," Ali said. "We're believers. Let's see if we can make believers out of them."

It was late Saturday afternoon. Josie Gutierrez and Frank Edwards, the two on-duty detectives in the Sexual Assault Unit, were both out in the field. It took some talking on Ali's part to bring them back in to headquarters, and they weren't particularly happy about it when they got there.

"What's this all about?" Detective Gutierrez wanted to know.

"It's about Crystal Holman," Ali told them.

"The Amber Alert from this week?"

Ali nodded.

"But I heard she came home yesterday," Detective Edwards said. "I thought everything was fine."

Ali handed Edwards the CD Chris had made. "Take a look at these files," she said, "then you tell us if everything's fine."

The two officers disappeared into the bowels of the building. A few minutes later, a grim-faced Detective Gutierrez returned. "You'd better come with me," she said. "We have a few questions. Who the hell is this asshole? Where was the video shot? Who did the enhancement? And who the hell are you? In reverse order."

Initially, Detective Gutierrez took the same position Larry Marsh had—that civilian involvement was a no-no. As far as she was concerned, Athena should never have entered Masters's office because it was far too dangerous, and she and Detective Edwards alone should be the ones to interview Crystal and her family.

"Look," Ali said. "You wouldn't have a clue about any of this if it weren't for us. I've been through a hell of a lot with Crystal Holman in the last few days, and I think I have some credibility with her. And with Roxie, too," she added.

"You know the mother?" Gutierrez asked.

"She came to see me in Sedona just yesterday afternoon," Ali said, choosing to edit out the exact nature of that visit.

The detective turned to her partner. "What do you think, Frank?"

Edwards shook his head. "With kids it can go either way," he said.

"Chris and Athena don't have to go," Ali added, "but if you don't take me, I'm prepared to show up on my own—with or without your permission."

The detectives finally relented. They drove in a two-car caravan with the two officers leading the way. When they arrived at the Jackpot Dune's Mobile Home Park in North Las Vegas, the place was every bit as desolate, grim, and uninviting as Ali expected. It reminded Ali of that old Roger Miller song lyric, "No phone, no pool, no pets." She was surprised they even allowed children. No wonder Crystal hated it.

While Chris and Athena stayed in the car, Detective Gutierrez led the way up the obviously new wooden steps and knocked on the mobile home's metal door. When Roxanne Whitman opened it, though, she ignored the police officers and looked straight at Ali.

"What are you doing here?" she demanded. "Has something happened to Dave?"

"It's about Crystal," Ali said. "We need to talk to her."

"She's in the shower, but tell me. What's wrong?"

A tall man appeared beyond Roxanne's shoulder just as Detective Gutierrez held up her badge. "What is it, Roxie? What's going on? Why are the cops here?"

"Do you mind if we come in?" Detective Gutierrez asked.

Shrugging, Roxie and Gary Whitman stepped aside and let the two cops and Ali enter their small but spotless living room.

"You still haven't said what this is about," Gary said, once they were all seated.

"Do you happen to know someone named Richard Masters?"

"Of course, I know Pastor Masters," Gary Whitman said, answering for both of them. "He's the youth minister at our church. He's a great guy, and great with kids."

"Has Crystal had any interactions with him?" Detective Gutierrez asked.

"Yes," Gary said. "Definitely. When she started having difficulties at school, we sent her to him for counseling."

"And did the counseling sessions seem to help?"

"Well, no," Gary admitted. "Not really. Things have been getting worse instead of better. But she's a teenager. You know how they can be."

"Did she indicate whether or not she was happy with the sessions?"

"She did say she didn't want to go anymore," Roxanne pointed out. "She said that a couple of weeks ago."

"And I told her she didn't have a choice," Gary said. "She needed to clean up her act, or else."

Ali's heart constricted. In her own way, Crystal had tried to tell someone. She probably hadn't told anyone the whole story, but she had asked for help, and no one had listened. Her parents hadn't listened, but Ali had. And now something was going to be done about it.

"I hate to have to tell you this, Mr. and Mrs. Whitman," Detective Gutierrez said. "We have reason to believe that Mr. Masters is a sexual predator who has had inappropriate sexual contact with your daughter. We need to talk to her about it."

"Why, that son of a bitch!" Gary Whitman exclaimed, his whole body rigid with absolute outrage. "That low-down son of a bitch! Let me at him. I'll tear him limb from limb!"

Just then Crystal appeared in the doorway to the living room. She was wearing a robe. A damp towel was wrapped around her head. "Mom? Gary?" she asked uncertainly, looking from one face to another. "What's going on?"

Roxanne leaped off the couch and hurried to her daughter's side. "Oh, my poor baby," she murmured, gathering Crystal into her arms. "Come in here. I think we need to talk."

# { CHAPTER 21 }

On Wednesday of the following week Rudyard Kipling Hogan was laid to rest in the cemetery of his hometown of Kingman, Arizona. Ali, along with everyone else, was surprised when it turned out to be a far larger funeral than anyone—including the mortuary—had expected. A standing-room-only crowd turned out to bury him as if paying their respects to a departed hero. As the local paper had editorialized, regardless of who had actually killed Kip Hogan, he was as much a victim of that long-ago but not forgotten fire as the men who had perished in the actual inferno. It had simply taken a lot longer for him to die.

Elizabeth Barrett Hogan came home for her son's funeral, accompanied throughout the services by both Sandy Mitchell and Jane Braeton. Ali heard several people speculating about who was who and most especially wondering about the two very protective women who never left Elizabeth's side, but since Elizabeth wasn't telling, neither was Ali.

She was standing nearby when, at the end of the graveside ceremony, Ali's father went over to Elizabeth's wheelchair and handed her an envelope. Ali knew what it was. Bob had found it in the LazyDaze when he had cleaned it out. It was a letter Kip had written to his mother only a few months before his death, one that bore the U.S. Postal Service's inarguable determination—*Return to Sender.*

"Kip tried to write to you," Bob Larson said. "But it was too late. The forwarding address had run out by then, and it came back."

Elizabeth held the envelope up to the sunlight and peered at it from several different angles. Then she stowed it, unopened, in the purse that rested on her lap. "Thank you for this," she said, smiling up at him. "If Kip wrote it, it's not too late. And thank you for being his friend."

Bob patted her shoulder wordlessly and then hurried away, but not fast enough that his wife and daughter failed to see what was going on. Edie Larson hurried to her grieving husband's side. "Come on, Bobby," she said. "Let's get out of here before you make a complete fool of yourself."

• • •

A week after Arabella Ashcroft's arraignment, Ali received a surprise call from the woman's attorney, Morgan Hatfield. Ali knew from news reports that Arabella had pled innocent to one charge of vehicular manslaughter in the death of Billy Ashcroft. She knew, too, from Dave that additional charges were pending in other jurisdictions, including involvement in the deaths of the nurse and patient who had perished in the fire at the Mosberg Institute and the woman who had run an institution called the Bancroft House near Carefree. In the mid-sixties the director had gone for a horseback ride, had been reported missing, and had been found dead months later. At the time, no one had connected her death to Arabella Ashcroft's being incarcerated there. Now they had.

It occurred to Ali that this was a time when pleading insanity might actually be the right thing to do, but she didn't mention that to Mr. Hatfield.

"Arabella would really like to see you," Morgan said. "She's in the new high-security jail on South Fourth in Phoenix."

Arabella had lied to Ali on so many occasions about so many things, that Ali wasn't eager to go another round. "Why?" Ali asked. "What does she want?"

"I'm not sure, but you know Arabella. She was quite adamant."

Two days later, still filled with misgivings, Ali drove herself to Phoenix. Arabella came into the visitors' room wearing shackles and a bright orange jail jumpsuit.

"The food here is dreadful," Arabella said, as soon as she sat down opposite Ali behind a Plexiglas window. "Have you heard of nutrition loaf? It's where they mix all the food together in a terrible conglomeration, bake it, and serve it as a meal."

As jail fare went, nutrition loaf was fully balanced and amazingly cheap. "I've heard of it," Ali said.

"Oh, what I wouldn't give to have one of Mr. Brooks's dinners about now," Arabella said wistfully. "He did a particularly wonderful job with lamb chops. Have you heard from him, by the way?"

"No," Ali said. "I haven't."

"I haven't either, not directly," Arabella said. "He must be terribly angry with me. I'm afraid I've been a naughty, naughty girl."

*That's the understatement of the century,* Ali thought.

"I've also heard rumors that there's only one person interested in buying my house," Arabella continued. "He's a developer, of course. He's planning on tearing it down. The real estate agent warned me that, if he does make an offer, it'll probably be for only a fraction of what the place is worth—pennies on the dollar."

"So?"

"I'd like you to buy it," Arabella said. "For this."

Using a pencil, she jotted a sum down on a three-by-five card and shoved it through the opening under the window that separated them.

Ali looked at the amount and put the paper down. "That's ridiculous," she said. "That's pennies on the dollar, too."

"Yes, it is," Arabella said. "But you wouldn't tear it down. And anything that's left after I pay off Mr. Hatfield will go to a good cause—to the scholarship trust fund—which I'm hoping you'll administer, by the way. You'd like that, wouldn't you?"

Ali shook her head. The amount was something she could well afford, but she didn't think she'd have the energy to tackle the kind of wholesale remodeling that would be necessary.

"I don't think so," she said. "It's far more house than I need."

"Please," Arabella said quietly. "I'd really like for you to have it. And I know Mother would, too."

Ali stood up. "I'll think about it," she said. "But I'm not making any promises."

"Wait," Arabella said. "Don't go yet, please. I need to ask you. How's your friend—the little girl who ran away?"

"The guy who molested her is in jail," Ali said. "And she wasn't his only victim."

"So, did I help?" Arabella asked.

"What do you mean, did you help?"

"Did you tell her about me? Did you use me as an example so she'd go to the police?"

Ali looked at Arabella—a pathetic, damaged, delusional old woman—and she could not deny her that one bit of satisfaction.

"Yes," Ali lied. "Yes, I did."

On the drive back to Sedona, Ali felt little satisfaction for having lied and allowed Arabella that one small triumph. Driving through town, Ali saw her mother's Alero parked outside the Sugarloaf. The Bronco wasn't there. Wanting some private time with Edie, Ali stopped and knocked.

"Are you all right?" her mother asked as soon as she saw her face.

"I saw Arabella Ashcroft today," Ali said.

"Oh," Edie said. "No wonder you look a little green around the gills."

"She wants me to buy her house."

"Arabella has a lot of nerve calling it her house," Edie said. "She may have lived in it, but it was always her mother's house. Anna Lee Ashcroft was a nice woman. And if you do decide to buy it, that's how I'd think of it—as Anna Lee's, not as Arabella's."

Ali was quiet for a moment. Finally she said, "I never really knew that Aunt Evie and Arabella were good friends. From what Arabella told me, I guess they were. She said it was because of that friendship that she and her mother started the scholarship thing—that to begin with, the whole point was to benefit me."

"Arabella was always a conniver," Edie said. "I think she was after your Aunt Evie and saw you as a way to get Evie into her clutches. She might have succeeded, too, but Anna Lee warned Evie away. And then she went ahead and set up the scholarship fund so other girls would benefit from it, too, not just you."

"Wait a minute," Ali said. "What kind of clutches? What do you mean?"

"Oh, forever more, Ali," Edie said with a laugh. "Just because your Aunt Evie stayed in the closet all her life, don't tell me you didn't know about it."

• • •

Learning that bit of Aunt Evie's history hit Ali hard. And knowing how Richard Masters and Curtis Uttley had used the Internet to victimize and ensnare Crystal didn't help. The whole chain of events had cast a pall over Ali's life and over her interest in cutloose as well. She could no longer look at what happened on the Internet as being harmless and she wasn't sure if she was helping or making things worse.

She drifted into a strange lassitude. Her interest in blogging seemed to have dissipated, but she had no idea what she was going to do instead. She did some random posting, but without having her heart in it. When she finally heard from Velma T, she read the message with a heavy heart.

> *. . . so the second opinion concurs with the first one—that there's not that much to be done for me. There are experimental protocols—expensive procedures—that I could possibly qualify for, but most of those wouldn't be covered by insurance. So, my son and his golfing buddy doctor were right about my prognosis and their why-bother attitude, but I will insist to the death—which may be sooner than later—that they were* ABSOLUTELY WRONG!!! *not to tell me. It's my life. My decision.*
>
> *So, here's what I'm going to do. I've got that book about a thousand things to do before I die, and I've also looked into one of those luxury round-the-world tours that will hit a bunch of them at one fell swoop.*

*There's one that leaves Las Vegas, Nevada, on March first and lasts for twenty-five days. Private jets and first-class hotels all the way. By the time it's over, if I'm not dead or dead broke, I should be close to it.*

*Maybe,* Ali thought, *I was wrong to be worried about Velma's financial situation.* She continued reading:

*When I called to inquire about reservations, it turned out that there was only a single pair of accommodations left on the trip. Since I was a single, I thought that left me out, but then the reservations lady came up with a wonderful idea. It seems there was another person who had inquired about that same trip, another single, who's a retired schoolteacher from Washington State. So we ended up booking our trip together. Her name is Maddy Watkins. She's quite a bit younger than I am, but we've been e-mailing back and forth, and she sounds delightful.*

*Thank you for encouraging me not to stand around waiting for life or death to happen. If I die somewhere along the way, my son can damned well pay to have me shipped home. And if I get home and I'm still feeling well enough and have any money left over, I may book a cruise, too.*

*I miss your blog. I know something bad must have happened, and I know you're not ready to say what it is. Just know that you've made a huge difference in my life and probably in lots of other lives, too.*

*Love,*

VELMA T IN LAGUNA

• • •

On a sunny evening in March, Dave Holman came by for dinner. While Athena and Chris laughed and cooked in the kitchen, Ali and Dave sat outside on the front porch on the swing, sipping some of Paul Grayson's very expensive wine. They were spending more and more time together these days. Ali wasn't sure where the relationship was going, but for now she was comfortable with it.

"The custody hearing's next week," Dave said, draping one arm around her shoulder. "We've hammered out an arrangement that seems reasonable, and we're pretty sure the judge will go along with it. Richey will be a senior next year, and he'll stay in Vegas to finish high school. After that he's planning on joining the Marines."

"Like father like son," Ali said.

Dave nodded. "And the girls will spend half the summer there, then they'll come live with me and go to school here. They're thrilled. Of course, it means I'll have to find somewhere else to live, but with Roxie paying child support . . ."

Ali was astonished. "She's agreed to pay child support?"

"That's what I said. It's a reasonable arrangement. And I have to give Gary Whitman credit. He's the one who came up with the idea and convinced Roxie that it was doable. After what happened to Crystal, I think he wants the girls out of Vegas even more than I do. When Richard Masters agreed to a plea bargain and Crystal no longer faced having to testify, Gary was so relieved that I thought he was going to burst into tears."

Ali said nothing. After a pause, Dave added, "It really chaps my butt."

"What does?"

"Gary and I aren't ever going to be friends," Dave said. "But he isn't that bad a guy. Maybe he's not the best businessman who ever came down the pike, but he's a better husband to Roxie than I ever was, and she's happier with him than she was with me. I just have to make sure he's not a better father."

Again Ali had nothing to say. She found that happened to her often these days.

"Speaking of fathers," Dave continued, "I saw yours today. Bob's worried about you."

"He is?" Ali asked.

"And so am I," Dave said. "You're depressed, Ali. You're not yourself. You're not even blogging anymore. You've been through a lot. Have you ever heard of post–traumatic stress disorder?"

"Of course, I've heard of PTSD," Ali said dismissively, "but it's got nothing to do with me."

"Yes, it does," Dave argued. "Your father and I have both been around it. We know the signs. You need to see someone. You need help."

"No, I don't," Ali declared, ducking out from beneath Dave's arm. "All I need is some sleep. You and Dad need to mind your own business. And since I'm not feeling very sociable at the moment, maybe you should just go."

"No deal, Mom," Chris said, materializing silently in the open doorway behind them. "Dinner's on the table, and Athena and I say Dave isn't leaving."

• • •

The next day, it was all Ali could do to drag herself out of bed. By midafternoon, she was still in her robe and worrying about getting dressed before Chris came home from school when the doorbell rang. When she looked through the peephole, she was surprised to find Leland Brooks standing there in all his rhinestone cowboy glory. He looked tanned and fit and surprisingly chipper. The Rolls, shiny as ever, was parked in the driveway behind him.

At first Ali wasn't going to open the door. He rang the bell again though, and she opened the door.

"I hope you'll forgive me for dropping by this way," he said. "I came over from Prescott to check on the house, and I wanted to see you."

Grudgingly, Ali invited him inside.

"I've had a letter from Miss Arabella," he said. "Several of them, in fact, all of them asking that I intercede with you on her behalf and beg you to reconsider your decision about purchasing her place."

"I thought that was all set," Ali said. "I thought a developer was going to take it and tear it down."

"He thought so, too," Brooks said, "but that was before some of the neighbors got together and had it placed on the National Historical Record. The house is considered second-generation Frank Lloyd Wright and all that. Then there was another possible buyer, but his offer fell through. The house failed the inspection—rather miserably, I'm afraid, and his bank wouldn't approve it."

"What does any of this have to do with me?"

"Miss Arabella wanted me to let you know that we'll take less than she told you earlier, although I'm not sure what that amount was. She said that if you'll make an offer somewhere in that neighborhood, as long as the offer is from you, the real estate agent and I are both directed to accept it. She also said your offer should include the house's contents. That way, when you refurb it, you'll be able to use as many of Mrs. Ashcroft's original furnishings as you wish. You'll be able to bring the house back to what it once was—what it never was with Miss Arabella living in it."

Ali was tired—more tired than she'd ever been in her life. "Look," she said. "I don't really care what Miss Arabella wants."

"It's what I want, too," Brooks said. "And I'd be more than willing to come help oversee the remodeling project. I know where the original blueprints are, and believe me, I know what's wrong and what needs fixing. I suppose you could say, in a manner of speaking, that I know where the bodies are buried."

With his eyes twinkling, Brooks seemed to be waiting for Ali to smile, but that was more than she could muster.

"I've spoken to Mr. Holman about this," he said finally. "He thinks it would be a good idea for you to take on a project."

More meddling on Dave's part. Ali was suddenly angrier than she had been in months. "This is none of his business!" she exclaimed. "And it's none of yours, either."

"Oh, but it is," Leland Brooks said. "Has anyone mentioned to you that you look quite dreadful?"

"How kind of you to point that out," Ali said.

"Here it is, late afternoon, and you're not even dressed."

"Excuse me," Ali said. "This isn't any of *your* business, either."

"Yes," he said. "I believe it is. Do you know much about the Korean War?"

"No," Ali said. "Not really."

"I was in it," he said. "I was in Forty-one Commando Royal Marines—a cook. So I saw a lot of action but I didn't do much fighting. I fed the guys who did, but I didn't think I was worth much. I came home from the war and I was ready to just sit around and do nothing, but then a miracle happened—two of them actually. Someone sent me his Silver Star."

"Like a war medal?" Ali asked.

Brooks nodded. "It belonged to a guy named Arthur Reed, whose life I happened to save when his vehicle crashed through some ice and he almost drowned. He sent me the medal when the war was over. Said he never would have been alive to receive it if I hadn't saved his sorry butt to begin with." Brooks fell quiet for a moment and then continued.

"I was always a bit different back home. My family wasn't keen on having people of my persuasion hanging about. After the war I tried going home where my own parents treated me like an outcast. For a while I sat around wallowing in self-pity, but after Art sent me that medal, I made up my mind to come here to the U.S. in hopes of starting over. Once I got here, the other guy, the second Marine, heard that Anna Lee was looking for a bodyguard and driver, and he put me in touch with her. So that was the second miracle. The rest is history."

"Why are you telling me all this?" Ali asked.

"Because, according to what Mr. Holman tells me, you've been through your own kind of war, Ms. Reynolds. And I think you've earned your own kind of medal. When the police release it from evidence, I want you to have it."

"I can't possibly . . ."

"Yes, you can," Brooks insisted. "I'm like Art Reed, you see. I had no idea how far gone Miss Arabella was. If it hadn't been for you, chances are, I'd be dead now, too, right along with Mr. Ashcroft the third. That's why I'm determined to pass it along. And now I'd like you to get dressed and come with me. I want to take you for a ride."

"A ride," Ali echoed. "Where to?"

"To the house," Brooks said. "To Anna Lee Ashcroft's house. To what I hope will be your house someday. I'd like to show you some of the changes I think are in order. Come on now, Ms. Reynolds. Let's go."

"Wait a minute," Ali objected. "I know what you're doing. This is exactly how you used to treat Arabella—how you'd talk your way around her and get her to do what you wanted. It's how you got her to be . . . normal."

"Exactly," Mr. Brooks said with a smile. "It worked for Miss Arabella, and I'm quite sure it will work for you as well."

• • •

**CUTLOOSEBLOG.COM**
*Saturday, April 1, 2006*

Happy April Fool's Day. I woke up this morning laughing. What's so funny? Well, let's see. I've bought a house that needs everything—new plumbing, new wiring, new roof, new windows. How could any of that even remotely be construed as hilarious? For one thing, I've never built anything in my life.

I'm sure I'll have plenty of help. My father is itching to get his hands on the place. So is my son, Chris. So is Leland Brooks. So is Dave Holman. They're all brimming over with suggestions about how to do this and that, and I'm prepared to take their ideas under advisement. But if this is going to be my house, I'm going to be the one with the final say. Next week I'll be traveling down to Phoenix to interview several architects, and we'll see if one of them measures up.

People who've lived through their own remodeling projects tell me that tackling this kind of job is no laughing matter, but this morning I beg to differ. The clouds finally seem to have lifted. Fixing Anna Lee Ashcroft's house is going to be dreadfully hard work, but I'm looking forward to it. In fact, I can hardly wait.

After months of living in a fog of grief, I'm finally ready to step back out into the sunlight.

Demolition? Plaster dust? Building permits? All I can say is, "Bring it on!"

*posted by Babe,* 9:27 A.M.

## ABOUT THE AUTHOR

J.A. Jance is the Top 10 *New York Times* bestselling author of the Joanna Brady series, the J.P. Beaumont series, three interrelated thrillers featuring the Walker family, and the Ali Reynolds series: *Web of Evil* and *Edge of Evil*. Born in South Dakota and brought up in Bisbee, Arizona, Jance lives with her husband in Seattle, Washington, and Tucson, Arizona.

*For a recipe for Sugarloaf Café sweet rolls please go to www.jajance.com and check the recipe page.*